"FLYNN, EH?"

Inspector Wattle motioned to Sergeant Daub. "Check the IRA terrorist files. Plenty of connections in America."

The inspector turned back to Judith. "See 'ere, Mrs. Flynn, or whatever your real name is, don't try to lead us down the garden path. Why 'ave you made contact with the Ravenscroft 'ousehold? You and your cousin, that Mrs. Jones—she could be one of those Welsh separatists. They're a dangerous lot too—you wait until the old lady's on 'er last legs, then you come flying in to get your share of the family fortune?"

Judith's patience snapped. "That's ridiculous! We hardly know any of these people in the family! We're definitely *not* related!"

Wattle looked at Daub. They seemed to be sharing a private joke.

"We found 'er will," the inspector said. "It seems that Miss Ravenscroft left you and your cousin this fancy old 'ouse. Now what do you think of that as a motive for murder?"

Other Bed-and-Breakfast Mysteries by
Mary Daheim
from Avon Books

MURDER, MY SUITE
MAJOR VICES
A FIT OF TEMPERA
BANTAM OF THE OPERA
DUNE TO DEATH
HOLY TERRORS
FOWL PREY
JUST DESSERTS

n of Avon Books. This work
is a novel. Any sim-

Auntie Mayhem

AVON BOOKS ◆ NEW YORK

AUNTIE MAYHEM is an original publicatio
has never before appeared in book form. This work
ilarity to actual persons or events is purely coincidental.

AVON BOOKS
A division of
The Hearst Corporation
1350 Avenue of the Americas
New York, New York 10019

Copyright © 1996 by Mary Daheim
Inside cover author photo courtesy of Images by Edy
Published by arrangement with the author
Library of Congress Catalog Card Number: 95-94926
ISBN: 0-380-77878-5

First Avon Books Printing: March 1996

AVON TRADEMARK REG. U.S. PAT. OFF. AND IN OTHER COUNTRIES, MARCA
REGISTRADA, HECHO EN U.S.A.

Printed in the U.S.A.

RA   10   9   8   7   6   5   4   3   2   1

ONE

JUDITH GROVER MCMONIGLE Flynn climbed into a taxi, collapsed onto the leather jumpseat, and told the driver to take her to Buckingham Palace. The vehicle zipped into London's madcap traffic and hurtled pell-mell down Pall Mall.

"Buck House, yes?" the driver said, accelerating around a double-decker bus.

Judith had expected to hear the Cockney accent of her previous trip to England some thirty years earlier. Instead, the driver's voice was layered in rich Middle Eastern tones. It seemed to Judith that nobody in London spoke the Queen's English anymore.

"You see changing guard?" the bearded driver asked cheerfully.

Judith didn't remember taximen talking at all in 1964. "I will?" she replied in surprise. Her intention was to meet Cousin Renie in front of Buckingham Palace at 11:30 A.M. She hadn't realized that their rendezvous would coincide with the changing of the guard.

"Many visitors, much crowd," the cheerful driver said as he whizzed past Marlborough House.

"Oh, dear." Judith squirmed on the small seat. How would she find Renie in such a mob? On this Tuesday in April, her cousin had gone to breakfast with a former graphic design colleague. Judith had spent the morning with her husband at the National Gallery. They had

1

parted company in Trafalgar Square, with Joe Flynn heading for a tour of Scotland Yard.

"American?" The driver was looking at Judith in the rearview mirror. The taxi drifted perilously into the next lane of streaming traffic. "Canadian?"

"American," Judith gulped as they screeched to a stop at St. James Street.

"Ah!" The driver turned to give Judith a big grin. "I have cousin in New York. Mustafa. You know him?"

"Uh—no. I don't know New York," Judith admitted, having visited the city only once. "I'm from . . . somewhere else." There was no point in trying to explain U.S. geography to foreigners. Outside of New York, they never seemed to know anything except Los Angeles, which Judith couldn't explain to herself. At present, she was still trying to comprehend London. There were new high rises, though they hadn't yet overwhelmed the skyline. But signs of change were everywhere, from the golden arches of McDonald's to the homeless pushing grocery carts. The world was not only growing smaller, it was becoming too similar.

Buckingham Palace and the Victoria Memorial loomed before her. So did several hundred milling tourists, some of whom were forced to leap out of the taxi's way as the driver squealed to a stop by Green Park.

Nervously, Judith counted out the proper fare in English money, added what she hoped was an adequate tip, and thanked the driver. She also thanked God for arriving in one piece.

Feeling forlorn, Judith scanned the crowd. Cousin Renie was nowhere to be seen. Every nationality seemed to be represented, with Africans in flowing robes and Indian women in elegant saris. There were Americans, of course, but these days it was hard to identify them by sight. The visitors in jeans and T-shirts could just as well be Germans, Swedes, Aussies, or Argentinians.

Indeed, as Judith accidentally bumped into a middle-aged Chinese man in a dark suit, she apologized in careful English. "Please excuse me, sir. I'm so sorry."

"No biggie," he replied. "This place is worse than BART at rush hour."

"Oh!" Judith grinned at the reference to the Bay Area Rapid Transit system. "You're from San Francisco!"

The man shook his head. "San Mateo, actually. But I work in The City. I'm here for a shrink convention. In fact, I'm playing hooky from the morning session. I figured this was something I had to do, just like the tourists in San Francisco can't go home without riding a cable car."

Judith's dark eyes widened at the man's reference to the convention. "You're attending the International Mental and Neurological University Therapists Society convention, too? That's why I'm here. I mean, my cousin's husband is attending it."

The man from the Bay Area nodded. "It's a big deal. IMNUTS brings together academic psychologists and psychiatrists from all over the world. It's an honor to be invited."

Judith knew that Renie's Bill had been gratified by the invitation. Indeed, his attendance had prompted the trip to England. Back in January, when Renie and Bill Jones had decided to attend the conference, Judith and Joe Flynn had jumped at the chance to go along. One of Joe's brothers, Paul, was posted to the American embassy in London. Joe had three weeks' vacation coming on his job as a homicide detective for the metropolitan police force. Except for Easter weekend, which had already passed, April wasn't exceptionally busy at Judith's bed-and-breakfast. If ever the Flynns and the Joneses were to visit England during good weather, it was in the spring.

The guard-changing ceremony had begun. The man from San Mateo was swallowed up by the crowd. Trying not to get swept away, Judith dug in her heels in front of the Victoria Memorial. Again, she peered at the colorful crowd, which was constantly shifting for camera shots and better views.

If only, Judith thought, *Renie wasn't so small.* At almost five-nine, Judith had always been grateful for her height. In middle age, she also had grown comfortable with her statuesque figure. An extra five pounds was never cause for concern. But at present, she would have liked to add another foot in order to see over the tourists. She realized she could do just that by climbing the memorial's steps. The seated sculpture of Queen Victoria seemed to demand a curtsy. Judith let her eyes stray to the golden angel that stood atop the monument. The angel looked more amiable.

But the new vantage point didn't seem to help. Judith saw the red jackets and black beaver hats move in precision. A regimental band was playing, bold, brassy notes from a military march that Judith vaguely recognized. The scene was impressive. But the guards weren't assisting in the search for Renie. Judith moved cautiously around the memorial with its solemn plaques and heroic figures. Scanning the crowd beyond a group of tall blonds who were probably Scandinavians, but might have been from Minnesota, she heard a faint voice. It was behind her, possibly above her, floating out over The Mall.

Judith turned. She heard the plaintive voice again. It was familiar.

"Coz!" It was Renie. She was perched on the back of a fierce bronze lion, while a heroic bare-chested victor waved a torch toward the heavens. Compared to the imposing statuary, Renie looked smaller than ever. "Help! I can't get down!" Her round face was terrified.

Frowning, Judith considered the situation. If she climbed a few more steps, she could reach the platform that held the bronze statues—and Renie. It wasn't impossible. Several young people, mostly raucous teenagers, were also draped around the massive memorial at various levels. But Judith and Renie were old enough to be their mothers. The only saving grace was that they weren't. With a mighty lunge, Judith heaved herself up to the lion's paws.

The descent wasn't as dangerous as it looked. Once Renie had Judith's hand to steady her, she moved nimbly off the lion. Moments later, the cousins were safely back on the ground.

"What the hell were you doing up there?" Judith asked, more relieved than annoyed.

Renie dusted off her beige slacks. "A couple of kids from New Zealand helped me up. I wanted to make sure I could see you. Who was driving your taxi—A. J. Foyt?''

''Mustafa's cousin,'' Judith retorted. Seeing Renie's puzzled expression, she waved an impatient hand. ''Skip it, we're both alive. Let's get out of here before everybody else does.''

Proceeding down Buckingham Palace Road, Judith and Renie spent the next hour soaking up London's West End. The city was abloom with daffodils and tulips and crocuses. They admired Belgravia's handsome Greco-Roman houses, goggled at Harrod's exotic wares, and dropped their jaws but held on to their bank cards as they gawked their way through the chic shops of Knightsbridge.

Turning back onto Brompton Road, they picked up the pace as they headed for St. Quentin, the restaurant where they were to meet their luncheon date.

''What's her name?'' Renie asked for the fourth time.

''Claire,'' Judith answered a bit sharply. ''Claire Marchmont.'' Her feet hurt, and so did her pride. Judith, who had made untold sacrifices during eighteen years of marriage to Dan McMonigle, suddenly found that taking the trip of a lifetime with the man of her dreams still wasn't enough: She had a terrible urge to buy out Saint-Laurent and Elle and Charles Jourdan. Maybe her feet would feel better in a four-hundred-dollar pair of shoes. Then reality sank in, and so did repentance. ''Sorry, coz. I'm fighting an urge to indulge myself and wear nice clothes when I live in the poor house. What I really need are Band-Aids for my blisters.''

''I know walking is the real way to see London, but it wears me out,'' Renie panted as they passed a BP station. ''How did we do all this thirty years ago?''

''We didn't.'' Judith gave Renie and the service station a wry look. At home, on Heraldsgate Hill, she traded at the local BP, which, she recalled, stood for British Petroleum. The commercial invasion cut both ways. ''If you'll recall, I got halfway from Green Park to Grosvenor Square and threatened to go home if you didn't put me into a taxi.''

Renie smiled at the memory. In 1964, Judith had only recently met Joe Flynn, rookie policeman. Despite five years of dreams and plans to visit Europe, Judith had been reluctant to part with Joe for three months. She had developed a form of migraine headache that had proved almost disastrous to their trip.

"So Claire is your pen-pal Margaret's sister-in-law," Renie said, deciding to drop the subject of Judith's earlier romantic tribulations. "I remember Margaret's brother. He was about fourteen and had spots."

"He's probably over them by now," Judith replied. The morning clouds, which had threatened rain, were now drifting away and the sun was coming out. At the moment, it promised to be a warm afternoon. Unless it rained. Even the weather reminded Judith of home. "I'm so sorry that Margaret and her husband left last week for Prague. It would have been fun to see her again after all these years."

Renie nodded in agreement. "Margaret's kids were just tiny then. In fact, didn't the youngest girl come along soon after we were here?"

"That's right. She's teaching ballet now." Judith's expression was nostalgic. "Goodness, but a lot has happened since then. We weren't married; you hadn't met Bill. I'm glad Margaret and I kept writing. At least I think I am. I'm not sure what we're getting into with her sister-in-law Claire."

The cousins again strolled past the expansive front of Harrod's. "It sounds like fun. A weekend in an English country cottage has always been my fantasy. What could be better as long as Bill and Joe are off fishing in Scotland?"

Judith arched a dark eyebrow. "Going with them? We fish. We might even catch something."

Renie shrugged. "We'll meet them in Edinburgh next week. Then we'll have eight more days to sightsee as a foursome. Let them do the male-bonding thing. With Bill's teaching schedule and private patients, and Joe's crazy hours as a cop, the only time they see each other is at family gatherings where they're both pretending they like their in-laws. This gives them a chance to bitch about us and our mothers."

"Fishermen don't talk," Judith countered. "All they ever say is 'Any luck?' and 'Nice fish.' "

Renie laughed. "True. But that's still bonding."

Judith sniffed. "You forget, it's a working weekend for me. I'm supposed to give advice."

"So? You can write the trip off as a business expense. We will. Why else did you come, if not to outwit the IRS?"

They had reached St. Quentin, where Judith stood outside, shifting from one tired foot to the other. "I know," she admitted. "Joe and I wanted to come along so much, and Margaret's relatives' plan to turn Claire's family home into a bed-and-breakfast was a real bonus. But three weeks is a long time to leave Hillside Manor. And Mother."

"*Mothers,*" Renie corrected, unwilling to stand around and listen to the cacophony of traffic and pedestrians. "My mother is sure we'll be bombed by IRA terrorists. Or, as she so quaintly puts it, sold into white slavery."

Trudging into the restaurant's foyer, Judith let out a long sigh. She thought of Gertrude, her own mother, who had griped and groaned and grumbled as if her daughter were deserting her for a three-year trip to Mars instead of three weeks in the United Kingdom. She thought of Hillside Manor, which had been left in the capable hands of Arlene Rankers, friend, neighbor, and substitute hostess par excellence. She also thought of her son, Mike, who was working as a forest ranger in Idaho's Nez Perce National Historical Park. All should be well with mother, son, and B&B. But life had taught Judith to expect the worst.

The reservation was in Claire Marchmont's name. A thin-lipped maitre d' led the cousins to a table covered with a crisp white cloth. Claire had not yet arrived.

"We're four minutes early," Judith announced, glancing at her watch. "Claire and her husband have a flat in town. I don't think they spend much time at Ravenscroft House."

"So you said." Renie's tone was indifferent. She had glommed onto a menu, and, as usual, was absorbed in the concept of food. Renie was still studying the selections and making little purring noises when Claire Marchmont arrived in a breathless state.

"Delightful!" she exclaimed in a well-bred voice. Her grey eyes darted from cousin to cousin. "Oh, my! Which of you is . . . ?"

Judith put out her hand. "I'm Judith McMonigle Flynn. And this is my cousin, Serena Jones. We call her Renie."

"Renie!" Claire's oval face seemed dazzled by the idiosyncrasy. "*Renie!* My!" She sank into the chair between the cousins. "Delightful!" she repeated, but now her tone was subdued.

While Claire appeared to be almost as tall as Judith, she was very slim, with a pale face and a delicate air. Mid-thirties, Judith guessed, and pretty, though her features were faintly pinched, as if from worry.

"So kind," Claire murmured after their order was taken for a bottle of Vouvray. "So very kind. Of you. To offer."

Judith smiled encouragingly. "But Margaret and I've been writing since we were in our teens. We only met once, when Renie and I were here in 1964. We got started with our letters through a program sponsored by my junior high school." Renie had also gotten involved with a pen-pal. But hers had stopped writing after running off at seventeen with an RAF pilot nicknamed Zipper. Margaret had proved more stable.

While sipping their wine, Claire apologized a half-dozen times for Margaret's absence. She also tried to update the cousins on her sister-in-law's recent past. Judith, who had received a lengthy letter in mid-March, didn't interrupt. Meanwhile, Renie rubbernecked around the other tables, looking not only for Princess Margaret, who was said to be a regular, but at the other customers' entrees.

"So there it is," Claire said, a bit wistfully, and Judith realized she'd lost the conversational thread. "A pity. Actually."

"Ah . . ." Judith struggled for an appropriate remark. "I suppose so. Life's full of ironies."

It seemed that Judith had inadvertently struck the right chord. Claire nodded enthusiastically. "Indeed! On the one hand, it's marvelous. That Aunt Pet has lived to such a great age. On the other, it's frustrating. To have so little say about things. Except for Charles, of course."

Charles, Judith recalled, was Claire's husband and Margaret's brother. Now middle-aged, Charles was, she hoped, without spots. He was a businessman, which was why the Marchmonts lived in London. As for Aunt Pet, Judith drew a blank. Margaret had never mentioned her.

". . . twins away at school." Claire was looking worried, agitating her wavy red hair with long, thin fingers. "They so love horses."

Claire and Charles Marchmont had twin boys, as Judith knew from Margaret's letters. "How old are they?" Judith asked, wishing Renie would stop trying to look over the shoulder of a bulky man in Harris tweeds at the next table.

"Nine," Claire answered, now smiling with maternal pride. "Such fine boys. Very keen on soccer. So convenient having twins. It's fortunate that they run in the family."

Renie was tapping one of the broad Harris tweed-covered shoulders. "What *is* that?" she asked.

The man glared at her from under sparse white eyebrows. "Turbot," he snapped, and swiveled back into place.

Renie wrinkled her pug nose. "Turtle? Did he say *turtle*? What next, donkey sandwiches?"

Looking apologetic, Claire explained the selections on the fixed-price menu. Renie smiled sheepishly, confessing that she understood most of the brasserie offerings but was more accustomed to salmon and trout and halibut. After the three women finally decided on steak *frite*, Judith tried to reconstruct Claire's conversation. As usual, she relied on logic to piece together the snatches she'd garnered from their hostess, as well as what she knew from Margaret's letters.

"You live in London," Judith said, savoring the Vouvray.

Claire nodded. "St. John's Wood."

Judith and Renie both recognized the neighborhood; some of the Grover ancestors had lived there in the late nineteenth century. "But you spend weekends at Ravenscroft House," Judith noted.

"Oh, yes," Claire replied with a tremulous smile. "At least some. London makes me nervy." To prove the point, Claire looked as if she were on the verge of an anxiety attack.

Renie was nodding. "We've got a cabin in the woods,

about an hour outside of town." She referred to the ramshackle structure that had been built a half-century earlier by their fathers and Grandpa Grover. "Of course it's sort of falling down. We don't go there very often."

Claire put a hand to her flat breast and leaned back in the chair. "Oh! I know! These old houses are so stress-inducing! The heating, the electrical, the plumbing!"

"Actually," Renie murmured, "we don't exactly have plumbing. Or electricity or heating. The outhouse is collapsing, too."

Claire sympathized. "Outhouses! My! We call them outbuildings. But I know what you mean about repairs. Such a challenge! Judith—may I call you that, I hope? Thank you so. Margaret said you renovated your family home. The one in the city. Into a bed-and-breakfast. I shall hang on every word. I swear."

Judith assumed a modest air. "I'll do my best. Hillside Manor had some serious problems, too." Fondly, she pictured the Edwardian house on the hill, with its fresh green paint and white trim, the bay windows, the five guest bedrooms on the second floor, the family quarters in the expanded attic, and the enclosed backyard with the last few fruit trees from the original orchard. There was a double garage, too. And the remodeled toolshed where her mother lived. Gertrude Grover had refused to share a roof with her son-in-law. She didn't like Judith's second husband much better than her first one.

"It *was* a challenge," Judith finally said, thinking more of coping with Gertrude than of the renovations. "It's expensive. I had to take out a loan."

Claire's high forehead creased. "My word! A loan! Charles should hate that!"

Trying to be tactful, Judith made an effort to put Claire's mind at rest. "I'm sure my situation was different. I'd been recently widowed and had no savings." Dan McMonigle had blown every dime on the horse races or the state lottery. "My husband wasn't insurable." Dan had weighed over four hundred pounds when he'd died at the age of forty-nine. "We had no equity in our home." After defaulting on the only house they'd ever owned, the McMonigles had lived in a series of seedy rentals, and had been about to be evicted when Dan had, as Judith put it, conveniently blown up. "In fact," she went on, feigning serenity, "I had no choice but to move in with my mother. That's when it occurred to me that it didn't make sense for the two of us to rattle around in a big old house. My son was almost ready for college."

"How true!" Claire positively beamed, revealing small, perfect white teeth. "That's precisely what I've told Charles. Why maintain a second home with so many expenditures and taxation? Why not turn it into something that will produce income?"

"Exactly," Judith agreed. "The main thing is to figure out if you're going to run it or let someone do it for you."

Claire's smile evaporated. "Oh, no. The main thing is Aunt Pet," she insisted, her rather wispy voice now firm. "First of all, she has to die."

TWO

PAUL FLYNN HAD shown his brother and his sister-in-law a good time since their arrival in England on Saturday, April seventeenth. Of course Paul's leisure time was limited by his busy schedule doing whatever diplomats did at the Court of St. James. "Translations," Joe had told Judith with a wink. He had never given Paul much credit for hard work, insisting that his brother got by on charm.

But Paul had picked up the hefty dinner tab at Jason's Court on Wednesday night. Meanwhile, Renie and Bill had joined some other IMNUTS conferees at La Gavroche. The gathering's finale was set for Thursday evening, and Bill had managed to finagle tickets for the Flynns. The cocktail reception and dinner were to be held at the Barbican Centre.

En route to the festivities, Renie, who had a passion for British history, acted as the quartet's self-appointed tour guide. "There's the Old Bailey," she cried, bouncing on the taxi seat. "It was built on the site of Newgate Prison. You wouldn't believe the horrors that went on there."

"Perps will be perps," Joe Flynn murmured, adjusting the black tie on his rented tuxedo.

"I mean the treatment they got," Renie said. "It was incredibly cruel."

"That's right," Joe retorted. "Coddle the criminals.

Treat them with kid gloves. Whatever happened to brass knuckles and the rubber hose?''

Renie ignored Joe. "There! Where those post office buildings stand now, that was once Grey Friars, the Franciscan church."

"Franciscans wear brown," Judith put in, more concerned with her own garb than monks' habits. She was trying to tame the long purple silk scarf that hung down the back of her simple matching gown. Even on sale, the floor-length dress had fetched an exorbitant price. Judith had rationalized away the tab, assuring herself that she would be able to wear it not only on the trip, but afterward. Maybe. If she and Joe ever went anywhere formal. Which they didn't. Judith tried not to think about how much the dress had cost, and concentrated instead on the conversation.

"Yesterday afternoon a paper was presented on St. Francis," Bill Jones noted, "by a woman from the University of Ottawa. Her premise was that St. Francis could penetrate the human soul and analyze behavior objectively. Had he devoted himself to the field, he could have made enormous contributions to the study of psychology."

"Aldersgate!" exclaimed Renie, after the taxi had turned into St. Martin's Le Grand. "It's gone now, but in 1603, King James entered London through it to claim the throne after Queen Elizabeth died."

As the taxi came to a stop in line behind the queue of vehicles arriving at the Barbican's conference headquarters, Judith turned to Joe. She hesitated for a split second, drinking in his presence. In middle age, the receding red hair had streaks of gray; there was the hint of a paunch under the black cummerbund. But Joe Flynn was otherwise still fit, and the green eyes retained their sparkle. Most of all, the round, engaging face had lost none of its charm for Judith.

"Joe," Judith said plaintively, "don't let my tails drag."

Joe looked puzzled, then grinned. "Oh, your scarf. Sure, I'll keep an eye on your tail . . . s." The grin turned faintly wicked.

"Now remember," Bill cautioned Judith and Joe, "the

conferees are unwinding. They've put in a very intensive four and a half days. You may see them in—''

''The nude.'' Renie gave Bill a sweet smile. After almost thirty years of marriage, the Joneses were accustomed to interruptions. Or, if not accustomed, they had stopped trying to kill each other. Most of the time. ''What Bill means is that these people may sound like a bunch of pedantic stuffed shirts, but underneath all their academic titles and honors, they're—''

''Just as wacked-out as you are,'' Bill finished smugly, with a slap on his wife's crepe-de-chine-covered knee.

The taxi pulled into the unloading zone. Bill paid the driver, who spoke no English of any kind, and followed the others into the centre.

''This had been the outer fortification of the City of London, going way back,'' Renie announced, bumping into a kilted gentlemen whose tartan tam was knocked askew. ''Henry III leveled the tower in the thirteenth century, but it was rebuilt. The area was almost wiped out by German bombs in World War II. This complex was completed in—''

''Ten minutes,'' Bill said, grabbing hold of Renie and steering her between some French Canadians and a pair of New Zealanders. ''We're ten minutes late. It must have been all that traffic on the Holborn Viaduct.''

''Then everybody's one drink ahead of us,'' Joe remarked as Judith got a high heel caught between the stones of the entrance floor. ''And my wife's already having problems walking.''

''I'm afraid of tripping over my scarf,'' Judith complained.

Joe squeezed her shoulders. ''You look terrific, Jude-girl. Purple is almost as good on you as red. Or black or blue or green.''

His use of her despised nickname was forgotten in the pleasure of his compliment. Briefly, she snuggled up next to him. ''I can't believe how handsome you are in that tux. It reminds me of our wedding day.''

Renie jammed her elbow into Judith's bare arm. ''Cut the cooing crap,'' she said out of the side of her mouth.

"You're acting like newlyweds and embarrassing Bill and me. Jeez, you've been married for almost three years. Have a fight or something normal."

Joe stopped admiring his wife long enough to survey the reception room with its banks of spring flowers and ornate chandeliers. "Nice," he remarked. "It reminds me of the city employees' cafeteria at home. Here comes a giant cockroach now."

The giant cockroach was actually a waiter clad in silver livery, bearing a tray of hors d'oeuvres. Renie grabbed two of everything while Bill pretended he'd never seen her before in his life. The crowd milled about, chattering in various forms of the English language. Judith, who was an inveterate people-watcher, found herself bedazzled by the delegates who came from all over the Commonwealth and the United States. The IMNUTS members and their guests did indeed seem to be unwinding as the laughter flowed on a rising tide of spirits, both potable and exuberant.

At the open bar, everyone in the Flynn-Jones party ordered Scotch except Renie, who was elated to discover a store of Kentucky bourbon. Nodding at a goateed man with a cane in one hand and a margarita in the other, Bill brushed crumbs off his wife's metallic tunic with a practiced hand.

"There's the keynote speaker, Alfred Fortescue, looking down the front of that redhead's dress," Bill said in his carefully modulated voice. "Fortescue is behavioral."

"Yes, he is," Joe agreed. "Who's the tall blond woman in the long sarong doing the tango with the midget?"

Bill followed Joe's gaze. "The midget is Karl Herkendorfer from Columbia University. He's into dreams. The blond is Ursula Renfrew-Smythe from Cambridge. She's sexual deviation."

Joe lifted one reddish eyebrow. "Has Ursula met Alfred?"

"They're married," Bill replied, somehow keeping a straight face. "He's at Cambridge, too."

Judith was craning her neck to see around several people who were mesmerized by a swarthy man balancing a silver cream pitcher on his head. "Who's the guy dressed like

Elvis?'' she inquired, discreetly gesturing in the direction of a spangled and sequined figure who wriggled his hips near the long table that held the punch bowl and more hors d'oeuvres.

Bill peered through his glasses. ''It's Elvis. Or so he says. Vanderbilt University. His specialty is delusions.''

''No kidding,'' said Joe very softly. ''And here I was, thinking about arresting all these delegates for impersonating real people. It would—'' A loud explosion caused Joe to slam a hand into Judith's back. ''Hit the floor! Cover me, I'm going in!''

Calmly, Bill sipped his scotch. ''It's all right, Joe. Sir Angus MacDougall set off a firecracker in that suit of armor by the far wall. Unfortunately, Alonzo Devlin was inside. He's memory, University of Wisconsin.''

''He's history, if you ask me,'' Renie remarked, as several people attempted to pry Alonzo out of the armor. She poked her husband in the chest. ''Hey, are all these people really crazy? I mean, you're not. At least not often. But let's face it, this bunch strikes me as bizarre.''

''They're acting out,'' Bill said, at his most unflappable. ''It's good for them. Tomorrow, they'll head home, go back to their mundane lives, teach classes, advise students, see patients, take out the garbage.'' His voice dropped with every phrase, then he grabbed Renie by the arm. ''Come on, there's Sidney Weinstock, Stanford. He's depression. I need to talk to him.''

''You sure do,'' Renie muttered as Bill led her away.

Judith was trying to rearrange her long purple scarf. ''Maybe we shouldn't have come,'' she muttered. ''This place is goofy.''

But Joe was no longer hovering at her side. Ever the policeman, he had rushed off to attend to Alonzo Devlin. Judith sighed and decided to replenish her drink.

''Don't let these high jinks disturb you,'' a distinguished man with silver hair and a mustache to match said calmly. ''You have no idea how dedicated these people are. They need diversion.''

Judith eyed the man a bit warily. ''I suppose. But it's awfully rowdy. For grown-ups.''

The man cupped his left ear. "Eh? Rowley? For turnips? How d'you do, Mrs. Rowley. But I think they're serving peas. Swinford, Woodley Swinford. But call me Doodles. Delighted, of course." He shook hands with a mighty grip.

"Flynn," Judith shouted, one eye on a man who was dangling from the chandelier. "*Judith Flynn.*"

"Jewish Finn? Didn't know there were any. Very nice, very nice." Doodles Swinford beamed under the mustache, his big teeth making him look like a cross between Bugs Bunny and Adolf Hitler.

Judith surrendered the task of trying to explain herself. Doodles paid no heed to the dangling man. "Don't know about you, but I haven't the foggiest what these people are talking about. It's m'wife who's the delegate. London University, amnesia. What's your specialty, Mrs. . . . Sorry, didn't catch your name. Finnish, I suppose, with all those 'Ns.' "

"Sort of," Judith muttered, then took pity on Doodles Swinford's deafness. "My husband is with the police."

"He's with a valise? Where?" Doodles's glance darted around the room. Two men were carrying Alonzo Devlin away on a stretcher. "Is your husband a doctor? I rather hope so. They could use one about now."

Judith winced. "The *police*," she all but screamed. "In the States."

"The police!" Doodles looked vaguely alarmed. "You don't say! Do excuse me, I'm a bit hard of hearing. Just as well. These fetes are such a bore. Much prefer staying home and watching the telly. You Yanks must find England very dull."

Since the man on the chandelier had just fallen into the punch bowl, Judith couldn't agree. "Goodness, I think he cut himself," she gasped.

"Possibly," Doodles allowed with a vague glance at the long table. "I'm in insurance. Glad I don't carry *his* accident policy. No rider for punch bowl injury."

Joe, Bill, and three other men who seemed to know what they were doing had now converged on the man who had fallen out of the chandelier. Judith scanned the crowd for

Renie. She was at the other end of the table, stuffing can-
apés in her mouth.

"Insurance," Judith said in an odd voice. "Oh, yes, I
see. How interesting."

To Judith's surprise, Doodles Swinford nodded vigorously. "It is indeed. You'd be flummoxed. I'm primarily
into animals."

The large room with its swirl of glittering guests and
masses of flowers and hyperactivity under the chandelier
seemed to swim before Judith's eyes. "Animals?" she echoed faintly.

Doodles nodded as he sucked on his daiquiri. "Exotic
pets. Pedigreed dogs and cats. Racehorses. Have you any
idea what the annual premium is on a hedgehog?"

Judith hadn't. She was admitting as much when she saw
Joe and Bill help the chandelier man to his feet. A moment
later, she felt a tap on her shoulder. It was Renie, looking
remarkably composed.

"Guess what?" said Renie. "It's time for dinner. As
soon as they remove the latest carcass, we can go into the
banquet hall."

"Is that good?" Judith asked with a nervous expression.

"Dinner is always good," Renie replied. "At least as a
concept. Here come Bill and Joe, back from their recent
emergency run. I think we're having prime rib."

Dazedly, Judith looked around her. Doodles Swinford
had disappeared, but Joe was almost immediately in front
of her.

"Ready?" he asked, offering his arm.

Judith stared at her husband. "Yes. No." She saw the
magic gold flecks dance in the green eyes and relaxed a
bit. "Yes, I'm ready." She sighed, slipping her hand
through his arm. "But after all this, I'm a just a little . . .
a-Freud."

Once again, Joe arched his eyebrow. "That, Jude-girl, is
because you're too Jung."

Following Renie and Bill, they advanced to the banquet
hall.

                    *   *   *

Judith and Joe Flynn were in bed. Room service had delivered breakfast, complete with hot toast, excellent sausages, country eggs, and surprisingly delicious coffee. Judith nestled back among the pillows and savored the last morning of their stay in London. The Abbey Court was not so much a hotel as it was a home, a restored Victorian mansion tucked between Bayswater and Notting Hill. Judith had studied the nineteenth-century structure closely, hoping to get some ideas for Claire's conversion of Ravenscroft House. Taking a sip of her coffee, Judith turned to Joe.

"Bangers." She sighed. "Only the English and the Germans make them properly. And Italians and Austrians."

Joe, who was wearing a semi-hideous plaid bathrobe that his mother-in-law had chosen from a mail-order catalog as his Christmas gift, arched an eyebrow at his wife. "Bangers?" he inquired. "As in sausages? Or," he went on, coming over to kneel on the bed and kiss his wife's forehead, "as in me?"

As ever, Judith melted. Thirty years later, Judith was still under Joe Flynn's spell. "I love you," she said simply. "I loved you in 1964, when Renie and I stayed at a—guess what?—a bed-and-breakfast in Clarges Street for eight dollars a night. It's been torn down. But you're still here. So am I."

"So's London," Joe Flynn remarked, nuzzling Judith's temple. "So's the rest of England and Scotland and Ireland and Wales. The only difference is, this place is costing us about twenty times as much. And they call it 'moderately priced.' Why don't you jack up your fees so that we can actually afford this trip?"

Judith let Joe's hands explore the curves of her body. "Jack what?" she asked in a wispy voice.

Joe chuckled, the low, rich sound that Judith loved so much. "At least we'll get a tax break. I've worked all the Scotland Yard angles, including six hours at a desk, giving them my useless Colonialist opinion on unsolved cases. I didn't solve anything, but I'll get a written thank-you to show the IRS. Now you strut your stuff at that old house in . . . where is it? I forget." The fact didn't seem to perturb him. He buried his face in the curve of Judith's neck.

"Somerset." Judith spoke dreamily, with one hand maneuvering the breakfast tray onto the floor. "You'll catch . . . fish."

"Salmon," Joe replied in a muffled voice. "In a stream. Nice."

"Very." With a rapturous tremor, Judith dismissed salmon, Somerset, and spending from her mind. Everything was forgotten, including the soft rain that fell outside the Abbey Court. Within the hour, Judith and Joe would be parted. The separation would last a mere week, but for Judith, who had pined for Joe on her previous trip to England thirty years earlier, the loneliness seemed to hover over her like the leaden skies of London.

Even after they had made love, Joe Flynn sensed his wife's lingering melancholia. "Jude-girl," he said, "what's wrong? You seem off your feed. How can that be? You ate like Renie and you carried on like Madame de Pompadour."

The comparison, at least to Madame de Pompadour, made Judith roll her eyes. "It's nothing to do with you, Joe. It's the weekend at Ravenscroft House. I'm supposed to be some expert at fixing up old dumps with bad plumbing and inflammable electricity. Just because I did it with Hillside Manor doesn't mean I can duplicate the renovation of some English country cottage. Besides, the Marchmonts can't do anything until Claire's ninety-four-year-old aunt dies. She's got control of the money, and from what Renie and I gather, she's kind of . . . difficult."

Joe was heading for the shower. He turned, his green eyes dancing. "A difficult old lady who actually owns the family house? What's wrong? Don't they have a tool-shed?" Joe disappeared into the bathroom.

"Mother's not ninety-four," Judith shouted after her husband. There was no reply. "Not yet." A rush of water ensued. "She doesn't have any money," Judith added, but to herself.

Pouring a last cup of coffee from the silver pot, Judith started to put on her makeup. People were truly the same, all over the world: stubborn old ladies and put-upon middle-aged men and worry-prone wives who wanted to please everybody. Judith sympathized with Claire Marchmont. Claire was probably fifteen years younger, but she was in the same boat as Judith, with a cantankerous oldster at one end and, presumably, a much-loved husband at the other.

Judith got dressed, kissed Joe good-bye, and joined a sleep-eyed Renie for the taxi ride to Waterloo Station.

The cousins didn't mind the rain that fell on London's urban sprawl. It was April, and it was probably raining at home. The high-speed train they were taking wouldn't stop until they reached Slough, the spur to Windsor and Eton.

"They must have enough bedrooms at Ravenscroft House so we won't have to sleep together," Renie remarked, shrugging out of her black trenchcoat and sticking to her agenda of creature comforts. "You always try to push me out of bed."

"I haven't done that since we were kids," Judith replied indignantly. "But you're right. The Marchmonts—or should I say Aunt Pet?—must have extra space or they wouldn't be thinking about turning the place into a B&B."

Three days had passed since Judith and Renie had lunched with Claire Marchmont. While Bill attended the conference sessions and Joe observed Scotland Yard, Judith and Renie trooped all over London, from Wapping Wall to Windsor, from Hampstead Heath to Hampton Court. They had seen the Tower of London, the Houses of Parliament, St. Paul's, Westminster Abbey, the silver vaults, the Cloth Fair, Temple Bar, Somerset House, Clarence House, Lancaster House, and the House of Donuts. By the time they kissed their husbands farewell, the cousins were reeling. Just sitting quietly on the train was a blessed relief.

"I wonder if the Marchmont place has a thatched roof," Renie mused as they roared through London's old urban blight. Rows and rows of smoke-blackened houses lined bleak narrow streets. The only color was provided by brave, bright window boxes filled with spring flowers. "Thatch has to be changed every hundred years, you know."

Judith grimaced at Renie. "Gee, lucky me, I don't have to worry about that. Claire said they were by a river."

"Just like our cabin." Renie was now looking out through the rain-spattered windows at some of the newer suburbs. Though they were painted from a brighter palette, the lack of imagination made them as drab as the dwellings from the previous century. "Do you suppose Aunt Pet is about to croak?"

"It didn't sound like it. She was ninety-four on April first, but the joke's on the relatives. Except for arthritis, the old girl's got the constitution of an ox." Judith stretched out her long legs and admired the updated version of British Rail. The high-speed train traveled at ninety miles an hour, which seemed only a fraction slower than the taxi she had taken to Buckingham Palace. "And, as Claire hinted in her well-bred way, Auntie has control of the money, and thus of the entire family."

"Are there a lot of them?" Renie inquired.

Judith reflected. "I don't think so. Over the years, I vaguely remember Margaret writing about various shirttail relations who had died. I assume they were Claire Ravenscroft's kin."

The train was now zipping through patches of green. Apparently, they had finally left London's suburbs. Renie stared out the window for a few moments, then turned back to Judith. "Are they rich? Claire's family, I mean. I know the Marchmonts weren't."

Judith gave a shrug. "Mr. Marchmont was a fishmonger. Remember how we visited the docks with Margaret and got fresh plaice for supper? Oh, her father did very well, and I gather Charles went to university someplace. I don't know about Claire's background. Maybe Charles married up."

For some time, the cousins sat in silence. Judith considered Charles Marchmont, the kid brother who had spoken in shy mumbles but had dreams of becoming an architect. It seemed that he had changed his mind. Or Fate had changed it for him. A lot had changed in thirty years. Judith and Renie had changed; England had changed; the world had changed. Upon her return from Europe in 1964, Judith knew she wanted to marry Joe Flynn. Fortunately, he wanted the same thing. The following year, they had become engaged. Judith had finished her degree in librarianship. Joe was no longer a rookie, but a seasoned vice squad cop. With their education behind them, Judith and Joe planned to get married. And so they did, but not to each other.

Joe may not have been a novice, but he hadn't yet developed the tough shell that protects veteran policemen from life's cruelties. The spectacle of two teenagers who had overdosed on drugs had sent Joe Flynn reeling off to a nearby bar. He had drunk himself stupid, and let a voluptuous lounge singer drag him off to a justice of the peace in Las Vegas. Judith was devastated, and retaliated by marrying Dan McMonigle. It hadn't been a satisfactory revenge; instead, it was eighteen years of penance. Then she had found Joe again, and life was once more worth living.

"Look!" Renie exclaimed, after the stop at Slough. "Fields! Farms! Foals! England as we knew it!"

Sure enough, the pastoral scene slipping by the train window was as lush as it was tidy. Low stone fences separated properties, and Judith glimpsed an occasional wooden stile. Smoke spiraled from the chimney of a farmhouse nestled in a vale. New lambs frisked across satiny grass. "This is more like it," Judith said with a contented sigh. "Do you remember what a goose I was when we saw London the very first time?"

Renie laughed. "You blubbered like a baby. I think you even forgot about Joe for a while. We'd come up from Southampton on the boat-train, and the minute we saw Big Ben and the Houses of Parliament, you burst into tears and said, 'Oh, my God, I've come home!' I figured you'd been watching too many old British movies on TV."

"But," Judith persisted, still vaguely embarrassed by the memory, "I really felt that way. It was some atavistic thing, going back to Grandpa Grover."

"Grandpa hated England," Renie pointed out. "He used to call the English 'those goddamned Limeys.' "

"That's because he *was* English," Judith countered. "Once he took out his American citizenship papers, he hated everybody who was different. It was the English way. Insular. Prejudiced. Superior."

At Reading, two young men wearing lots of leather and

studs sat down next to the cousins. Their magenta and chartreuse punk haircuts didn't endear them to Judith and Renie. Neither did their conversation, which seemed to be made up of brief bursts that sounded like "naffy-fook-fudder!"

Twenty minutes later, Judith and Renie were glad to change trains at Newbury. The express moved at a mere sixty miles an hour, but the cousins weren't sorry. They were now deep in the countryside, crossing the North Wessex Downs, which rolled in every direction, gently green, and infinitely peaceful. Judith studied her map of the area and smiled at the quaint place names: Inkpen Hill. Buckleberry Common. Wayland's Smithy. And, to her librarian's delight, Watership Down.

Their route kept close to the Kennet and Avon Canal, where speckled ducks paddled downstream on what had been a bustling waterway in the Victorian age. The rain had almost stopped by the time they reached Pewsey.

In the Vale of Pewsey, newly plowed wheat fields resembled rich brown ribbons. There were sheep, of course, munching the wet new grasses. The train raced across the Salisbury Plain, and Judith wished she could visit Stonehenge, which, according to the map, seemed near the railroad line.

"Maybe next time," she murmured.

"What?" Renie was jarred from her admiration of yellow and blue wildflowers growing up the sweep of Westbury Hill.

Judith was rueful. "We missed so much the first time we came to England." She waved at the passing countryside. "This whole area, for instance. I'm already feeling bad about what we won't see on this trip."

Renie made a face. "Gee, you're a lot of fun, coz. Think of what we have seen. *Will* see. And when's lunch?"

Chastened, Judith checked her watch. "We're due in at Castle Cary shortly before noon. The local line leaves in fifteen minutes. Claire says it'll take less than half an hour to get to Little Pauncefoot. Ravenscroft House is right on the edge of the village. Maybe they intend to feed us when we get there."

Renie brightened. ''Good. Remember all the great food we had when we stayed with Margaret and her husband? Plus tea. A minimum of four meals a day. The English have the right idea about eating.''

''Well . . .'' Judith recalled some of the less savory meals they'd eaten in 1964. On a list of international cuisine, English cooking would have ranked near the bottom in those days. ''Claire or Charles will meet us, I think. They drove down from London last night. Aunt Pet had a spell, or something.''

The train that took the cousins from Castle Cary to Little Pauncefoot was a far cry from Brit Rail's high-speed and express models. It was old, it was small, it was independently owned and operated. Still, it creaked its way from village to village right on schedule. By the time they stopped at Little Pauncefoot, a hint of sun was poking through the clouds.

Judith and Renie were the only passengers to disembark. The station was tiny and seemed deserted. They hauled their luggage out to the road, but there was no sign of a waiting car.

''Now what?'' Judith gingerly sat on her big suitcase.

Renie leaned against the white railway crossing gate. ''The town must be over there somewhere,'' she said, pointing down the road, ''just past those shops and the pub.''

Judith consulted the hand-drawn map Claire had given her. She grimaced. ''That *is* the town. Or village. The village green is behind the shops, then there's another street— no, it's a lane of some sort—and Ravenscroft House. It's actually very close. See that wall?''

Renie turned. Not twenty feet away was a barrier of mellow gold stone, perhaps five feet high. Beyond, they saw trees and what looked like a turret.

''Is that the church?'' Renie asked.

Judith again studied the map. ''Maybe,'' she answered. ''The church is in that direction. St. Edith's.''

A soft wind was ruffling the plane trees. Renie gazed at the old wall. ''It curves there. And I can see a bridge just behind the station. That must be the river. The house can't be very far away.''

"Right, Ravenscroft House is on the river. But we can't climb over that brick wall. At least not with our suitcases.'' Judith took another look at their surroundings. There wasn't a franchise in sight. The only things that moved besides the trees were two older women shuffling into a shop, and a limping brown dog. "We'll have to walk down the street and double back.''

The old brown dog collapsed about ten yards away from the cousins. Before Renie could pick up her suitcase, a red Alfa Romeo convertible roared down the High Street. The dog dragged himself onto the sidewalk and collapsed again. The sports car stopped within inches of Judith and Renie.

"Yo!'' cried the young man who was behind the wheel. "Are you the Yanks?''

"*Yo?*'' Renie gave Judith a look of dismay. "Whatever happened to 'I say, old thing'?''

But Judith was already dragging her suitcase up to the Alfa Romeo. "We're Mrs. Flynn and Mrs. Jones. Are you . . . ah . . . from Ravenscroft House?''

The handsome young man with the jet-black hair and the mocking black eyes slapped the steering wheel. "In a manner of speaking. I'm Alexei Karamzin, Claire's cousin. Hop in.''

"But . . .'' Judith indicated their luggage. The car was a two-seater. "Should we leave these and come back later?''

Alexei's dark eyebrows arched. "Bloody bad idea. Bikers buzz through these quaint old places and steal everybody blind. England isn't what it used to be.'' With the press of a button, he flipped the trunk open. "There, give those bags a toss into the boot.''

"What about *these* bags?'' Renie pointed to herself and Judith. "How are we going to fit into this squirty little car?''

Clearly, Alexei hadn't thought ahead. His response was limited to running a lean, brown hand through his hair. After stowing the luggage, Judith tried to sit on one haunch and make room for Renie. As Alexei rocketed off down the High Street, Judith slid into Renie, who fell into the

well between the seats. Alexei grabbed Renie's arm instead
of the stick shift. Renie tumbled under the dashboard and
landed on Judith's feet.

"Don't fret, it's not far," Alexei said, his longish hair
blowing over his shirt collar. "The house is just on the
other side of the green. Drink?" With one hand, he deftly
produced a leather flask from somewhere on his person.

"Ah—no thanks," Judith replied. Faintly appalled, she
watched Alexei take a hefty swig.

"Nothing like a little pick-me-up," he said blithely,
looking at Judith instead of the road. "Weekends with the
relatives require fortification. I must be charming, especially to Aunt Pet."

Judith made no comment, silently willing Alexei to pay
attention to his driving. As Renie wallowed about on the
floor, Judith glimpsed a pub, a tea shop, and a greengrocer.
Then they swung around a corner, and for what seemed
like split seconds, were traveling a country highway. "To
Great Pauncefoot" and "To Yeovil" read the weathered
sign. A moment later they had turned again, and were slowing down. A small stone church was on their left; Judith
presumed it was St. Edith's. She made some quick mental
notes: Ravenscroft House was close to the railway station,
a decent highway, a house of prayer, and some conven-
iences. Hillside Manor was situated similarly, even though
it was in the middle of a big city. The comparison gave
Judith heart.

Trees surrounded the village green, which was calm except for a mother pushing a pram and an elderly man leading a cat on a leash. Judith thought of Sweetums. She
thought about putting him on a leash. She thought about
Sweetums's reaction. She thought about being clawed to
shreds. She decided to stick to thinking about converting
Ravenscroft House into a B&B.

Judith saw a pillar in the middle of the grassy expanse,
and then another piece of granite at the far end of the green.
War memorials, she thought, then realized that Alexei had
slowed down again. Renie had the opportunity to squeeze
herself into a crouch. Trying to rearrange her legs, Judith
saw a continuation of the same mellow wall that had run

past the railway station. But, just ahead of the Alfa, the wall itself was bisected by a charming building made from the same golden stone.

"It's a gatehouse!" Judith exclaimed, and her mind began to race with possibilities. The two floors, with the top story built over the drive, probably wouldn't accommodate more than three guest rooms. The kitchen was bound to be small, and extra baths would present a problem. But the setting was wonderful, just off the village green and apparently close to the river. So wrapped up in her plans was Judith that she didn't at first realize they hadn't come to a full stop. Instead, they were cruising up a curving gravel drive lined with plane trees, narcissus, and jonquils. At the crest of the gentle slope, Alexei finally braked.

"Ravenscroft House," he said in a careless voice. "I do hope they've sent out for pizza."

Judith scarcely heard Alexei. Her mouth fell open. This was no cozy thatched cottage. Ravenscroft House was magnificent. Judith felt like pinching herself. Instead, she merely stared. And stared some more.

THREE

The structure that lay before her was three symmetrical stories of late-Elizabethan limestone, with wings at each end, a projecting porch, and great mullioned windows that reflected the afternoon sun like gold nuggets on a chamois cloth.

Alexei had punched the button to open the trunk and was now jerking the keys out of the ignition. "Quite the old pile, eh?" He jumped from the Alfa and began striding toward the entrance.

"Holy Mother!" Judith breathed. Her eyes traveled from the statuary that stood in niches along the top floor to the Renaissance lozenge over the entrance. At the rear of the house, the hint of turrets rose over the roof and its various chimneys. Judith was utterly dazzled.

"Hey!" Renie clawed at her cousin's navy slacks. "Move it, you twit! I haven't been in a position like this since I was a fetus!"

"Oh!" Startled, Judith fumbled with the door, then struggled to get out of the low-slung car. She stopped gawking long enough to help Renie.

Unfolding herself, Renie started to chide Judith, then caught sight of the magnificent building. "Oh, good Lord! Is this . . . *it*?"

Dumbly, Judith nodded. The cousins both stared, drinking in the four-hundred-year-old house, the manicured grounds, the splashes of spring flowers, and the

29

enormity of finding themselves in such a place.

"Ravenscroft House," Judith murmured. "It's like something out of *Country Life*."

"Or my dreams," Renie said in a hushed voice.

But Ravenscroft House was real enough, and as if to prove it, a stately butler appeared just after Alexei went inside.

"Harwood, at your service." He spoke in a precise wheeze, and his bow was almost imperceptible.

"Thanks, Harwood," Renie replied. "We've got two suitcases. They're big and they're battered, so don't worry if you drop them."

Harwood looked askance, if only for a split second. Then, much like a racing yacht bending into the wind, he proceeded to remove the cousins' luggage, one case at a time.

As Judith and Renie ascended the three steps that led to the enclosed porch, Claire Marchmont rushed out to greet them. "Oh! You're here! Thank goodness! Oh! This is . . . delightful!"

Judith felt almost as disconcerted as her hostess. She tried not to gape at the tapestries and paintings that lined what she assumed was the original screens passage but now served as the entry hall.

"This is breathtaking," Judith declared, tearing her eyes away from the larger-than-life statues of Minerva, Venus, Aurora, and Diana. "I had no idea Ravenscroft House was so . . . vast. It's much grander than Hillside Manor." The understatement almost choked her.

Claire, however, didn't take the remark as a compliment. "That's the very problem. It's going to require a great deal of work and expense to make it into a guest house. Eventually," she added quickly, and looked over her shoulder as if someone were eavesdropping.

No one was, unless it was Harwood, who was carrying Renie's black suitcase as he wheezed his way out of the entry hall and disappeared.

"I'll show you your rooms," Claire said, remembering her duties as a hostess. "Then we'll lunch."

Renie gave Claire an uncertain smile. "Has the pizza truck arrived?"

Claire's oval face puckered slightly, then she laughed, a light, tentative sound. "Oh, Alexei! He's a bit of a tease. Though he *is* fond of pizza. And yes," Claire continued, leading them through a stone screen decorated with Corinthian columns and ornate strapwork, "they definitely deliver to Ravenscroft House. You'd be surprised at how things have changed here over the years."

"I would," Judith replied. "I *am*." They were passing through what appeared to be the main hall with an impressive collection of antique furnishings and portraits that spanned at least four centuries. Ruffs, perukes, muttonchops and cloches marked the passing of time as well as fashion. Even the more modern school was represented with an abstract painting, presumably of a woman in red. Or maybe it was a British phone booth. Judith wasn't sure. More easily recognizable was a youthful Claire Marchmont in white tulle near the door that led to the main staircase. Judith was particularly taken with two paintings of what she guessed was the same young woman, a beautiful brunette who had posed in her teens wearing classic chiffon with a brocade bodice. The butter-yellow gown reminded Judith of her own high school prom dress. Later, in maturity, the brunette wore emerald-green satin and a bouffant hairstyle. Again, Judith felt a whiff of nostalgia.

"The portraits are wonderful," Judith remarked, pausing by the brunette beauty's paintings. "Did the family commission local artists or bring them in from London?"

A faint look of alarm crossed Claire's face. Judith wondered if it was an expression of genuine dismay or a nervous habit.

"Oh!" Claire exclaimed, putting a tentative hand at Judith's elbow, "I can only speak for my own sitting. An artist who summered at Lyme Regis was recommended. He was very bad-tempered. But good. As a painter. That is."

Claire had steered Judith to the staircase. "We're lucky here. I suppose," Claire continued, speaking rapidly. "Unlike so many villages closer to London, Little Pauncefoot hasn't been spoiled by mini-marts and gas stations and housing developments.'' Her voice held a note of doubt as they ascended the stairs amid walls lined with more Flemish tapestries. ''It's really quite unchanged from what I remember as a child. Between here and Great Pauncefoot, there are still farms and orchards. But in the other direction toward Yeovil, there is almost no distinction between the village and the town. We're just five minutes from Taco Bell.'' The idea seemed to please Claire, whose delivery had slowed.

It didn't have the same effect on Judith. She said nothing, as they traipsed along a paneled corridor. Harwood was coming through a door, looking as if he were about to collapse. He gave Claire a deferential nod in passing.

Claire hesitated, her eyes flitting from cousin to cousin. ''Oh! That bag was . . . ?'' Renie waggled a hand. Claire looked relieved. ''Then this is your room . . . *Renie*.'' The nickname tumbled off her tongue as if she were tasting it to make sure it wasn't too spicy. Claire indicated the door across the wide corridor. ''This is yours, Judith. Ordinarily, we have five extra rooms, but with Alexei and Natasha spending the weekend, we have only three. I hope they'll do. Unfortunately, there are just two baths on this floor. I've already spoken with Alex and Nats about sharing.''

The cousins agreed that sharing was fine. Each of their appointed bedrooms was large, airy, and full of furniture that looked as if it should be housed in a museum. Renie had a nineteenth-century sleigh bed; Judith's curtained and canopied four-poster probably had come with the house.

Trying to contain their elation at such luxury, the cousins bounded back and forth between the elegant bedrooms. Claire, however, was apologetic.

''Things are not what they once were,'' she lamented. ''Auntie has had to cut staff. Or, I should say, not replace them. Harwood and Auntie's maid, Dora, are all that's left of the old servants. Dora's very frail, and Harwood's never been the same since his knee was shattered at Messina during the Second World War. But of course the family was elated to get him back after he was invalided out of the service. The war took a terrible toll on the servant class. They wanted to do other things after demobilization. It's been very hard on people like Aunt Pet. Nowadays, we have to make do with Mrs. Tichborne, the housekeeper, and dailies from Great Pauncefoot. The same is true with the gardeners. The Beaker brothers come only once a week. Luckily, there are four of them.''

Judith was still smiling. ''No problem, Claire. The only help I have at Hillside Manor is a cleaning woman, Phyliss Rackley. She's a daily, too. I guess.'' Phyliss, with her fundamentalist credo and rampant hypochondria, was sometimes a daily pain in the neck. But she worked hard, and Judith couldn't run the B&B without her.

Harwood had reappeared, staggering down the corridor with Judith's brown suitcase. Figuring him for over seventy, Judith at first wanted to offer to carry the luggage for him. But she realized the man had pride; a simple *thank-you* tumbled from her lips as he wheezed into the bedroom.

''By the way,'' Judith said, going to her suitcase, ''we brought you a couple of small hostess gifts from home.'' She rummaged through her belongings, finally hauling out an assortment of Moonbeam's exotic coffee beans and three boxes of Fandangos, Donner & Blitzen Department Store's prized chocolate truffles. The presents had been intended for Margaret, but it was only fitting to hand them over to Claire.

''Oh! Thank you!'' Looking somewhat bewildered, Claire juggled the bags and boxes. ''That's ever so kind! Charles will be delighted.'' Still appearing ill-at-ease, she suggested that the cousins rest a bit before luncheon.

Renie demurred. ''Rest? From what? Sitting on our dead duffs? We can eat any time as far as I'm concerned.''

''Well . . .'' Claire seemed flustered. ''I'm not sure when Charles will get back from his appointment. And I don't know where Nats is.''

''Nats?'' Judith recalled the earlier reference. ''That's . . . who? Another cousin?''

Claire nodded. ''Natasha Karamzin, Alexei's sister. I had no idea they were coming down for the weekend until they arrived this morning in Alex's car. I hope you don't mind. They're rather engaging. Once you get used to them. Maybe.''

RAVENSCROFT FAMILY TREE

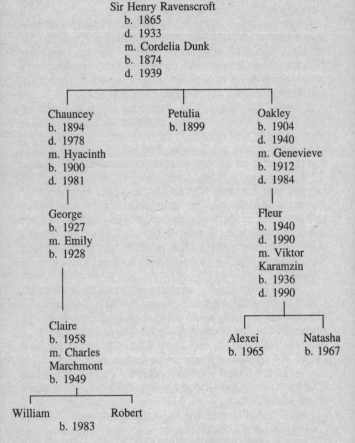

Sir Henry Ravenscroft
b. 1865
d. 1933
m. Cordelia Dunk
b. 1874
d. 1939

Chauncey
b. 1894
d. 1978
m. Hyacinth
b. 1900
d. 1981

Petulia
b. 1899

Oakley
b. 1904
d. 1940
m. Genevieve
b. 1912
d. 1984

George
b. 1927
m. Emily
b. 1928

Fleur
b. 1940
d. 1990
m. Viktor
Karamzin
b. 1936
d. 1990

Claire
b. 1958
m. Charles
Marchmont
b. 1949

Alexei
b. 1965

Natasha
b. 1967

William

Robert
b. 1983

Judith couldn't pin Natasha or Alexei Karamzin on the family tree. They were obviously related to Claire, not Charles. Ordinarily, Judith would have been forthright in asking about the relationship. But out of respect for British reserve, she said nothing.

Renie, however, had no such qualms. "Those are Russian names," she remarked. "How come?"

Claire sighed as she led her guests back to the main staircase. "It's rather complicated. My grandfather's brother, Oakley, married a Frenchwoman. He was killed at Dunkerque. Two months later, his widow, Genevieve, gave birth. Genevieve spent the rest of her life at Ravenscroft House." Claire paused halfway down the stairs, glancing back at Judith. "She had the room you're using, as a matter of fact. She died nine years ago. A most charming woman was Great-Aunt Gen." Claire gave the nickname a French pronunciation, as if had been "John."

The cousins followed Claire through the big hall. "Great-Uncle Oakley and Great-Aunt Gen's daughter, Fleur, married Viktor Karamzin, a Russian emigre. They were killed in an auto accident in Switzerland three years ago." Claire glanced at Renie. "You have what was their room. Alex and Nats are their children."

Judith recalled that Margaret had mentioned the deaths of Genevieve and the senior Karamzins in her letters. In Judith's mind, more sprigs were added to the family tree.

The dining room was paneled in handsome mahogany, but was more intimate than Judith had expected. The craftsmanship also seemed to date from a later period than the rest of the house. At the trestle table, Claire indicated chairs for the cousins.

Anticipating the arrival of a savory meal, Renie watched the door with eager brown eyes. But when a figure entered the dining room, it wasn't a servant carrying steaming covered dishes, but a middle-aged man wiping his brow. He stopped as soon as he saw the cousins, and turned very red.

"My word! Our guests! I say, I hope you haven't waited for me!" Charles Marchmont hurried forward to shake hands, first with Judith, then with Renie. "I would have known you anywhere," he insisted. "You haven't changed one whit since I saw you in . . . ah, what was it?''

Judith supplied the year of their previous trip. She and
Renie both expressed appreciation for their host's gallantry.
The words weren't true, of course, nor would the cousins
return the compliment. Charles Marchmont was a far cry
from the diffident, awkward adolescent they had met in
1964. Now that he was in his mid-forties, his light brown
hair was beginning to recede, he was thickening around the
waist, and his blunt features stopped just short of being
coarse. But, Judith noted, he had no spots.

Charles demanded to hear everything about the cousins'
trip thus far, their impressions of England, and what had
happened with them during the thirty-year interval. But
while he graciously posed questions, he never gave either
Judith or Renie a chance to finish a sentence:

"We flew from home the Friday after Easter—'' Judith
began.

"My word!" Charles wagged a stubby finger. "I do
hope you didn't pay full price. Air fares are exorbitant.
Knew a chap at Lloyd's who spent two thousand quid on
a flight to Toronto. Imagine!"

"Actually," Renie said, one eye cast wistfully on the
door that seemed to lead into the kitchen, "our bank cards
allow us credits we can put toward airline—''

"These banks!" Charles exclaimed. "Shocking interest
rates! Had a mind to buy a new Land Rover last winter.
Thought it might be wise to pay for it on time. Nonsense!
Much better to pay cash. Usury, that's what I call it."
Again, Charles turned very red.

Claire, however, turned not a hair. Apparently, she was
accustomed to her husband's bluster. Before anyone dared
make a further comment, the kitchen door finally swung
open, and a stout woman with graying red hair scattered
every which way on her head, huffed and puffed into the
dining room. She carried a huge tureen and had two soup
plates tucked precariously under each elbow.

"There you go, ducks," she announced, plunking the
tureen down on a hot pad hastily improvised by Claire.
"Leeks you wanted, leeks you get. Anybody for bread or
a handful of crisps?"

"Oh, Millie," Claire said in a meek voice, "don't trouble yourself. We'll be just fine. Though perhaps some tea? Or coffee?" She glanced inquiringly at her American visitors.

"Tea's fine," Judith said hastily.

Millie's broad face frowned at her employer. "I've no time to make tea. I'm due at the colonel's in ten minutes. It's my day to buff him up."

Claire's face fell. "Oh. Well, certainly. I'm sorry, Millie. I'll put the kettle on myself."

"You just do that," Millie said, waddling out of the room.

To Judith's surprise, Charles Marchmont didn't seem fazed by the part-time cook's breezy manner. Indeed, he had gotten to his feet and was ladling out soup. Pale green in color, it had the consistency of bathwater. Judith tried to ignore Renie's grimace.

"Your sister, Margaret, served us wonderful meals," Renie said in a pathetic little voice. "Every so often, I dream about them. Like now."

Charles frowned, but didn't look at Renie. "Margaret? Yes, fine cook, Margaret. She had no help then, of course. Bootstraps, that's what it was. Brought myself up through hard work and diligent effort. Fishmongering was well and good for Margaret's husband, but I wanted to make something of myself. Architecture, that was the thing—until I realized I didn't have the head for it. So I made my way in The City, and we've done well by one another, if I do say so myself." Charles's chest expanded along with his paunch.

"I understand," Judith said in a mild voice, "that Donald has carried on the fishmongering business very successfully. He and Margaret travel quite a bit."

"Yes, yes," Charles agreed, sitting back down. "Donald has a good head on his shoulders. Computerized the operation and all that. The pater wouldn't have turned everything over to his son-in-law if he hadn't. But I set my own sights higher. Couldn't stand the reek of fish, frankly. Money smells much nicer." He chuckled into his spoon.

They had just begun sipping their soup when a loud crash

resounded from the direction of the kitchen. Claire jumped, spilling the contents of her spoon onto her lap. Fortunately, the soup was lukewarm.

Shouts ensued, Millie and another female, both angry and hurling insults. Charles patted his mouth with his napkin and gave his wife a faintly chiding look.

"Really, m'dear, you ought to speak to Mrs. Tichborne. It would be much better if she tried to put a good face on it and cooperate with Millie. She's all we've got when it comes to cooking."

"She *is*?" Renie was horrified.

"Not really," Claire said quickly, her hands trembling slightly as she mopped up her lap. "That is, Mrs. Tichborne—the housekeeper—does the evening meals. She's very good."

Renie slumped in her chair, apparently relieved. The shouts from the kitchen continued, and Charles looked as if he was about to rise when a door slammed, ending the fracas.

Claire fanned herself with an extra napkin. "Oh! Millie's gone! I'm so glad! She might have been late for the colonel! He can be rather beastly when it comes to tardiness."

"The colonel?" Judith asked, not out of curiosity but to steer the conversation onto a more neutral course.

"Colonel Chelmsford," Charles replied, seemingly happy with his soup. "Chummy, we call him. Old bugger, really—excuse my language—but county through and through. Years ago, his grandfather, Bertram, was quite the big noise around these parts. Dead now, of course. The Chelmsford property borders ours."

Given the standards of Ravenscroft House, Judith wondered if the colonel lived in a palace that resembled Sandringham. She was searching for yet another conversational gambit when a tall, gaunt woman in a severe gray dress entered the dining room. Her colorless eyes flickered over the cousins, locked briefly with Charles's bland blue gaze, and then came to rest on Claire with the force of a branding iron.

"She must go. Or I will." Without another word, the woman went out through the other door.

Charles gave his wife a questioning look. Claire held up two shaky fingers. "Twice. Mrs. Tichborne's only threatened to quit twice today."

Charles uttered a harrumphing sound. "Not bad. Not at all. Perhaps they'll become quite matey. Millie's toast is almost never scorched."

Somewhat desperately, Judith spooned in more soup. She prayed that, for once, Renie would exercise tact. Her cousin's reaction to the meager, tasteless meal was bound to be critical.

But there was no opportunity for Renie to explode. Alexei and a beautiful young woman, who looked enough like him to be his sister and probably was, sauntered into the dining room. Renie's face fell when she saw they were each carrying crumpled paper bags bearing the Burger King logo.

"Still lunching?" Alex inquired. His usual breezy manner was a trifle smug.

Renie's reply was very low: "Not really."

Her comment was ignored. Claire introduced Natasha Karamzin to the cousins. Natasha lowered herself onto one of the high-backed chairs and dropped her paper bag in the open soup tureen.

"So you're the hostelry experts," she said in a languid voice. "What do you think—partition all the bedrooms, box up the valuables, and add four more baths and a Jacuzzi in the turret room?"

Claire had put a finger to her lips. "Hush, Nats. We aren't to speak of this. Yet."

Nats waved a hand. "Oh, bilge! Auntie can't hear. She's up in that tower of hers, watching the world go by."

Alex had turned one of the matching chairs around and was straddling it, an insouciant grin on his handsome face. "The world passed her by a good while ago, if you ask me. What's the point to being ninety-four?"

"Now, Alex . . ." Claire began, her cheeks turning pink.

Defiantly, Natasha twirled a lock of dark hair in her slim fingers. "I spent six months in L.A. last year. I've got tons of ideas for revving up this place. A theme park, maybe. Dinosaurs or vampires." She gave her brother a taunting smile. "You'd look marvelous in a cape, Alex. But you'd have to drink blood instead of hundred-and-fifty-proof liquor."

Alex was nonchalant. "Then why bother? I much prefer turning the place into a speedway. I could buy a Lotus and race it. A fast course, plenty of stands, concessions, advertising sponsors—who could ask for more?"

"How about an ambulance?" Renie inquired under her breath. She stared down at her soup plate. "How about a straw?"

Alex had gotten up and gone over to a cupboard that was built next to the sideboard. He opened what turned out to be a small refrigerator and removed a bottle of beer. Wrenching off the cap, he winked at Judith. "My sister's mad for anything from California. She'd like to turn the High Street into a shopping mall. Why not? Who needs a tea shop when you can have The Gap?"

Nats nodded enthusiastically, her languor replaced by the prospect of Los Angelicizing England. "A Ramada Inn, a Radio Shack, maybe even a Wal-Mart. We could make Little Pauncefoot into a real hot spot."

"I think I'm going to be sick," Renie murmured.

Again, no one but Judith seemed to hear her. Charles pounded the table with his fist. "Now, now! Enough of pipe dreams. We have *guests*."

"Precisely," Nats replied. "*American* guests who can tell us what to do with this old jumble of rock and make some money instead of pouring every farthing into upkeep."

Despite Claire's dismay, Charles gave a short nod. "Apt, very apt. I'll admit, this house is a parasite. It drains away everything. Taxes. Maintenance. Staff. When you can get them."

Nats rolled her dark eyes. "Staff! You call that creaking old Harwood and dithering Dora *staff*? They've been here for about a hundred years. As for Mrs. Tichborne, she's a mean-spirited old cow. The rest come and go, like the weather. Millie used to be a hooker in Yeovil until she got too long in the tooth and fat as a hog."

"Nats!" Claire was aghast. "That's not so! Millie ran a . . . a boardinghouse!"

Nats laughed, a brittle tinkling sound. "It was a whorehouse, Claire. Walter told me."

"Walter!" Claire seemed shaken. "How would *he* know?"

Nats shrugged her slim shoulders. "He's been the Ravenscroft steward for over ten years and worked as a stablehand before that. Why shouldn't Walter know?"

Claire lowered her head, seemingly absorbed in her soup plate. "It was a *boarding*house," she whispered. "Most respectable."

"Well," Renie said brightly, "it couldn't have been a restaurant. I'll vouch for that." She assumed her middle-aged ingenue's expression and laid her soup spoon next to her plate.

"The point is," Nats said in her melodic, careless voice, "we're interested in turning a profit on this place. How long do you think it would take to renovate it, or should we tear it down and start over with a condominium highrise? I saw some terrific examples in the Hollywood Hills." Her limpid black eyes rested on Judith.

"Oh, no," Judith answered quickly. "That would be . . . sacrilege. This is a marvelous house. It has tremendous possibilities. Not everybody wants modern glitz. Of course you needn't limit yourselves to a B&B. You could consider turning it into a small luxury hotel."

Again, Claire was looking alarmed. "Please. Not now. Auntie might be . . ." She shifted in her chair, staring at the door that opened onto the entry hall.

"Oh, stow it, Claire," Nats said sharply. "Auntie almost never comes downstairs during the day. Or do you think she's put a wire in the chandelier?"

Claire looked as if she wouldn't doubt it. "Auntie likes to know what's going on," she said to Judith, with her eternal air of apology. "That's why she spends her days looking out the turret window. She can't read much any more. She never watched the telly."

Alexei tipped the beer bottle to his lips. "Auntie can't walk. Auntie can't see. Auntie can't eat anything but thin gruel. Do tell me the point of it all,'' he demanded in a querulous voice. ''Why doesn't the old buzzard get it over with and die?''

Claire let out a little squeal; Charles muttered his disapproval. But Nats tossed her head, the short, chic raven tresses dancing. ''Oh, do be honest!'' She turned to first one Marchmont, then the other. ''You both feel the same way. This family doesn't mark time by counting the days until Whitsunday or Michaelmas or Harrod's annual clearance sale. We're all sitting around waiting for Aunt Pet to die. We live off her every whim, we jump whenever she cocks a furry white eyebrow, we couldn't afford tinned tuna if she didn't dole out the money. We're like marionettes, jerked about on strings. We wish she were dead because as long as she's alive, we're her hostages. Well?'' Nats's small, molded chin shot up. ''We are, aren't we?''

Nobody said a word.

FOUR

IT WAS WITH some trepidation that Judith and Renie ascended via the turret backstairs to the tower bedroom where Petulia Ravenscroft was ensconced. Between the unflattering portrait of Aunt Pet and the embarrassing exchange in the dining room, the cousins felt as if they were about to enter the lair of a dragon.

Nor did their first encounter reassure them. The tiny, decrepit maid who showed them into Aunt Pet's suite was Dora Hobbs, who, along with Harwood, was the other longtime servant Natasha had mentioned at lunch. The room itself appeared to have been virtually unchanged since the reign of Queen Victoria, and was furnished with heavy dark oak, heavy velvet drapes, heavy damask bed hangings, and ugly, sentimental knickknacks cluttering every possible surface. The only saving grace was a pair of oriel windows that let in the sunlight and apparently provided Aunt Pet with her view of the village's comings and goings.

As Dora fussed and fretted, Judith tried to find Aunt Pet. Through an open door, she could see a sitting room that appeared as laden with furnishings as the bed chamber. But Claire was fidgeting in the vicinity of an imposing bureau some ten drawers high. Finally Judith realized that the old woman was sitting in a brocade-covered chair by the window. Only the top of her white head could be seen over the high back.

"Well?" The voice was surprisingly strong. "What is it, Dora? Have you got Claire with you?"

Dora was clearly too intimidated to reply. With a tentative step, Claire moved away from the bureau and approached Aunt Pet with the deference due an empress.

"It's me, Auntie. I've brought guests. Americans. Friends of Margaret . . . and Charles."

"Didn't know Margaret and Charles had any friends," muttered Aunt Pet. "Especially American friends. Now how can that be?"

Petulia Ravenscroft turned slightly, with effort. She looked up at Judith and Renie, and apparently didn't much like what she saw.

"Pants! Why must you women wear pants, except to hunt? Don't you own a skirt?" Her bright blue eyes raked over Claire. "You, too—what's this? You been riding this morning? Only excuse for pants. Better not see you come to dinner in that ungodly outfit!"

Claire kneaded her smart gray flannel slacks as if she could erase them with her fingers. "I was . . . surveying the formal gardens. Of course I'll dress tonight. Silk."

Aunt Pet's severe white eyebrows arched. "Long?"

Claire nodded in a jerky manner. "Long. Naturally. Very long."

"And pearls." Aunt Pet seemed assuaged, then suddenly swerved her head to pierce the cousins with a look that could have cut brick. "And you? Silk or chiffon?"

Judith stammered. "Ah . . . well . . . I'm not sure. Yet."

Renie nudged Judith. "We have to brush our clothes," she said. "Or sponge them. I forget."

"Then remember," Pet huffed, but she seemed somewhat pacified. "Americans, eh? Why?"

"Ah . . ." Judith was still at an uncharacteristic loss for words.

"It was an accident," Renie explained. "Our great-grandparents thought they were just on a trip. To the Chicago Exposition. But they sort of got lost and ended up staying for . . . the rest of their lives."

The account was true, if abbreviated. Along with their son and daughter, Great-Grandfather and Great-Grandmother

Grover had set sail from England to visit America for a few weeks. But their great-grandfather's extravagances had led them into debt and put them to work. An ill-fated venture into Nebraska had left the Grovers at the mercy of bandits. Impoverished and indignant, they had fled West, avoiding more work and a growing number of creditors. By the time they reached the Northwest corner, they had been forced to stay with émigré relatives. It had literally taken an Act of Congress to make restitution for the hold-up, but by that time it was too late. The son and daughter had both married and started families of their own. The Grovers had never gone home.

"Excusable," allowed Aunt Pet. "That was—when?"

Renie considered. "In 1895, I think. I'm not much at math."

Pet snorted. "You're not much at clothes, either. Where did you get that outfit?"

Renie gazed down at her modified sweatsuit. "I forget. Costco?"

Aunt Pet looked pained. With equal disfavor, her shrewd sapphire eyes raked over Judith's cotton blouse and slacks. "Scandalous," she declared. "Women have no pride these days. Who can blame the world for being in such a disreputable state? It's up to the women to set the tone. Look at you!"

Judith, however, was looking at Petulia Ravenscroft. She was sitting ramrod-straight, white hair piled high on her head and kept in place with a plethora of ivory combs. Her fine white skin was stretched taut over good bones, exhibiting surprisingly few wrinkles. Pet's sharp features, particularly the down-turned nose, suggested a falcon, waiting to pounce on its prey. Petulia Ravenscroft had never been a beauty, Judith judged, but she must have been striking. Indeed, the old lady was still handsome, in a fierce, forceful kind of way.

Noting Aunt Pet's long black dress with its high collar and cameo brooch, Judith sought a more neutral topic than female apparel. "This house is wonderful. And your view is lovely."

Indeed it was, taking in the gardens at the rear of the

house, the outbuildings and a corner of pastureland, the walnut trees that lined the property, and almost all of the village green with its shield of horsechestnuts and holly. But if Aunt Pet was pleased by Judith's remark, only the merest flicker of her eyelids betrayed the fact. "Old houses require constant care. I refuse to allow any sign of neglect. You Americans build and tear down, create and destroy. No sense of history, no pride. Serves you right when people riot. Might as well burn your cities. What's the point in saving trash?"

Claire put a hand on the brocade chair. "Now Auntie—" she began.

But Renie interrupted. "You're absolutely right, Miss Ravenscroft. My husband, Bill, says that one of the biggest problems with America's inner cities is the property tax structure. The worse shape a building's in, the less the tax. Landlords—slumlords—get a break by letting their holdings fall apart. If local governments reversed the system, then owners would be forced into making repairs and stopping the decay that contributes to unrest among—"

"—my souvenirs," Judith put in, with a firm nudge for Renie. As Judith knew all too well, when Renie got launched on one of Bill's hobbyhorses, the ride could take all day. "Photos, I mean. Of the house, to take home and show our friends and family." She winced a little, thinking of Gertrude's reaction to the Ravenscroft estate. Judith's mother would either take the English to task for wasting money on white elephants or ask what the hell their hosts were doing living in a mental hospital.

Aunt Pet ignored Judith. Instead, she fixed Renie with those hard blue eyes and offered the hint of a smile. "Astute. Very astute. Where is this Bill? I'd like to meet him."

Renie gave Aunt Pet a helpless look. "He went fishing. In Scotland."

"Scotland! A backward place. Can't understand a word they say. Doubt if it's English." Feebly, Aunt Pet moved her hands in an attempt at scorn. But the fingers were stiff and the joints were swollen. Carefully, she rested first one hand and then the other on the brown and yellow afghan that covered her lap. "Why would Bill do such a thing? He sounds so sensible, otherwise."

Happily, Renie was spared an explanation. Aunt Pet had turned to the windows, her gaze caught by a figure out on the green. "See there? Colonel Chelmsford, the old black-guard, heading for The Hare. Three o'clock. Every day, off to drink the pub dry, set your watch by him. Jackanapes."

Sure enough, a stiff-legged figure in varying shades of brown was trudging across the village green toward the lane. "Goodness," said Judith in admiration, "your eyesight must be very keen, Miss Ravenscroft."

Aunt Pet snorted. "At a distance, it's still usable, especially with eyeglasses. I didn't bother with them until two years ago. Troublesome, that's what they are. Always getting mislaid and Dora can never find them. You'd be astounded by some of the sights I've seen out this window. People think no one's watching. Some of them behave in a most shocking manner. Worse than shocking." For a brief moment, her sharp features quivered, as if in revulsion. Then she lifted her pointed chin and gave the cousins a rueful look. "Can scarcely see a thing up close. Had to give up reading and solving the jumble puzzles. A great nuisance, but nobody's written a decent book since R. L. Delderfield. And even he was inclined to smut. Won't tolerate smut. Life's full of ugliness—why write about it?"

As Judith recalled, R. L. Delderfield's works were very tame. But that was by her own standards, not Aunt Pet's. Maybe, if she thought hard enough, she'd remember that he'd used such provocative words as "thigh" and "lips."

Aunt Pet had turned away from her view. She was eyeing Claire suspiciously. "Well? Why are you looking like that?"

Claire's nostrils twitched. "Ah . . . I believe I smell smoke."

Aunt Pet was now also sniffing, the beaklike nose taking on a life of its own. "Where's Dora?"

Judith smelled smoke, too. Claire practically galloped out of the room. Judith started to follow her, but Aunt Pet called out in a crisp voice:

"Claire will tend to it. Dora's inclined to set fires. It's probably *The Times*. No great loss."

A swift perusal of the room showed no signs of a smoke detector. At home, that would be the first requirement for a hostelry. Judith gave Aunt Pet an inquiring look. "Does Dora do it often?"

Aunt Pet shrugged. "Whenever she feels threatened. You're strangers. She's probably frightened."

"*I'm* frightened," Renie put in. "I'm not crazy about the idea of having a pyromaniac loose."

But Aunt Pet scoffed at Renie's fears. "My eyes and ears may not be what they were, but I have a very keen sense of smell. I always know when Dora's playing with matches. The most we've ever lost is a velvet cushion."

Breathless, Claire had returned. "It's all right, Auntie. It was only an antimacassar. One of the ugly ones. I insisted Dora make herself a nice cup of tea."

Aunt Pet nodded, then turned to the cousins. "Dora has a hot plate in her quarters, on the other side of my sitting room. And no," she went on, taking in Renie's expression of horror, "she's never set a fire with it. Matches, that's what I said. That's what I meant." Now she swiveled in Claire's direction. "I always say what I mean, don't I, child?"

Claire nodded jerkily. "Oh! Definitely! You're not one for falsehoods. Or exaggerations. Or . . . any of those things." Claire's voice died away.

"I don't take things back, either." Aunt Pet did her best at folding her crippled hands in her lap. The sharp profile tilted upward. "Never make threats you don't intend to carry out. Never go back on your word. Never *give in*."

An uneasy silence fell between the four women. At last, Judith spoke up. "Sometimes," she said quietly, "life requires compromise."

But Aunt Pet shook her head. "No, it doesn't. Compromise is a sign of weakness. People who compromise don't believe in themselves, let alone anything else. If you stand firm, the opposition will surrender. If they don't, then the cause wasn't worthy. Honor, that's what life's about. If you can't live with yourself, there's no point in living." For the briefest of moments, what might have been uncertainty seemed to flicker across the stern old face. But before Judith could be sure, Aunt Pet eyed Claire with reproach. "Well? What are you waiting for? It's time for Dora to fix my tonic. Be off with you, shoo!" Aunt Pet motioned Claire and the cousins out of the bedchamber. Dora was last seen skittering around the tower room like a frightened mouse.

"You mustn't pay too much attention to Auntie," Claire cautioned in her apologetic voice. "She doesn't mean half of what she says. Well, a third, perhaps. Or maybe a—"

"I like her," Renie put in as they left the suite via the sitting room, with its faded silks and brooding landscapes.

"You would," Judith muttered under her breath. But Claire had heard the comment. Judith gave their hostess a feeble smile. "Your aunt reminds me of my mother. Kind of contrary. Critical, too. It's part of being old, and hanging on to what little independence is left. Sometimes Renie gets along better with my mother than I do. It happens that way with aunts and nieces. Parents and children don't always have the same latitude. They're too close."

Eager for harmony, Claire agreed. "Oh! I know! Though I get on splendidly with my own parents. Of course I almost never see them," she added a bit wistfully, leading the cousins out into a long gallery that seemed to run the length of the house's core. "They're missionaries in Swaziland."

The gallery contained yet more fine tapestries, classical sculpture, beautifully carved chests, and exquisite paintings. The cousins goggled. Claire, however, kept walking, albeit slowly.

"More guest rooms?" she whispered, indicating the mullioned windows and parquet floor. "Or as Nats suggests, a video arcade?"

Judith gasped. "Oh, no! Why, this is glorious! Wherever did you get all these art treasures?"

Claire was drifting between what might have been a Rubens and what looked like a Tintoretto. "Oh—I couldn't say, offhand. Various owners acquired these things. I suppose. And Great-Grandfather was quite a collector. The house was built by Dunk."

"Dunk?" Renie had stopped in front of a marble bust of Charles II. She seemed transfixed, either by the lifelike rendering or by the possibility that the old rogue was flirting with her.

"Sir Lionel Dunk." Claire had wandered off to stand by a French Renaissance table that held a trio of what looked like Fabergé eggs. "Sir Lionel was Master of the Revels under Queen Elizabeth I. Unfortunately, he reveled rather too much and came a cropper. That's why Little Pauncefoot holds its annual April All Fools Revels."

"Did we miss it?" Renie asked hopefully. She had finally torn herself away from King Charles, giving him a parting pat on his marble curls.

"I'm afraid so," Claire replied, now moving along the gallery at a brisker pace. "It's on April first, naturally. Everyone turns out, from Great Pauncefoot and even Yeovil. It lasts two days, and sometimes things get a bit out of hand. Drink, you know. And other things."

"What's the premise?" Renie inquired, no doubt to make amends for her earlier attitude. "Besides get high, I mean."

Claire was looking very serious. "The entire festival has an Elizabethan theme. There's always a short play, usually based on an historical incident. They give readings, too, from writers of the period—Shakespeare, Ben Jonson, Sir Philip Sidney. And music and food and fortune telling and games. It's all based on the last half of the sixteenth century. Oh, the men dress up as women, and vice versa."

Judith arched her eyebrows. "A cross-dressing festival? How . . . interesting."

"Not really," Claire said without enthusiasm. "Sir Lionel—the original builder—was caught wearing Queen Elizabeth's wig and one of her court dresses, farthingale and all. The Queen was furious. She dismissed Sir Lionel and sent him packing. Back here where the house was a-building. It seemed he'd never be able to complete the project. But Elizabeth died a short time later. King James I came to the throne. He found Sir Lionel very amusing. So the King reinstated him at court. Of course James had some rather extraordinary ideas about . . . amusements."

The King's alternative lifestyle was forgotten as Claire opened the door at the far end of the gallery. "This is our hideaway," she said, a trifle embarrassed. "Especially when the twins visit Auntie."

The homely room struck a familiar chord. While some of the furniture was old and possibly valuable, the rest included a two-piece sectional sofa, a recliner, a coffee table, and a stack of TV trays. The carpeting was a serviceable wall-to-wall shag, and the only art featured dinosaurs drawn by the twins. The large-screen television, the elaborate stereo setup, and the VCR all had been imported from Japan. The room was just like home.

"You can't have children—especially boys—playing Power Rangers in the drawing room," Claire explained. "The back stairs from the kitchen and the servants' hall come up through the nursery wing and end here. It's very convenient."

Reflecting on the layout, Judith nodded. "We have our living quarters on the third floor. You could convert all of this and use the gallery as a combination living and dining room without spoiling it too much."

Claire seemed dubious. "It's a great deal of space. I doubt that Charles and I would actually live here. He prefers London, if only because—" At a sound from the far end of the gallery, she gave a start, then turned quickly.

It was Dora, teetering outside Aunt Pet's suite. "Oh, Mrs. Charles!" the maid cried, her thin voice echoing off the artworks. "Please! I'm all undone!"

Claire hurried to intercept the elderly servant. Renie grabbed Judith's arm. "I don't smell smoke. Do you suppose she misplaced her matches?"

Disengaging herself, Judith gave Renie a withering look, then hurried after Claire. Reluctantly, Renie followed, too.

"What is it, Dora?" Claire inquired. "Has Auntie had a spell?"

But Dora shook her head, the wisps of gray hair falling limply around her wrinkled face. "It's angry she is, and all because Cook's out of biscuits."

Claire frowned. "Auntie's not supposed to eat biscuits. Dr. Ramsey has forbidden sweets."

Dora's faded brown eyes widened. "As if I didn't know, Mrs. Charles! But your aunt will have her way. If it's biscuits she wants, it's biscuits she'll have, mark my words! Why, she says I must be off to the village to fetch the sort with sugar sprinkles!"

The shapeless gray dress that hung on Dora's frail frame seemed to be held up by a starched white apron. The maid's tiny hands clawed at the air and her small chin trembled. If Aunt Pet was a falcon, Dora was a sparrow.

Noting Claire's indecision, Judith intervened. "My cousin and I are going for a stroll through the village." The fib tripped off Judith's tongue. "We'd be glad to get the biscuits."

Dora practically crumpled with relief. "*Could* you? *Would* you? I'd be ever so grateful." A sudden expression of alarm crossed her pinched little face. "But such cheek! You're Mr. and Mrs. Charles's guests!"

"It's no bother," Judith assured the maid. "We were just leaving. We'll be back shortly."

Two minutes later, the cousins were downstairs in the entry hall. Claire was still protesting their generous offer. "Besides," she added, "Auntie really shouldn't eat sugar biscuits."

Renie waved a hand. "Hey, she's ninety-four. A couple of cookies won't kill her. Or," Renie asked, her savoir-faire momentarily shaken, "is she diabetic?"

"No, no, it's not that," Claire answered as the door chimes sounded. "It's her digestion. She's supposed to be on a strict, bland diet. Of course she badgers poor Dora to bring her things she shouldn't eat. Auntie's quite the scamp."

The last words came from over Claire's shoulder as she hurried to the front door. Judith and Renie held back, waiting for the caller to come in.

Claire's reaction, however, wasn't exactly welcoming. "Oh! Colonel Chelmsford! Whatever are you doing here?"

Beyond Claire, Judith could make out the figure on the porch. Colonel Chelmsford was wearing a tan Norfolk jacket, brown breeches, brown boots, and held a brown and black checkered snap-brim cap in his hands along with a small parcel. His luxuriant ginger mustache had traces of silver and his complexion was florid. He looked to be in his late sixties, possibly older, but stood at military attention.

"It's Miss Ravenscroft I wish to see," Colonel Chelmsford said in a gruff voice. "Most urgent."

Claire's hands fluttered in agitation. "Oh! But I think not. Auntie won't be pleased."

"Bother Auntie!" the colonel bellowed. "The woman hasn't been pleased in ninety-four years! Come, come, let me pass."

"But . . ." Despite the protest, Claire stepped aside. Colonel Chelmsford marched into the entry hall, then came to a halt in front of the cousins.

"What's this?" he demanded, his hazel eyes hard as agates. "Reinforcements? Stand back, I'm on the move!"

Obediently, the cousins stepped out of the colonel's way. He clomped forward, then again came to an abrupt halt. "I say, where are those blasted stairs? I haven't been in this house since 1955."

Hastening to join the colonel, Claire led him toward the main staircase. "This way . . . I believe the stairs have always been here, though the corridor range in the rear was added around 1785 . . ."

Left on their own, the cousins exited the house. A moment later, they were following the curving drive that led around the house to the main gate.

"Wow!" Renie exclaimed as they caught sight of the formal gardens held in the lap of the hill that sloped toward the river. "What a place! All that art—it must be worth a fortune! Why would they be fussing about opening a B&B? They could sell one of those Titians or Van Dycks and use the money to keep up the house for years."

"You'd think so." Judith tore her eyes away from the neatly ordered rows of red, white, yellow, and purple tulips. "Of course we can't really judge. A setup like this is completely outside the range of our experience."

Renie gave a little shrug as they approached the gatehouse. "True. I don't suppose we spend more than two hundred bucks a year on seeds and bulbs and slug bait."

"Don't forget the fert," Judith said with a grin.

"Don't forget the cookies. Or biscuits," Renie reminded Judith. "If we can get them at the tea shop, we might be able to cadge a decent meal. I'm still starved."

Judith didn't try to dissuade Renie. She, too, was hungry. They slowed their step as a man appeared from the vicinity of the small orchard beyond the gatehouse. He was bareheaded, under forty, wearing jeans and a denim workshirt. A brief wave of one hand indicated he wanted to speak to the cousins.

"Sorry to trouble you," he said with a diffident air. "Did I see Chummy going up to the house?"

"Chummy?" Judith frowned.

The man seemed faintly embarrassed, and clasped his hands behind his back. "Sorry. Colonel Chelmsford. From The Grange." His speech was consciously modulated, as if he had schooled himself.

Next to Judith, Renie was doing a little dance. "He went to see Miss Ravenscroft. You can catch him when they sound the retreat. 'Bye."

The man didn't budge. Indeed, Judith thought he seemed shocked. It was his voice that gave him away. The well-ordered features showed almost no emotion. Again, Judith had the feeling that he was not only self-disciplined, but self-conscious as well.

"That can't be," he said flatly.

Ignoring Renie's impatience, Judith waited for an explanation. But none was forthcoming. "Why is that?" she finally asked.

The man hesitated, giving Judith more time to study him. He was a shade over six feet, physically fit, and on the cusp of being handsome. The tawny hair was combed straight back to fall just below his collar. Sharp cheekbones and green eyes would ensure his attractiveness to women. But then Judith had always been a sucker for green eyes.

At last, the man made up his mind. "I'm Walter Paget, the Ravenscroft steward." He shook hands with Judith. Walter's grip was firm, but like the rest of him, noncommittal. Judith introduced herself and Renie, who was forced to retrace the twenty yards she'd covered in an effort to reach sustenance.

"In the twelve years I've been at Ravenscroft House," Walter explained without inflection, "I've never known Chummy to set foot on this property. If he's here, this is quite remarkable."

"But he's a neighbor, isn't he?" Judith said, pretending she didn't see Renie, who was again behind Walter and staggering around in the final throes of starvation.

"Yes, he is." Walter allowed himself a faint frown. "That's the problem. Or so it seems. The colonel and Miss Ravenscroft have had a longstanding feud over property lines. You'd think such matters would have been resolved after four hundred years."

Judith stared at the steward. "You mean they've been arguing since the sixteenth century?"

A slight smile played at Walter Paget's lean mouth. It was a very attractive smile. And a very attractive mouth, Judith noted. "Not precisely. Chummy's ancestors lived at The Grange even before Sir Lionel Dunk built what's now known as Ravenscroft House. The colonel moved back to his home after he retired from the army some twenty years ago. His father died in February. The old boy refused to deal with Miss Ravenscroft, which may have prolonged the quarrel."

Renie was now under the archway, reeling against the wall. With a hand to her forehead, she made as if to slip into oblivion.

"Ah . . . yes . . . well . . ." Judith tried not to be distracted by her cousin's antics. They were hardly new. Renie always seemed to be hungry. "But the Ravenscrofts aren't Dunks, are they?"

"They are, actually," Walter replied. Now, he seemed somewhat distracted, too. His green eyes narrowed in the direction of the main house. "Miss Ravenscroft's mother was a Dunk. She was an only child, the heiress to the estate. The family had fallen on hard times. Sir Henry Ravenscroft had made his fortune in The City. The Dunks were only too happy to welcome him—and his money—into the family. Excuse me," Walter said hastily, "I must be off."

Judith turned, watching the steward rush toward the house. She realized why he was in such a hurry when she also saw Colonel Chelmsford, who was rounding the curve in the drive, shouting and shaking a fist. It appeared that his visit had not been a success.

"It's about time," Renie said in a testy voice as Judith joined her in the lane. "I'm thinking steak and kidney pie."

Judith was hungry, too, but her mind wasn't on food. She was wondering about the rancor between neighbors. "We shouldn't take time to sit down and eat," said Judith as they passed the village green with its border of pansies, primroses, and thorn apple. "We promised Dora we'd be right back. Let's get some buns or something we can munch on the way."

"Buns!" Renie cried. "How about crumbs or gruel or some of your mother's dreaded clam fritters? Or," she added in sudden excitement, "do you think they'll serve high tea? You know, with little sandwiches and cakes and maybe a couple of meringues?"

"Well . . ." Judith winced. She had been studying the monuments on the green, which included a life-sized statue of a man in early seventeenth-century garb on a granite base, and the simple stone pillar she'd seen from Alexei's Alfa. At present, three small boys were chasing each other around the pillar, shouting their heads off. "I think Claire told us we should assemble around six-thirty for cocktails. Drinks have replaced high tea, it seems."

Renie practically jumped up and down. "That's crazy! Just drinks? No high tea? What's wrong with having *both*? I thought we were in England! We might as well be on Bora-Bora!"

With a lame smile, Judith steered her irate cousin past the stone church with its ancient graveyard. Early fourteenth century, Judith guessed, from the design of the windows and the spireless bell tower. Like Ravenscroft House and the other buildings in the village, St. Edith's was also made of the mellow golden stone that Judith assumed was indigenous to the area. Her smile widened as she saw great clumps of daffodils bending in the soft spring breeze. A dogwood tree was beginning to bloom next to what appeared to be the vicarage. And, in the cracks between the stone pavement that led to the High Street, sprigs of fairy flax poked up to greet the sun. Marauding bikers and Taco Bell notwithstanding, Little Pauncefoot seemed quite perfect on this April afternoon.

Or it was, until a large gray car, whose make Judith didn't recognize, almost mowed them down. Turning off from the High, its driver misjudged the curb, swerved to avoid a lamppost, and just missed the cousins.

"Hey, jerk-off," yelled Renie, "watch it! You want to get your butt sued?"

The errant driver killed his engine, either accidentally or on purpose. The result was the same: He was left to face Renie, who was in a vengeful mood.

"Please," said the offender, sticking his head out the car window, "I didn't mean to frighten you. My mind was on other things."

The long, thin face wore a harried look. The balding man in the conservative suit was about the same age as the cousins. Renie decided to grant mercy.

"Okay," she said in a grudging tone. "We're not used to people driving on the wrong side of the road. Besides, you were going pretty fast for a town this size. Don't they have speed zones here?"

The man's bony fingers tapped the side of the car. Clearly, he was anxious to be off. "Yes, of course. Are you certain you're not injured?"

Renie had now espied the tea shop just around the corner. "I'm fine. We're fine. If we aren't, we'll call the local lawyer."

The man cleared his throat. "I *am* the local lawyer. Solicitor, as it were." He pulled his hand back inside the car, fumbled around on the front seat, and proffered a business card to Renie. "Arthur Tinsley, at your service. If you'll excuse me, I'm late for an appointment."

"You're excused," Renie muttered to the departing vehicle. "Goofball. He could have killed us." She plunged across the High Street, then noticed that Judith was still standing at the curb. "Hey, come on. Let's eat."

But Judith's gaze had followed the big car as it turned into the lane and kept going past the church. There was only one place that Arthur Tinsley could be headed, and that was Ravenscroft House. Judith wondered why.

FIVE

JUDITH WAS RIGHT. The Marchmonts had dispensed with afternoon tea. The cousins were informed that Mrs. Marchmont was resting, Mr. Marchmont had gone out to the stables with Mr. Paget, and Mr. Karamzin and Miss Karamzin were playing tennis in Great Pauncefoot.

"Cocktails will be served at six-thirty in the drawing room," Mrs. Tichborne announced. "Dinner is at seven." With a supercilious expression on her gaunt face, the housekeeper headed toward the kitchen.

Renie tried to follow her, but Judith grabbed her sleeve. "Knock it off, coz. It's after four. That sardine sandwich will hold you just fine."

"Are you kidding?" Renie snarled. "That was one anemic sardine and the bread was the size of my thumb. I can't believe the tea shop was out of food."

"We're lucky they still had a half-dozen sugar cookies. Come on, let's take them to Aunt Pet."

Renie grumbled all the way up the main staircase to the third floor. The cousins came out into the gallery, just a few feet from Aunt Pet's rooms. Dora turned very pink when she saw Judith and Renie with their small bakery bag.

"You're ever so kind!" the maid exclaimed, reaching for the biscuits. "Thank you. I'm afraid I can't ask you in. Miss Pet has a visitor."

Judith leaned into the doorway. A swift glance told

her that the visitor must be in the other room, where Aunt Pet had received the cousins.

"Does Miss Ravenscroft have trouble walking?" Judith inquired in her most sympathetic manner.

Dora put the hand that didn't hold the bakery bag to her withered cheek. "Indeed she does. That arthritis plagues her something cruel. Poor lady, she can't take but a step or two on her own. That's why she keeps to her bedroom, except on special occasions. Like tonight."

"But," Judith protested, "your mistress doesn't need to come down to dinner for our sake. It sounds like an imposition."

Dora's brown eyes shifted away from the cousins. "I really couldn't say about that," the maid said evasively. "Miss Pet has made up her mind to dine with the family."

Renie muscled Judith out of the way. "Does she have tea in the afternoon? With a little something?"

Dora gave Renie a quizzical look. "She's having it now, with her visitor. That's why I must take her these biscuits."

Judith shoved Renie back. "Her visitor—that wouldn't be Colonel Chelmsford?" she asked, knowing that it wasn't likely he'd returned.

"My no!" Dora was horrified. "Miss Pet put a flea in his ear! Imagine! Such cheek!" With a quick glance over her shoulder, the maid lowered her voice. "It's Mr. Tinsley, Miss Pet's solicitor. I believe he's staying to dinner."

Judith tried to hide her surprise. "Really? But dinner isn't until seven. They must be having a long meeting. Or is it just a social call?"

Dora's expression became very prim. "I couldn't say, I'm sure." Then, feeling the bag of sugar biscuits, she grew more loquacious. "Mr. Tinsley is like one of the family. He and his father before him—Mr. Edward Tinsley that was, and his grandfather, Mr. Edmund Tinsley that was, all served the family. Very nice men they were—for being solicitors and all. Rest their souls."

An impatient tinkling bell cut short Dora's confidences. "Miss Pet," she whispered. "No doubt she's anxious for her biscuits." Giving the cousins a grateful smile, she closed the door.

Renie slunk away, still grumbling. "I should have pinched a couple of cookies. I'd have done the old girl a favor. Now she'll get a stomachache."

"You're giving me a headache," Judith chided. "Let's go to our rooms and air out our tiaras. We've got to dress for dinner."

The cousins rendezvoused in the hallway at six twenty-five. Fortunately, their large suitcases included the evening dresses they'd worn to the IMNUTS banquet. They eyed each other critically in the fading April light.

"That trailing scarf's dangerous," Renie said. "Don't let Dora near it with a cigarette lighter."

"Aunt Pet won't like that bronze shimmer," Judith retorted, referring to Renie's metallic tunic that went over the black crepe-de-chine skirt. "You glow in the dark."

"Screw it," said Renie, making for the stairs. "I'll tell her it's chain mail. She can't see up close, remember?"

The drawing room was on the opposite side of the main staircase from the parlor. The furnishings and decor were almost exclusively eighteenth century, elegant and graceful. Harwood was propped up behind the makeshift bar, mixing a martini for Claire. Charles, attired in a business suit, was already quaffing a scotch and soda. Judith requested the same.

"Hors d'oeuvres," Renie hissed. "Where are they?"

"They aren't," Judith hissed back. "Shut up and drink."

But Renie was once again thwarted. Harwood had neither American bourbon nor Canadian rye. Renie was forced to settle for a screwdriver.

"Alex and Nats are late," Claire fretted, glancing at the Breguet clock on the Palladian mantel. "They have no sense of time."

"Or courtesy," Charles put in. "They roar down here once every two months, spend five minutes with Auntie, drink all the good liquor, and then go off to parties with their young set. What they both need is a job."

Claire carefully set her glass down on a small mahogany pedestal stand. "They *have* jobs, Charles."

"Rubbish!" snapped her husband. "Alex tests sports cars when he feels like it, and Nats offers interior decorating advice when she's in the mood. I don't call those 'jobs.' "

"Well," Judith remarked affably, "they're still young, and if they can support themselves—"

"Nonsense!" Charles exclaimed. "They can't. That's why they come to Ravenscroft House, to wheedle funds out of Auntie." His blunt features grew sly. "But this trip may be in vain. Auntie's of a mind to cut them off at the pockets."

At that moment, a commotion erupted outside the drawing room. Judith heard a groan, followed by a grunt, and then the shrill voice of Aunt Pet: "Do be careful! You're jostling my spine! Put some leg into it, Arthur! I'm not a rag baby! Walter, mind the doorway! You'll scrape my elbows!"

Aunt Pet was being carried into the drawing room by a red-faced Walter Paget and a pale Arthur Tinsley. She was seated—or tilted, at the moment—in a Sheraton armchair. Judging from her bearers' state of near-collapse, they had hauled their burden all the way downstairs from the third-floor bedchamber. Staggering to a place by the hearth, they lowered Aunt Pet onto the floor.

"Bother!" muttered Aunt Pet. "In my day, men were *men*! They hefted a hundred pounds of equipment into the African bush. They slung tigers over their shoulders out in India. They bagged elephants in Ceylon with only a—"

"—lift," Claire was saying softly. She stood next to her aunt's chair, proffering a glass of sherry. "I can't think why you won't let us install a lift, Auntie. It would be such a help. To you. To Dora. To all of us."

Aunt Pet clutched the sherry glass in both gnarled hands. "Such extravagance! Did the Dunks need a lift? Did my father, Sir Henry Ravenscroft? Or either of my brothers, poor sticks that they were? Bother!"

Taking Judith's advice to heart, Renie had already polished off her screwdriver and was chewing on the ice she'd insisted that Harwood add to her drink. "What was wrong with your brothers?" she demanded. "Couldn't they find a rhino to wrestle?"

Aunt Pet started to look affronted, then burst into a high-pitched cackle. "Those two couldn't find a dik-dik in the petit fours," Pet said when her glee had subsided. "Chauncey and Oakley were pitiful excuses for real men." Her hard blue eyes narrowed at Renie. "You're a saucy one, Miss Renee. You've got spunk. I like that. Good to find kinfolk with spunk, even if they are Americans."

"But . . ." Renie exchanged a puzzled look with Judith.

"My father," Aunt Pet went on with vigor, "Sir Henry Ravenscroft to you—was a self-made man. Rich as Croesus and wise as Solomon. He knew better than to entrust the family fortune to his sons. No spunk, you see. Oh, Oakley was brave—and foolish. He saw nothing but romance in war, and got himself killed in the process. Was he shot in an artillery attack? Was he felled by hand grenades? Not Oakley. He slipped on a wet tin of pilchards, fell down a flight of stairs, and broke his neck. Dunkerque, indeed! He never got out of England!"

Charles's gasp of protest went unheeded. "As for Chauncey, he was the dreamer. Yearned to be a poet—or a priest. Silly man passed his foolishness on to his son, George." The blue eyes glinted at Claire. "So your father runs off to Swaziland to convert the half-clad natives. Waste of time. Better off worshipping tree stumps. Ever see pygmies holding a church bazaar?"

"They're not pygmies," Claire countered in an agonized tone. "Really, Auntie, a very large portion of Swaziland's population is Christian. I know, I grew up there . . ."

In response, Aunt Pet shoved her empty sherry glass at her great-niece. "Medicinal, this. Keeps my blood circulating. Come, girl, move along."

Since Claire seemed frozen in place, Renie took the sherry glass from Aunt Pet. "I'll get us both a refill," she said.

With unveiled admiration, Aunt Pet watched Renie walk to the bar. "Fine female specimen, that Renee. But why do her clothes light up?"

Judith was spared concocting an answer. Alex was strolling across the room, wearing a suit and tie, and looking none too pleased about it.

Yet when he came up to Aunt Pet, his chiseled features

broke into a charming grin. "How's my favorite girl?" he asked, leaning down to kiss her cheek.

"Fine as frog hair," Pet replied. "All things considered. Why aren't you and Charles in dinner jackets? Young Paget, too. Arthur has an excuse. He's been working." One eye almost closed, and there was an edge in Aunt Pet's voice.

Alex straightened up. "He has?" His gaze took in Arthur Tinsley, digested the solicitor, and appeared to spit him out. "Doing what?"

Aunt Pet wagged a crooked finger. "Never you mind. You'll learn soon enough. Ah, here's my sherry." She accepted the glass from Renie.

Somehow, Judith had been maneuvered next to Walter Paget. For want of anything better to say, she inquired about the Ravenscroft stables.

The query seemed to plunge Walter into gloom. "The Marchmonts aren't horsemen. They don't understand. Miss Ravenscroft does, of course. But she thinks in terms of the past. Especially when it comes to money. The pound doesn't buy what it once did."

Even though she wasn't sure what Walter was talking about, Judith was sympathetic. The elderly seemed incapable of comprehending inflation. Gertrude quoted Depression era prices for hamburger, the cost of shoes during World War I, and housing sales that were roughly the same as contemporary annual property taxes. Judith's mother refused to spend more than five dollars on a birthday present, and when informed that her grandson Mike had shelled out fifty bucks taking his girlfriend, Kristin, to a baseball game, she wanted to know if he'd come home with the ball, the bat, and a couple of utility infielders. As far as Gertrude Grover was concerned, the dollar was as sound as it ever was—in 1910.

"Old people get fixed ideas," Judith said somewhat vaguely.

Still gloomy, Walter nodded. "We can't maintain the bloodstock at this rate. What's the point of keeping hunters if no one wants to pay stud fees? They'll go elsewhere, to farms with first-class animals. These days, people want to show their horses, not just ride them to the hounds.''

Slowly, Judith was becoming enlightened. ''Has this always been a stud farm?''

''No,'' Walter answered, after taking a sip from his gin and tonic. ''Only for the last hundred years. Before that, the farm was more diversified. They had tenants then. But Sir Henry Ravenscroft was a great one for the hunt. So were several of the Dunks before him, but their own stables had declined. Sir Henry wanted the very best of everything. He had the money to invest in excellent stock and decided to use it not merely for pleasure, but for profit. The estate flourished for years. It's only in the last decade that things have begun to go downhill. Unfortunately, that trend started shortly after I began my tenure as the Ravenscroft steward.''

Across the room, Judith saw Natasha in the doorway. A vision in scarlet chiffon, she paused just long enough to entice Arthur Tinsley to her side. Judith sensed Walter Paget stiffen beside her.

''But Sir Henry didn't make his fortune breeding horses, right?'' she asked as Arthur escorted Nats to the bar.

''What?'' Despite his attempt at self-control, Walter seemed unnerved. ''Oh—no, Sir Henry was an investor. Machinery, mainly. He was fascinated by mechanical things. I gather he had a magic touch for making profitable choices. Excuse me, I must refresh my drink.''

Judith murmured her assent, though she knew that Walter's glass was still half-full. A moment later, he was speaking to Nats. Arthur appeared disgruntled. Then he saw Renie and became terrified.

Judith rushed to intervene. But Renie, well into her second screwdriver, was feeling magnanimous.

''Hey, Arthur,'' she said, slapping him on the back, ''no harm, no foul. I'm not the best driver, either.''

That, Judith thought, was putting it mildly. Upon occasion, Renie was appalling. More often, she was merely erratic. Back on Heraldsgate Hill, Renie drove the Joneses' big blue Chev as if it were part of an armored division.

''I don't think we've met, officially,'' Judith said to Arthur Tinsley. She put out her hand.

Arthur's grip was limp and vaguely clammy. "I had no idea you were guests of Ravenscroft House. I say, I am terribly sorry about this afternoon."

"It was the pits, all right," Renie agreed cheerfully. "You should have seen that sardine sandwich!" She leaned over the bar and waggled her empty glass at Harwood, who looked as if he might be legally dead.

Judith stepped on Renie's Via Spiga pump. "Knock it off, coz," she said under her breath. "We're about to go into dinner. I hope."

"Not a chance," Renie shot back. "We're never going to eat again. That's why I'm getting juiced. I'll pass out before I die of malnutrition."

But Harwood revived sufficiently to refill Renie's glass. Judith surrendered and requested a refill, too. Then Harwood left his post and walked woodenly into the entry hall. Trying to make conversation, Judith asked Arthur if he had an office in Little Pauncefoot.

"I do, actually," the solicitor replied in his dry voice. "I share space with Dr. Ramsey. But I live at Mon Repos, off the Great Pauncefoot Road. It's less than a mile from the village."

Judith nodded in a sanguine manner. There seemed to be a great deal more scotch than soda in her second drink. "This part of England seems quite unsoiled. *Unspoiled,* I mean." She felt her cheeks grow warm, for various reasons.

"Both," Arthur replied with a faint lift of one eyebrow. "Actually, I live five doors from the Giddyap Grill. It's Texas-style barbecue. Very messy. Lona refuses to dine there."

"Lona?" Judith forced her eyes to focus.

"My wife." Arthur didn't look very pleased at the concept. "She's delicate. Spicy foods distress her."

Renie had draped her arm around Arthur's neck, no mean feat, since he was half a head taller, even allowing for her Via Spigas. "Puny, huh? Or does she just get a lot of gas?"

Judith held her head, or tried to, but missed, the free hand sailing past her left ear. "Coz . . ."

Arthur, who was now white around the lips, attempted to free himself from Renie's quasi-hammerlock. "Lona suffers from colitis," he explained in an almost frantic voice. "That's why she's not here this evening. Dr. Ramsey felt she should stay home and rest."

Sagely, Renie nodded. "My mother has colitis. Sometimes she's really constipated, other times, she just lets loose and—"

Fortunately, a gong sounded from somewhere within the bowels of the house. Or at least that was how Judith interpreted the noise, given the topic of conversation. The entire group congregated behind Charles Marchmont, who offered Claire his arm, and led the way to the dining room.

The change of venue benefited Judith. She felt relatively sober as she was seated between Charles and Alex. Renie, apparently by special request, was across the table and down, next to Aunt Pet, with Walter Paget on her left. Miraculously, Renie also seemed reconstituted. No doubt the promise of food had erased the effects of alcohol. Judith knew her cousin had not only a bottomless stomach, but a hollow leg as well.

Dinner was served by a sullen, pigtailed teenager who didn't know and certainly didn't care from which side dishes should be presented or in what order. Judith, Charles, Claire, and Alex received green salads; Renie, Arthur, Nats, and Aunt Pet faced the soup. A bewildered Walter was left staring at poached halibut.

But nobody, not even Aunt Pet, complained. Judith's salad was crisp, with a tangy vinaigrette dressing. Judging from Renie's benign expression, the lentil soup was more than adequate. And Walter was lapping up halibut like a hungry house cat.

The company turned quite jovial. On her right, Alex talked animatedly about the various sports cars he'd tested. His conversation was vapid, if engaging, though Judith thought he seemed a trifle intoxicated. To her left, Charles related mildly amusing anecdotes about his colleagues in The City. Judith listened and smiled, smiled and listened, all the way to the saddle of lamb, which, fortuitously, was brought to everyone at the proper time.

"Mrs. Tichborne is a fine cook," Charles confided,

spearing fresh asparagus. "Bloody shame she doesn't do all the meals."

"The dinner is excellent," Judith enthused, noting that for someone on a strict diet, Aunt Pet seemed to keep pace with the rest of the diners. "Has Mrs. Tichborne been here a long time?"

Charles paused, fork in right hand, knife in left. Judith was reminded of Grandpa Grover's curious eating habits. "I believe she has. Twenty years, more or less. Good woman, under that crusty exterior."

Judith nodded, tasting the exquisite new potatoes with just a hint of garlic and parsley. "Is the . . . serving girl her daughter?"

To Judith's surprise, Charles shuddered. He wiped his mouth with a linen napkin, then shook his head. "No, no. That's some girl from the village. Not sure who. They come and go. Mrs. Tichborne's daughter . . . disappeared." He put the napkin back in his lap. "It was years ago."

The unknown teenager was now removing dinner plates from those who had finished. Judith swallowed the last bite of lamb and allowed her elegant piece of Wedgwood china to be taken away. On her right, Alex was chortling.

"Tichborne will hear about this," he said, lighting up a gold-tipped cigarette. "Saddle of lamb costs the world. Aunt Pet won't like it."

But Aunt Pet appeared to be in a festive mood. At the other end of the table, she was engaging Arthur Tinsley in a conversation that seemed to challenge his professional ambivalence. Renie, meanwhile, was speaking quite seriously with Walter Paget. Perhaps he was unburdening himself of his problems funding the Ravenscroft bloodstock.

Dessert was a chocolate mousse, with freshly baked ladyfingers. Judith marveled. It was no wonder that Mrs. Tichborne had been curt with the cousins. Obviously, she had had a great deal to do in preparing the dinner. In perfect contentment, Judith sipped her excellent coffee, and idly wondered if they'd all adjourn to the parlor for a rousing game of Happy Families.

But that was not what was on Aunt Pet's mind. After the dessert dishes had been taken away, the old woman tapped a spoon on her empty wineglass. Conversation evaporated, and all eyes turned to the far end of the table.

"This dining room used to seat many more family members than it does tonight," she said in her strong, clear voice. "We've had our share of tragedies, some too heartbreaking to mention. In the last few years, we've suffered terrible losses. That's why I always wear mourning." Pet's crippled hand trickled over the long black taffeta gown with its stark ornamentation of pearl ropes. The diners involuntarily bowed their heads. For a fleeting moment, Aunt Pet's eyes grew unnaturally bright. "So the family circle closes, getting smaller and smaller. I suppose that's not all bad for the rest of you."

Judith saw Claire cast a nervous glance at her aunt. Charles fumbled with his napkin. Alex and Nats exchanged wary, surreptitious looks. Walter seemed ill at ease, while Arthur made an effort to appear detached. Mrs. Tichborne had slipped quietly into the dining room.

"There's no point in being coy," Aunt Pet continued. "I'd be a fool not to know you're all wondering what will happen after I die. That's what Arthur here and I've been discussing this afternoon. Oh, I've made wills in the past, but I've had to revoke them. Too much outrageous behavior on the part of certain persons, too many of my beneficiaries up and died. Now I'm making a new will. Don't think I can't see through you. All of you. And before anybody gets their hopes up, I don't intend to meet my Maker just yet. I'm not going anywhere, except to bed. Good night."

With that remarkable speech, Aunt Pet signaled for Walter and Arthur to carry her upstairs. Naturally, they didn't dare demur.

For several minutes after Aunt Pet's departure, the only sound was the wind. The old house seemed to sigh. With a sudden shiver, Judith wondered if it yearned for peace.

She sensed that even at ninety-four, Aunt Pet preferred war.

SIX

Saturday brought drizzle, and an occasional glimpse of sun. It was typical for April, with weather that the cousins knew well. The climates of England and the Pacific Northwest were very similar.

Charles and Claire insisted on devoting their day to showing Judith and Renie the sights. The Marchmont Bentley purred along narrow roads, effortlessly carrying its passengers over the soft hills of Somerset. Small, almost perfect villages, many with thatched roofs and whitewashed walls, nestled in the valleys. There were inns and churches and farms, all brightened by spring flowers, blossoming fruit trees, lush shrubs, and that orderly chaos known as the English country garden.

They stopped to view the quietly imposing cathedral at Wells, the stark ruins of Glastonbury Abbey, the enduring magnificence of Dunster Castle. The cousins were awed by the sheer rock face of Cheddar Gorge, impressed by the heath-covered expanse of Exmoor, and charmed by the breathtaking panorama from Cothelstone Beacon.

By the time they returned to Ravenscroft House shortly after three-thirty, Judith and Renie admitted to fatigue. Claire was more frank:

"I must lie down for a while," she said with a guilty little smile. "There's so much to see in such a small area. Perhaps tomorrow we can go out again. You really should get to Devon and Cornwall."

Judith protested politely, though she knew that after a good night's rest, she and Renie would be delighted to see more of the nearby sights. Meanwhile, they were expected to take tea with Aunt Pet. The old lady wasn't coming down to dinner, and she'd extended the invitation before the cousins left in the morning.

Judith and Renie trudged up the main staircase. "Maybe we'll get a chance to unwind before cocktails," Judith said hopefully. "I envy Claire's afternoon siestas."

"The only time I ever nap is when I fall facedown on my drafting board," Renie remarked. "Claire's a lot younger than we are. I'll bet she doesn't work half as hard, either."

The cousins had almost reached the third floor when Natasha came hurrying down the stairs, her face a mask of fury. She paused, barring the way.

"If you're going to see the old dragon, forget it. She's got my brother in there. It's his turn to get bloody hell. I hope Aunt Pet chokes on her stupid tea!"

Nats started down the rest of the stairs, but Judith called after her. "Is something wrong? I mean, has something happened while we were out?"

Nats's dark eyes flashed. "Nothing that should concern you. It's strictly a family affair. Just be thankful the old bitch isn't trying to run *your* life!" She continued on her angry way.

Judith fingered the carved balustrade with its oak garlands and ivy. "We might as well go back to our rooms and change. We're wearing *pants.*"

But before they could reach the landing, a man's voice reverberated in the stairwell: "You're coldhearted, that's what you are! Family, my frigging arse!" A door slammed, and Alex appeared, hurrying as fast and furiously as his sister. He brushed past the cousins with only a muttered apology.

"Well?" Renie eyed Judith. "Shall we keep our pants on and take tea with Aunt Pet?"

Judith considered, then nodded. "It's four, and she's expecting us. We want to be punctual. I dare you to tell her your name isn't Renee, but Renie.''

"With her money, she can call me Beanie. Did you notice that Claire and Charles never mentioned Aunt Pet's State of the Union message?''

"English reserve," Judith declared, rapping twice on Aunt Pet's door. "It would also have been in poor taste.''

"So was the speech," Renie replied. "In a way. I mean, we're strangers, and Walter and Arthur aren't family. Neither is Mrs. Tichborne.''

Judith rapped again. "But Arthur's treated like a family member and I imagine Walter's been steward here long enough that he qualifies, too. Mrs. Tichborne has worked even longer as housekeeper.''

Dora opened the door a scant inch. She peered into the gallery, let out a sigh of relief, and admitted the cousins. "Forgive me, do. I thought you were Master Alex. Or Miss Nats. I was putting the kettle on.''

If Aunt Pet had suffered any ill effects from her confrontation with the Karamzins, she gave no sign. Her chair had been turned sideways so that it no longer faced the windows. A small table sat in front of her, and two other chairs had been drawn up. Judith and Renie sat down.

"Tired, are you?" Aunt Pet's assessment was astute. "Claire and Charles probably hauled you all over the county. Hope you weren't bored to tears.''

"Oh, no," Judith insisted. "It was wonderful. We saw some really fabulous sights.''

"Ha!" Aunt Pet was watching Dora fuss with the tea things. The cousins were watching Dora to make sure she didn't start a fire. "What's so fascinating about a pile of rubble like Glastonbury? Now if it were all of a piece, that would be different. But no, Henry VIII had to wreck the place, the greedy old fool.'' She craned her neck to see what the maid was doing. "Dora! You can't make the kettle boil by staring at it! Bring those scones and the cucumber and fish-paste sandwiches so we can start nibbling.''

Dora obliged, fluttering to the table with a Royal Doulton plate that held a dozen finger sandwiches. The cousins were careful to try the cucumber first. The scones were delivered next, in a covered wicker basket.

"I talked Tichborne into making these," Aunt Pet said, devouring one of the fish-paste concoctions. "Odd woman, that Hester. Can't blame her in some ways. Still, a person can't give in to tragedy. Might as well roll over and die."

Judith discovered that the cucumber sandwich was delicious. The filling included tomato, creamed cheese, and a dash of basil. "You're referring to Mrs. Tichborne's daughter?"

Aunt Pet seemed to be studying her second sandwich. "Well—yes. Janet, her name was. Flighty creature. Not the least like her mother."

"She disappeared?" Judith decided to dare eat the fish-paste. It was surprisingly tasty.

Aunt Pet was still avoiding eye contact with her guests. "That was the story at the time. Not that girls don't do that when they're young and headstrong. Foolish—so foolish. They ruin their lives." The tea kettle whistled, and Aunt Pet nodded with satisfaction. "Let it steep properly," she commanded Dora. "You tend to hurry the leaves along."

"Mrs. Tichborne is certainly a fine cook," Renie noted, gobbling finger sandwiches of both varieties. "What happened to Mr. Tichborne?" The question was idly phrased, for Renie was now slathering butter on a warm scone.

Aunt Pet wrinkled her faintly hooked nose. "He drank. Owned a pub, in fact, over in Taunton. Crude sort, probably beat Hester. Nobody mourned when he fell off a bridge and drowned. Years ago, of course. That was how we acquired Mrs. Tichborne. He'd mortaged the pub to the hilt, and she needed the post."

Judith also tried a scone, with a dab of damson jam. "So she and Janet moved in?"

Aunt Pet nodded. "That they did. Janet was raised here. Sample the orange marmalade. Tichborne puts it up herself."

Judith and Renie were more than willing. Despite a fine lunch at The Royal Oak in Ilminster, their excursion had made them hungry.

"What," Judith inquired as Dora poured tea, "did Janet do? Run away?"

But Aunt Pet's attention was fixed on her maid. "Mind that teapot, Dora. You'll spill into the saucer." She paused, waiting for Dora to pass the cups. "Where did you say your great-grandparents lived? Wiltshire?"

The cousins hadn't said. "Essex," Renie answered. "High Ongar. A great-great-great-grandfather was the curate there in the eighteen-thirties. Another great—not so far back as that—served in the Admiralty under Queen Victoria."

"Ah." The pieces of family history seemed to please Aunt Pet. "Good stock. Service to God and country. Delighted to have you as part of the family. Don't think I'll forget it when I finalize this new will." The old lady winked broadly.

"But . . ." Judith began, taken aback. "Great-Grandfather was a Grover who married a—"

"Jackass," Aunt Pet said amiably. "That was my own grandfather, the last of the Dunks. Drank, gambled, frittered away what was left of the family fortune. It took my father, Sir Henry Ravenscroft, to save this place. Cordelia, that was my mother. Cordelia Dunk-Ravenscroft. Beautiful woman, but no spine. She filled my brothers, Chauncey and Oakley, with too many pretty stories. Wandering knights and ladies a-pining. No wonder my father made me his heir. Or heiress. One has to be careful these days about nomenclature. Don't know why. A fool's a fool, regardless of gender. More tea?"

Renie offered her cup. "Sure, it's good stuff. I'm invigorated."

Aunt Pet nodded. "Tea's the thing. You've seen the library? Used to be the formal dining room until about a hundred and fifty years ago."

Claire hadn't yet shown them all of the second floor, but Judith had noticed the library was opposite the master bedroom. When Judith confessed that she was a trained librarian, Aunt Pet seemed mildly impressed.

"You'll appreciate the collection then," she said. "Several first editions, mostly nineteenth century. Lot of trash, too. The younger generations bought these so-called modern novels. Nothing but sex and gloom. Most depressing. Oh, there are some French and Russian works, too. Genevieve and Viktor saw to that. Personally, I can't read a word of Russian. Alphabet's all queer and backwards.'' Aunt Pet buttered another scone. Once again, the doctor's instructions went unheeded. ''Browse at your leisure. If Charles is working there, ignore him. Nobody else uses the library. You won't catch Alex or Nats reading a book. Even smut's too dull for their tastes.''

Judith's expression was rueful. ''It's sad when young people don't read. They miss so much.''

Aunt Pet snorted. ''Those two don't miss a trick. Opportunists, both of them. Think they can pull the wool over my eyes. More fools they!''

Judith assumed her most innocent look. ''You mean— they're schemers?''

''Swindlers is more like it.'' Aunt Pet chewed her scone with vigor. ''Not quite criminals. Alex hasn't the brains to be a crook. And Nats is too clever to break the law. More scones?''

The cousins, however, were replete. Aunt Pet turned to summon Dora, but the maid was nowhere in sight.

''Slips in and out like a wraith,'' Aunt Pet complained, picking up the silver bell from the nightstand between her chair and the elaborately hung bed. ''Listens at keyholes, too. Good thing her bedroom is on the other side of my sitting room. Otherwise, she'd sit up all night, listening to me talk in my sleep.''

But Dora scurried in through a door next to a heavy oak armoire. Judith figured it was the bathroom. When Aunt Pet imperiously ordered the maid to take away the tea things, Judith pictured the long, winding turret stairs and offered to carry the items down to the kitchen.

''No need,'' said Aunt Pet. ''There's a dumbwaiter. It comes out on the main floor by one of the back doors. Mrs. Tichborne will collect everything and take it to the kitchen. Now off with you. I've enjoyed myself, but I'm due for a nap. Can't sleep at night for more than two hours at a time. Most vexing.''

Offering their thanks, the cousins started out through the sitting room. But Aunt Pet called after them:

"Ring up Arthur, if you please. Tell him not to come by this evening." Her manner grew secretive, almost playful. "I'm not ready to see him yet. Sometimes it's more interesting to keep people in suspense."

Judith had stepped back into the bedchamber. "Would he be at work or at home on a Saturday afternoon?"

Aunt Pet was leaning heavily on the diminutive Dora. "At home, I should think. Don't know his number. I won't use a telephone. Never had one in my rooms. Nothing but a nuisance." Still clinging to the maid, she dragged herself to the bed. As the cousins left the suite, they heard Dora's high-pitched voice commiserating over her mistress's aches and pains. Aunt Pet told the maid to belt up.

As predicted, the library was empty. Its size, not to mention its inventory, surpassed what Judith had imagined. Books lined the walls, requiring ladders to reach the top shelves. The chimneypiece, with its Portland stone, could have been part of the original craftsmanship. Certainly the heraldic stained-glass windows showed signs of great age as well as ethereal beauty.

The volumes were wonderful, too, from Austen to Zola. At last, Renie had to forcibly drag Judith away. It was after six o'clock, and while Aunt Pet would not be at dinner, the cousins still needed to change out of their sightseeing clothes.

The cocktail interval was subdued compared to the previous evening. The Karamzins had gone off to a party in Yeovil, and Walter Paget was nowhere to be seen. Judith had called Arthur Tinsley from the library. He hadn't been at home, but a petulant female, who Judith assumed was the delicate Lona, promised to convey the message.

Dinner was also a more modest, as well as informal, affair. Charles monopolized the conversation, discussing his work, which seemed to consist of overseeing the Ravenscroft fortune.

"I started out as a clerk for Barclay's Bank," he explained. "The pater wanted me to go into the fishmonger business with him, but the stench put me off. A man needn't reek of fish to prove he's a man, I said, and how could the pater argue?''

With feigned modesty, Charles went on to relate how quickly he'd risen in The City. Basically, he loved money, but disliked banks. Or, at any rate, bankers. Managing investments was his forte. He had found himself more at home in a brokerage house. Consequently, upon his marriage to Claire twelve years earlier, Aunt Pet had asked— or commanded—him to take over the family's financial affairs.

"Incredibly, she'd handled most of the business herself until then," Charles said as they enjoyed Mrs. Tichborne's tender pork loin. "Aunt Pet had advisers, of course, but she made all the decisions. Then, when she became housebound, she felt it prudent to appoint someone who could be on the spot in The City. That's when I took the helm." Charles seemed to swell with self-importance, though he cast his eyes downward in an attempt at humility.

There was more, mostly about the complexities of doing business in a high-tech world. Aunt Pet would founder in the computer age, Charles asserted, but he was well-qualified, mainly because he took advantage of every seminar that came along.

"It's very fast-paced out there when it comes to commerce," he declared. "No room for slackers or those who hold back." Still, he admitted, there were pitfalls, even for the savvy. "Too much speculation in the last decade. A number of seemingly sound investments have soured. It's very difficult to forecast trends. But we'll pull through, mark my words."

Judith, who was a babe in the woods when it came to investments, gathered that the Ravenscroft fortune was being eroded. But Renie, whose graphic design business regularly felt the corporate pulse, was nodding in agreement.

"Software has made a lot of people—and unmade them," she remarked over the snow pudding. "I've watched any number of companies come and go. The marketplace exploded in the eighties and became overcrowded.

Several undercapitalized firms got squeezed out, especially in our part of the country.''

Briefly, Charles scowled at Renie. It was obvious that he didn't like having his thunder stolen, least of all by a woman. And an American at that.

It was Claire, however, who played the peacekeeper. She had listened to her husband's self-promotion with a patient demeanor that almost managed to mask her boredom. "Of course, everything will come out all right," she said with a tremulous smile for Charles. "You'll pull us through. Auntie, I mean. After all, it *is* her money."

The reminder seemed to cause Charles pain. "Of course it is. I'm not likely to forget." His face tightened, and he attacked his pudding with a vengeance.

The meal wound down, with Claire finally wresting a few pieces of conversation. She volunteered ten hours a week at a battered-women's shelter in Stepney. She was anxious for the twins' next vacation. She hoped that the rain, which had started to come down hard just before dinner, wouldn't spoil the proposed Sunday outing to Devon and Cornwall.

And when Mrs. Tichborne made her final foray into the dining room to remove the dessert plates, Claire treated the housekeeper with great deference, rather like a novice conductor coaxing a reigning prima donna. Mrs. Tichborne maintained a wooden mien but performed efficiently, if not graciously.

"She's off tomorrow and Monday," Claire said in a low voice after the housekeeper had returned to the kitchen. "She's such a hard worker, but of course when we're not here, her duties are rather light."

Charles grunted. "She's done very well for herself. Free room and board, a substantial salary, plenty of free time. Not that she doesn't earn her keep, but staff is a tremendous drain on household expenses. Worse yet are the responsibilities Auntie has taken on as lady of the manor. The church, the library, the All Fools Revels. Every event in the village falls on Ravenscroft House. Auntie is expected to foot the bill for everything from the flower boxes along the High Street to repairing the Dunk Monument on the green. *Droit de seigneur* indeed! The only privilege these days is signing checks to benefit others.''

Claire's smile was now faintly reproachful. ''Come now, Charles, the flower boxes don't cost but twenty pounds a year. They use seeds. And the Dunk Monument crumbled years ago, about the time we married. The only thing we do for the All Fools Revels is pay for clean-up and provide costumes. As for the vicar, he loathes asking for money.''

Charles wasn't placated. ''All the same, Aunt Pet is more than willing to offer it to him. You'd think she was buying her way into heaven. Not that she ever expects to go there. I do believe the woman's convinced she can live forever.''

The cousins made no comment. It seemed to Judith that while Aunt Pet wasn't immortal, she had a good chance of still being around in the twenty-first century. Certainly she had outlived not only her contemporaries, but many in the next generation as well.

As a prophet, Judith was about to be proved wrong.

After dinner, Claire suggested a rubber of bridge. Despite the long day, Judith felt it would be impolite to refuse. Renie, in fact, seemed eager.

''Hey, the only time we get to play is when one of our mothers' bridge club members has a stroke or dies or something and we have to substitute,'' Renie whispered as they returned to the drawing room. ''And you know what that's like. Your mother always jumps all over my mother for underbidding and my mother pouts for two days because your mother wins the quarters and your mother says it's because she plays her hand and doesn't sit there like a wart on a hyena's hind end and my mother says your mother cheats.''

Judith was indignant. ''My mother does *not* cheat at bridge.''

''I know she doesn't,'' Renie said equably as the Marchmonts supervised Harwood's laborious setting up of a card table and four chairs. ''My mother knows it, too. Sometimes she says your mother is just too lucky.''

''She is,'' Judith agreed, having been victimized by Gertrude all too often at cribbage. ''At cards, anyway.'' Gertrude would not agree that she was a lucky person in general. Having been widowed too young, suffering from arthritis, living in the toolshed—these were reasons that Judith's mother didn't consider herself "lucky." Her daughter understood, and made allowances.

After a lengthy rubber with many sets and several partial games, Judith stifled a yawn. It was almost eleven, and everyone looked weary. No one demurred when Claire suggested that it was time to retire.

The big bed with its blue damask hangings was very old, but the mattress felt quite new. The previous night at Ravenscroft House, Judith had slept soundly. She expected to do the same as she slipped between the hand-embroidered sheets around eleven-thirty. It had been a very long day, and the rain on the mullioned windows pattered in a comforting rhythm. Judith hadn't read more than four pages of the John Dickson Carr mystery she'd borrowed from the Ravenscroft library when she felt her eyes closing. She went to sleep without turning off the light.

When she was awakened by the sound of voices and hurrying footsteps, she didn't know where she was. Had Joe been called out on a case? Was one of the B&B guests having a crisis? Could Gertrude be in trouble—or merely causing it?

But Judith was not at Hillside Manor. Adjusting her eyes to the bedside lamp which seemed unnaturally bright, she sat up and listened intently. The sounds had stopped. A glance at her watch showed that it was after three. The rain was no longer streaming down outside the windows. Maybe she had dreamed the strange noises.

Now wide awake, she felt a need to go to the bathroom. Slipping into her robe, she headed out to the adjoining bath. The hallway was lit by gilt wall sconces with flame-shaped bulbs. In the bathroom, Judith thought she heard more footsteps, either overhead or on the turret stairs that were located on the other side of the wall.

Back in the corridor, she noticed that the door to the master bedroom stood open. A light was on inside, making a sallow patch on the hall floor. At that moment, Charles came rushing down the main staircase. Apparently, he didn't see Judith. With his silk robe flapping at his bare feet, he raced into the library.

Judith hesitated, then went across the hall to knock on Renie's door. There was no answer. Judith knew Renie could sleep through a performance by the Ohio State Marching Band. The knob turned at a touch. Judith flipped on a Flemish brass lamp. Only the top of Renie's chestnut curls could be seen above the covers.

"Coz! Wake up!" Judith nudged the sleigh bed with her knee.

Renie rolled over, then disappeared completely.

"Coz!" This time Judith shook Renie. "Something is happening! Get up!"

Renie burrowed so far down that her feet poked out at the other end. Judith sat on her. Renie let out a gasp, then a squeak, and finally started to swear.

"You creep! What the hell's going on? Are you trying to kill me?"

Judith stood up. "I heard a commotion. Charles ran into the library as if his p.j.s were on fire. I think there's some kind of trouble."

"There sure is," Renie said in annoyance. "It's the middle of the night, and I'm awake." She glanced at her travel clock. "Three-thirty? I didn't get up this early to deliver our three kids!"

Judith made as if to tug her cousin's arm, but Renie pulled away sharply. "Okay, okay! I'll put on my robe. But if this is a false alarm, you'll have to feed me."

When the cousins reached the hall, they saw Charles emerging from the library. He noticed his guests and staggered toward them.

"It's dreadful!" he cried. "It's worse than dreadful!" Charles swallowed hard, and in the pale glow of the hallway fixtures, Judith saw that his usually ruddy complexion was ashen. "It's Aunt Pet." He swallowed again, then suddenly, frighteningly, he laughed. "She's dying! Isn't that . . . incredible?"

Charles couldn't stop laughing.

SEVEN

DR. RAMSEY ARRIVED five minutes after the cousins entered Aunt Pet's sitting room. Charles and Dora were with the stricken old lady in the bedchamber. Claire was weeping and pacing, insisting she should be with her aunt.

"It's best we don't all crowd in there," Judith insisted. "We'll get in the doctor's way."

Claire's face was blotchy and her eyes were already swollen. "Then Dora shouldn't be there, either. She's hysterical."

Dora was indeed out of control. But her wails and screeches had forced Charles to get a grip on himself. Abruptly, Dora fell silent. Judith figured that Charles had given her a good shake.

The most shattering sound came from Aunt Pet, who let out a long, low moan that turned into a gurgle, and then stopped. Judith edged over to the bedchamber door. Dr. Ramsey, a balding, chunky man, was bending over Aunt Pet. Charles leaned against the bedpost. Dora had collapsed in her mistress's favorite chair. Despite her distress, she looked vaguely guilty about usurping Aunt Pet's place.

"She's dead." Dr. Ramsey's deep voice was brusque, yet not without compassion. "I'm sorry. There was nothing to be done." Gently, he pulled the snowy white sheet over Aunt Pet's face.

"Well." Charles stood up straight, then turned toward the door, where Renie and Claire had joined Judith. "Quite a run, really," he said in an oddly hollow voice. "It's a shock, but she didn't have to linger. Shall we adjourn to the sitting room? I believe Dr. Ramsey wants a word with Dora." Charles took his wife by the hand.

"We must call an undertaker," Claire murmured tonelessly. "The vicar, too. A cable should be sent to my parents . . ." The words trailed off among the sitting room's collection of Victorian bric-a-brac, framed photographs, satin pillows, and solid oak.

Judith watched Renie accompany Charles and Claire out of the suite. Lingering behind, she couldn't resist listening to Dr. Ramsey's interrogation of Dora Hobbs.

". . . heard her ring around midnight . . . A headache, she had, and a terrible thirst . . . Blurry-eyed, she claimed . . . Skin all hot and dry . . ." There was a long pause. Judith, who had been holding her breath, sucked in a lungful of air. She noted the telltale smell of smoke, very faint, but still present in the vicinity. Had Dora started another fire? Judith hoped not. She breathed again, just as the doctor gently urged Dora to continue.

"I gave her a big glass of water," the maid went on in a shaky voice. "She seemed to settle down, got drowsy-like, and went off to sleep. I went back to bed. Too much excitement, I thought, with all these guests. Later, maybe half an hour ago, I heard noises. I came back in, and the mistress was jerking around in the bed, ever so queer. Dreaming, I decided, and tried to rouse her. But I . . . couldn't." Dora began to sniff and sob. "That's when I went down to fetch Mr. Charles."

Dr. Ramsey spoke reassuringly to Dora. The sobs subsided. Judith stepped behind a screen painted with cupids sitting on a crescent moon. When the doctor had left the suite, she tiptoed back to the bedchamber and looked in on the grieving maid.

"Dora," Judith said softly, "would you like to come downstairs with me?"

Startled, Dora looked up. "Oh—no, thank you all the same. It wouldn't be decent to leave her alone." One small wrinkled hand gestured at the still form in the bed. "I've been with her for over seventy years, day in, day out. When I broke my leg in fifty-three, it was herself who took care of me. I'm not leaving her now." Almost defiantly, Dora resettled herself in the brocade chair. There was a curious dignity about the way she squared her narrow shoulders and lifted her little chin. In her mistress's cherished place by the windows, Dora no longer looked guilty.

Under ordinary circumstances, the parlor would have been an inviting room. The original stone chimneypiece was the mate to that of the library overhead. A plaster frieze of flora looked as if it were part of the original decor. The oak-paneled walls were covered with paintings of both the hunt and individual hunters, perhaps scenes and animals from the glory days of the Ravenscroft stables. Furnished with Elizabethan and Jacobean pieces, the room should have emanated comfort as well as beauty. But at a few minutes after four in the morning, the pall of death hung on the air. There was no fire in the grate, only two lamps had been turned on, and a damp chill seemed to settle over the mourners.

Mrs. Tichborne and Harwood had now joined the others. The pair looked unsure of their roles, whether they were expected to be fellow mourners or dutiful servants.

It was Charles who dispensed the brandy with a liberal hand. Even Harwood, incongruous in a gaily striped robe, accepted a snifter. After everyone was served and seated, Charles inquired as to the whereabouts of the Karamzins.

Claire uttered a small cry. "Oh! They can't have returned from their party in Yeovil! What a shock this will be for them!"

"Will it?" Charles set his mouth in a stern line. For some moments, nobody spoke.

And then police constable Colin Duff arrived, accompanied by Walter Paget. The steward was dressed, though it was obvious that he had thrown his clothes on in haste. He went directly to Claire and took both her hands in his.

"I'm so sorry . . . Mrs. Marchmont. I heard Dr. Ramsey's car, then I looked out and saw lights in the turret room. After I dressed, I met Constable Duff bicycling through the gate."

The rest of the household appeared shocked by the policeman's arrival. Charles had stepped forward and was eyeing Colin Duff in a bewildered manner.

"What's this? Who rang you? What's going on?"

Dr. Ramsey coughed. "I did, Mr. Marchmont. I felt it necessary to send for the police."

Charles seemed on the verge of exploding. "What? Are you daft, man?"

With regret, the doctor shook his head. "Miss Ravenscroft was basically healthy, despite her age. There were some . . . ah . . . suggestive symptoms as described by her maid. I've attended at least three children who suffered from the same sort of gastric distress. I'm not convinced that her death was natural. I must also recommend an autopsy."

Withdrawing her hands from Walter's grasp, Claire gaped in disbelief. "What are you insinuating, Dr. Ramsey? I don't understand."

The doctor gave a helpless shrug. "I'm not insinuating anything, Mrs. Marchmont. But I'm responsible for signing the death certificate. I'd be less than conscientious if I didn't consider all of the . . . possibilities." Dr. Ramsey's voice gained momentum. "Miss Ravenscroft was a woman with very high standards. She would want me to do the right thing. That's why I rang up the police."

"My word!" Walter murmured. "How very odd."

Police Constable Duff was young, sandy-haired, and freckled. He looked both awed and intimidated by his surroundings. "If you please," he said in a soft voice with a Scottish accent, "I must view the deceased."

With a sigh of resignation, Charles led the way. Dr. Ramsey trailed after the two men.

Claire wrung her hands. "Poor Dora. I hope the doctor will give her a sedative."

Hester Tichborne, wearing a tailored charcoal robe, was standing in front of a Flemish tapestry that depicted Circe, the Enchantress. "If he doesn't, I'll see to Dora." The housekeeper spoke in a clear, even voice, with the hint of a challenge in her manner.

But no one objected. In fact, Claire murmured that it was very kind of Mrs. Tichborne to offer. And then, as the first streaks of light appeared in the night sky, the squeal of tires could be heard in the drive. Raucous voices erupted—and then went dumb.

"What's wrong?" Nats demanded, charging into the parlor. She looked both disheveled and alarmed. "Why is everybody up?"

Ever the perfect servant, Harwood tottered over to take the newcomers' wraps. "There's been a tragedy, miss," he said in a doleful voice.

Alex, who was more unsteady than the butler, reeled against an Italian credenza. "Tragedy? What d'ya mean, tragedy? Someone pinch the Tudor salt cellar?"

Claire burst into fresh tears. It was left to Mrs. Tichborne to deliver the bad news. Judith sensed that the housekeeper somehow relished the task. "Your aunt died. It was very sudden."

"No!" Alex staggered, presumably from drink. But then he covered his face with his hands, slumped to a sitting position on the floor, and began to sob. To Judith's amazement, his reaction seemed unfeigned.

Nats, however, was made of sterner stuff. She was sobered by the announcement, and her dark eyes took in the entire room. "That's ridiculous," she said flatly. "Aunt Pet had an iron constitution. Something's not right here."

The uncertainty had been hovering in the shadows of the parlor for the last half-hour. That conclusion had occurred to Judith, to whom unnatural death was no stranger. But this time, given the victim's advanced age, she had hoped that life had come to a peaceful close.

That hope was dashed when Constable Duff reappeared with Charles and Dr. Ramsey. The policeman nervously fingered his regulation headgear as he addressed the gathering:

"I'm verra much afraid there will have to be an autopsy—and an inquest. I must speak with m'superiors, naturally, but there is reason that we canna rule out foul play.

I must ask ye all to bide close for the time being. Thank ye.'' He bobbed his head and took his leave.

"Absurd," Charles declared.

"Appalling," Claire murmured.

"I told you so," Nats said.

Judith and Renie kept quiet. The swift, rueful looks they exchanged conveyed dismay, sorrow, and resignation. This couldn't be happening to them. They were on their dream trip. They were houseguests. They hardly knew the Ravenscroft ménage. But as dawn crept in through the mullioned windows, harsh reality struck them both like an April squall. Old and beautiful though the house might be, they had no intention of staying past Monday. Joe and Bill expected to meet them Wednesday in Edinburgh.

Renie had sidled up to Judith. "Are you thinking what I'm thinking?"

"Probably," Judith replied. With a lifetime of closeness that was rare for cousins, and even unusual with sisters, Judith and Renie practically could read each others' minds. "We planned to leave tomorrow. I'm assuming that's still possible, despite what the constable said. I mean, even if Aunt Pet didn't die of a stroke or whatever, we can't be under any suspicion."

Renie nodded vigorously. "That's right, we're just a couple of booblike American tourists. Maybe we should offer to leave today."

Briefly, Judith considered. "You're right. If we stay, we'll just get in the way."

The cousins started to follow Claire out of the parlor. But she had gone into the entry hall to meet the ambulance drivers who had come to take away Aunt Pet's body. Judith glanced around to see who else remained in the room. Charles and Dr. Ramsey apparently had already returned upstairs. Nats had led Alex away. Mrs. Tichborne was gone, probably to look after Dora. Only Harwood and Walter Paget were still in the parlor. The butler was tidying up, and the steward was on the telephone.

"What do we do now?" Renie asked, a faintly forlorn figure in her voluminous velour bathrobe.

It was going on 5 A.M. "It's too late to go back to bed,"

Judith said. "It would seem pretty heartless of us. I couldn't sleep anyway."

"Neither could I," Renie agreed, somewhat to Judith's surprise. "I feel terrible about Aunt Pet. I really liked the old girl."

"Me, too," Judith replied. "I think." From the stairwell, she could hear voices. "Come on, let's get out of here. The ambulance attendants are bringing the body down. I don't feel like being a ghoul."

The cousins headed for the dining room, found it empty, and went into the kitchen. Alex and Nats were sitting at a much-scarred oak table. A coffeemaker was plugged in and a glass of what looked like Alka-Seltzer sat in front of Alex.

Nats looked up at Judith and Renie with only minimal interest. "If you want coffee, it'll be another five minutes," she said, sounding very tired.

"Thanks," Judith answered, gazing around what was probably the most renovated room in the house. The appliances weren't new, but they looked out of place in a kitchen that had once housed an open spit, huge baking ovens, and long worktables for a battery of scullery maids. Tentatively, Judith pulled out a chair.

"Go ahead," said Nats, then suddenly scrutinized both cousins closely. "Who are you? Really, I mean. I didn't pay much attention when we met Friday. Are you friends of Claire's or Charles's?"

Briefly, Judith explained the tenuous connection with the Marchmonts through her pen-pal, Margaret. Nats nodded absently; Alex was making faces as he consumed his bromide.

"This rather spoils your stay," Nats remarked as she rose to check the coffee. "Or does it?" Her dark eyes flitted from one cousin to the other.

Renie wore a faintly pugnacious look. "Meaning?"

Nats shrugged. "It gives you something to talk about when you get home. Not the same old dreary photos of Hampton Court and Big Ben and St. Paul's, but a dead body in an honest-to-God English country house. You'll be quite the celebrities, I should think. For a short time."

Judith had an urge to tell Nats that finding dead bodies

wasn't exactly a novelty for her and Renie. Judith's role as a hostelry owner had taught her to deal with all sorts of rude, unreasonable people. Besides, she'd been raised by Gertrude.

Judith's silence seemed to goad Nats, who was taking coffee cups out of a large hutch. "Dr. Ramsey and the constable think there's something odd about Aunt Pet's death," Nats said, sounding defensive. "I think so, too. Look how sprightly she was at dinner Friday night!"

Pushing aside his empty glass, Alex groaned. "Sprightly! Spitefully is what I call it! Whatever happened, she's dead. And I feel bloody awful!"

It was impossible to tell if Alex referred to his physical condition or his emotional state. Judith accepted a cup of coffee from Nats and listened as a vehicle drove away from the house. The ambulance, she guessed, and offered a silent prayer.

At that moment, Mrs. Tichborne entered the kitchen. She had changed into a plain black dress and had her graying brown hair pulled back into its usual tight chignon. "if anyone is hungry, I'll make breakfast," she said in her brisk voice.

Alex groaned again; Nats declined; Judith was about to do the same, but Renie spoke up in an eager voice: "Sounds good. Can I help?"

The housekeeper politely rejected the offer. "I work better alone," she asserted. Her colorless eyes surveyed the group at the kitchen table. "Completely alone."

Sheepishly, Judith and Renie took their coffee into the dining room. The Karamzins followed. Charles entered from the hall almost simultaneously.

"Ramsey's gone off to help with the autopsy," Charles said, still disconcerted by the idea. "Walter notified Arthur Tinsley. He'll be here shortly. I insisted that Claire go back to bed." Charles heaved a sigh as he sat down next to Judith. "Rum, this. You must think we're rotten hosts."

Judith assured him that wasn't so. "It's not your fault Aunt Pet died. It could happen to anyone. In fact, it does. Eventually." As soon as the words tumbled out of her mouth, she felt like an idiot.

But no one—except Renie—seemed to notice. Alex put down his cup and said he was going up to bed. After her brother had left the dining room, Nats inquired after Walter Paget.

Charles stirred sugar and cream into his coffee. "Life goes on. Walter went to the stables. The hands don't work Sundays."

Nats received the information without comment. But as the aroma of frying meat wafted from the kitchen, she rose from the table and unceremoniously exited the dining room. The cousins were left alone with Charles.

"Blast," he said, more to himself than to his guests. "We were going up to town tomorrow. I've afternoon appointments. What to do, what to do?" He thrummed his blunt fingers on the table.

Judith decided to raise the issue of their own leavetaking. Charles eyed her doubtfully. "The Sunday train schedule is limited," he said. "Especially the local. Besides, I thought we were all told to stay at Ravenscroft House."

"They can't mean us," Judith protested. "I mean, we're not . . . involved."

"But you are," Charles countered. "Now that Auntie's dead, we can make plans for the B&B. Claire needs your advice more than ever."

Judith was flummoxed. "But . . . she'll be up to her ears in funeral arrangements. She's grief-stricken. She won't want to move ahead with a major project so soon."

Charles, however, remained adamant. "The sooner, the better. Every day we put off, potential revenue is lost. See here, we're in a bit of a financial bind. I'm prostrated with grief, and all that, but Aunt Pet's death couldn't have come at a better time. I'm sure you understand."

Judith didn't. Instead, she was appalled.

Charles and the cousins were eating scrambled eggs, rashers of bacon, slices of ham, and toasted muffins when Arthur Tinsley arrived. It was not quite six o'clock, and the solicitor eyed the covered dishes on the sideboard with longing.

Charles paid no heed. He forked in a last mouthful of

ham and announced that he wanted to get right down to business. Arthur must join him in the library immediately.

The solicitor looked troubled. "I'm not certain . . . that is to say . . . really, Mr. Marchmont, the situation is most . . . awkward."

"Awkward?" Charles scoffed at the word. "Nonsense! I'm all undone by Auntie's passing, but death is part of life. We must go on. And do call me Charles. We've known each other for donkey's years."

Judith sensed that Arthur wasn't mollified. Nonetheless, he trooped off with Charles. Renie went to the sideboard, piling more eggs and bacon onto her plate. "Well? Are we coming or going?" she asked Judith.

"Going," Judith replied promptly. "I couldn't possibly sit down with Claire and hammer out a renovation plan under the circumstances. When we get home, I'll send her a detailed letter with my suggestions. Anyway, I need some time to think things through. This house is much more of a challenge than I expected." Frowning at her watch, she looked at Renie again. "What time is it at home?"

Renie calculated. "There's eight hours' difference. It must be after ten Saturday evening. Why?"

Judith stood up. "I'm going to call Mother. The rates will be down."

Renie looked bemused. "Good luck. I've already called my mother. Twice. I can't afford another transatlantic marathon. You know how my mother goes on. And on."

Judith did. Confined to a wheelchair, Aunt Deb spent most of her waking hours with the receiver propped up to her ear. But Gertrude was very different. Like Aunt Pet, she hated the telephone.

Judith poked her head into the kitchen. Mrs. Tichborne was wiping off the big stove. "Yes?" She peered over a pair of half-glasses. "What is it? Have we run out of something?"

"No," Judith replied. "Nobody else has come down for breakfast yet. I was wondering where I might use the phone. Mr. Marchmont and Mr. Tinsley are in the library."

The housekeeper pointed to a wall model at the end of

a row of cupboards. "Go on, use this. I'll fix a tray for Dora."

Judith thanked Mrs. Tichborne, then asked if she knew where a railway schedule might be found. The housekeeper thought there might be one in the library. Judith said she'd look for it after Charles and Arthur had finished their conference. Stalling for privacy, she next inquired if there was a Catholic church nearby.

Mrs. Tichborne paused in the act of placing eggs and ham on a plate, presumably for Dora Hobbs. "You're Roman Catholic?" she inquired, her high forehead creased.

Judith nodded. "It's Sunday. My cousin and I would like to go to Mass."

"As I recall," Mrs. Tichborne said, not very encouragingly, "there's an R.C. church in Yeovil. At least there used to be. A friend of my . . . of the family went there. Bridget was Irish. She had no choice."

Judith let the slur pass. She was more intrigued by the housekeeper's change of reference. "I could look the church up in the directory. How far is it to Yeovil?"

Mrs. Tichborne placed silverware and a napkin on Dora's tray. "Ten miles. It's a long walk."

Growing vexed, Judith went to the phone. By the time the call had been placed and charged to her credit card, Mrs. Tichborne had disappeared up the back stairs. Nine thousand miles away, in the cul-de-sac on the side of Heraldsgate Hill, the phone rang and rang. At last, a gruff hello sounded in Judith's ear. The transmission was so clear that Gertrude could have been in the next room. Judith was thankful that she wasn't.

"Where are you?" Gertrude demanded. "The airport? I figured you'd come home early. You and Lunkhead are broke, right?" A chortle rolled across North America and under the ocean to the green fields of England.

"No, Mother," Judith replied, grudgingly pleased to hear Gertrude's raspy voice. "I'm in Somerset."

"Sunset? What's that, a rest home? You have a fit or something?"

"*Somerset*. It's a county."

"Not as far as I'm concerned," snapped Gertrude. "Never heard of it."

"Renie and I came down for the weekend," Judith explained. "Joe and Bill are fishing in Scotland."

"I'll bet. I thought Bill was meeting a bunch of nuts. Instead, he's gone fishing with one? What next, taking tea with the Queen? Listen here, Judith Anne, did you and your numbskull husband have a fight?" Gertrude sounded pleasurably excited by the idea.

"No, Mother. I gave you a copy of our itinerary. Joe and Bill have had this fishing trip lined up for weeks." Judith discovered that her patience was slipping away. "Renie and I are meeting them Wednesday in Edinburgh."

There was a pause in the converted toolshed behind Hillside Manor. Judith thought she could hear pages being riffled. Gertrude probably had the itinerary right in front of her.

"No, you're not. You're supposed to be in Edberg. Where's that? It sounds like Norway to me. What are those lamebrained husbands of yours fishing for—pickled herring?"

"It's pronounced Ed-in-bo-ro," Judith said distinctly. "It's—"

"It's stupid. Either you go to England or you don't. That's the trouble with you young people, you say one thing and do another. Now you're in Sweden, watching the sunset. What if I have a stroke? How will anybody find you? Or would they bother? Those Swedes don't show much emotion, if you ask me."

Somewhat frantically, Judith looked around to see if there was someplace she could sit. But the phone cord didn't stretch to the chairs at the kitchen table. "Mother, you know that Renie and I can be reached through an American Express office in case of an emergency. But," she added, just to reassure Gertrude, "we're heading for London. We'll be there until—"

"London? You've already been there. It says right here," Gertrude declared, apparently poking a finger at the itinerary listings, "you were in London from April seventeenth to April twenty-third. This is the twenty-fourth."

"Actually," Judith said, "it's the twenty-fifth here. We're eight hours ahead of—"

"Ridiculous," Gertrude broke in. "You think you're in a time machine? It's Saturday, April twenty-fourth. You think I'd watch 'America's Most Wanted' on the wrong night? I just saw this crazy old fart who'd been married to five women at once, and he—"

It was Judith's turn to interrupt. "Mother . . ." She was clinging to the receiver as if it were a life preserver. She seemed to be drowning in a sea of maternal chaos. "This is costing money."

"You bet it is, Toots," Gertrude retorted. "I said all along you couldn't afford this trip. But off you went, leaving me alone with your dopey cat. And your rum-dum bed-and-breakfast guests! Don't blame me because they burned the place down. Half-wits, all of 'em! Now you'll have to live in the garage."

"What?" Judith was screaming into the phone.

"It's too soon for barbecues. That's what I told Arlene and Carl Rankers. But Arlene's stubborn as a mule. She thought it would be fun to toast some wienies outside. Well, she toasted her buns, too, and Carl's wienie ended up in the—"

"Mother!" Judith couldn't stand it another second. "Stop! What happened?" She lowered her voice, trying to sound calm. "What *really* happened?"

Renie, having heard Judith's raised voice, had come into the kitchen. She was munching a muffin and looking worried.

Gertrude sighed. "Carl turned the hose on and put the fire out before it reached the back porch. But you were darned lucky, kiddo. It could have been cinders. Your statue of St. Francis on the patio is scorched. He looks like he's got five o'clock shadow. All the feathers on his birds fell off, too."

The feathers were stone, as was the statue. Judith leaned against the cupboard and held her head. "I wish you wouldn't tease me like that, Mother. You know I get upset."

"*You're* upset! Ha! What about me, with this complete

paralysis? I'm lying on the floor while Sweetums sits on what's left of my bust and claws the only decent housecoat I own. Go ahead, enjoy yourselves in Finland. Drink and dance your way through Russia. It's not what it used to be, and neither am I. Write if you get work. You'd better, you'll need the money. G'bye." Gertrude slammed the phone in her daughter's ear.

Gingerly, Renie took a couple of steps toward Judith. "Ah . . . how's your mother?"

Carefully, Judith replaced the receiver. She ran both hands through her short, streaked hair. She gave herself a good shake, squared her shoulders, and forced a feeble smile. "Mother's fine. Is it too early to have a drink?"

It was, of course. Judith contented herself with a third cup of coffee. After relaying the unnerving conversation with Gertrude, she remembered to check the local phone book for church listings. Mrs. Tichborne was right: There was a Catholic presence in Yeovil, but the only weekend Masses were at five o'clock on Saturday and eight on Sunday morning.

"We can't walk," Judith pointed out, "and I don't think we should trouble the family to borrow a car."

Renie, however, didn't agree. "What do they care? There's the Bentley, the Alfa, and who knows what else parked out back. Nobody's using them at the moment. Let's ask Harwood for the keys. I'll drive."

"No!" Judith had horrifying visions of Renie behind the wheel, trying to cope with the left-hand roadways. Of course she often veered into the wrong lane at home; maybe they wouldn't get killed after all.

But common sense and courtesy told Judith to leave well enough alone. "Besides," she added, ignoring Renie's look of annoyance, "if we return to London today, we can go to church this evening. And if we don't make it, God isn't going to turn us into pumpkins."

"True," Renie allowed, and then yawned. "When do we get out of here?"

Judith admitted that she didn't know, and wouldn't, until the library was vacated by Charles and Arthur. Renie

glanced at her watch as they returned to the dining room.
"It's not quite seven. Ordinarily, I'd still be asleep. If we
aren't taking off within the hour, I've a mind to go back
to bed."

Judith scowled at Renie. "I thought you were distraught
over Aunt Pet's demise."

Renie arched her eyebrows. "The word is 'saddened.'
And I am, I liked her. But let's face it, coz, we hardly knew
her. Or any of the rest of these people. I'm not going to
pretend to be desolated. I'll leave that to the relatives."

Judith's expression turned quizzical. "I wonder . . ."

But there was no opportunity to complete the thought.
Charles was shouting in the hall, apparently berating Arthur
Tinsley. The cousins hurried to the door and peeked out.
Arthur had his arms over his head, protecting himself.
Charles was making wild windmill swings at the solicitor.

"You're a bloody moron! Incompetent! Unethical! I'll
sue! Where are the police when I really need them?" He
swung again, missed, and lost his balance. Charles sprawled
on the parquet floor.

"Really, Mr. Marchmont," Arthur said meekly, "it's no
good. Being angry with me, that is to say." Kneeling, he
helped Charles to regain his feet. "I was merely acting on
Miss Ravenscroft's instructions. There wasn't time to
change the will. And even if there had—" He stopped
abruptly, seeing Judith and Renie step into the hall.

Judith's smile was tense. "Are you two okay?"

Charles was brushing himself off. "No," he replied
sharply.

"Yes," Arthur answered, then back-pedaled away from
Charles, who was still looking thunderous. "That is to
say . . . there's some . . . ah . . . confusion."

"About what?" The voice belonged to Mrs. Tichborne,
who had apparently returned from serving Dora and was
standing in the door to the dining room. She regarded both
men as if they were a pair of schoolboys fighting on the
playground.

Charles let out a heavy sigh. "Aunt Pet—Miss Ravenscroft—had a puckish sense of humor." Scathingly, he
glanced at Arthur Tinsley. "She was in the process of

changing her will. But in the meantime, she left everything to God. Or at least to her nephew, George, and his mission in Swaziland. It seems she really did intend to buy her way into heaven. But,'' he went on, raising his voice and his fist, ''I'll be in hell before I see that will hold up in a court of law!''

EIGHT

JUDITH COAXED RENIE out of her proposed nap. A brisk walk would do them good. If Alex woke up in time to drive them to Yeovil, they could catch the one o'clock train to London. Meanwhile, they would escape the tense atmosphere of Ravenscroft House by exploring the neighborhood.

A fine mist hung in the air as they strolled down Farriers Lane. Risking wet feet, they crossed the deserted village green to examine the flower beds and the memorials. As Judith had guessed, the simple pillar commemorated Little Pauncefoot's dead in both world wars. Given the village's small population, there were fewer than three dozen names. Nevertheless, Judith recognized one of the deceased soldiers: Oakley Ravenscroft, born 1904, died 1940.

Following a dirt path to the larger monument, Judith noticed that many of the spring flowers were still drooping from the hard rain. The damp air didn't smell as fresh as Judith would have thought fitting for the English countryside.

"Is this mist—or smog?" she asked as they approached the statue, which depicted a man in Jacobean attire.

As church bells pealed, Renie wrinkled her pug nose. "It can't be smog. Or can it? It's something rancid."

Judith gave a shake of her head. "I suppose there's a

tire factory or a pulp mill in yonder vale. We can't seem to get away from progress.''

The large base on which the statue stood apparently bore the Dunk coat-of-arms. The shield displayed a vertical band decorated with three lions rampant. To Judith's left were three batons with bells, presumably signifying Sir Lionel's post as Master of the Revels; to her right, a trio of money bags bearing the pound sterling sign attested to the family wealth. The inscription below read "Sir Lionel Dunk, 1567–1621. The best plan is to profit from the folly of others." The quote was attributed to Pliny the Elder.

"I guess you could say that Sir Lionel did just that," Judith remarked, wandering around the other side of the monument. "I'm surprised the statue's not wearing a dress.''

"So what about Lady Dunk?" Renie inquired, staring up at the stone figure in its high-crowned hat, wide ruff, slashed doublet, and hose. "Fetishes aside, Sir Lionel must have been married. The line continued down through Aunt Pet's mother, Cordelia.''

Judith started back along the path. "They must be buried in the village church. We should explore the crypts and the graveyard.''

But St. Edith's was holding its early communion service. The bells in the ancient tower stopped just as the cousins saw a couple of late arrivals hurry through the lych-gate. One of them was Colonel Chelmsford, marching as to war.

"Hmmm," Judith murmured.

"What?" Renie had already strolled over to the burial ground with its crooked crosses and tilting headstones.

"Well . . ." The mist was beginning to evaporate, as if dispersed by the church bells. She waved one hand in an uncertain gesture. "Should we?"

Renie scanned the scarred oak doors, the wavery glass in the windows along the nave, the statues of the Four Evangelists who had stood in their niches for seven hundred years. "What the heck," said Renie. "It *used* to be Catholic, before Henry VIII got a bug up his bodkin. And I wouldn't hike ten miles into Yeovil if the Pope was saying Mass in tennis shorts.''

Discreet stares greeted the cousins as they entered the small but exquisite old church. While Judith and Renie understood the difference in substance between the Catholic and the Anglican faiths, they couldn't make much of a distinction in style. The Book of Common Prayer had been modernized by no less a butcher of the English language than whoever had updated the Roman liturgy. Carnage by committee, Judith figured, and let herself become absorbed in the community of faith.

The vicar, whose name was Dunstan Truebone, was a pale, angular man of sixty with a plummy voice. His homily seemed to be about lust, which didn't seem particularly apt for most of the congregation, which was made up of plain-as-pudding women with limp gray hair. Judith noticed, however, that Colonel Chelmsford paid strict attention, as if his field marshal were giving him combat orders.

It was at the conclusion of the service that Vicar Truebone announced the death of Petulia Ravenscroft. "As you all know," he said, diluting the plummy tones with a note of sorrow, "Miss Ravenscroft was a devout and longtime member of St. Edith's. I ask you to remember her in your prayers."

Judith could have sworn that under his breath, Colonel Chelmsford said, "Pshaw."

Renie wanted to walk in the direction of the High Street to admire the row of almshouses that had been converted into pricey condos, but Judith insisted on dogging the colonel's footsteps.

"We ought to get a glimpse of The Grange," she declared as they tramped along the Little Pauncefoot Road. "Do you think it's anywhere near as grand as Ravenscroft House?"

"Sheesh." Renie moved well off onto the roadway's verge as a family of five drove by on their way from the church service.

"What does *that* mean?" Judith demanded. Fifty yards ahead, in the bend of the road, they could see the colonel's stiff figure. He was marching along so smartly that the distance was ever widening.

But Renie didn't reply. Two minutes later, Colonel Chelmsford had turned in, presumably entering his property. The cousins had just reached the mellow stone wall that marked the boundary between Ravenscroft House and The Grange.

Unlike those of its neighbor, The Grange's gates were locked. The moldering glass panes of a greenhouse could be seen off the winding dirt lane. Fifty yards beyond, the cousins could just make out a roof with a crooked weathervane. Perhaps that was a barn or stables. Judith and Renie peered off in the other direction, through walnut and paper birch trees. The colonel's house appeared to be two-storied, half-timbered, and possibly from the early Tudor era. The Grange was far more modest than Ravenscroft House.

"It probably has its charms," Judith mused as they started back toward the village.

"I'm surprised you didn't try to vault the fence," Renie remarked as a few drops of rain came down. "I thought you wanted to collar Colonel Chelmsford."

Judith glanced inquiringly at her cousin. "Why would I want to do that?"

"Gee," Renie replied, sounding slightly cranky, "I don't know. Maybe it's because you have a natural curiosity about other people. Maybe it's because you want to find a date for your mother. Maybe it's because you're *sleuthing.*"

Judith retained a placid air. "Maybe it's none of those things, coz. Hey, it's going on ten. We'll go pack and see if Alex—or somebody—can drive us into Yeovil."

The church bells were ringing again as the cousins approached St. Edith's. Judith couldn't resist a stroll through the cemetery. But she found neither Dunks nor Ravenscrofts among the older headstones.

"Of course they aren't there," Renie said, leaning against an alabaster angel. "They're in the church. Didn't you see the crypt in the side chapel?"

Judith hadn't. As usual, she'd been too busy studying the living to worry about the dead. "We can't go in now,"

Judith lamented. "The ten o'clock service is about to start."

Renie, however, hauled her cousin by the sleeve. "Come on, we've got five minutes. They'll just think we're obnoxious American tourists. We're wearing *pants,* for Pete's sake."

The side chapel was actually in the west transept, under a stained-glass rose window depicting a haloed nun with a royal crown suspended above her bowed head. Judith assumed it was St. Edith. An inscription on a timeworn stone in the floor said something about "forsaking the world, rather than knowing it." Judith guessed that Edith had entered the convent at an early age and decided it was a good place to hang out. Maybe, given the state of the world now or a thousand years ago, she'd had the right idea.

"Dunks," Judith whispered as worshippers filed into the nave. "All sorts of them, from the sixteen hundreds up to the nineteenth century. Lots of Sidneys, Johns, and Dorothys."

Renie sniffed. "They took Lionel's house and money, but not his name. It figures. Sidney and John didn't look good in an Empire waist. Or a bustle. Ah! Here's the original Dunk tomb, back behind this little altar."

Sure enough, just as the organ began to play the entrance hymn, Judith saw the effigies of Sir Lionel and Lady Eleanor Dunk. They lay side by side, enshrined forever in smooth white marble. Unlike the more imposing granite on the green, Lionel looked vaguely fey in repose. His wife wore a faint smirk, as if she knew a delicious secret.

"Gee," Renie whispered as the vicar appeared on the altar, "Eleanor was only twenty-two when she died in 1591."

Judith noted the birth and death dates. "Childbirth, probably. Puerperal fever. Here's their son. Two of them, in fact."

As discreetly as possible, the cousins slipped out through a side door, ending up in the vicarage garden. After some confusion, they made their way around the back of the church and found themselves once again in the cemetery. They stopped in their tracks. Someone was bending over one of the graves, placing a bouquet on a headstone. It was Walter Paget, and his head was bowed in prayer.

Judith and Renie waited. At last, Walter straightened up and went on his way. Cautiously, the cousins tiptoed over to a sloping section of the graveyard where the steward had left his large bunch of jonquils and cherry blossoms.

The markers were relatively new in what was apparently an added section of the cemetery. The graves lay next to the fence that ran alongside the Great Pauncefoot and Yeovil Road.

"Fleur Ravenscroft Karamzin," Judith said in wonder. "Born 1940, died 1990. I wonder why Walter put the flowers on her grave?"

Renie was half-kneeling above the adjacent marker. "Here's her husband, Viktor Karamzin, born 1936, died the same year as his wife. They were Nats's and Alex's parents who bought it in a car crash, right?"

Absently, Judith nodded. "The rest of them are here, too. Fleur's mother and father, Oakley and Genevieve Ravenscroft. Chauncey and Hyacinth Ravenscroft, Claire's grandparents."

Renie straightened up. "And thus, their son, George, who is Claire's father, has inherited all this." She made a sweeping gesture in the direction of Ravenscroft House, on the other side of the village green.

Judith grimaced. "I wonder if he knows. Or cares."

"Claire will tell him," Renie said, starting back towards Farriers Lane. "Charles can rant and rave all he wants, but the Swaziland contingent will have to be notified."

"I guess." Judith sounded dubious. The rain was coming down harder, and the cousins walked swiftly along the lane. The village green was still deserted on this Sunday morning, which seemed fitting. The great house which lay beyond the holly and horsechestnut and hornbeam trees was in mourning. Though Judith and Renie could not see the chimneys and turrets from Farriers Lane, they knew that in some atavistic way, the Ravenscrofts, together with the Dunks before them, and the Marchmonts who came after, exerted a deep, if subtle, influence on Little Pauncefoot. As the heavy clouds hung low over the river valley, it was almost as if the heavens wept.

Alexei Karamzin was still asleep. "My brother has never met a drink he didn't like," Nats declared when Judith asked if Alex might be able to drive them into Yeovil to meet the one o'clock train. "I don't expect him to wake up until dinner." Then, as an afterthought, she asked if the cousins would like to have her take them to the station.

"Oh, yes, thank you!" Judith bordered on obsequiousness. "It's almost eleven. We'll run up and pack. Would it be all right to leave around noon?"

While not enthused, Nats had no objection. The cousins scurried upstairs, each to her own room. At precisely eleven-twenty, they emerged in the hallway, suitcases in hand.

"Now what?" Renie inquired. "We've got over half an hour to kill."

"Don't use that word," Judith retorted, only half-kidding. "Maybe we can round up a cup of coffee."

"How about a sandwich?" Renie asked, lugging her suitcase down the corridor. "It's been a long time since breakfast."

Judith was about to agree when Claire opened the door to the master bedroom. She was still wearing the pale blue peignoir and negligee that she'd had on in the wee small hours.

"Oh! What's this? You're leaving? Oh, no!" She looked as if she were going to faint.

Judith assumed a contrite air. "We didn't intend to run out on you. Nats is going to take us into Yeovil around noon."

Claire's mouth worked in agitation, but no words came out. At last she stumbled into the hall and caught Judith by the arm. "No, no! You must stay! You promised to be here until tomorrow!"

Judith winced. "I know, but that was before . . . Aunt Pet died. Now, Renie and I are excess baggage, so to speak. You've got tons of things to do, and we'll get in the—"

At that moment, Charles came charging up the main

staircase. His face was very red and he was panting.
"Duff's here, with Ramsey. And a couple of coppers from
Great Pauncefoot. Get dressed," he urged his wife. "We've
got terrible problems. It seems that Aunt Pet was poisoned!"

The cousins left their suitcases in the hallway. By the
time they entered the drawing room, Mrs. Tichborne was
serving tea and coffee to Arthur Tinsley, Dr. Ramsey, P.C.
Duff, and the policemen from Great Pauncefoot. The only
member of the household on hand was Nats, who looked
annoyed.

Charles had stayed upstairs with Claire, who was undone
by the latest development. Constable Duff politely refused
Mrs. Tichborne's offerings, and mumbled that he must be
getting back to his regular duties.

"M'bike's outside," he said, and with an air of relief,
the young policeman bowed himself out of the drawing
room.

The large, pompous man in the cheap suit took a step
forward and cleared his throat. "Wattle, 'ere. Claude Wattle, of the Great Pauncefoot force." He pointed to the small,
uniformed man at his side. "This 'ere's Daub. Alston Daub,
my sergeant." Under heavy lids, Claude Wattle's icy blue
eyes settled on the cousins. "And who might you be? The
dailies?"

Seeking to forestall an outbreak of ire on Renie's part,
Judith stepped in front of her cousin. "We're visitors," she
said, astonished by the squeak in her voice. "Americans.
I'm Judith Flynn, and this is my cousin, Serena Jones."
Warily, she moved just enough so that Wattle and Daub
could see Renie.

Wattle glowered at the cousins, then glanced at Daub.
"You got that?" Scribbling in a notebook, Daub nodded.
Wattle looked again at Judith. "That's 'Flynn' with an
'F'?"

Judith's jaw dropped. "Ah . . . yes."

Renie was pulling her hair. "That's 'Jones' with a 'J.'
The 'H' is silent."

Wattle shot Renie a dark look. "What?"

But Renie wasn't going to prolong the farce. She was at the credenza, pouring herself a cup of tea from the tray that Mrs. Tichborne had left. "Grandpa Grover always warned me against marrying a Welshman," she muttered. Luckily, no one but Judith seemed to hear her.

Indeed, there wasn't anything to hear from anyone for the time being. Judging from Wattle and Daub's expectant manner, they were waiting for the rest of the Ravenscroft ménage. Mrs. Tichborne returned, this time with a plate of wafers and cheese. Charles entered the room, apologizing for his wife, who would be with them presently. She was getting dressed. And a moment later, a sleepy-eyed Alex Karamzin ambled in and headed straight for the liquor cabinet. Arthur Tinsley was eyeing him with apprehension. Indeed, Arthur seemed to eye everyone with apprehension. Given his legal charge from Aunt Pet, Judith didn't much blame him.

Walter Paget arrived only moments ahead of Claire Marchmont. The only missing person, as far as Judith could tell, was Dora Hobbs. But as family and friends settled into their places, the little maid appeared, looking wan and woebegone. Judith, who was sitting near the door, got up to give Dora her chair.

It was Dr. Ramsey who took charge, apparently at the behest of Wattle and Daub. "The autopsy was completed about half an hour ago," he said in his most professional manner. "While the chemical analysis won't be finalized until tomorrow, it's accurate to state at this time that Petulia Ravenscroft died from a lethal ingestion of hyoscyamine. We cannot be absolutely certain in what form Miss Ravenscroft consumed the poison, but the stomach contents thus far have yielded several possibilities. Despite my medical advice to the contrary"—here Dr. Ramsey coughed in an apologetic fashion—"Miss Ravenscroft partook frequently of all manner of food and drink. However, by tomorrow, we should have a fair idea how the poison was administered."

Claire shuddered. "Oh! 'Administered!' Such an awful word!"

Dr. Ramsey's broad shoulders slumped. "In this context,

it is. But it can't be helped. I was afraid of such a conclusion. The symptoms indicated something other than a seizure or apoplexy as the cause of death." Fleetingly, his gaze rested on Dora Hobbs.

"Humbug," Charles said. "How can you be sure? People eat all sorts of things these days. Health foods. Flowers. Foreign stuff, with names you can't even pronounce. The supermarkets are full of them. And now you expect us to believe in . . . *science?*"

Dr. Ramsey was looking uncomfortable, rubbing his hands together and appealing to Inspector Wattle. "This is how it's done," the doctor said in a humble voice. "I had to follow procedure . . ."

Wattle finally thumped to the rescue, planting a big paw on Ramsey's shoulder. "And so 'e does. Daub and I are in charge now, thank you very much. Like Constable Wotsisnyme said, you're all to stay close by. Anyone who does a bunk will be considered 'ighly suspect." The chilly blue gaze flickered over the gathering.

Judith was trying to figure out the best method of making a getaway when Renie spoke up: "My cousin and I aren't doing a bunk, but we are leaving. We've got a one o'clock train to catch in Yeovil. If nobody minds, we're on our way. Thanks for everything and so long."

But before Renie could get to the door, Sergeant Daub blocked her passage with his small, wiry form. "Sorry, ma'am," he murmured. "The inspector means what he says."

Renie, who was almost as tall as Daub, attempted to stare him down. "Hey, do you have any idea who I am?" she demanded.

Daub tried to look dignified. "No, I do not."

"Good," Renie said. "Then you won't give a rat's ass if I take a hike. Come on, coz, let's blow this joint."

But it was Arthur Tinsley who prevented the cousins' flight, and it was done in the most unexpected of ways:

"Er . . ." he stammered, half-rising from his chair, "it's not in your best interest . . . that is . . . I mean . . . you really must stay on. Miss Ravenscroft intended to remember you in her will. After all, you *are* family."

Daub grabbed Renie by the arm; Wattle made a dive for Judith.

The cousins were stuck at Ravenscroft House. Judith wasn't entirely surprised.

But she was certainly chagrined.

nine

WATTLE AND DAUB didn't want to hear the cousins try to explain that they weren't actually related to Aunt Pet or any of the other Ravenscrofts or Marchmonts or Dunks. The investigation was under way, and within moments, a half-dozen uniformed policemen had also arrived at the house, ostensibly to search the crime scene.

Judith and Renie, along with the rest of the household, were temporarily confined to the drawing room. Mrs. Tichborne boldly suggested that she would go into the kitchen and prepare lunch. The idea was greeted half-heartedly by Nats and Charles. Renie was still pouting.

Judith had remained standing next to Dora. The little maid was looking upset and confused. Judith patted her frail shoulder.

Dora looked up. "Poison!" she whispered. "I can't believe such a thing! Who would have thought it?"

Judith leaned down. "Have you any idea how Miss Ravenscroft might have gotten hold of . . . whatever it was that had this stuff in it?" she asked in a low voice.

But Dora looked blank. "Not in the least," she whispered back. "Mrs. Tichborne it was who fixed her meals. Excepting the ones I did."

"What about Millie the daily?" Judith was aware that Charles and Claire were both staring.

"Millie!" Dora made a scornful gesture. "I wouldn't let her feed a cat!"

Judith already had considered Aunt Pet's eating habits. In the past twenty-four hours, the old lady had wolfed down everything put before her, including many items that were common to others in the household. But she also had meals brought to her. Then there was the tonic, and presumably other medications as well.

Wattle and Daub returned to the drawing room. They would conduct their inquiries in the parlor. Charles was asked to come along first. He glowered at the policemen, but accompanied them without further ado.

Nats had joined her brother in his foray on the liquor cabinet. "This is all too stupid," she asserted, pointing an empty glass at Claire. "Have you cabled Uncle George and Aunt Emily in Swaziland with the good news?"

Claire wouldn't meet Nats's belligerent gaze. "Walter—Mr. Paget—was kind enough to send the cable off to my parents. Really, Nats, how can you call it good news?"

"It is, for Uncle George and Aunt Emily." Deftly, Nats mixed herself a martini. "They haven't been back to England in—what, ten, twelve years? Whenever you and Charles were married. You could hardly say they were close to Aunt Pet. So now they inherit an enormous fortune, with very little grief to show for it."

"That's not fair." Lifting her head, Claire gave Nats a resentful look. "My father and mother have devoted their lives to God. They've done wonderful things with the natives. Education. Health care. Work skills. I was raised there until I was seventeen. I saw firsthand the sort of contribution Mummy and Daddy are making. You've no right to criticize. What have you—or Alex—ever done to improve mankind?"

Claire's fervor surprised Judith, though it didn't seem to faze Nats. "I deal in aesthetics," she replied with a toss of her head. "I make showplaces out of people's homes. It gives them pleasure, and thus a sense of well-being. There's nothing wrong in that."

"I drive cars very fast," Alex put in, "and run over a

lot of small animals. Roadkill is very important to keeping a balance in nature.''

Judith didn't know if Alex was teasing or not. Judging from Walter's look of disgust, he took Alex seriously. So, apparently, did Arthur Tinsley, whose thin lips were compressed in revulsion.

''Well?'' Nats demanded of Claire. ''Are your pious parents coming home for the funeral, or will they stay in the jungle and wait for the money to arrive in big bags marked 'booty'?''

Claire's spurt of outrage had faded. ''They're not near Mbabane, the capital, so it takes some time for them to receive messages. Swaziland is rather primitive. Communications are limited.''

Nats sniffed. ''It sounds like a very stupid place. Why haven't your parents introduced fax machines along with all their other bountiful oblations?''

Before Claire could respond, Walter Paget spoke up: ''I don't think you understand the problems, Miss Karamzin. Swaziland is extremely small. They reverted to a monarchy after receiving their independence, and progress in general has been difficult. Personally, I find it commendable that Mr. and Mrs. Ravenscroft have done so much with so little all these years.''

''Well,'' Nats snapped, ''they're about to do it with a lot more. If Swaziland is such a pokey place, they can buy fax machines for everybody. And televisions and hot tubs and Cuisinarts and . . .''

Renie finally caught Judith's signal to decamp. The cousins slipped into the hall. If not unnoticed, at least their departure wasn't prevented.

''I can't stand listening to family wrangling,'' Judith said, vexed. ''Haven't we had enough of that with our own shirttail relations?''

They had indeed, and not so long ago, with their Uncle Corky's in-laws. The quarrels had erupted over money then, as they did now at Ravenscroft House. Judith's patience with grasping relatives was very thin.

''Let's see if we can help Mrs. Tichborne in the kitchen,'' Judith said, crossing into the dining room. ''If she can roam the house, so can we. Now how could anybody think we're related to this bunch?''

"It's Aunt Pet,'' Renie replied. "Somehow, she got a notion that we were connected by blood.''

"Well, she was mistaken.'' Judith opened the kitchen door. To her surprise, Mrs. Tichborne was sitting at the table crying. When the housekeeper heard the cousins come in, she looked up, dismay and embarrassment writ clearly on her usually austere face.

"Forgive me,'' she said, hastily wiping at her eyes with a handkerchief. "I can't think why . . . I was just finishing these . . .'' One hand indicated a large silver tray that was piled high with a variety of sandwiches. On the nearby cutting board, several buttered slices of bread sat faceup.

Judith and Renie joined Mrs. Tichborne at the table. "You've been bearing the brunt of the last few hours,'' Judith said in a sympathetic voice. "We came to see if we could help. Maybe you ought to lie down for a while. We'll serve lunch.''

It cost Mrs. Tichborne to marshal her self-control, but she managed. "Foolish, that's what I am,'' she murmured. "What good are tears? It was all so long ago.'' She crumpled the handkerchief and put it into the pocket of her black dress.

Judith tipped her head to one side, the picture of polite curiosity. "What was? You can't mean Miss Ravenscroft.''

"Oh, no.'' Mrs. Tichborne's voice was now steady, if not as brisk as usual. "That is, I feel very badly about her passing. Especially if''—the housekeeper gulped—"she was murdered. Greed, that's what it is, plain and simple. Every one of her relatives has been lying in wait to lay hands on her money. And don't they need it! Charles and Claire, living beyond their means. Natasha and Alexei, refusing to hold down decent jobs while lavishing luxuries upon themselves. Even Walter Paget, constantly harping about his horses—yes,'' she went on, noting the cousins' quizzical expressions, "his horses. He doesn't particularly care about the hounds and the poor fox, but he cherishes the bloodstock as if it were his own. Of course, it's in his veins. Walter is obsessed with breeding fine hunters." Wearily, Mrs. Tichborne sighed.

A brief silence filled the kitchen. Then Judith tried to steer the housekeeper back to the original topic of conversation. "But your distress—is it merely for Aunt Pet and the family?"

A veil seemed to come down over Mrs. Tichborne's colorless eyes. But she wasn't yet ready to retreat into herself. "You're strangers here, for all that your ancestors may have been related to the family." She ignored the protest forming on Judith's lips. "Where's the harm? It was in April that my Janet disappeared. Twelve years ago, during the All Fools Revels. A day doesn't go by that I don't think maybe I'll hear some word of her. It wasn't like Janet to run off without so much as a by-your-leave. What I'd give to know what happened to her! Then I could close the door and be done with it."

Renie was trying to keep her eyes off the sandwich tray. "How old was Janet?"

"Seventeen. Ever so pretty, and had brains, when she felt like using them. She planned to be a hairdresser." Mrs. Tichborne was tucking a few stray strands of hair into her chignon. Apparently, the reference to her daughter's vocation had impelled her to tidy her own coiffure. "She'd 'prenticed to a shop in Great Pauncefoot. But her goal was to work in a London salon. The city had a great pull for Janet. She felt buried in the country."

"Do you think she went to London?" asked Judith.

Mrs. Tichborne resettled her half-glasses on her nose. "At first, I did. But she didn't take any of her things with her, and there was no word. Ever. That wasn't Janet's way. She could be moody, girls are like that in their teens, but we were on good terms. She would never have gone off and not let me know where she was."

Another silence fell between the three women. It was broken by the appearance of Charles, who was looking harassed. "I say," he said in an irascible tone, "are we going to eat or not? Claire has finished with the police and is lying down, but the rest of us are getting hungry."

With a resumption of her usual efficient manner, Mrs.

Tichborne rose from the chair and began placing sliced turkey on the buttered bread. "We'll be there in two minutes," she promised. "Would anyone care for soup or salad?"

But sandwiches sufficed. Renie accompanied the housekeeper to the drawing room. Judith remained behind to prepare a tray of coffee and tea. The tea canister was empty. Checking the kitchen cupboards, Judith couldn't find any new tins. Indeed, there seemed to be no staples of any kind on the shelves. It occurred to her that there must be a storage area off the kitchen.

There was, next to the back stairs. A small pantry had been built into what had probably once been a coat closet. Judith found the tea, then glanced out through a window that looked onto the herb garden. A figure was hurrying up the drive. It was Claire, wrapped in her beige raincoat, with a paisley scarf over her head.

Puzzled, Judith returned to the kitchen, where she poured the tin of fresh tea into the canister. She was putting out the teaspoons when Nats wandered into the kitchen, cradling her martini glass.

"You must think I'm dreadful." The careless flounce of her body suggested that Nats was indifferent to Judith's opinion, but the sulky voice revealed injured pride.

Judith looked up from her tally of teaspoons. "What I think really doesn't matter much, does it? I've witnessed family rows before. Believe me, fighting isn't peculiar to this side of the Atlantic."

Nats leaned against the work counter. "But don't you care? You and your cousin got cheated, too."

Judith gave Nats a wry smile. "We never expected to get anything. We don't deserve anything. We're just ... guests."

"Not according to Aunt Pet." Nats sipped her martini. "Or so she told that dry stick of an Arthur Tinsley. I wish to God I'd known that Auntie had changed her will. Up until last August Bank Holiday, everything was just fine."

Judith started to pick up the beverage tray, then set it back down. It was heavy, and she had a feeling that there would be no quick escape from Nats. "Oh? What happened?"

Nats made a face, then finished her drink. "It was all too silly. We'd come down for the better part of a week—Charles, Claire, the twins, Alex, and I. It was to be our usual summer holiday gathering. It was terribly hot, and Aunt Pet despised warm weather. She was testy from the start. Then Charles mentioned that he was glad it was August. At least nothing too dreadful could happen when everyone in The City was away on holiday. Aunt Pet pressed him. He admitted that the Ravenscroft investments were suffering some reverses. Aunt Pet pitched a fit and said maybe she should regain control—Charles seemed to be mucking things up. Charles got angry, Claire tried to defend him in her inept way, and then Alex volunteered to take over. That didn't go down at all well with Charles, and the next thing we knew, Walter had shoved Alex's face into the blanc mange." Nats paused for breath.

"Walter?" Judith was mystified. "Why did he do that?"

Nats shrugged. "I think it was something Alex said to Claire. A free-for-all broke out, and Harwood got in the thick of things. He ended up being hauled off to the hospital in Great Pauncefoot. The George III epergne fell on him when the table went over."

"Goodness!" Judith was aghast. "It sounds like a real melee!"

"It was. Aunt Pet said we were all a great bunch of uncivilized animals and unworthy of the Ravenscroft name. Unfortunately, I pointed out that nobody was named Ravenscroft anymore, except her. At least not any of the family who were on hand at the time. She told me that was precisely her point, the family line was diluted with foreigners and middle-class interlopers. We could all go to the devil. Or words to that effect."

"So she changed her will?"

Nats nodded. "She must have. But not the way she'd intended before the August debacle. I'm not sure how her previous will was drawn up, but it had been made almost twenty years ago, by Arthur's father, Edward Tinsley. In the meantime, Grandmother Genevieve had died. Then my parents were killed in that awful auto accident. They were all mentioned in the original will, so Aunt Pet had to change it. She gave us to understand that Charles and Claire would get the property, and a fair amount of money. The main stipulation was that the house, its furnishings, and artworks had to stay in the family. That was a bit of a sticking point, but with sufficient funds for maintenance, no one could carp.''

It became clear to Judith why Charles and Claire wanted to convert Ravenscroft House into a B&B. Nats's explanation also provided the reason for the family's inability to sell off the occasional painting.

"Trusts would be set up for Alex and me, with annual allowances," Nats went on after a brief pause. "Claire's parents would be remembered, but I got the impression that the amount would be rather modest. Aunt Pet had never quite forgiven George and Emily for going off to Swaziland and staying there. If Aunt Pet ever made that will, she changed it later, after she got so mad last August. And that's too rotten—Uncle George and Aunt Emily will spend it on Bibles or put it in the bank, and then Charles and Claire will end up with everything after all." Now it was Nats who seemed on the verge of tears.

Renie breezed into the kitchen, stuffing her face with a tongue sandwich. "Where's the tea and coffee? Tichborne's with the police, and Arthur Tinsley is ready to drink out of the hose nozzle in the formal garden." She caught sight of Nats and stopped dead. "Excuse me, I didn't realize I was interrupting a therapy session. Bill hates it when I do that, especially when he's counseling a true sociopath. They tend to get rambunctious."

Nats wiped at her eyes and glared at Renie. "Obviously, I've said too much. Aunt Pet always told me I tended toward indiscretion. In many ways." With another flounce, Nats rose from the chair and started out of the kitchen. At the door, she turned back to look at Judith. "I'm sorry to be such a bore. Maybe it comes of losing your parents when you're still young. There's no one left to talk to. Alex is fun, but he's totally self-centered. I envy people with understanding parents and sympathetic siblings. They have all the luck." Nats flew off into the dining room.

Judith gazed at Renie. "Our dads have been dead for years. We have no siblings. And our mothers are—"

"—our mothers," Renie finished for her. "Nats should stop feeling sorry for herself."

Picking up the tray, Judith let Renie hold the door for her. "You're forgetting something," Judith murmured. "We've got Joe and Bill and our kids. We've also got each other."

Renie grinned. "Nats is right. Some people do have all the luck. Like us."

If the atmosphere in the drawing room hadn't exactly lightened, at least the verbal sniping had stopped. Everyone seemed absorbed in the sandwiches. Only Charles and Arthur were engaged in conversation, huddled together on a matching pair of Chippendale chairs. Charles dominated the conversation; Arthur shifted uneasily in his seat.

Mrs. Tichborne returned, indignant and offended. "The police ask so many pointless questions! How should I know if Miss Ravenscroft had any enemies? I'm told she caused quite a stir with her anti–Labor Party letters to *The Times*!"

Charles interrupted his tête-à-tête with Arthur. "Come, come, Mrs. Tichborne—Inspector Wattle is the soul of tact. Or tries to be. He was most deferential with me."

But the housekeeper didn't agree. "Cheek," she murmured, taking inventory of the sandwich tray. "Wattle's predecessor was a much superior man. No wonder he was promoted." With a sniff, Mrs. Tichborne left the drawing room.

Dora Hobbs already had been led away by Sergeant Daub. Judith felt sorry for the maid, fearing she might go to pieces under questioning. "How old *is* Dora?" she asked of no one in particular.

Walter Paget was pouring himself a cup of coffee. "Dora's seventy-six, I believe. She's been in service here since . . ." The steward hesitated. "I'm not really sure."

Again, Charles broke off his conversation with Arthur. "Forever. *Tante* Genevieve once said she couldn't recall a time when Dora wasn't at Ravenscroft House. Quite the old-fashioned sort of servant. Alas, such loyalty has gone out of vogue.''

Mrs. Tichborne returned with a fresh pot of coffee, then beckoned to Alex, who was on his third drink and humming to himself.

''The inspector would like to see you,'' the housekeeper said briskly. She leaned down to speak in Judith's ear. ''I'm taking Dora upstairs. She's quite worn out. If anyone needs anything while I'm gone, would you mind seeing to it? I'd be ever so grateful.''

Judith assured Mrs. Tichborne that she could count on the cousins. Alex swaggered off, singing ''The Wild Colonial Boy'' in a loud, yet surprisingly melodious, voice.

Walter was checking his watch. ''It's going on one o'clock. I do hope the police hurry. I must go down to the stables.''

Judith took a chicken salad sandwich from the tray. ''Say, do you think we could come with you to see the horses? We haven't actually toured the farm.''

For a fleeting moment, alarm seemed to cross Walter's stolid face. ''Well . . . later, perhaps. I've no help working today. I'm afraid I'll be quite busy.''

''That's okay,'' Judith said, though she knew she sounded disappointed. ''We may still be here tomorrow. As it is, we've missed our train.''

Renie's expression was droll. ''Surprise, coz. Did we really believe we'd get out of here today?'' With a resigned air, she checked the silver teapot. ''I'm going to get some more hot water. Want to help me turn on the faucet?''

Judith was willing. As the cousins entered the hall, two policemen were coming down the main stairs. One of them carried something in a plastic evidence bag. He and his companion headed for the parlor and knocked on the door.

Renie kept going across the entry hall's wide expanse, but Judith gave her a push in the direction of the pedestal that held Minerva, with her marble helmet and spear.

''We're hiding,'' Judith whispered to a startled Renie. ''Don't breathe.''

Renie rolled her eyes, but complied. Sergeant Daub

opened the parlor door. "We need to see the inspector," said the policeman with the evidence bag.

Wattle came out into the hall, closing the door on Alex's raucous laughter. "Well? What's this?"

"A box of chocolates," the policeman replied, holding the bag out to his superior. "Half of them are gone, sir. It looks as if at least two of the others may have been tampered with. We found them under a pile of magazines in the nightstand in Miss Ravenscroft's bedroom. We think they could be the method by which the poison was introduced."

Claude Wattle didn't speak for several seconds. "Good work," he allowed at last. "Take it to the lab. But no jumping to conclusions, eh? It's early days, and we need the chemical analysis first."

Judith and Renie couldn't avoid being seen by the policemen on their way out of the house. "Hi," Judith said brightly. "Seen any good clues lately?"

Scowling, the officers continued on their way. They didn't respond.

Renie sighed. "They think we're nuts."

Judith shook her head. "They know we're Americans."

"Same thing," said Renie.

Upon Alex's return, he promptly passed out in a Louis XVI lyre-backed chair. When he slid onto the carpet, everyone in the room tried to pretend that nothing had happened. It occurred to Judith that maybe Alex's behavior was taken for granted.

Nats was now in the parlor with the police. Arthur Tinsley had gotten to his feet, carefully stepping over Alex.

"There's nothing more I can do here," he said in an abject voice. "That being the case, I should go home to check on Lona. She had a migraine when I left this morning."

Charles objected. "Sorry, old man. I imagine the inspector will want a word with you, too. The will, you know."

Arthur's high forehead wrinkled. "Yes, but . . . you know all about that. Really, I must be—"

"Nonsense," Charles broke in. "I'll insist that they take you next. The interview won't last more than ten minutes. Walter won't mind waiting."

But it was clear that Walter did mind. He opened his mouth to protest, but Charles cut him off, too. "A quarter of an hour will do the horses no harm. Relax, Walter. It's aggravating, but we must make the best of it."

It seemed to Judith that Walter's taciturn manner was about to disintegrate. A moment later, Nats returned, and Arthur resignedly went off to the parlor. Walter mumbled that he would wait his turn in the hall.

Nats was regarding her brother with disapproval. "I do wish Alex would come 'round," she complained. "He's drooling on the Aubusson carpet." None too gently, she nudged him with her foot. Alex snuffled, but didn't wake up. "Bother," breathed Nats. "I'm going for a walk."

It was after two before Judith's presence was requested in the parlor. Neither Arthur nor Walter had returned after their interviews, and presumably Harwood had been summoned ahead of the cousins. Judith thought that Inspector Wattle was showing signs of strain.

"Name," he barked from his place behind the heavy Elizabethan trestle table.

Judith answered promptly.

"Residence." Wattle didn't look up from the papers before him.

Judith gave her full address, stating that she was an American citizen.

Wattle emitted a sound that was half-sigh, half-groan. "Americans! Nothing but violence wherever you go. Flynn, eh?" He motioned to Sergeant Daub. "Check the IRA terrorist files. Plenty of connections in America. Money, arms, the rest of it." The inspector turned back to Judith. "Know anything about bombs?"

Judith gaped. "Bombs? As in the kind that explode? Heavens, no. We've got a new city ban on fireworks. We can't even light off pinwheels or Mr. Parachute."

The inspector's eyes narrowed under the heavy lids. "Mr. Parachute? Is that a code name?"

"No, certainly not. Mr. Parachute is from Taiwan. You

light him off and there's this big blue flash and then he flies up and lands with his parachute in the lilac tree. Or on top of the garage. One year, he fell in my mother's potato salad. She ate him.''

"Your mother *ate* Mr. Parachute?" Wattle was now looking startled, as well as confused. "See 'ere, Mrs. Flynn, or whatever your real name is, don't try to lead us down the garden path. Why 'ave you made contact with the Ravenscroft 'ousehold? It is to be a new 'eadquarters, or just a drop-off point?"

"You're not serious." Judith shed all pretense of naïveté. "If you've done your job, and checked my cousin and me through Interpol, you know perfectly well we're exactly what we say we are—American tourists."

Wattle remained skeptical. "Your cousin's name is Jones. She could be one of those Welsh separatists. They're a dangerous lot, too. Refuse to use vowels, like proper folk."

In agitation, Judith rubbed her temples. "She's not. We're not. In fact, we've never been to Wales or Ireland. At home, we don't even belong to the same political parties. I'm a Democrat and she's a Republican."

"Well, now!" Wattle smirked as if he'd made a startling discovery. "All for Mr. Clinton, are you? Or is it all for yourselves?"

"Huh?" Judith felt lost.

"The will," Wattle said. "You and Mrs. Jones thought there was something in it for you. So you wait until the old lady's on 'er last legs, then come flying in to get your share."

Judith's patience snapped. "That's ridiculous! We hardly knew any of these people until this week. Our only connection is through my pen-pal, who happens to be Charles Marchmont's sister. We're definitely not related to the family. And even if Aunt Pet had wanted to leave us a little remembrance, she didn't because her previous will was drawn up some time ago, and I understand that she didn't have time to make a new one before she . . . ah . . . died."

Wattle looked at Daub. They seemed to be sharing a private joke. Judith suddenly felt uneasy.

"That's what the solicitor said, all right," Wattle agreed, his manner a trifle too jolly. "But solicitors don't know everything. This will 'e mentions is nowhere to be found. 'E's gone off to look for it among 'is papers. Curious, though—we found another will in the deceased's bedroom desk. It was drawn up yesterday, and the contents will cause quite a stir. It seems that Miss Ravenscroft left you and your cousin this fancy old 'ouse. Now what do you think of that as a motive for murder?"

TEN

AS MOTIVES WENT, Renie agreed that it was a good one. A quarter of an hour later she emerged from the parlor to find a disconsolate Judith standing in the hall next to the statue of Aphrodite.

"Here," Judith said abruptly, handing Renie her jacket. "Let's go outside. I need fresh air. My brain has turned to pulp."

Renie suggested a stroll through the Ravenscroft farm. But Judith reminded her of Walter Paget's objections. "I wouldn't want him to think we were barging in on whatever it is he's doing with the horses," Judith said. "Let's wander around the village."

"What *is* he doing?" Renie asked as they headed out into the gray afternoon.

Passing Wattle and Daub's black and white police car in the drive, Judith let out a long sigh. "I don't know what anybody's doing around this place. Walter seemed pretty antsy this afternoon. And Claire didn't take a nap after her session with the police. I saw her leave the house while I was making more tea."

"Where was she going?" Renie inquired as a breeze ruffled the plane trees that grew next to the stone wall.

"This way," Judith replied, then pointed to the path that led to the rear of the house. "She must have left through one of the two back doors, either off the main hall or by the turret stairs."

"The stables are in the other direction," Renie reflected as they passed under the gatehouse. "So she could have been leaving the property altogether. Maybe Claire was like us, going for a walk."

"Maybe." But Judith didn't sound convinced. "I don't like the sound of this new will. It can't be valid. Arthur Tinsley didn't know anything about it." Judith kicked at some of the small, downy nuts that had fallen from the plane trees. "Or did he?"

They were again passing the village green. Despite the overcast skies, there were clusters of parents and children putting the open expanse to playful good use. Renie smiled at a teenager who had climbed up to pose beside Sir Lionel Dunk's statue.

"What do you mean?" she asked as Judith turned off from Farriers Lane onto the Little Pauncefoot Road.

"I mean," Judith explained, "that Arthur Tinsley knew Aunt Pet wanted to change her will. They'd discussed it when he visited her Friday. Presumably, he knew her intentions. That's why he was so muddled when Charles asked him about the will."

Renie mulled over Judith's words for a moment, then stopped in her tracks. "Hey—wait, coz. I thought we were going to explore the village. We're headed for The Grange."

Judith gave her cousin an innocent look but kept going. "Oh—are we? Well, why not? Wasn't it your father who always wanted to see what was around the next bend or on the other side of the hill?"

Cliff Grover had possessed a sense of adventure as well as a keen curiosity that covered just about everything he encountered. Not wanting to disavow her patrimony, Renie trudged along beside Judith.

"I have a feeling we're going to call on Colonel Chelmsford," Renie muttered. "He won't like it."

"We're merely going to engage him in friendly but possibly revealing conversation," Judith answered blithely. "Just follow my lead. You know," she went on in a more serious tone, "I'd like a peek at that new will. I can't believe Pet would leave us the house. It has to be a hoax."

A fresh-faced young couple on bicycles pedaled by the cousins. "Do you think the rest of the family knows?" Renie asked.

"It doesn't seem like it," Judith replied as they passed the stone wall that marked the boundary between the Ravenscroft and Chelmsford properties. "We would have heard a huge reaction if they did. I suspect the desk wasn't searched until just before you and I were brought in."

"Maybe," Renie suggested, "that's why Wattle and Daub were still there when we left. They wanted to tell Charles and Claire about the will. And Nats and Alex, assuming he ever comes to."

"Probably," Judith agreed as they approached The Grange's locked gates. "But what's the point? That's the part I don't get. Is a handwritten will legal in England? I don't even know if it would be at home."

Aunt Deb had been a legal secretary for over forty years. Renie grimaced as she tried to recall her mother's many admonitions on the law. "If it's not witnessed, it's probably not foolproof. But it would be up to the courts to decide, especially if the attorney—Arthur Tinsley, in this case— could swear that the new will was what the deceased really wanted. There might be a strong argument from the heirs of the previous will, but since Claire's parents are altruistic missionaries in Swaziland, I suspect they wouldn't fight too strenuously." She paused while Judith tried to figure out how or if they could get Colonel Chelmsford's attention. "If you're thinking about motive, then I'd say everybody at Ravenscroft House had one. *If* they knew that Aunt Pet wanted to change her will and leave them her fortune."

The gate had an old-fashioned padlock. There seemed to be no method of communicating with the two-story, timber-framed house that sat among the trees. Just as Judith was about to give up, two large sheepdogs ran up the winding drive. They stopped at the wrought-iron gate, settling in on their haunches and barking their heads off. The cousins winced at the noise, but decided to wait and see if the dogs' master would appear.

He did. As before, Colonel Chelmsford was dressed in

brown tweeds and a snap-brim cap. He was carrying a shotgun.

Judith and Renie exchanged anxious glances, but held
their ground. The colonel's arrival put an end to the barking, though the dogs remained in place, tongues protruding
and panting heavily.

"What's this?" Colonel Chelmsford demanded in a bark
no less grating than that of the dogs. "Lost your way, have
you?"

Judith smiled engagingly. "No. We met you the other
day at Ravenscroft House. Sort of," she amended. "We
heard you served with Uncle Corky in North Africa."

The shotgun, which had been more or less aimed at the
cousins, now wavered. "Colonel Corker? Don't recall.
Might have done. Which regiment?"

Fleetingly, Judith wondered whether to elaborate on the
lie or revert to the truth. "Uncle *Corky*. Lieutenant Charles
Grover, served under Generals Patton and Bradley. Tall,
dark, big teeth. *Show him*," Judith said under her breath,
with a nudge for Renie. "Like that." Judith pointed as
Renie drew back her upper lip.

"Frightening," mumbled Chelmsford, wincing at Renie's overbite. But sticking to the facts generated interest, if
not recognition. "Ought to remember anyone who looked
like *that*. The fellow would have had Rommel shaking in
his boots."

"Well," Judith conceded, "it was a long time ago. I
suppose in some ways, it seems like yesterday to you."

"Quite," Chelmsford agreed, now staring off into the
distance. "Hot. Dry. Dusty."

"That's because it was the desert," Renie said, now restored to her normal appearance. "You wouldn't mind letting us in . . ."

"Fuel, that was the thing," Chelmsford went on, rubbing
at his bristling ginger mustache. "The Jerrys needed petrol
badly. And there we were, raw recruits just up from . . ."

Renie leaned against the wrought-iron bars; Judith was
forced to stay planted in the muddy drive. She felt the
dampness seep into her feet. She wondered if her leather
flats were ruined yet. She reflected that Colonel Chelmsford

would have to shut up eventually because World War II had lasted only six years.

". . . Blimpy Forstwick, that was the chap's name. Only had nine toes. Don't recall which was missing, shouldn't think he'd have been allowed to sign on, but there it was . . ."

Renie's eyes had all but disappeared, and her cheeks looked sunken. Judith marveled at how her cousin achieved such a state, while she herself could do no more than to sink slowly into the soft earth of England.

". . . If Monty hadn't been a bit of an ass, don't you see. But there I was, at El Alamein, and wouldn't you know, one of these Egyptian chappies, hardly spoke a word of the King's English, brown as a berry, and no sense of hygiene . . ."

Somehow, the war in North Africa wound down. As usual, the Allies won. When Colonel Chelmsford stopped for breath, Judith was ready:

"What a fascinating life you've led!" she exclaimed, trying to free her shoes. "I can't help but think that in ninety-four years Miss Ravenscroft, too, saw so much! You'll miss her, I imagine."

Colonel Chelmsford appeared to linger in triumph over the Afrika Korps. "Eh? Miss who?"

"Petulia Ravenscroft." Judith enunciated the name carefully. "I mean, you've been neighbors for years."

The chilly hazel eyes said it all: Neighbors weren't necessarily friends. Not in Little Pauncefoot. Colonel Chelmsford looked as if he'd just as soon have had Generalfeldmarschall Erwin Rommel living next door for the past half-century.

"Pigheaded woman," the colonel finally said, more to the dogs than to his visitors. "Took to notions and wouldn't let go."

"Oh," Judith said, still forcing charm. "You're referring to the boundary dispute?"

Colonel Chelmsford frowned. "That—and other things."

Renie, whose patience was never as unflappable as Judith's, gave a futile yank on the iron bars. "What is this place, anyway? A farm? A retreat house? A rehab center?"

The colonel regarded Renie with mild curiosity. "What became of your teeth? They've gone."

Renie gave an impatient shake of her chestnut curls. "Never mind my teeth. Your house looks very old and rather lovely. But what's with all the grounds? You seem to have a large piece of property and not much to show for it."

Sadly, Colonel Chelmsford shook his head. "Plowed under. No one wants to farm another man's land these days. Only thing I grow is vegetable marrows. Gives me room for practice shooting. Clay pigeons. Keeps my eye sharp."

Judith's smile finally faded. "Oh," she said in a hollow voice, then waited a full minute. "I suppose we ought to be going."

The colonel didn't protest. The dogs began to bark again. Judith and Renie moved quickly up the road.

"Old futz," muttered Renie. "How could you encourage him to launch his war stories?"

Two energetic race-walkers breezed by the cousins. "How else could I get him to talk at all? Besides, Uncle Corky *was* in North Africa."

"I know that. But you didn't learn anything," Renie pointed out, "except how Chummy Chelmsford got rocks in his socks at Tobruk."

"I learned more than that," Judith said with equanimity. "You must pay closer attention and exercise your little—"

"Shove it," Renie snapped. The smile she bestowed on a redheaded woman pushing a pram was definitely forced. "Okay," Renie went on in a calmer tone, "so what did your previously pulplike gray cells pick up from Colonel Chelmsford?"

Judith slowed her step, watching the woman and the baby stroll past the church toward the Great Pauncefoot Road. "What? Oh—mainly that the grudges between the Chelmsfords and the Ravenscrofts go further back than the current boundary dispute. Didn't you catch that part about Aunt Pet's 'notions'?"

"Were they what foiled the German Panzer attack?" Renie inquired dryly.

Judith glanced at Renie in mock reproach. "What I'm saying is that Chummy dismissed the boundary argument as if it were minor compared to 'other things.' That indicates bigger controversies, probably dating back to . . ."

The cousins had reached The Old Grey Mare Inn, which faced the Great Pauncefoot–Yeovil Road and took up the space between Farriers Lane and the High Street. Judith was hesitating over which direction to take when a black and white police car bumped down the lane. It came to a complete, abrupt stop at the intersection.

Sergeant Daub was in the driver's seat; Inspector Wattle rolled down his window, calling to the cousins:

"You're to remain in the village," he shouted. "We're off to Great Pauncefoot to get the lab report. We'll expect to see you both at Ravenscroft 'ouse when we return. Meanwhile, we'll be checking your bona fides." With a curt nod, the inspector signaled for Daub to drive on.

"Touch my bona fides and you're a dead man!" Renie yelled. Fortunately, the policemen didn't hear her. But several other people out and about in the village did, including the redheaded woman who was now pushing the pram across the road in the direction of the converted almshouses. She turned to stare. Judith was tempted to hail her, but mother and child moved on, turning up a walkway lined with hyacinth and primrose.

"Don't tell me you know her," Renie said as they wandered into the High Street.

"Of course not," Judith said.

"Then why the fascination?"

"She's got red hair."

"So? Lots of people do. Claire, for one. Your husband, for another."

"That's right." Judith nodded. "Joe has red hair. That's why I'm fascinated."

The tour of the High Street didn't take long. Since it was the Sabbath, except for an antiques shop that also sold used books, none of the stores was open. Between the inn and the tea room, Judith noticed the offices of Arthur Tinsley, solicitor, and Lawrence Ramsey, M.D.

"Cute," Renie remarked, following Judith through the splashes of sunshine on the main road. "Very Olde English. Except it really is. Imagine Nats wanting to mall it over with contemporary claptrap! The buildings are mostly sixteenth century, maybe earlier. The inn has got to be pre-Tudor."

"How's that?" Judith asked as they reached the first of the dozen almshouses.

"The Old Grey Mare is a reference to Elizabeth Woodville, Edward V's queen," Renie explained. "She was a commoner."

Dutifully, Judith deferred to Renie's knowledge of English history. As a master of librarianship, Judith's forte was literature. "So circa the Wars of the Roses?" she asked.

"And thus pre–Richard III," Renie said. "Or maybe during his reign. It might have been a knock on Richard's sister-in-law. He wasn't too keen on Elizabeth and her family." Renie paused, momentarily lost in the mists of Bosworth Field. "Where are we going?" she inquired in some surprise.

Judith feigned ignorance. "The sun's out. We haven't walked this way, toward Great Pauncefoot. Nice old houses. Pretty gardens. The town isn't more than three miles away."

"*Three miles?*" Renie was horrified.

Naturally, Judith had no intention of going to Great Pauncefoot. Her aversion to covering long distances on foot was almost as great as Renie's. Yet there was something in the spring air that goaded Judith. Perhaps it was the English penchant for walking. Or the freshness of the afternoon, with bright periwinkles, bluebells, and wood anemones clustered under stands of oak and ash. There was very little motor traffic, even along the route to Great Pauncefoot. After crossing an ancient packhorse bridge, the cousins found themselves flanked by orchards bursting with blossoms. They climbed the softest of hills to view the vale below with its neat green fields bordered by hedgerows and copses. The vista stretched before them to the horizon, tranquil and timeless, essentially English.

"My feet are killing me," Renie said. "We must have walked five miles. Can we go back now? Or is there a bus?"

"Oh, good grief!" Judith cried. "We haven't gone more than half a mile!"

"Good. Then we won't have more than half a mile to walk back." At the side of the road, Renie did an about-face.

But Judith kept going. There were more houses now, bearing discreetly lettered names such as "River's Bend," "The Willows," and "Xanadu." Renie yelled at Judith to stop, but got no response. Indeed, a hundred feet up the road, Judith turned off.

By the time Renie caught up, Judith was at the door of a two-story thatched and whitewashed cottage with shrubbery that looked as if it had been clipped with a scalpel. A small sign bearing the words "Mon Repos" hung from the little roof over the porch.

"What in the world are you doing?" Renie demanded in annoyance. "Or," she added, brightening, "is this the bus depot?"

Before Judith could explain, a middle-aged woman with unnatural gold hair and tight facial features opened the door. There was nothing wrong with the prim little mouth, the turned-up nose, or the sky-blue eyes. But any kinship with beauty was spoiled by the sour expression. In addition, the woman looked at Judith and Renie as if they were virulent germs.

"Mrs. Tinsley?" Judith said in her warmest voice. "Is your husband at home?"

"No." The small, red mouth grew even tighter and the little nostrils flared.

"Oh." Judith's disappointment overflowed. "Oh, dear!"

Lona Tinsley's small, slim body was encased in a black pleated skirt, a navy-blue pullover, and the hint of a white blouse, the collar of which lay chastely at her throat. She seemed quite unmoved by Judith's obvious despair.

"When do you expect him?" Judith finally asked.

Mrs. Tinsley's short lashes fluttered ever so slightly. "I really couldn't say."

Again, Judith waited, hoping to goad Mrs. Tinsley into speech. But no further words were discharged by those prissy little lips. Judith sighed heavily.

"It's extremely urgent," she said, all pleading earnestness. "May we leave a message?"

Mrs. Tinsley didn't actually unbend, but she permitted a muscle to twitch along her jawline. Judith wondered if it showed interest. Or if the woman had a tic. "May I ask who is calling on Mr. Tinsley?" inquired his spouse.

Judith's nod was eager. "Certainly. I'm Mrs. Flynn, and this is Mrs. Jones, my cousin." Judith ignored the fact that Renie was now sitting on the steps with her back turned. "We must talk to Mr. Tinsley at once about"—she lowered her voice and coughed discreetly— "the will. We're leaving tomorrow, you see."

Mrs. Tinsley looked as if tomorrow couldn't come too soon. "Then you'd best go back where you came from," she said. "That is, to Ravenscroft House, I assume? Mr. Tinsley returned there a quarter of an hour ago."

"Ah!" Judith sounded relieved, even as she strained to get a look at the interior of Mon Repos. From what she could see of the hallway and a corner of the parlor, the house was immaculately maintained and scrupulously well-ordered. Mrs. Tinsley no doubt considered visitors messy by definition. If the mistress of Mon Repos suffered from bouts of ill health, possibly they were triggered by over-zealous cleaning. "You're right," Judith agreed, "we ought to head back to Little Pauncefoot. We walked. Maybe we passed Mr. Tinsley on the road and didn't realize it."

"Perhaps." Mrs. Tinsley was indifferent. It was clear that she didn't care if the cousins had passed a Gypsy caravan, a traveling circus, or Sherman marching through Georgia. "Good day," she said, and quietly, if firmly, closed the door.

On feet of lead, Judith descended the three stairs that led to the front porch. "Rats," she muttered, starting down the walk with its close-cropped privet hedge. "Now we'll have to . . ."

But Renie was still sitting on the step. She pretended to ignore Judith, her gaze fixed somewhere in the direction of the river that flowed in back of Mon Repos.

"Come on, coz," Judith finally said in exasperation. "You're the one who wanted to go back to Ravenscroft House."

Slowly, Renie turned. "I think I'll stay here and take tea with Mrs. Tinsley. She's such fun. Maybe we can bond and become bosom buddies. Of course, she doesn't have any. Bosom, that is. I'm always suspicious of flat-chested women." In a sudden burst of anger, Renie flew off the steps. "Now you tell me what that was all about or I'll bust your chops. Why the hell did we have to walk damned near a mile to get the deep freeze from Arthur Tinsley's dry-as-dog-food wife?"

Judith had the grace to looked chagrined. "I thought he was home. That's where he said he was going. And he did," she added with a dash of fervor. "It's not my fault he went back to Ravenscroft House. He probably found the previous will. As for the new one, it's a cinch that nobody else is going to tell us about it."

The cousins were now both hoofing it along the road, almost running past "The Larches" and "Shangri-la" and "Chez Boothby." A lone jogger passed them at his peril. The gentle rise they had ascended earlier suddenly seemed as steep as the hills in their native heath. Overhead, gray clouds scudded across the sky to obscure the late afternoon sun.

"Listen, you idiot," Renie panted, "you're supposed to be the one for whom logic is an icon. If the cops only found the will before they saw us, Arthur Tinsley wouldn't have known about it. He left before that, remember?"

"Shoot," Judith gasped, now going downhill and regaining her breath, "that's true. But he should have known. He's the solicitor, right?"

"Right," Renie agreed, her ire cooling with the weather. "Except that Aunt Pet hadn't signed the blasted thing. So maybe he never saw it, either. So why do we care? We don't know if the thing's valid."

"We care," Judith said, slowing down at the stone

bridge, "because we're murder suspects. We care because we're meeting Joe and Bill in Edinburgh Wednesday night. We care because we don't want the ugly blot of divorce on our family escutcheons."

For at least a full minute, or until they reached the pastel perfection of the orchards, Renie was silent. "Does that mean you're seriously sleuthing? I should have known."

"You bet," Judith responded. "Oh, I'm not discounting Inspector Wattle and Sergeant Daub. I have the greatest respect for the English police. Goodness knows, I've read enough mystery novels. But time is of the essence. We could leave Ravenscroft House as late as Wednesday and still get to Edinburgh on time. I'd rather not cut it so close, though. We're supposed to be gone tomorrow so that we can shop till we drop."

"I'm about to drop now," Renie admitted as they approached the outskirts of Little Pauncefoot. "I'm also starving. Will Tichborne have any sandwiches left?"

"I think," Judith said, as they passed the almshouses and headed for Farriers Lane, "she'll have to make more to go around. E'en now, as they say in English literature, the police draw nigh."

Sure enough, the black and white car had turned into the lane. So did the cousins, wondering what hath the lab analysis wrought.

ELEVEN

AMID THE LENGTHENING afternoon shadows, the household reassembled in the drawing room. Judith and Renie were the last to arrive, breathless from their gallop down Farriers Lane. A belligerent Charles glowered behind his wife's chair. Claire looked nervous as she fingered the long gold chain that hung over her black cashmere sweater. Alex was bleary-eyed, and Nats wore a full-fledged pout. Walter Paget registered no emotion, while Arthur Tinsley seemed to fade into the Flemish tapestry. Mrs. Tichborne sat next to Dora Hobbs. The housekeeper was vigilant, as if primed for trouble; the maid cowered, tiny hands clenched in her lap. Harwood, as usual, exhibited all the animation of a waxworks dummy.

Inspector Wattle displayed due deference, though Judith detected an underlying relish as he made his announcement: "We have the lab findings. The quantity of 'yoscyamine in Miss Ravenscroft's system was sufficient to kill 'er. Further testing will determine if other toxic substances were involved. We're told that the poison was most likely contained in at least one of the four chocolate liqueurs she consumed in the last twelve 'ours of 'er life. The same poison was found in two of the remaining chocolates in the box we removed from 'er bedroom. The inquest, which is a mere formality, will be 'eld tomorrow at ten A.M. in the meeting 'all at the village library."

135

A brief silence ensued. It was Claire who spoke first: "Oh! Chocolates! Auntie wasn't supposed to eat chocolates! How naughty of her!"

Alex stirred himself to a derisive laugh. "Served her right then, eh, Claire? She might have died even if somebody hadn't laced the chocolates with hyo ... whatever it's called."

"Oh, Alex," Claire cried, close to tears, "that's very cruel!"

Alex sneered. "Not so cruel as whoever poisoned Aunt Pet." His black eyes came into focus as he gazed around the room. "Who was it? Not me, I can tell you that much."

Inspector Wattle loudly cleared his throat. "This isn't the place for a row, if I may say so. Does anybody 'ere know 'ow Miss Ravenscroft came by those chocolates? They're St. Cloud brand, available anywhere."

The candy maker's name meant nothing to Judith and Renie, who presumed that St. Cloud didn't export to the States. But all eyes had turned to Dora. The little maid blushed furiously and wrung her hands. "*I* don't know! Chocolates, indeed! I never once saw Miss Petulia eat chocolates!"

Nats stood up and went to the bar. "She didn't take them in an IV drip. How well do you see, Dora?"

Dora's hands now fluttered every which way. "Really, I ... My sight's not what it once ... Still, I'm not blind ..."

"You mustn't blame Dora," Mrs. Tichborne broke in, her voice like steel. "If Miss Petulia wanted to eat the armoire, there would have been no stopping her. She was a most determined woman."

"But *who*?" Claire wailed. "Who would do such a terrible thing? It was thoughtless enough to give Auntie chocolates, but to put poison in them is wicked!"

The understatement riled Charles. "Of course it is! Unless," he added, lowering his voice, "Aunt Pet bought them herself."

Grasping a bottle of Beefeaters' gin, Nats scoffed. "She wouldn't poison herself. Not like that."

Alex eyed the gin bottle covetously. "She wouldn't poison herself in any event. She was having too good a time making the rest of us miserable."

"Oh, hush up!" Nats ordered her brother, with a warning glance. "Don't go digging a hole for yourself, you twit!"

Once again, Inspector Wattle was forced to intervene. " 'Ere now, let's be calm. My men and I must get on with the investigation. But first, there's the matter of the wills." His small, piercing eyes rested on Arthur Tinsley. "Did you find the previous document among your papers, sir?"

Arthur Tinsley appeared overcome by embarrassment. "I did not," he responded in a fragile voice. "I searched both at my office and my home. My recollection is that Miss Ravenscroft kept one copy and I had the other. Yet both have now . . . disappeared." He lowered his eyes, studying the high gloss on his black oxfords.

"Well, now." Wattle fingered his stubby chin. "That leaves us with the 'andwritten will. Now that you've seen it, what's your legal opinion, Mr. Tinsley? Qualified, of course. I know 'ow you fellows operate."

Arthur actually ran a finger inside his shirt collar. "Well . . . It's what Miss Ravenscroft intended to formalize at our next meeting, which was scheduled for tomorrow. Or so she indicated on Friday. Basically, it's the same document she had me draw up for her in April of last year. With . . . ah . . . one exception." He studiously avoided looking in Judith and Renie's direction.

"And?" Inspector Wattle prodded.

Arthur moved three steps to the bar and poured himself a glass of water from a lead-crystal decanter. "The addition was the bequest to Mrs. Judith Flynn and Mrs. Serena Jones. They were to receive the gatehouse."

"The *gatehouse*!" The words were echoed by several people, including the cousins.

Charles was more specific, his face set in stone. "Not *this* house, then?" He saw Arthur give a shake of his head. "I should think not!" Charles asserted, trying to tone down his triumph. "Then the remaining property goes to me? And my wife, of course."

"That was Miss Ravenscroft's intention," Arthur said primly. "As I mentioned a moment ago, except for the gatehouse, the handwritten will is otherwise the same document that was in effect from April until last August when my client became . . . vexed, and drastically changed her mind. As I believe most of you know, Mr. and Mrs. Marchmont were to inherit Ravenscroft House and the land on which it stands, as well as a percentage of the estate. Trusts were to be set up for Miss Karamzin and Mr. Karamzin, and turned over to them upon marrying or reaching thirty years of age, whichever came first. Meanwhile, they would be permitted to draw on the interest. There was also a trust for each of Mr. and Mrs. Marchmont's twin boys. Mr. and Mrs. George Ravenscroft were to inherit shares in a profitable electronics firm. Miss Hobbs, Mrs. Tichborne, and Mr. Harwood were also provided for, as were various charities, including St. Edith's Church.'' Arthur stopped to take a long drink of water.

Charles seized the opportunity to urge the solicitor to get to the point. "Dammit, man, is this new will legal or not?"

Arthur swallowed hard. "Naturally, under the circumstances . . . er . . . there must be some . . . ah . . . question of its validity. The will was signed, but not witnessed. The first step would be to prove that the handwriting was indeed Miss Ravenscroft's and not a . . . um . . . forgery." The solicitor looked as gloomy as a man going to the gallows tree.

"Bilge," snapped Nats. "Nobody had handwriting like Aunt Pet. It was that old-fashioned spidery kind. Did she revoke the previous will or not?"

This time, Arthur's nod was almost imperceptible. "She so stated. Miss Ravenscroft was very precise, very thorough. But there's still the matter of the will which was made last August and duly—"

Alex spun around to confront Arthur. "We have only your word for it that a different will existed. See here, Tinsley, unless you can produce a copy of the revised August document, we're closing ranks against you." The glance that Alex gave his relatives found no opposition.

Arthur folded, literally, hunched over on a Chippendale chair. "It's a point well-taken, Mr. Karamzin. I shouldn't fight you over it. Only my honor and my ethics are at stake."

Charles administered a hearty slap to Arthur's back. "We believe you, Arthur. But having the interim document turn up missing is a blessing in disguise. It was obviously a whim of Aunt Pet's after the dust-up during August bank holiday. We can all pretend it never existed, eh? Think of the trouble it will save!"

The deep creases in the solicitor's high forehead indicated he wasn't in complete agreement. But his manner was meek as he replied: "Well ... yes ... seeing that Miss Ravenscroft didn't intend to let it stand. Of course there's the matter of Mr. and Mrs. Ravenscroft in Swaziland. If you wish, I can write to them. I shall have to anyway, whatever the outcome. Perhaps you'd be so kind as to provide me with their address ..."

"Gladly," Charles all but shouted. In a lightning move, he produced a pen and a piece of paper, handing both to the solicitor. "Claire, give Arthur your parents' address. You must know it off the top of your head."

Claire did. She recited slowly, as Arthur wrote in his neat, if cramped, style. "Until we have a ruling from the probate court, I shall inform them that they are co-heirs," he said, putting both paper and pen into the inside pocket of his suitcoat.

"Bugger probate court!" Charles boomed. "Why do we need it? If you can't find Aunt Pet's August prank, no one need know. It's pure fiction! And give me back my pen, Tinsley." Charles narrowed his eyes at Arthur, though his mouth was curved in a smile. "You legal chaps make enough off your fees without stealing clients' property."

Arthur blanched, then handed back the pen. "Awfully sorry. I tend to become distracted sometimes. Really, I must recommend that we go through proper channels ..."

Ignoring Arthur's anxious protests, Nats turned to Claire. "Your parents won't contest the will. They're a zillion miles away, and they have no resources except for beads and bones and whatever else they use for money in Swaziland. They don't even have a fax machine."

Walter Paget had stepped forward, offering a shield between Nats and Claire. "Of course they don't. I've already explained the primitive conditions. Besides, they're dedicated missionaries. They'll see this as God's will."

"It's Aunt Pet's will, not God's," Nats sniffed. "If she'd wanted to keep the August will, she wouldn't have written a new one. It must have been very hard for her, with her arthritis."

Charles was looking smug. "She made the August will in a fit of temper. Common sense must prevail. It would be unthinkable not to abide by her last wishes."

A murmur of assent rumbled around the room. Only the cousins were silent. Or so it seemed, until Judith realized that there was one other exception: Walter Paget remained frozen in place. He had also been frozen out of the will.

The other servants had been at Ravenscroft House longer, but the steward had at least a decade of service. It didn't seem right for Pet to exclude him. Judith wondered why.

The police had gone about their business, including a thorough search of the entire house and grounds. Given the size of the property, Judith assumed they'd be combing through storerooms, pastureland, and cellars for days.

Nor did she know what they expected to find. More chocolates, perhaps, or the source of the poison. After the family group had partially dispersed, Judith put the question to Mrs. Tichborne.

"How should I know?" the housekeeper asked in a testy tone. "It's just as well that Miss Ravenscroft is dead. If she were alive, she'd hear all about how I haven't kept up every nook and cranny of this big old place. How can I, with only daily help?"

Judith nodded in sympathy. "I've been meaning to clean our basement ever since the remodeling seven years ago. If I ever get around to it, I'm sure I'll find stuff that's been there since the house was built in 1907."

Mrs. Tichborne huffed. "Think 1597. Your home is comparatively new." She wrestled a large ham on the kitchen counter. Supper preparations were under way, and the cousins had volunteered to help. Mrs. Tichborne didn't reject the offer this time. Officially, it was her day off, and she wasn't inclined to prepare a hot meal. Instead, the family would be served a cold collation. "Maybe," the housekeeper went on, her ire cooling, "they'll turn up the jewels Mrs. Ravenscroft swore were stolen."

Momentarily, Judith was puzzled. "*Mrs.* Ravenscroft? Now which one would that be?"

With a scowl at Renie who had already filched a slice of ham, Mrs. Tichborne brandished the kitchen knife. "Genevieve Ravenscroft, the Frenchwoman. Even in her dotage, she ranted about how she'd had her diamond choker and ruby earrings stolen. Miss Ravenscroft—her sister-in-law—didn't believe it for a minute. She said Mrs. Ravenscroft was careless. She'd put them somewhere, and couldn't remember."

Renie was licking her lips over the last morsel of ham. "Diamonds and rubies, huh? That sounds like pretty expensive forgetfulness."

The housekeeper shrugged. "Lady Cordelia had plenty of other pieces that were handed down to the next generation. I'm told that Sir Henry Ravenscroft doted on his wife. The French daughter-in-law got most of them. Chauncey Ravenscroft's wife, Hyacinth, was too godly to wear gems, and Miss Petulia didn't care for anything showy. Anyway, I don't think the missing pieces ever turned up. I would like to see them find Bothwell, though."

Judith paused in putting sweet pickles on a three-tiered server. "Bothwell? What was it, a family pet?"

"No, no," Mrs. Tichborne replied. "It was a costume for the All Fools Revels. Participants dress up as actual characters from the Elizabethan period. Sir Walter Raleigh. The Earl of Essex. Bess of Hardwicke. And of course Mary, Queen of Scots, and the Earl of Bothwell. The costumes have all been copied from portraits and are very authentic. The Ravenscrofts always store them here." Suddenly, her face sagged. "My Janet got the blame for Bothwell's disappearance. She wore the costume that year. And didn't it suit her, with those long, lovely legs! How she and her partner danced! The galliard, I think it's called. They do it every year."

The housekeeper bit her lip in an effort at self-control. "But of course she didn't take the Bothwell costume with her. Why would she do such a thing? Ever since, whoever plays Queen Mary has had to make do with the Earl of Darnley."

"So did Mary," murmured Renie, swiping another piece of ham while Mrs. Tichborne looked away.

"Forgive me," the housekeeper said, turning back to the cousins. Her eyes were overbright. "I try so hard not to dwell on Janet. It's best to think of her as living a wild life in London than accept the fact that she might be . . ."

Emboldened by the other woman's misery, Judith reached out to pat her arm. Mrs. Tichborne stiffened, but didn't recoil. "That's possible," Judith said kindly. "Teenagers do very foolish things. By the time they realize it, they're too embarrassed to admit their mistakes. That takes real maturity. I know, I've raised a son, mostly on my own, just as you did with your daughter. Mike was eighteen when my first husband died, but during the last ten years of his life, Dan didn't play an active role in our family." As in, thought Judith, all four hundred pounds of him lying on the sofa stuffing his face with Ding-Dongs and slugging down shots of vodka while berating his wife for forgetting to pick up the chocolate mud pie on her whirlwind trip between two jobs. Dan McMonigle had been a terrible husband, but he really hadn't been a bad father. At least not if you defined inertia as a virtue.

Mrs. Tichborne had brightened a bit. "How true. Raising children is difficult, under any conditions. Janet wouldn't be the first to run off. Or so I've heard." Her voice suddenly took on a dark edge.

Curiosity piqued, Judith started to ask Mrs. Tichborne what she meant. But the two policemen who had searched Aunt Pet's suite earlier in the day entered the kitchen. They intended to give it a thorough going-over. Mrs. Tichborne bridled.

"Can't you wait? We're serving supper. Come back in an hour."

The policemen didn't persist. They withdrew politely, but their superior bustled in on their heels. Inspector Wattle eyed the sliced ham with longing. Renie neatly stepped in front of the platter.

"Hi," she said. "Find the poison yet?"

The inspector stared at her with distaste. "No need to be flippant," he chided. "I have some questions for all three of you."

Mrs. Tichborne was slicing cheddar cheese off a large brick. "You questioned us earlier. What now?" Her voice was tired.

Wattle was undaunted. "Did any of you know that Miss Ravenscroft had actually drawn up a new will?"

"No," replied the housekeeper. "Certainly not."

"She talked about it at dinner Friday night," Renie allowed.

"Have you asked Dora?" Judith was trying to sound reasonable.

Wattle snorted. "Dora 'obbs 'as the brains of a chicken. Scatty, that's what she is. She didn't see Miss Ravenscroft eating chocolates, she didn't see 'er making out a will, she didn't see 'er 'and before 'er face!"

Once again, Mrs. Tichborne waved the knife. "Mind me, Inspector, you show Dora some respect. She's elderly, and her hearing and her sight aren't keen. But she's far from scatty."

Wattle remained skeptical, but he whipped out a small photograph from his inside pocket. "Then why didn't she recognize this chap? 'E must be somebody from 'er era. Who is it?"

While Mrs. Tichborne studied the wallet-sized studio photograph, Judith craned her neck to get a look. The man was young, or had been, probably around the First World War. His thick, straight hair appeared to be light in color, and only a weak chin marred his otherwise handsome features.

"I don't know him," Mrs. Tichborne declared. "He's not part of the rogues gallery in the entry hall."

The inspector gave Mrs. Tichborne a withering look. "We already checked the family portraits," he said, putting the photo back in his pocket. "We found this in the drawer where the chocolates were 'idden."

Strangely enough, Judith thought there was something familiar about the man in the picture. But that was impossible. She decided to change the subject:

"Excuse me, Inspector, but what is hyoscyamine? I've never heard of it."

"No reason why you should." Wattle gave Judith a quizzical look. "Not a chemist, are you? Never know these days with women, especially Americans. They take some peculiar posts." Seeing Judith shake her head, Wattle became almost avuncular. "By definition, it's a poisonous white crystalline alkaloid. Nasty stuff, but it can also be used medicinally, as an analgesic and as a sedative. Except this wasn't in its processed form. We're dealing with hyoscyamine in its raw state. In other words," the inspector added in sepulchral tones, "we mean *plants.*"

"*Plants?*" Mrs. Tichborne was aghast.

Wattle nodded gravely. "Plants. That's why my men are going through the gardens."

If Mrs. Tichborne was startled by Wattle's indictment of local flora, Judith was not. She had encountered garden-variety poisoning on another occasion.

"Do you know what kind of plant contains hyoscyamine?" Judith inquired.

Wattle's heavy eyelids drooped. "There's several that do. Never fear, we're working on it."

Judith didn't doubt it. The inspector took his leave, and Mrs. Tichborne began carrying food out to the sideboard. Renie picked up a platter of ham, a basket of bread, and a covered butter dish, but Judith forestalled her.

"Coz—what on earth are we going to do about the gatehouse?"

Renie's shrug was inhibited by her juggling act. "Nothing. It'll never happen. Trust me."

"What do you mean?" Judith spoke in a whisper. "It sounds as if the new will could be valid. We'll end up with the gatehouse."

But Renie was firm. "No, we won't. Even if the will is proved, we'll give the gatehouse away. We'll have to. Between death duties, the IRS, and living nine thousand miles away, we can't afford it. Let Walter Paget have it. He lives there anyway, and he didn't get zilch.''

Judith's forehead creased. ''I know. That's odd. I wonder why Walter was left out. He's been with the family for years.''

Renie had no explanation, and the bread basket was slipping out from under her arm. She hurried into the dining room just as Harwood sounded the gong. Judith picked up a plate of sliced tomatoes and a bowl of fruit. She supposed that Renie was right. There was no point in fretting over their putative inheritance. It hadn't happened yet.

But the family members behaved as if it had. Claire and Charles were in excellent spirits, while Nats and Alex were almost giddy. Somebody had opened two bottles of French wine. Nats proposed a toast:

''To Aunt Pet—she may have driven us crazy, but she didn't take us for a ride. Cheers!''

The others raised their glasses, though both Judith and Renie were tentative. It was then that Judith realized neither Arthur nor Walter was present. When she asked where they had gone, Charles answered in an unusually jocular manner:

''Old Arthur went home to his ball-and-chain. Walter had to send another cable to George and Emily, canceling their unexpected fortune. Or most of it. Tsk, tsk.'' He burst into laughter.

Claire tried to look shocked. ''Now Charles, we mustn't be disrespectful. We've got a funeral to plan. We should set it for Thursday, don't you think? That way, it won't spoil the weekend.''

Charles's attempt at solemnity was only a partial success. ''I'll go 'round tonight and see the vicar. Have those blasted policemen left yet?''

Nats jiggled her wineglass. ''They have not. Two are up in the storerooms, two more are outside, and Wattle and Daub are in the wine cellar. Or so Harwood said when he fetched this 1983 Mercurey Chateau de Chamirey.''

''Sod all,'' Alex muttered, but good-naturedly. ''Coppers are a bloody great nuisance. I say, Charles,'' he went on with a sly look in his dark eyes, ''just how much do you figure we'll get straight away? You know the family finances, after all.''

"Well." Charles cleared his throat and squared his shoulders. "I shouldn't like to hazard a guess just now. I'll go over everything in the next few days. Then I can be more precise. It doesn't do to conjecture when it comes to money."

Apparently something in Charles's manner had disturbed his wife. She leaned forward at the opposite end of the table, whispering as if they were the only two people in the room.

"It *is* all right, isn't it, Charles? I mean, there are no . . . surprises?''

Charles laughed again, but somehow he didn't sound quite so hearty. "Certainly not, m'dear! Everything's right as rain! Oh, as I mentioned earlier, there have been a few reversals, but that's the way of high finance. No need for you to worry your pretty head."

Nats rested one elbow on the table. "What about *my* pretty head, Charles?''

Charles speared a slice of cheese. "Nor you, Nats. The worst that can happen is that your interest from the trust might be a trifle smaller than it would have been a year ago. But when it comes time for the trust fund to be turned over to you, you'll be in clover.''

"I should hope so." Nats shot Charles an arch look. "The time is now." She paused for only a beat, luring all eyes in her direction. "I may not reach thirty for a few years, but I *am* getting married. Now that Aunt Pet is dead, we can set the date.''

Claire blinked several times, then put a hand to her breast. " 'We'? Who is 'we,' Nats?''

"I'm one-half of 'we,' Claire.'' Nats took a sip of wine, then smirked. "The other half is Walter Paget. Isn't everybody happy for us?''

It appeared to Judith that they were not. Alex dropped his fork, Charles let out an agonized growl, and Claire fainted dead away.

TWELVE

IT WAS HARWOOD who revived Claire by pouring a glass of water over her head. She spluttered and Charles protested, but the butler was unmoved.

"Young ladies used to swoon a great deal," he said woodenly. "Years ago, it was considered fashionable. Smelling salts are quite nasty. Water works just as well. Excuse me, sir, you're stepping on Mrs. Marchmont's hair."

Clumsily, Charles removed his foot which had been planted in Claire's wet auburn tresses. "Sorry, old girl," he mumbled. "Are you all right?"

With her husband's help, Claire struggled up on one elbow. "I think so. Oh! I feel dreadful! And dampish!" She ran a hand through her hair, which was now limp and plastered close to her head.

Charles accepted Judith's offer to help put Claire on her feet. "I'm feeling a bit peaked myself," he confessed. "Shall we take you into the parlor or would you rather go upstairs?" he asked his wife.

Harwood coughed. "I believe the police are still using the parlor as their temporary headquarters, sir. May I suggest the drawing room? A bit of brandy might be in order. And a towel. I'll fetch one at once." Harwood creaked off to the kitchen.

Alex sprang for the door. "Brandy! What a jolly good idea! I'll pour." He was halfway across the hall before

Judith and Charles could start dragging Claire out of the dining room.

Renie was consolidating what was left of the cold collation. "Waste not, want not," she said to Nats, who was calmly finishing her wine. "Grab a tray. We'll take this into the dining room. And tell me why Claire passed out because you're getting married."

Nats gave Renie a wry look as they slowed their step behind Judith, Charles and Claire. "Don't ask me," Nats said, then pointed to Claire, who seemed to be a dead weight between her bearers. "Claire?" Nats called, mischief dancing in her dark eyes. "Don't you think Walter and I make an ideal couple?"

Claire's only response was to sag even more in the clutches of her husband and her guest. Nothing further was said until the group reached the dining room, where Claire was eased onto a Hepplewhite-inspired divan.

"So embarrassing," Claire sighed, a hand over her eyes. She rallied when Alex proffered brandy. "Just a sip. Oh! That's very strong! This day has been such an ordeal! Can Auntie still have been alive twenty-four hours ago?"

In truth, it seemed more like a week than a day to Judith as well. Reflexively, she accepted a snifter from Alex, then turned to Charles. "Should you call Dr. Ramsey?"

Charles looked uncertain, but Claire brushed the idea aside. "Don't disturb him. The doctor's had a long day, too. I'll be fine." She gave Harwood a wan smile as he presented her with a kitchen towel.

Judith waited for Charles to assist his wife, but he was pouring himself a brandy. Claire was making an ineffectual effort at rubbing her hair.

"Let me help," Judith offered, setting her snifter down on a side table.

"How kind," Claire murmured. As Judith worked with the towel, she felt Claire's head turn toward the far end of the room, where Nats seemed absorbed in studying the marquetry work on a Boulle desk. When Claire spoke again, her voice was unnaturally loud and self-possessed. "Nats— you and I must talk privately, and soon. This is a very serious business."

The only acknowledgment by Nats was a twitch of her slim shoulders. Judith finished fluffing up Claire's coiffure. At the bar, Alex poured himself another brandy.

"Maybe," he said to the room at large, "I should get married, too. There's Clea—but models are so vain. Dee-Dee is amusing, but a bisexual wife could present problems. Erica's quite wonderful in every way, except for her husband. What to do, what to do." Alex continued communing with his brandy snifter.

Sergeant Daub entered, wearing humility like a badge. "The inspector would like to interview everyone again. It shouldn't take long, since he doesn't wish to trouble you, and he's anxious to go off-duty. He'll see you in pairs to expedite matters."

This time, Judith and Renie were summoned first. Only two desk lamps were turned on in the parlor, evoking the pale glow of rush lights and tapers that must have illumined the room four hundred years earlier. Judith could almost see Sir Lionel Dunk sitting at the big oak desk in his doublet and hose. Or a dress.

Now seated in the lord of the manor's place was Claude Wattle. Either because he was tired or because he had settled into the mechanics of the case, the inspector was less contentious than he had been earlier in the day. His attitude toward the cousins was now businesslike, rather than confrontational.

"You arrived at Ravenscroft House Friday afternoon, I understand. You 'ad not met any of these people until then, except Mrs. Marchmont, who lunched with you in London earlier in the week. Correct?"

Judith and Renie affirmed the statement. Sergeant Daub wrote assiduously in his notebook. The inspector continued: "Given that you 'ad no prior knowledge of Miss Petulia Ravenscroft, 'ow did 'er manner strike you?"

Judith fielded the question. "She was a very forceful personality. Stubborn, demanding, critical—but basically kind. She had very high standards, and wouldn't make allowances for how the world had changed. Deteriorated, she might have said. We're told she tried to run the lives of her relatives, particularly through the use of money. It was her only weapon, really. Old people lose so many physical powers, which makes them resentful because it means a loss of independence as well. That would be particularly hard for a proud, willful woman like Aunt Pet who was used to having her own way. Confined as she was, it was only natural for her to resort to money as manipulation.''

Daub looked as if his hand was cramping, and Wattle wore a dazed expression. The inspector took a deep breath. ''I'm asking about 'er state of mind, not the story of 'er life. How did she *behave?*''

Judith was embarrassed. ''Oh—I'm sorry. Well, she acted the way I'd expect a person such as I just described to act. She was impatient, opinionated, and autocratic.''

''She was in good spirits,'' Renie put in, then gave the inspector a self-deprecating smile. ''My husband's a psychologist, so I know what you're driving at.'' Renie ignored Judith's baleful look. ''Aunt Pet wasn't nervous or depressed or anxious. I'd have to guess that her behavior was normal—for her. There was no indication that she expected trouble. Bill—that's my husband—would point out that she talked a lot about family members who had died. He might tell you that didn't indicate a desire for death on Aunt Pet's part so much as for—''

''Thank you very much, Mrs. Jones,'' Wattle broke in, wiping his brow with a big handkerchief. ''Now wot's this about Miss Ravenscroft taking the family to task at dinner Friday night?''

This time, neither cousin answered. Instead, they were exchanging sheepish glances. Finally, Inspector Wattle prompted Judith.

''Aunt Pet said she was devising a new will.'' Judith spoke carefully, trying to be exact. ''She mentioned making other wills, but having to revoke them for various reasons. She also warned the family that she knew they were anticipating inheritances, but that she had no intention of dying soon, so they'd have to wait.''

Wattle nodded slowly. ''But maybe they didn't. Wait, that is. 'Ow did they react?''

Judith nodded in Renie's direction, letting her take a turn.

Renie, however, shrugged. "Nobody did much of anything. Aunt Pet went up to bed."

The inspector absorbed this information, then glanced at what appeared to be some notes on the desk. "No one made threats? Did anybody seem unduly upset or angry?"

Judith grimaced. "Well . . ."

Renie uttered a lame little laugh. "People don't mean what they say."

"Such as?" Wattle leaned forward in his chair.

Renie wasn't exactly flustered, but her usually flippant manner had disappeared. "What I mean is, people exaggerate, to work out antagonistic feelings."

"And who would these people be?" Wattle inquired.

Reluctantly, Renie recounted the cousins' meeting on the stairs with Nats and Alex Saturday afternoon. "They were both angry with Aunt Pet. They didn't say why. I suppose it had to do with money. She probably refused to give them any."

Judith wanted to be helpful. "Nats said something about Aunt Pet trying to run her life. Or all their lives. I forget exactly. But we didn't hear either of the Karamzins actually threaten Miss Ravenscroft."

Wattle nodded again. "And what about Miss Ravenscroft's other visitor? Not Tinsley—we know about him. I mean the colonel, from The Grange."

This time it was Judith who showed signs of unwillingness to tattle, though she didn't know why. "He wasn't a regular caller," she hedged.

"So I gather," Wattle said dryly. "Mrs. Marchmont indicated a property line dispute. Did you see Colonel Chelmsford at Ravenscroft House Friday afternoon?"

"Yes," Judith replied, "we saw him arrive. And leave. We heard that Aunt Pet wasn't happy to see him."

"Did you 'ear why?" the inspector queried.

Judith glanced again at Renie. "No," Judith said, "I don't think we did. It seems as if the colonel and Aunt Pet were never on very good terms."

Wattle once more referred to his notes. At last, he looked up. "You two brought some chocolates as a gift. Now why would that be?"

Renie bristled. "Fandangos aren't mere chocolates. They're truffles, in different flavors—mint, rum, extra dark, white, orange, latte . . ." Renie was practically salivating as she recited the different types of Fandangos. "Oh, we brought coffee, too. Real coffee, from Moonbeam's."

The inspector was looking skeptical. "The coffee's unopened. But the—watchacallits?—'ave been consumed. Sergeant Daub found the empty containers in the kitchen. Now wot 'ave you got to say for yourselves?"

Renie gave off a little shudder. "Once you eat a Fandango, you can't stop until they're all gone. That's no mystery."

Noting Wattle's dissatisfaction, Judith tried to clear the air. "Fandangos aren't hollow. I don't think it would be possible to inject any kind of poison into them. They're solid chocolate, and each one comes individually wrapped in cellophane to ensure its freshness and delicious taste." To her dismay, Judith's own mouth was watering.

The inspector, however, still didn't appear convinced. "We'll 'ave someone check out these Durangos. We've only got your word for wot they are." Wattle's face became a mask of professional neutrality. "Thank you. That will be all for now. Would you please send in Mrs. Tichborne and Mr. 'arwood?"

Judith and Renie gladly acquiesced. Five minutes later, they were outside, strolling down the path that presumably led to the stables.

"I couldn't face the family again," Judith admitted. "They must be tired of having us around, too."

"We'd all better get used to it," Renie said with a bitter note in her voice. "We're stuck until they find the killer."

"I've got confidence in Wattle," Judith asserted, cautiously descending a dozen stone steps that led through the gardens. Night had fallen, but there was a bright three-quarter moon riding just above a bank of clouds. "I don't know if he's got any leads yet, but the number of suspects is pretty limited."

Renie emitted a cross between a chuckle and a choking sound. "The only problem is, we happen to be two of them."

"But we can eliminate us," Judith noted as they followed a path that ran between the rose arbors and the sunken garden. The scent of lilacs followed them from the upper terrace. "That leaves the Marchmonts, the Karamzins, and maybe Mrs. Tichborne. Walter Paget has no money motive."

"You're forgetting Dora and Harwood," Renie pointed out.

"No, I'm not," Judith replied as the stable roof appeared before them. "I honestly can't picture Dora poisoning Aunt Pet. Not Harwood, either. What would be the motive? A small legacy? No, that doesn't play for me."

There were lights on behind the stable windows. "What about Colonel Chelmsford?" Renie asked.

The cousins had entered the paddock. Judith slowed her step as they approached the stable entrance. "You're right, we shouldn't forget him. He's the only person we know of with a motive other than money." Some ten feet from the unbolted double doors, she stopped. "I just remembered, coz. Colonel Chelmsford had a package with him when he came calling on Aunt Pet."

Renie eyed Judith with curiosity. "He did? Yes, I think you're right. Oh, my."

"It wasn't very big," Judith said in a wondering voice. "In fact, it was the size of a box of chocolates."

At that moment, the moon disappeared behind the clouds. A horse neighed, a loud, harsh cry that conveyed pain. A side door to the stables was flung open and a figure raced to the far end of the paddock, then fled in the direction of the river.

Walter Paget's voice called out from somewhere in the night. Judith couldn't hear what he said, but his tone was desperate. A shot rang out, ugly and alien on the English spring air.

Judith and Renie ran for their lives.

Separated by the formal gardens, the front entrance was nearest to the stables. Judith and Renie pounded on the door, got no immediate reply, and discovered it was unlocked. Panting and gasping, they lurched into the entry hall. Alex was hurrying down the main staircase.

"What's going on?" he demanded, looking almost sober. "I thought I heard a shot! Where are those coppers?"

Distractedly, the cousins recounted their startling adventure by the stables. For once, Alex seemed thoughtful.

"I should go down there," he said somewhat dubiously. "But if the police are still here, it's really their business. That is, it might have actually been a shot. Who do you think you saw running away?"

But neither Judith nor Renie could be sure. "There wasn't any moon," Renie explained. "It had just gone behind a cloud. I couldn't tell if the figure was a man or a woman. All we saw was a shadowy . . . *form.*"

Alex resumed his pensive attitude. "Well. This probably calls for a drink. Shall we?" He indicated the drawing room.

Judith didn't feel right about encouraging Alex's propensity for alcohol, but she was still shaken. "Okay," she agreed in a weak voice and a weaker moment. "I could use a scotch."

Settling into the drawing room's plush upholstery, the cousins allowed Alex to serve them. The trio had drinks in hand when an ashen Nats made a staggering entrance.

"Oh, my God! Get me a drink!" she cried. "I hate guns!" Nats collapsed onto the Louis XV settee.

Alex jumped in his armchair. "Nats! Did someone shoot at you?"

But Nats shook her head in a frenzied manner. "No, of course not, you ninny! Walter had to shoot Balthazar. He broke a leg. I'm sick—he was my favorite." She put her head in her hands and kicked off her shoes.

Judith sat up on the sofa. "Oh! Then you were the . . . and Walter fired the . . . I see."

Nats darted a reproachful look at Judith. "No, you don't see anything. How could you? Have you ever ridden Balthazar? He was magnificent."

A commotion had erupted out in the entry hall. Judith recognized Inspector Wattle's voice, then Charles in response. Nats still held her head, but finally revived when her brother handed her a drink.

"Blast!" she exclaimed, getting up and spilling some of the beverage on the Aubusson carpet. "I have to make a phone call. I'll be right back."

Alex wore an expression of alarm. "A phone call? Who, Nats?"

Still in her stocking feet, his sister glanced over her shoulder. "To the insurance fellow. Walter gave me his name." She paused on the threshold, digging into the pocket of her suede jacket. "Doodles. Silly name, but that's it. Doodles Swinford."

The insurance agent's name struck a familiar chord with Judith. It took a few seconds for her to remember why.

"I met him," she explained to Renie and Alex, "at the IMNUTS cocktail party."

Renie frowned. "Was he the one who fell out of the chandelier?"

"No," Judith replied with a shake of her head. "In fact, that's how we got on the subject of insurance. We were talking about the various injuries sustained during the cocktail party. You know, the fall and the explosion and all that. Doodles mentioned that he insured pets. I suppose that includes horses." She gave Alex an inquiring glance.

Alex, however, was more interested in the cocktail party. "I say, it sounds like a real bash. How did I miss it?"

Before the cousins could explain, Charles entered the room, glowering. "Pushy, that's what the police are. What else can we tell them? Now they're threatening to bring in the Yard. And all because Aunt Pet was rich."

Refreshing his drink, Alex was unperturbed. "They won't ask for help from the Yard. The local coppers hate to do that. It makes them look stupid."

An uneasy sensation settled over Judith. "Are they trying to tell us that they haven't any leads?"

Behind the bar, Charles all but shoved Alex out of the way. "That's what I gather," he muttered, pouring himself a brandy.

Alex's handsome face contorted in what Judith guessed was an effort at deep thinking. "It's obvious, isn't it? The one person with a grudge shows up at Ravenscroft House for the first time in donkey's years. He brings Aunt Pet a box of poisoned chocolates. The next day, she's dead." Alex shrugged. "What's so difficult?"

Charles was fingering his chin. "Colonel Chelmsford? I wouldn't put it past the old bugger. But killing Aunt Pet doesn't solve his legal dilemma. The courts must do that."

Alex gave Charles a patronizing look. "Chummy's disagreeable. He'd been on bad terms with Aunt Pet for years. He wanted to get even with her for causing problems. Maybe he figured that if she was dead, the rest of us wouldn't fight him in court." Alex draped himself on the Chippendale chair. "Has anybody got a better solution?"

The contempt on Charles's face changed to distress. "No, actually," he admitted. "You're quite right, Alex. It must have been Chummy. If not . . ." His entire body gave off a small shudder.

Nats was back in the doorway. Apparently, she had overheard some of the exchange between Charles and her brother. "If not, what? Go ahead, say it—if Colonel Chelmsford didn't poison Aunt Pet, then it had to be one of us." Her dark gaze roamed from Alex and Charles to Judith and Renie. "Well?"

The bald truth didn't elicit any response.

Renie wanted to know why Judith had insisted on leaving the drawing room and going upstairs. Judith refused to explain until they had reached the sanctuary of her guest bedroom.

"Things are looking bleak," she announced, putting her feet up on the canopied bed while Renie collapsed in a curved Italian armchair. "Alex may not be the swiftest blade on the ice, but he's right about the police—if they're talking about the Yard coming in on this case, Wattle and Daub don't have a clue. Literally."

"Jeez!" Renie was more angry than upset. "What's wrong with Alex's theory? You're the one who said Chummy was carrying some kind of parcel when he called on Aunt Pet Friday. What, if not chocolates?"

Judith didn't respond immediately. She was writing something in the haphazard journal she had determined to keep for the trip. So far, the only entries were "Lined tartan slippers for Mother—sole grippers," "Mike—Jaeger corduroy blazer?" and "Dead ringer for Sweetums, stalking birds in vicinity of Marble Arch."

"I'm making a note of Doodles Swinford," Judith explained. "His real first name was Woodley. I remember it because it was like Joe's partner, Woodrow Price."

"Woodrow isn't like Woodley," Renie countered. "And Joe's partner is called Woody, not Noodles or Poodles, or whatever track your suddenly illogical train of thought is taking. Why do you care anyway?"

Judith refused to be nettled. "I don't know. But that episode at the stables was upsetting. I'm merely filing Doodles Swinford's name away for future note." Slipping off the bed, she poked Renie. "Let's go see Dora. It's not yet nine o'clock. She'll still be awake."

With a put-upon air, Renie followed Judith to the third floor. While still up, Dora was attired in a dark blue flannel bathrobe. Her gray hair hung in a single braid over one shoulder. She seemed startled, but not displeased, to see the cousins.

"It's so lonely up here," she lamented, inviting Judith and Renie to sit down in Aunt Pet's overcrowded sitting room. "I can hardly bear to go into the mistress's bedroom. But I must, eventually. I'll have to arrange her things for the funeral." Tears glistened in the maid's tired eyes.

Judith had assumed her most sympathetic expression. "You'll have to be very strong over the next few days," she said. "Miss Ravenscroft depended on you while she was alive, and so she will do even in death."

The doleful words actually seemed to buoy Dora. "Well, yes, now isn't that the case? My usefulness isn't over, is it? Hester said much the same thing earlier."

"Hester?" It took a moment for the name to register with Judith. "Oh—Mrs. Tichborne. That's right, you have a lot of responsibility. It's a good thing you're accustomed to it. Miss Ravenscroft must have been very dependent on you."

Despite herself, Dora preened just a bit. "Well now, I must admit she was fairly helpless. Getting her dressed, fetching her meals, doing her hair, helping with the bath—

yes, it was all on my shoulders. Not that I minded. That was my job, and as the good Lord knows, I'd done it since I was a girl. But then what else could I do?'' Her gaze shifted into the shadows and her small face sagged.

Renie, for whom sentiment was a wasted emotion, tapped the arm of her mohair chair. ''Teacher? Nurse? Secretary? Brain surgeon?'' Noting Dora's astonished reaction, she offered a self-deprecating smile. ''My mother's older than you are, Dora. She was a legal secretary for more than forty years. Judith's mother was a bookkeeper for some doctors. Even a half-century ago, there were choices.''

Though true, the declaration didn't sit well with Dora Hobbs. ''Your mothers are Americans,'' she said in a defensive manner. ''It was different here. Especially for me.'' Again, the maid looked away.

Judith was about to intervene, but Renie never gave up easily. ''Why was that?'' she asked. As usual, her sympathy seemed forced, even when it was sincere.

Backed into a corner, Dora lifted her chin. ''Because it was charity, pure and simple. I was brought into this house under a cloud. Miss Pet took pity on me. She gave me a post as her maid. And why not, I ask you? I've done my job, and done it well. Should I be ashamed?''

If not always compassionate, Renie was basically reasonable. ''No. Of course not. But I get annoyed by women who pretend that until the last twenty years, their only job opportunities were being a housewife or a hooker.'' Seeing Dora blanch, Renie waved a hand. ''No offense. I was curious, that's all.''

While some sort of minor alarm bell had gone off in Judith's head, she felt it was imperative to rescue the conversation. ''I'm curious, too,'' she put in, smiling at Dora and wishing Renie would stick her head under the mohair cushions. ''On Friday, when Colonel Chelmsford came by, what did he bring for Miss Ravenscroft?''

Dora was clearly puzzled. ''The colonel? Why, nothing. He wouldn't bring the mistress anything but trouble!''

Judith persisted. ''He was carrying a parcel when Claire let him in.''

Dora's frown deepened. ''So he was. I'd forgotten.''

Her pinched face grew stricken. "Oh, my! You don't think . . . ? Surely not!"

"Anything's possible," Judith said evenly. "Could it have been a box of chocolates?"

Dora floundered in the wingback chair. "How horrible! But somebody must have done . . . No, not Colonel Chelmsford! I remember now, I threw the empty box away myself."

"*Empty* box?" Judith echoed. "What sort of box?"

Calming herself, Dora reflected. "It was . . . just a box. Brown or tan. Unless the police took it, I suppose it's still in the wastepaper basket in Miss Petulia's room. The daily doesn't empty the trash until Monday."

"Let's look," Judith suggested, getting up. She noted Dora's hesitation. "Do you mind?"

Dora put a hand to her head. "But why?"

Judith admitted she didn't know. "It could be important. If nothing else, it might prove that Colonel Chelmsford didn't poison Miss Ravenscroft."

Without Aunt Pet's presence, the bedroom seemed not only empty, but a little shabby. Dora went over to the wastebasket that stood next to an escritoire. The contents had been removed from the basket, presumably by the police.

"I know the box was empty," Dora insisted. "Miss Petulia said as much. She wanted to be rid of it."

Judith nodded, noting that the inside of the metal wastebasket was badly scorched. "But the box wasn't empty when Colonel Chelmsford arrived. I wonder what it held?"

Renie was examining the escritoire, which was from a somewhat earlier era than most of the other furniture in the suite. "You didn't stay in the room after the colonel arrived?" she asked Dora.

The maid looked vaguely affronted. "My, no! It wasn't my place. Not that Colonel Chelmsford stayed long. Miss Petulia sent him packing after about five minutes."

"I don't suppose," Judith said innocently, "you happened to hear any of the conversation. The colonel speaks rather loudly sometimes."

Dora looked pained. "Well . . . that he does. Quite the

shouter is the colonel. I was in the sitting room, mending. It would have been impossible *not* to catch a word or two.'' Dora looked rather defensive.

''Such as?'' Judith said encouragingly.

Dora's pained expression grew more pronounced. ''That's the problem. It didn't make sense. The police already asked me. And of course, I am a wee bit hard of hearing. The only words I heard Colonel Chelmsford say were 'clutches' and 'moonstruck' and 'ingratitude.' The mistress said something about 'duty' and 'betrayal.' I can't think what either of them could have meant. Can you?''

Neither Judith nor Renie could. ''Whatever it was,'' Judith said, ''it doesn't sound like a property dispute. You didn't hear anything about boundary lines or fences or variances?''

Dora slowly shook her head. ''No—not that I was *listening*, of course. Still, one couldn't help but overhear.'' Her eyes widened. ''What was it you said? Valences?''

''Variances,'' Judith repeated. ''They have something to do with property, at least in the States.''

Again, Dora grew puzzled. ''That wasn't the word . . . It was like that, though. Cadence, maybe.''

Now Judith was looking mystified. ''I don't get it.'' She turned as Renie scraped open a drawer in the escritoire.

''Excuse me, Dora,'' Renie said with an apologetic smile. ''I'm saving my cousin the embarrassment of being a sneak. Maybe there's something in this desk that will enlighten us about the new will.''

Judith shot Renie a wry look. ''If there is, Wattle's got it. Why do you think I'm not already pouncing on the furniture?''

But Renie wasn't giving up. Judith and Dora joined her. The drawers yielded very little. Unused stationery, postcards saved as keepsakes, a book of spiritual devotions, bottles of ink, Scotch tape, scissors, stamps, a tablet of lined paper, and unsharpened pencils seemed to be all that was left from the official police perusal. The only thing that seemed out of place was a tiny scrap of paper, caught between the side and the bottom of the lower right-hand drawer. Renie tugged it free.

"This was torn off something," she said without interest. "It's just a date. The twenty-seventh of April."

Dora studied the tiny fragment. "That's Miss Petulia's handwriting. Oh, my! To think she'll never write anything again!"

"Hard to do when you're dead," Renie murmured under her breath. Fortunately, Dora didn't hear her. The maid was now watching Judith go through the drawer in the nightstand next to the bed. Apparently, it finally dawned on the old woman that the cousins were being a trifle forward.

"Pardon," Dora said in a meek voice, "but are you allowed to do this? That is, wouldn't Mr. or Mrs. Marchmont object?"

Renie obligingly ran interference for Judith. "Now, Dora," she began, "if they cared, would they let us come up here? They're as anxious to find out who killed Miss Ravenscroft as we are. This may surprise you, but my cousin here is actually *married to a policemen*."

Dora was aghast. "You don't say! Oh, my!" She gave Renie a tremulous smile. "Had I but known . . . by all means, do what you will!"

"I'm doing it," Judith said in a somewhat aggrieved tone, "but it isn't getting us anywhere. There's nothing in this drawer but junk. Uh . . . *stuff*, I mean. Magazines and odds and ends." To prove her point, she waved what looked like a broken gold chain at Dora.

Dora, however, was transfixed. "What *is* that? I've never seen it before!" The maid grabbed at the chain, jerking it out of Judith's hand with a surprisingly strong grip.

With some trepidation, Judith sat down on Aunt Pet's bed. Dora either didn't mind or was too mesmerized to notice. "Goodness," the maid said in a soft voice, "wherever did this come from? It wasn't there Friday."

Judith dug into the drawer again. "What about this?" she inquired, holding up what looked like a small jewel case or a pillbox.

Dora stared. "Nor that! It's a cufflink case. Miss Petulia never had one of those! It's for men."

The drawer also revealed brushes, two tie clasps, and a tooth mug. Dora swore she had never seen them before in her life. When Judith hauled out a double picture frame, the maid finally nodded.

"That belonged to the mistress. But the rest . . ." Her voice trailed off. "I don't understand. I was in and out of that drawer ever so often. Miss Petulia kept her eyeglasses there when she wasn't using them."

Judith was opening the picture frames, which had been held shut with a simple clasp. The posed photographs that looked out at her were of the same young woman. Somehow they seemed familiar.

"Ah!" Judith exclaimed, showing the pictures to Renie and Dora. "This is the girl in the entry hall portraits. She must be about my age. Downstairs, she's wearing a dress like my prom outfit, and later a satin gown I'd have killed for in my twenties. Who is it?"

Dora, however, was still frowning at the items she didn't recognize. "This is ever so odd. Why would Miss Petulia have a tooth mug in her drawer? Or these other things? I rummaged through here Thursday trying to find an emery board."

Realizing that Judith and Dora were talking at cross purposes, Renie intervened: "It seems to me that everything in the drawer that's new belongs to a man. For instance, a cufflink case and what looks like a watch chain. Could those be the items that Colonel Chelmsford had in the brown box?"

Dora's attention was finally captured. "Well . . . maybe. It was fairly deep. It could have been a boot box. But why?"

Judith was trying to think. "Souvenirs? Something that was borrowed? What ties did the colonel have with this family besides being the next-door neighbor?"

Dora was bewildered. "None, that I know of. He hadn't been near Ravenscroft House in forty years."

As usual, Judith was applying logic. "But if none of these items was here Thursday, it makes sense to assume that they could have been brought by the colonel on Friday. Something was in that box. And because this stuff is innocuous, the police left it here. They wouldn't consider a tooth mug as evidence."

Distractedly, Dora nodded. "It's possible. But I can't think why."

Judith couldn't either. She shoved the framed photographs in front of Dora. "Who is this? She's very lovely."

Dora gave a start and drew back. "That's Fleur, Miss Natasha and Master Alexei's mother." Judith started to nod, but the maid hadn't finished. "She's on the right. The one on the left is her twin sister, Aimee. They're both dead, poor things. Or so I've been told."

Dora began to cry.

THIRTEEN

JUDITH SHOULD HAVE known. In alluding to her own two sons, Claire had mentioned that twins ran in the family. Yet there had been no other reference to them. Certainly Margaret's letters had never mentioned twins as a Marchmont phenomenon. But they had shown up in the Ravenscroft line, and not just in the youngest generation. Fleur Ravenscroft Karamzin had had a twin sister, Aimee, and apparently both women were deceased.

"What happened?" Judith asked when Dora had finally wiped her eyes and becalmed herself. "No one has ever mentioned Aimee."

"I'm not to tell," Dora said in a miserable voice. "It's a family secret."

Briefly, Judith recalled the two portraits in the entrance hall. She had assumed they were of the same young woman. But now she realized that one of the sisters had been painted in adolescence, and the other a decade later.

"Aimee," Judith breathed, recalling Claire's eagerness to move away from the paintings. "Aimee ran away as a teenager."

Dora was startled. "How did you know?"

Judith shrugged. "Because she isn't more than sixteen in either of the two pictures I've seen. Fleur is. And since she's Nats and Alex's mother, I know she stayed around until she and her husband, Viktor, were killed in the car crash. So it must be her twin, Aimee, who took off. Just like Janet Tichborne.''

But Dora shook her head. "No, not like Janet. Not in the least. Miss Aimee eloped. She was fifteen. Miss Petulia didn't approve of the match. Miss Aimee and her young man left the country. They became Bohemians.''

"What?'' Renie made a face. "Legally? Or do you mean spiritually?''

Dora seemed confused. "I mean, they went to Paris. They lived in an attic or something like that. They were poor. Isn't that what Bohemians do?''

Slowly, Judith nodded. "They did that mostly in the nineteenth century. But in the mid-twentieth, they were called Beatniks. At least they were in the States. What happened to Aimee and her husband?''

Dora dabbed at her eyes with a handkerchief. "I don't know. I heard they died. Strong wine, I suppose. Isn't that how Bohemians meet their untimely end?''

"Drugs,'' Renie stated. "This isn't Puccini, it's Kerouac.'' Noting Dora's blank expression, she waved a hand in dismissal. "Never mind. I don't suppose this has anything to do with Aunt Pet being murdered. How long ago did Aimee and Mr. Pot-Zen croak?''

"Potson?'' Dora had gone beyond bewilderment. "There never was a Potson in Little Pauncefoot. He was a Somerset lad, but I didn't know his name. It wasn't my place to ask.''

Feeling somewhat at sea, Judith also felt obligated to sort out the family tree. "But you must know when Aimee and her husband passed away.''

Dora's vague expression sharpened a jot. "It was ten years ago. No, more than that—fifteen or twenty, even. Time goes by ever so quick. Miss Petulia got a letter from Paris. She said it served them right. Miss Aimee had stolen from the family. Jewels, to finance her Bohemian life abroad.''

Judith recalled the robbery which had been claimed by Genevieve Ravenscroft. Aunt Pet had argued otherwise. Perhaps she had known that Aimee had stolen from her own mother. The truth might have been too cruel for even Aunt Pet to admit.

"Interesting," she remarked, finally closing the drawer to the nightstand. "So this is also where the box of chocolates was found?"

Dora grew chagrined. "They were underneath the other things," she asserted. "I wouldn't have seen them. All those magazines were on top. You can't accuse me of *snooping*."

Judith patted Dora's small hand. "We wouldn't think of it," she said, suppressing a yawn. The fright at the stables and the session in Aunt Pet's bedroom had not only frustrated Judith, but made her tired. "We'll leave you in peace now. It's getting late, and we've all been up since before dawn."

Dora didn't argue, though she seemed eager to quit her mistress's bedroom. A few moments later, the cousins were back downstairs, seeking their guest quarters.

"I hope Dora's not too upset," Renie said in a worried tone. "I don't like the idea of her starting a fire in the middle of the night. Aunt Pet's not around to raise the alarm."

Judith acknowledged the fact with an apprehensive look. "Something was burned in that wastebasket. Recently, too." She held up a smudged index finger. "I wonder what it was?"

Renie raised both eyebrows. "Chummy's box?"

But Judith shook her head. "Dora may be a pyromaniac, but she's not a liar. Or an amnesiac. She was sure the police took the box away, and I believe her." Judith yawned. "I'm beat. It's only ten o'clock, but we didn't get much sleep last night. I'm turning in."

Renie nodded. "Me, too. We should get up for the inquest tomorrow, I suppose."

Judith sighed. "Right. It won't help much, though."

"No," Renie agreed. "But it'll be a new tourist experience." She tried to give Judith a bright smile.

Judith couldn't quite manage to reciprocate. Twenty minutes later, she was in bed. Twenty seconds later, she was asleep. It was shortly after 2 A.M. when Harwood banged on her door, wheezing his way through an announcement of an overseas call for Mrs. Flynn.

Mentally fogged in, Judith struggled to put on her robe and stagger down the hall to the library. Despite her semiconscious state, a sense of disaster crept up her spine. Grabbing the receiver, she expected the worst of news.

She was almost right. The voice at the other end of the line belonged to Gertrude.

"Say," Judith's mother began, sounding far too sprightly for the middle of the night, "if you're going to Sweden, how about picking up some of those Christmas chimes. You know, the little angels that fly around the candles and look like they're setting their nighties on fire."

Judith knew she must be dreaming. Her mother couldn't possibly have called her at 2 A.M. from nine thousand miles away to ask her to buy Swedish Christmas chimes.

"Since this isn't real," Judith said in a wispy voice, "let's pretend I already bought them. They're in your refrigerator, next to the blue ham and the rusty lettuce."

"Listen, fathead," Gertrude rasped, "I didn't make this phone call to joke around. I'm eating ham right now, for my supper. Want to hear me snap my dentures?"

Sinking down behind the mahogany desk, Judith blinked against the light from the green-shaded lamp. "This is truly you and not my worst nightmare?" Or, she asked herself, is it both?

"Who else would it be, dummy? I got the number from Deb. Renie gave it to her. Deb said the rates are down all day Sunday, so I'm saving money. What are you having for supper? I'll bet you a quarter it's not as tasty as this ham."

Briefly, Judith considered enlightening her mother. It wasn't suppertime in England. It was no longer Sunday. But Gertrude refused to accept the eight-hour time change.

"Mother, we're not going to Sweden," Judith said at last. "I can get those chimes for you at home. How are you . . . otherwise?"

The pause that followed was almost imperceptible. "Well—now that you ask, I guess I'd better tell you." Gertrude sounded unusually solemn. "My butt fell off."

"*What*?" Judith jiggled the phone as if she could correct what she'd just heard.

"I don't mean it fell off of *me*," Gertrude explained. "It fell off of the couch. Unfortunately, I was still attached to it. I cracked my tailbone. I'm in the hospital. They brought my ham supper twenty minutes ago. Breakfast and lunch were pretty good, too."

Now shocked into full consciousness, Judith was upset. "Mother, are you okay? Exactly what happened?"

Gertrude's chuckle was faintly subdued. "It was about ten-thirty last night, and I was watching John Wayne in that movie where the Japs get so nasty and then he wipes 'em all out at the end and we win the war. You remember that?"

"I remember the war. Barely. I was two at the time." Judith wondered if Charles kept any scotch in the library.

"You'd turned four by V-J Day, dopey," Gertrude reminded her daughter. "Anyway, they got to the part where the Duke—I forget the name of the guy John Wayne was playing—is in the bushes and these Japs are sneaking up behind him and they're about to riddle him with their machine guns, and I yelled, 'Look out, Duke!' and I sort of jumped up and the next thing I knew, I fell off the couch."

"Off the couch," Judith echoed. The short fall shouldn't have done more than shake up Gertrude. But of course she was old and her bones were brittle. "So how did you get up?"

"I didn't," Gertrude replied. "My butt hurt too much. Besides, I had to make sure that the Duke would shoot all those Japs. Then I tried to call Arlene Rankers, but I couldn't find the phone."

Judith was puzzled. "You couldn't . . . ? How come?" Over her mother's protests, Judith had recently bought her a cordless phone which she could carry along with her cigarettes in a small bag on her walker. When Gertrude watched TV, she always kept the phone next to her on the couch.

"That's what *I* wanted to know," Gertrude answered indignantly. "Your dumb cat's never figured out how to use the phone, so who else would've taken it? It isn't like I've got a steady stream of people coming through my so-called apartment to howdy-do me. How many could I fit into a hatbox anyway? I'll tell you one thing, kiddo, when my time comes, you won't have to buy a coffin. Just nail up the door to this place, tip it over, and slide me down Heraldsgate Hill. 'Course you better make sure you've dug a hole at the bottom first. I don't want to end up out in the bay.''

"Mother . . ." While too familiar with Gertrude's self-pitying diversions, Judith could practically hear the phone bill mounting. "How did you reach Arlene? Did you yell?"

"You bet. And bless her heart, she heard me because she was just coming home from a wedding reception at church. Well, you know how she fusses over me—she insisted I see a doctor, just in case I'd busted something. So she and Carl got me into their car and we went to the emergency room. They took some X rays, and along about midnight, they told me I'd broken my tailbone. Then, seeing as how I'm old and infirm and my only living daughter is off gallivanting around Finland, the doctor thought I should stay here for a couple of days. Unless you and Lunkhead want to fly home and nurse me, of course. *Do you?*''

The question caught Judith off-guard. "Ah . . . well . . . we can't\ . . . even if we wanted . . . I mean, our tickets were prepurchased for certain dates. And besides, Renie and I are sort of . . . stuck.'' There was no scotch in any of the desk drawers. Judith decided to skip telling her mother about Aunt Pet's murder.

"Aha!" Gertrude cried. "I knew it, you won't come back to take care of me! Off to the pest house! I can just lie here and rot, right? Did I say this ham was good? I lied. It stinks. I think it's made of wrapping paper. You know, the plain unmarked brown kind your Aunt Ellen uses for her Christmas presents.''

"Mother—if you're really in a bad way, maybe I could fly home tomorrow or the day after. I mean it, I won't let you suffer alone.'' Judith paused as she noticed a handwritten sheet of paper in the last drawer she'd opened. The spidery text in deep blue ink looked very old-fashioned. Judith slipped the single sheet under the desk lamp. "Let me talk to the nurse. Are you in pain?"

"Am I a pain? Very funny, Judith Anne. And no, you

can't talk to the nurse. She's busy." Gertrude's voice suddenly became muffled, as if she'd put her hand over the receiver.

"When will they send you home? Can you take care of yourself? What kind of medication are you on?" Judith's voice grew more frantic as she tried to divide her attention between Gertrude and what was obviously the original copy of Aunt Pet's handwritten will.

"They're giving me something—something with codeine. I forget, it's a long, goofy name." Gertrude was again coming through loud and clear. "Listen, rumdum, I've got to go. The nurse needs me."

Judith gave a start. "The nurse needs *you*? What for?"

Gertrude chuckled, a faintly evil sound. "It's my turn to shuffle the cards. We're playing crib. I'm winning."

Judith held her head. "Mother! What about the phone? Did you ever find it? You can page it, you know, by going to the base and pushing the button that says—"

"Of course I found the phone," Gertrude snapped. "That's how I cracked my tailbone. I sat on it when I fell off the couch."

"Oh." Judith's voice had grown faint. "I see. I guess. Okay, Mother, I'll check back with you later today. I'm glad you told me about your accident, but you shouldn't have spent the money to call."

"What money?" Gertrude replied in a testy voice. "It's not *my* money. I called collect. So long, sucker. Fifteen-two, fifteen-four, and a pair is—" The phone clicked in Judith's ear.

Judith leaned on the desk. It wouldn't be right to wake Renie up at two-twenty in the morning. It wouldn't be smart, either. Disturbing her for the second night in a row might provoke Renie's violent tendencies. The news about Gertrude could wait. So, Judith realized, could Gertrude. Obviously, she was not seriously harmed. For all Judith knew, her mother might have fallen off the couch on purpose. The Rankerses would supervise Gertrude's wellbeing. And that of Sweetums. Or so Judith hoped. Given the circumstances, she couldn't do much else. Carl and Arlene had earned a lavish present. Vaguely, Judith wondered how they'd like a bone china meat platter. But after thirty-seven years of marriage and five kids, they probably had at least three of them. Judith would shop for something else in Edinburgh. If she ever got there.

Trying to put aside the image of Gertrude suffering in a lonely hospital bed, or worse yet, Gertrude haranguing the benighted staff into submission, Judith read through Aunt Pet's Last Will and Testament. Or at least her intended final will.

For apparently this was the document that the police had found in Petulia Ravenscroft's bedroom. Judith assumed they had made copies and left the original with the family. It was indeed Aunt Pet's desire to leave Ravenscroft House to Claire Ravenscroft Marchmont and her spouse, Charles Marchmont. There followed the other bequests, to Natasha and Alexei Karamazin, to the Marchmont twins, to George and Emily Ravenscroft, to the faithful servants, Hobbs, Tichborne, and Harwood. And, at the bottom of the page in an even shakier hand, Aunt Pet had written the fateful words:

"That in gratitude for their friendship and their family's service to God and country, I do hereby devise and bequeath to Judith Grover Flynn and Serena Grover Jones the gatehouse that stands on the same property as . . ."

Judith sighed. The gesture was appreciated, but in fairness, the gatehouse should have gone to Walter Paget. The steward was definitely omitted from the will. It was impossible not to wonder why. Certainly Walter had served the family faithfully for over ten years, maybe more. Judith glanced at the date below Aunt Pet's florid signature: 24 April. Saturday had been the twenty-fourth of the month. Obviously, this was Aunt Pet's most recent wish for the division of her estate. Judith smoothed the paper with her right hand before replacing it in the drawer.

It was then that she realized there was something not quite right about the paper itself. It was from an ordinary writing tablet, probably the one Judith and Renie had seen in the escritoire. But somehow it looked odd. Judith stared at the sheet, but couldn't figure out why. Maybe she was imagining things. That would be easy to do at two-thirty in the morning. With a shake of her head, Judith put the will back in the drawer, turned off the desk lamp, and carefully made her way out of the library.

Surprisingly, she went back to sleep. It was almost eight o'clock when she woke up. At the bathroom door, she heard Renie cussing.

"What's wrong, coz?" Judith called.

"Shut the hell up," Renie shouted back. "I'm flossing. It makes my gums bleed. I'm offering it up to St. Apollonia. She's in charge of teeth."

Judith leaned against the door. She was always startled by Renie's devotion to various saints and her urge to offer up whatever physical affliction she was suffering at the moment.

"Which saint's in charge of butts?" Judith inquired after a long silence. "Mother fell off the couch and dented hers. I think she's okay, but she's in the hospital."

"What?" Renie yelled back, then yanked open the door. "Your mother's in the hospital? What happened?"

Judith explained. Renie shuddered. "Oh, great! Now my mother will try to top her. What will she do? Roll her wheelchair down the stairs of her apartment and crush Mrs. Parker and her repulsive poodle, Ignatz?"

"Probably," Judith replied, scooting past Renie. "I'm going to shower. By the way, I saw the will."

Renie made a dive for Judith, but missed. Judith closed the bathroom door almost but not quite shut. "No surprises," Judith said, peering at Renie through the crack. "It's lucid, signed and dated. Ergo, it may hold up in court." The door clicked into place.

At precisely nine o'clock, Judith and Renie arrived in the dining room for breakfast. Except for Alex, the rest of the family was already seated.

"Millie didn't show up," Charles announced in a grumble. "She handed in her notice. Mrs. Tichborne is serving under duress."

"Good," Renie retorted, piling lamb kidneys and kippers and tomato slices onto her plate. Noting the startled looks on her hosts' faces, she smiled apologetically. "I mean, Mrs. Tichborne knows how to cook. That is, she makes delicious meals. Not that Millie wasn't just fine and dandy, but ...'' With a helpless shrug, Renie sat down next to Nats, who was openly sulking.

"I wonder," Judith said to cover the awkwardness caused by Renie's implied criticism of the Marchmonts' daily help, "if the police have talked to Millie."

Claire jumped in her chair. "Millie? But why?"

Charles, however, understood the question. "They may have. But Millie hadn't been with us long." He glanced inquiringly at his wife. "A month? Two, perhaps? She wasn't here during the winter. Prunes did for us at holiday time, eh?"

"Yes, that's so." Claire dabbed at her mouth with a napkin. "Prunella Raikes. Then there was Myra Stodgely. Or was she between Prunes and Millie? I can never keep track—Aunt Pet had a stream of dailies. So difficult to get good help. Auntie was hard to please. Rest her soul."

Judith, who had dished up eggs, bacon, and toast from the sideboard, mentally scratched Millie from her list of suspects. Not, she knew from unfortunate experience, that you could ever completely dismiss anyone. But from what she knew of Millie, the woman lacked not only motive, but cunning.

"What's going to happen at the inquest?" Judith asked, looking beyond Nats's sullen face.

Charles slathered raspberry jam on his toast. "Couldn't say, really. I suppose Dr. Ramsey will give his statement, as will the police. I doubt that any of us will be called. Except Dora, perhaps."

Somewhat stiltedly, Claire passed the jampot to Nats, who snatched it away and gave her cousin a venomous look. "Dora shouldn't have to testify," Claire asserted. "It's too much to ask of her. And whatever could she tell them?"

"How should I know?" Charles snapped. "I don't know what they'll ask."

Alex breezed into the room, looking only somewhat the worse for wear. "Sorry I'm late. Any kippers left?" He lifted the silver lids in turn. "I say! Kidneys! Tichborne does them to a turn!"

"Of the stomach," Judith said under her breath with an ironic glance at Renie. The cousins had a longstanding argument over whether grilled lamb kidneys were fit for human consumption. Judith thought not. Renie was even now stuffing half a kidney in her mouth.

Nats seemed to echo Judith's revulsion, but in a more general way. "I'm sick of all of you," she snarled, speaking for the first time since the cousins had entered the room. Abruptly, Nats stood up and started out of the dining room. "Go to the inquest without me. I'll walk." She banged the door behind her.

Charles pitched his napkin onto the table. "Dash it all! What's gotten into Nats now?"

Claire was wearing an aggrieved expression. "I told you, Charles, she's upset about Walter. Nats and I had a little talk last night. I informed her that the engagement was impossible."

Charles's face had grown impassive. "I see," he said woodenly. "That, of course, explains it. Yes, that's it exactly." Nodding to himself twice, he relaxed and drank his coffee.

"Explains what?" Claire asked on a note of sudden anxiety.

Charles put down his coffee cup and made as if to rise. "Millie wasn't the only one to give notice this morning. Walter tendered his resignation, too." Excusing himself, Charles left the dining room.

Although they hadn't realized it at the time, Judith and Renie had seen the local library on their walk the previous day. The post-World War II building was across the road from the converted almshouses, and its architecture was so nondescript that the cousins had assumed it was a storage complex or the local telephone exchange.

The inquest was held in a room that was obviously used for civic and fraternal meetings. It looked to Judith like a small lecture hall, with folding chairs, a long table, and an elevated lectern off to one side. The ventilation was poor and the overhead fluorescent lighting lent a sickly pallor to everyone present.

And everyone *was* present, it seemed to Judith. Almost all of Little Pauncefoot was crammed into the meeting room, including the vicar, the woman who ran the tea shop, and the redheaded mother who stood at the back, gently rocking the pram to and fro. However, two people Judith expected to see were missing: Walter Paget and Colonel Chelmsford weren't in the audience.

Judith poked Renie in the ribs. "Can you spot the media types?"

Renie scanned the room. "Two print, one male, one female. No TV. Or radio, unless the old coot in the deerstalker is holding a tape recorder up to his ear."

Judith regarded the elderly man in the deerstalker. "That's a hearing aid, coz. I wonder why there isn't more coverage? In mystery novels, reporters always descend on the scene of the crime like locusts."

"You're in a time warp with your mother," Renie whispered as someone who looked like a magistrate ascended the makeshift dais. "Those books were written fifty years ago, when murder was a novelty. The public's jaded here, just like at home. They'd rather read about cabinet members in a love nest or soccer riots or the royals exposing their private . . . whatevers." Renie turned her attention to the front of the room. Judith followed suit, though she tried to keep the family members within her purview. Charles and Claire sat in the second row with Alex right behind them. Across the aisle, Mrs. Tichborne, Harwood, and Dora huddled together, appearing to seek comfort from each other. Or, Judith realized, perhaps it was an illusion caused by Harwood listing this way and that. Nats had distanced herself from the others by sitting at the back of the room, not far from a nervous-looking Arthur Tinsley. Lona was at his side, wearing a suitably solemn expression. Judith wondered if Mrs. Tinsley ever smiled.

The proceedings went just as Charles had predicted. Dr. Ramsey gave his evidence, as did the police medical examiner, Constable Duff, and Inspector Wattle. To Judith's relief, Dora Hobbs was not called to the stand, nor were any of the other members of the Ravenscroft household. After a mere twenty minutes, the inquest was adjourned

with the expected verdict of "willful murder by a person
or persons unknown."

Judith exchanged a bemused glance with Renie. A
shocked communal whisper ran through the meeting room.
Inspector Wattle was the first one out the door. Caught up
in the crowd, the cousins heard snatches of conversation.

"Imagine! Here in Little Pauncefoot!" "Just like the
telly, only more real . . ." "Well, I never! Gave me a turn,
it did . . ." "Murder! Why bother, when the old girl would
have bought it before long anyway?"

Why indeed, thought Judith. If she knew *why,* she'd
know *who.* But at the moment, she felt as if she knew next
to nothing.

FOURTEEN

OUTSIDE, ON THE plain concrete walk that led to the road, Judith noticed the inspector in deep conversation with a heavy-jawed man wearing a black mackintosh. Wattle's superior, she mused, or perhaps someone from Scotland Yard. Sergeant Daub stood off to one side, looking deferential. Judith considered approaching him, but was diverted by the woman with the pram.

"Pardon," she said softly, rolling past the cousins. By chance, one wheel of the pram struck a pebble, derailing mother and child. Judith raced to the rescue.

The young woman let out a squeak of concern, but the chubby redheaded baby was squealing with delight. Judith helped right the pram back onto the walk. The grateful mother thanked her.

"That's okay," Judith said with a bright smile. "Your baby is adorable. What's his name?"

"Maureen," the woman replied.

"Oh!" Judith's smile went awry. "Sorry, he ... ah ... she looks so robust! I always assume that such ... *husky* babies are boys. How old is she?"

"Six months." The young woman was now smiling and cooing at the child. "Thank you again."

Judith kept pace with the pram, though she was forced to walk on the grass. Renie trailed along behind the woman, looking mildly annoyed. The cloudy sky had brought a soft drizzle to Little Pauncefoot.

"You must be Bridget," Judith said, holding her breath for the answer.

The pram jerked to a partial stop. "Why, yes! Bridget Horan. How did you know?" The young woman's blue eyes were wide under the wealth of red curls.

Renie's eyes were also wide, just before they rolled up into her head. Doggedly, she kept moving; the exiting mass of villagers were now crowding along the walk, abuzz with excitement over the shocking murder that had disturbed their usually placid little world.

"Janet's mother told me," Judith said, not daring to look at Renie. "You know—Mrs. Tichborne, the Ravenscroft housekeeper."

For just a moment, Bridget's entire body seemed to give off a small shudder. Or, Judith thought, trying not to be too fanciful, she'd encountered another pebble.

But when Bridget Horan spoke, her manner was composed. "My, I haven't thought about Janet Tichborne in quite a while! I suppose it's because of the baby. They take so much time and energy." Bridget's expression was fondly focussed on the gurgling infant.

They had reached the road, but were forced to wait while several vehicles came out of the library car park. "We're staying at Ravenscroft House," Judith explained. "It's been quite an experience."

Bridget's plain but pleasant face turned sympathetic. "I should say so! How terrible for you! Are you frightened?"

"Frightened?" The question caught Judith off-guard. She glanced at Renie, who emitted a shiver of mock terror behind Bridget's back. "Well—not really." Judith grimaced. It was hard to explain the cousins' previous encounters with murder and mayhem to a stranger.

"I see." Bridget had grown wary. There was a break in the traffic. "Pardon, I must be getting home. Maureen needs to be fed."

"No, she doesn't," Renie muttered as Bridget and baby crossed the road. "That kid has enough food stored up for the next six months." She gave Judith's jacket sleeve a tug. "What was that all about? And how come you knew who she was?"

The cousins began ambling away from the library area. Despite Nats' defection, there hadn't been enough room in the two cars for the cousins. Consequently, they had volunteered to walk the short distance to the inquest.

"I told you—and Bridget. Mrs. Tichborne mentioned that her daughter had a friend named Bridget. She was Irish-Catholic. So many Irish—like Joe—have red hair. How many women in Janet's age bracket of their late twenties have that coloring in a village the size of Little Pauncefoot? If she wasn't Bridget, she'd know who was." Judith walked purposefully across River Lane.

"Okay," Renie said reasonably. "So why do we care?"

"I'm not sure we do," Judith answered candidly. "But I have to wonder why Janet disappeared. What happened to her? Where did she go? Now it turns out that two young women have run away from Ravenscroft House. Is that a coincidence?"

"I doubt it, since Aimee and Janet took off twenty-five years apart," Renie noted, pausing to gaze at the butcher's offerings of fresh pork, lamb, beef, and chicken. The cousins had entered the High Street, which was unnaturally peopled this Monday morning by the crowd dispersing from the inquest. The drizzle had turned into a full-blown spring shower. Passing the greengrocer, Judith looked across the way to the gabled office building that housed the doctor and the solicitor.

"I wonder if Dr. Ramsey is back in his surgery," Judith said, more to herself than to Renie. "You got any pains, coz?"

"Only you." Renie made a face at Judith, but trotted dutifully alongside her cousin. April rain neither daunted nor disturbed the pair of native Pacific Northwesterners; the cousins didn't own an umbrella between them. "Why are we worrying about side issues?" Renie demanded. "Isn't a big estate sufficient motive to bump off Aunt Pet?"

"It isn't the only motive," Judith replied, pressing the buzzer above the brass plate that read "*Lawrence Ramsey, M.D.*" The common entryway to the law and medical offices was faced by white doors with small mullioned windows. "From what I can tell, nobody knew she'd changed

her will to favor the family and servants. Money notwithstanding, Aunt Pet ran their lives. I wonder if she knew
about Nats and Walter Paget.''

''Are you thinking what I'm thinking about Walter and
Claire?'' Renie asked.

But Judith had no chance to answer. A stout woman
wearing a white smock over a blue pantsuit opened the
door. The small brass name tag on her smock identified her
as ''*Eleanor Robbins, Receptionist.*''

Judith and Renie went through the ritual of identifying
themselves, admitting they had no appointment, but ex-
pressing grave doubts about the state of their health.

''It's my ankle,'' Judith said.

''It's my neck,'' Renie said. Unfortunately, they spoke
at the same time.

Eleanor looked dubious. ''You're both in pain?''

''It's all this stress at Ravenscroft House,'' Judith explained in a beleaguered voice.

''We can't sleep,'' Renie put in vaguely, then gave herself a shake. ''That's it! *We can't sleep.* We need sleeping
pills.'' She gave Judith a poke in the arm.

Eleanor Robbins consulted her appointment book.
''Since Doctor had to attend the inquest, we didn't book
anyone until eleven. I can squeeze you in now if you don't
think it would take too long.'' She gazed at the cousins as
if she figured whatever ailed them could be cured by a
couple of swift kicks.

''That sounds terrific,'' Renie enthused. ''We'll go in
together to save time.''

''Actually,'' the receptionist began, ''I don't think . . .''
She stopped, shrugged, and opened the door behind her
desk area. ''Dr. Ramsey, the Americans are here to pry
about Miss Ravenscroft's death. Can you see them before
Mr. Pettigrew comes in for his eleven o'clock?''

The cousins trudged sheepishly into the doctor's office.
Obviously, there was no need to go into the examining
room. Ramsey eyed them with a hint of amusement.

''You understand that I can't betray any professional
confidences?'' he remarked, offering them each a solid,
worn wooden chair. Ramsey's work space was crowded,

with a jammed roll-top desk, a scuffed leather couch, and glass-fronted bookcases. The rough whitewashed walls were virtually covered with snapshots, mostly of newborn babies and smiling toddlers.

"Oh, yes," Judith agreed, trying not to feel foolish. "We're in kind of a spot, Doctor. The police don't want us to leave Little Pauncefoot until they find the murderer. I don't suppose you have any idea who might have given Miss Pet those poisoned chocolates?"

All trace of humor fled from Dr. Ramsey's face. "No, I don't. If I had, I would have told Wattle and that sergeant of his. The St. Cloud brand is a common one and, according to the police, all but impossible to trace. They're sold throughout England, though not in Little Pauncefoot. I believe they're available in Great Pauncefoot, however, as well as Yeovil. The only thing I know for certain—and I did tell Inspector Wattle—is that Miss Ravenscroft has been eating chocolates for some time."

Judith blinked at the doctor. "Meaning . . . ? Oh, I see!" she said as enlightenment dawned. "Whoever gave them to her may have been doing it quite a while. Unless he—or she—knew Pet ate chocolates on a fairly regular basis."

The doctor nodded. "Frankly, the chocolates didn't do much harm to her digestion, as long as they weren't full of nuts. But if she overindulged—which she vehemently denied—she'd break out in hives. That's how I knew she was sneaking sweets. Last spring, she had quite a spell. I had to prescribe an antihistamine. I also lectured her about eating chocolate in any quantity."

"But," Judith inquired, "Miss Ravenscroft didn't say who had given her the chocolates in the first place?"

Dr. Ramsey uttered a small chuckle. "My, no. She wouldn't even admit she'd eaten any. Rather, she insisted one of the dailies had sneaked cocoa powder into her dinner. Miss Ravenscroft was many things, but she wasn't a good liar. Too used to being frank, I suppose."

While Judith mulled over the doctor's information, Renie posed a question of her own: "What about Dora? Wouldn't she have some idea who was bringing candy to her mistress?"

But Ramsey shook his balding head. "I took her aside and asked at the time. Dora swore she'd never seen any sweets in her mistress's room. And she certainly didn't know who'd brought them. I believe Miss Ravenscroft hid the chocolates in the bottom of her nightstand. It would be hard for Dora to look through that drawer. She and her mistress were rarely out of the room at the same time."

Judith's head shot up. "But they were the night before the murder. Aunt Pet joined us for cocktails and dinner. Dora stayed upstairs."

It was Dr. Ramsey's turn to look thoughtful. "That's so. I suppose there were occasions when . . . But surely you don't think . . . ?" He let the monstrous suggestion trail off.

"Not *that*," Judith put in hastily. "I'm not accusing Dora of poisoning Aunt Pet. But there were opportunities for the maid to search her mistress's things. And yet," she added in a puzzled voice, "she didn't. I'm sure of that."

Both Renie and Dr. Ramsey were now regarding Judith with curiosity. Judith, however, waved a hand. "Sorry, I was just trying to figure out something. Later, maybe. Doctor, how does anybody get hold of hyoscyamine?"

The doctor arched his thick eyebrows. "You mean a layperson? After consulting with the police medical examiner, I understand that the poison was in its raw state. But of course you probably gathered as much from the inquest."

Judith hadn't. Between the M.E.'s thick Cornish accent and the medical jargon, she and Renie had hardly understood a word of his testimony.

"Where do you find hyoscyamine in its raw state?" Judith asked. "Inspector Wattle mentioned plants."

"True," Ramsey replied. "There are several varieties indigenous to this area which produce the poison. In another form, hyoscyamine is quite common commercially. I prescribe it often for bladder infections."

Judith recalled the inspector's earlier comment about hyoscyamine's useful properties. "So it can be harmless?"

Dr. Ramsey nodded. "Many so-called poisons are not only harmless when properly used, but beneficial. If Miss Ravenscroft had ingested hyoscyamine in a processed form, it might be thought that she'd accidentally overdosed.

But," he continued gravely, "that wasn't how it happened. Nobody would dream of having the stuff around in its native state."

"I suppose not," Judith remarked rather absently. Her brain was concentrating on something the doctor had said earlier: Aunt Pet had developed hives the previous spring . . .

". . . smells dreadful," the doctor declared, tapping a fountain pen against his desk blotter. "Now if you'll excuse me, Mr. Pettigrew has probably arrived." Ramsey smiled politely at the cousins.

Even as Eleanor Robbins acknowledged Judith and Renie's departure with a sardonic twitch of her lips, Judith was still frowning in concentration. Mr. Pettigrew, who looked to be about as old as Aunt Pet, hobbled across the waiting room on a cane. The cousins quietly took their leave.

Renie had paused in the entryway. "Hey," she called after Judith, "are we pestering Arthur Tinsley, too?"

Judith hesitated, then shook her head. "No, not now. What smells?"

Renie sniffed. "Nothing." She sniffed again. "Oh— that's fish and chips. Hey, want to eat lunch at the pub?"

"Not yet, it's too early." Judith tugged at Renie's sleeve. "*What smells?* I missed that part."

Renie's face lighted up. "The hyoscyamine, in its natural state. Or is it the plant itself? Or plants?" Renie became hazy. "I forget. You know me, I was always poor at science. And math."

The rain had stopped and the sun was out, if briefly. The High was now all but deserted, except for two women and an elderly man who appeared to be doing the morning marketing.

Judith admired the bright geraniums and petunias and pansies in the baskets that swung from the wrought-iron lampposts. "Let's go buy some stamps," she suggested, nodding at the post office which was directly across the street. "I should write a letter to Mike."

Renie looked askance. " 'Dear Son: Found a dead body. Under suspicion of premeditated homicide. May be in mortal peril. Having a wonderful time. Love, Mom.' You can't write Mike a real letter. Besides, you won't have time until we get out of here. You're sleuthing.''

Judith was wearing a quirky smile as they crossed to the post office. ''Don't you remember how in English murder mysteries the sleuths always quiz the talkative old woman who sells stamps and postcards? They always know everything in the village. Let's give it a try.''

The woman behind the counter was in her early twenties, with a spiky pink punk haircut and three paper clips in her right earlobe. She eyed the cousins as if they'd just been turned down by a museum for quaint antiquities.

Judith, however, was undaunted. ''Hi, there. I need some stamps. Did you go to the inquest this morning?''

The pale face under the pink hair sported burnt-brown lipstick. ''What inquest?'' The voice was bored down to the depths of its husky hue.

''Miss Ravenscroft's,'' Judith said, her friendliness dropping just a jot. ''You know, the old lady who was poisoned.''

The young woman looked blank. ''Poisoned? That's what happens when you don't do the good stuff. You get what you pay for.'' With a disinterested shrug, she removed a sheet of postage stamps from a leather-bound book and pushed them at Judith. ''How many?'' she finally asked, still bored.

''Ummm . . .'' Judith tried to concentrate on calculating the denomination into a U.S.-bound air letter. ''Three?''

The young woman tore off four and waited for Judith to pay. But Judith had never quite mastered the new English currency system. She handed over a five-pound note. The young woman made change, then turned her back on the cousins. Judith and Renie started out of the post office. Colonel Chelmsford was just coming in. A flicker of recognition crossed his florid face, but he merely nodded and continued up to the counter.

''Morning, Miss Comet,'' he said to the young woman. ''Make me up a postal money order for three hundred pounds, will you?''

Judith reluctantly closed the door on the colonel and Miss Comet. ''There's one way to find out what Chummy brought in that box,'' Judith said, lingering near the entrance. "We could ask him."

"Go ahead," said Renie. "You were such a roaring success with the drugged-up post office woman. Maybe you'll get really lucky with Chummy and he'll deck you under yonder pub sign."

Judith glanced up at the wooden sign on the adjacent building. The letters that spelled out "The Hare and the Hart" were well-weathered, as were the crude depictions of a running deer and rabbit.

"Let's treat Chummy to a pint," Judith said. "Then we can grab some lunch. I have a feeling Mrs. Tichborne isn't going to put out three meals today."

Colonel Chelmsford marched out of the post office. This time, Judith spoke up: "You missed the inquest," she said in her friendliest manner. "Of course it wasn't very dramatic."

The colonel fixed Judith with a reproachful eye. "Why should it be? What's dramatic about dying? Nothing unique—everybody does it. Seen men do it often enough in battle."

"I'll bet you have," Judith said, her voice fairly palpitating with interest. "What's it like to be surrounded by whizzing bullets and exploding grenades?"

"Well now." The colonel cleared his throat, then peered off in the direction of the train station at the end of the High Street. His eyes grew cloudy, as if he were envisioning a troop transport, somewhere in the war-torn Netherlands. "There we were, Stinky Crowther and I, crawling on our bellies towards the bridge at Arnhem . . ."

Renie's eyes had already glazed over. Judith let the colonel ramble on, her mind elsewhere. A very old Morris rumbled along the High as the sun disappeared behind a bank of pale gray clouds. Out on the road, a shiny new mini-van headed for Great Pauncefoot. A local bus followed shortly after. Then a small sedan, a motorcyclist, and a livestock carrier.

As if on cue, Colonel Chelmsford whirled. "My word! I must be off! I'll finish up later with how we put old

Stinky's leg back on.'' The colonel bustled off down the High Street.

"Nice work," Renie said in sarcasm. "Unless, of course, you think Stinky Crowther killed Aunt Pet."

Judith was chagrined. She began to make excuses for herself, but interrupted them with a sudden burst of anger. "Damn! We're going nowhere!" In contradiction, she started off down the street.

"Hey, wait!" Renie called, running after Judith's long, swift strides. "I thought we were going to eat at the pub."

"That was only if we could pump Chummy. Let's go to the inn. They should have a better menu."

The Old Grey Mare's restaurant was small and empty. The cousins reassured themselves by noting that they were early for lunch. It was eleven-thirty when they sat down at a round wooden table.

A plump woman with flyaway brown hair indicated a blackboard. "Those are the specials," she said without enthusiasm. "They're always the specials."

"I'll have the Ploughman's Platter," Judith said.

Renie ordered the Shepherd's Pie. "I hope she can cook," Renie whispered after the woman had thumped off into the inn's nether regions. "Now tell me what's bugging you."

"Everything," Judith answered, still testy. "There are so many missing bits and pieces. Think about last night— what did you hear after we got back from the stables?"

Renie frowned. "You mean in conversation?"

"No," Judith responded. "I mean otherwise." Noting her cousin's lack of comprehension, Judith clarified, "I'm being unfair. You *didn't* hear anything, and that's my point. I know we went to bed early, but by ten o'clock we should have heard a truck pull up at Ravenscroft House. I realized that just now when I saw the livestock hauler go down the road. Either there's still a dead horse in the stable, or . . ." Judith made a gesture with her hands. "I don't know."

At last, Renie understood. "You mean they'd haul the carcass away. But it was a Sunday night. Maybe the glue factory isn't open on weekends. Or," she added with a sudden inspiration, "the truck you just saw was going to Ravenscroft House."

But Judith shook her head. "It would have been slowing down to make the turn into Farriers Lane. The truck I saw was doing close to thirty miles an hour. No, coz, there's something fishy about Balthazar. I've read enough English mysteries to know they don't actually shoot horses anymore. They do something more humane, like a bolt of some kind. We should drop by the stables on our way back. I'm betting we won't find a dead horse."

"Let's hope not." Renie made a face. "Ugh, I'm about to eat."

But Renie was wrong. The hostess returned to the dining room, walking slowly in her flat-footed manner. "We're out of Ploughman's Platter," she announced, not without a trace of pleasure.

Judith paused. "Okay, I'll have the Shepherd's Pie then."

"We're out of that, too." It seemed very difficult for the woman to keep from smiling in triumph.

The third item on the blackboard was a meat pasty. Renie regarded the woman hopefully. "Do you . . . ?"

"No, we don't." Folding her arms across her big bosom, the hostess finally indulged herself in a victory laugh. "Flat out, that's what we are. Unless you'd care for poached eggs on toast. Or soup," she added somewhat doubtfully.

"What kind?" Renie inquired.

The woman turned back to the door which presumably led to the kitchen. "Which soup?" she called. "Millie? You there?"

Renie screamed. The woman stared. Both cousins fled.

Once they were outside, Judith had second thoughts. "We should have quizzed Millie. She might know something."

"Cooking isn't one of them. Let's hit the tea shop." Renie was already halfway down the street.

Since Judith couldn't think what to ask Millie except if she'd eaten all three boxes of Fandangos, lunch at the tea shop seemed like a good idea. The cousins were encouraged by the sight of a dozen women, mostly middle-aged or older, already sitting at tables covered by fresh white cloths. Small vases of spring flowers sprouted everywhere, lending the shop a garden air. The menu wasn't much longer than the inn's, but it was considerably more adventurous. Judith selected chicken breast in a white cream sauce; Renie chose fresh grilled trout.

"Okay," Renie said after a Royal Albert teapot had been brought to their table, "other than beating a not-so-dead horse, what else bothers you?"

"Motive," Judith said, aware that some of their fellow patrons were discreetly staring at the strangers in their midst. "Yes, the money is definitely number one. Let's face it, except for Charles, nobody in the family has a real— excuse the expression—*job*. And even Charles is—was— dependent on Aunt Pet for his employment. But if the heirs thought the old will from August that excluded them was still in effect, none of them would have killed Aunt Pet so soon. They'd have waited until she had signed her new will."

"Unless," Renie speculated, stirring sugar and cream into her tea, "one of them knew she had drawn up the new document and figured it would stand up in court. Or maybe they just assumed that because Arthur Tinsley had spent such a long time with Aunt Pet on Friday, the new will was ready to roll."

Judith sipped from her steaming cup. "That's all possible. But the wrinkle is that whoever gave Aunt Pet those poisoned chocolates couldn't know when she'd eat the ones that killed her. I'm assuming she was greedy about sweets. But she wouldn't want to give herself another case of hives. So we have to figure that she'd go slow, maybe two or three at a time. Was the killer guessing at the dosage? Or was the time element really important? Now if the allergic reaction she had last spring was caused by chocolates from the same person who poisoned this latest batch, why did whoever it was wait so long? Did the poison idea come later?"

Renie considered. "You mean that whoever gave her chocolates on a regular basis meant well in the beginning?"

Judith nodded. "It could be. It could also be that the person who brought the candy wasn't the same one who poisoned it. But that scenario doesn't work. Aunt Pet wouldn't admit she ate chocolates, not even to her doctor."

"And Dora didn't know." Renie stopped talking as their waitress brought the entrees. "You were right," she went on after they'd been served, "about Dora being alone in the suite Friday night. But she obviously didn't snoop if she didn't know about the men's stuff in the nightstand drawer."

Judith tasted her chicken breast, which was delightfully tender. "She didn't snoop in the nightstand, let's put it like that. Dora's no actress, and a poor liar. But she's nosey. She's lived vicariously, and people who lead those kind of closed-in lives are always poking about in what's not really their business. Despite being a bit deaf, she eavesdrops. She probably goes through the mail, too. You can bet she—" Judith stopped, her fork halfway to her mouth. "She did snoop, I'd bet on it." Judith had lowered her voice still further, and was smiling slyly.

Renie didn't bother to look up from her plate. "The desk? The will? The *motive*?"

Taken aback, Judith's smile evaporated. "How'd you guess?"

Renie lifted one shoulder. "Easy. The desk and the nightstand are the only places where Aunt Pet kept important stuff. It doesn't take Sherlock Holmes to figure it out. Do you think Dora told anybody about the will?"

"Before Aunt Pet was killed?" Judith saw Renie nod. "She might have. Mrs. Tichborne, maybe. They seem close."

"Neither Dora nor Tichborne are getting enough of an inheritance to kill for," Renie pointed out. "Besides, Dora is going to be lost without Aunt Pet, especially if the family turns the house into a B&B."

A shaft of sunlight came through the windows with their white lace curtains. Renie waved a fork at Judith. "What about the fire in the wastebasket? Was that merely Dora having fun, or did she actually burn something?"

But Judith didn't know. "If it happened before Aunt Pet

was poisoned, Chummy's box would have been there. In fact, if the wastebaskets are emptied only every few days, there would have been quite a blaze.'' In confusion, Judith shook her head. ''Something's not right. I wish I knew what it was.''

For several moments, the cousins ate in silence. After finishing her new potatoes, Judith finally spoke again. ''One of the problems is that the motive doesn't fit the method. I almost like the control concept better. There's no specific time element involved.''

Renie didn't argue. ''So what about Nats and Walter? If Pet was against the match, maybe one of them did her in so they could marry.''

Judith wasn't keen on the concept. ''Pet couldn't stop them. Oh, she could threaten to cut Nats out of the estate, but that had already been done, in effect. And as far as we know, Walter was never in it. Besides,'' Judith went on, leaning closer so that she could whisper, ''it's Claire, not Pet, who opposed the match. If Claire has a thing going with Walter, it would explain all her so-called naps. I saw her with my own eyes going toward the gatehouse yesterday when she should have been upstairs in her room.''

Their waitress removed the plates and inquired about dessert. Judith and Renie tried not to look at the pastry case, but their eyes were drawn like magnets.

''A simple eclair,'' Renie said simply.

''A slice of the chocolate mousse cake,'' Judith said, feeling a bit like a moose.

The tea shop now had people waiting for tables. Since it appeared to be the only viable eatery in the village, Judith wasn't surprised.

''The thing is,'' Judith said, getting back to the topic at hand after their waitress had departed, ''Claire doesn't show any signs of leaving Charles. So what's the point of keeping Walter single if she doesn't want to marry him?''

''No distraction?'' Renie suggested. But the doubt in her voice left room for quibbling.

''Nowhere,'' Judith murmured. ''That's where we are. Absolutely—'' She leaned sideways in her chair, eyeing the door. Bridget Horan and another young woman had just entered the shop. Judith jumped up and went over to the entrance. Renie, exuding more than her usual share of patience, calmly poured more tea.

"Really," Judith was saying to a startled Bridget, "we're at a table for four. You're going to have to wait at least ten minutes. Why don't you and your friend join us for dessert?"

Bridget gave her companion an uncertain look. "Well . . . I don't know . . . Of course the sitter costs the world . . ."

At last, the two young women trooped after Judith and sat down. Bridget introduced her friend, a perky brunette whose name was Elena Dodd. Elena was also a recent mother, but she and Bridget went way back.

"Grew up together, we did," Elena said in her cheerful, piping voice. "Lifelong chums. Married within a year of each other, babies three weeks apart. Everything in synch, eh, Bridie?"

Bridget smiled, though she still seemed ill-at-ease in the cousins' company. "Our husbands work together at Frosty-Cold Frozen Foods in Great Pauncefoot."

"How nice," Judith enthused. "Do most of the young people stay in the village or do they head for London?"

Elena's piquant face burst into laughter. "*Most?* There weren't more than a half-dozen of us girls in the same age group. Little Pauncefoot is *little.* There was Bridie and Tammy and Kristen and Gigi and Janet and yours truly. Tammy and Kristen went off to university. Gigi moved to Manchester. And Janet—well, Janet disappeared."

Judith's quick glance noted that Bridget was again looking uncomfortable. "We heard about it from Janet's mother," Judith said in a quiet voice. "She insists she doesn't know what happened to her daughter. I'll bet you two have some idea, though. Girls always know what's going on with other girls."

Elena gave Bridget an inquiring look. Judith thought that Bridget's shuttered expression was intended to convey a warning. But the cousins' desserts arrived and the waitress took the newcomers' lunch orders. As Bridget mulled over her choices, Elena turned to Judith and Renie.

"Never mind Bridie," she said, with an expression of

fond disdain. "She has a guilt complex about Janet. Bridie always felt she should have talked her out of whatever it was Janet got into."

"No, I didn't," Bridget asserted, her smooth cheeks turning pink as the waitress walked away. "I never said that. I just wish I *could* have done. But Janet was headstrong. She wouldn't listen."

Judith made a logical guess. "Seventeen-year-old girls are like that when it comes to boys."

But Bridget turned faintly scornful. "Boys! He was no boy. He must have been twenty-five, at least, maybe older. Or so Janet made him seem."

Renie, who had been making cooing noises at her eclair, looked up long enough to pose the obvious question: "Who was this guy? A local?"

Bridget slumped in her chair. "That's just it—I never knew who he was. Janet wouldn't say. She loved secrets."

"Oh, yes," Elena put in. "Everything was a secret with Janet. Her favorite rock group, her favorite movie star, what she was going to wear the next day—Janet would never let on. She was mad for being mysterious."

Bridget's nod showed agreement. "That's right, she made everything into a riddle. We'd have to guess. It was to get attention, I suppose. She had no father."

Life for a housekeeper's child at Ravenscroft House struck Judith as lonely and stultifying. "Janet must have had an unusual upbringing," Judith remarked. "I suppose she felt isolated in that great big house."

"Oh, never!" Elena cried. "There were Natasha and Alexei Karamzin who were around her age, and when Claire Ravenscroft—Mrs. Marchmont now—came back from Africa, she was like a big sister to Janet. Mr. and Mrs. Karamzin were so good to all the children, taking them on picnics and hikes and to the sea. Of course the old ladies were another matter." Elena's mouth turned down.

Standing corrected, Judith considered the rest of the household twenty years ago: Petulia Ravenscroft; Chauncey and Hyacinth Ravenscroft; their widowed sister-in-law, Genevieve; Genevieve's daughter, Fleur; and her husband, Viktor Karamzin.

"It was quite a group," Judith noted. "Did George and Emily Ravenscroft come home very often in those days?"

Briefly, the two young women looked puzzled. Bridget faced Judith with a slight frown. "You mean the missionaries? Hardly ever. They sent Claire to school in England when she was in her teens. She went back to Africa later, but didn't stay on. She'd gotten used to being here. And then she married Mr. Marchmont."

"Yes," Judith said, still reconstructing the former family circle. Aimee Ravenscroft would have been gone for twenty years. Chauncey, Hyacinth, and Genevieve died in the next decade. And the senior Karamzins had met their fate in a car crash at the beginning of the nineties. "Claire and Charles were married—when?"

Again, Bridget and Elena exchanged quizzical looks. "Twelve years ago in June, I think," Bridget finally said. She seemed to have overcome her uneasiness at being with the cousins. "Yes, early June. It rained."

Judith recalled when Charles married Claire Ravenscroft. Margaret Marchmont had described the wedding at length in a long letter. For the first time, Judith realized that Margaret had been very impressed by the match her brother had made. The subtleties of social class had been lost on Judith's American mind. "Claire and Charles must have been married not long after Janet disappeared," Judith noted in what she hoped was a casual tone.

Both young women seemed surprised. "That's so," Elena said in wonder. "Janet ran off during All Fools. The Marchmont wedding was two months later. Life's like that—sad, happy, happy, sad—there's no predicting which comes when."

Renie had finished her eclair and wore a sated expression. "Was Walter Paget working at Ravenscroft House then?" she asked, brushing a few stray crumbs from her green linen shirt.

Bridget's red eyebrows came together. "Walter Paget— the steward? Yes, I think so. He's been there quite some time."

"Local?" Renie pursued.

Elena shook her head. "Not him. He popped up, as it

were. Hired through an ad, I'd guess. The old one—I don't remember his name—died, didn't he?'' She turned to Bridget.

''They put him out to pasture, so to speak.'' Bridget dimpled, amused by her own small joke. ''Pettigrew, that was his name. He lives with a niece in Great Pauncefoot.''

Judith tried to show no more than mild interest. But a swift glance at her cousin showed that Renie also recognized the name of the elderly patient at Dr. Ramsey's surgery.

''So,'' Judith said after she'd swallowed the last lethal bite of cake, ''neither of you ever guessed who Janet's beau was?''

''Oh, we guessed! Precious good it did us!'' Elena giggled, throwing her head back and revealing a swanlike neck above the beige lambswool sweater. ''Robby! Devin! Miles! But they were all no more than nineteen, and Janet kept hinting that Mr. Utterly Fab was *older*. He may have been, too. He gave her presents, nice things, like Chloe perfume and a Monet bracelet.''

Renie appeared puzzled. ''Yet you never saw them together? How long did this romance last?''

Again, the young women looked uncertain. Elena hazarded a guess ''Three months? Janet never went with anybody for long.''

Bridget was still working her way through the query. ''It was more like four. She got the bracelet for Christmas and the scent on St. Valentine's Day. But in late November, she was still going with Eddie Clayton. I remember, because they were together at Mrs. Ravenscroft's funeral. Mrs. *Chauncey* Ravenscroft, that is.''

It occurred to Judith that the ancient concept of the manor house still lingered. If life no longer revolved around the lord and lady, Ravenscroft House remained in the villagers' marrow. Despite change, the family's rites of passage were entwined with their neighbors. Ravenscroft weddings, funerals, and births were milestones in Little Pauncefoot, keynotes to other, more mundane events.

But Janet Tichborne's disappearance hadn't been mundane. Renie reiterated her question about how Janet and her suitor could have eluded the villagers.

Elena laughed again. "Frankly, we figured he lived somewhere else and had a wife. Why ever would Janet sneak about with him otherwise? Once she got over her first infatuation, whoever she was seeing didn't have to be a secret anymore."

The waitress returned, bearing Bridget and Elena's entrees, as well as the cousins' bill. Judith waited to speak until their companions had been served. "Mrs. Tichborne said her daughter wasn't really boy-crazy. But that doesn't sound quite accurate."

Elena shook her head. "Janet wasn't. Not in that sense. She never chased boys. She let them chase *her*. It was the conquest that mattered. She had to be loved and admired. After they succumbed to her charms, she moved on to the next. Isn't that so, Bridie?"

Bridget nodded. "It wasn't sex with Janet—it was power."

Judith picked up the bill, trying to figure a proper tip. "What do you think happened to Janet?"

Elena buttered the roll that had come with her lunch. "Janet was keen on feathering her nest. She's living in one of those swank London condos on the Thames with a famous rocker."

But Bridget didn't agree. Carefully, she set her teacup down in its saucer. "I wish I could think it. But I can't." Bridget lowered her eyes. "Holy Mother help me, I think she's dead."

FIFTEEN

UNDER A FITFUL sun, Judith and Renie were standing at the edge of the village green. Several old folks provided a stately counterpoint to the sprightly melody of mothers with their children. The figures moved and shifted beneath the trees and along the stone walk. Gossip, slow-paced and hopeful of comment, fell on half-deaf ears among the oldsters. The mothers called out in reproach or encouragement. In the borders and the small circular plots, daffodils, tulips, hyacinths, lilies, and crocuses dazzled the eye. Judith allowed herself to be charmed, though she couldn't completely fight off the distractions that tugged at her mind.

"What smells?" Renie's pug nose was wrinkled in dismay. "That's really disgusting."

Annoyed at having her reverie broken, Judith made a face at her cousin. "I was feeling like Wordsworth. You know—'I wander'd lonely as a cloud . . . ' "

"Whatever it is, it *reeks*," Renie interrupted. "Let's cut across the green."

Not only did Renie's complaint sink in, but so did her words. Judith stopped in her tracks. "You're right. Something smells really vile." She waved at the border of bright spring flowers that was interspersed with large clumps of greenery. "It's this green stuff. Why would they plant something that smelled so bad along with all the bulbs and shrubs?"

Still wrinkling her nose, Renie approached one of the offending plants. "Gack! You're right, that's what it is. But look, it's got buds. The flowers must be pretty or nobody'd go to the trouble."

Backpedaling, Judith frowned. An avid gardener, she recognized all but the most exotic flora. "I'd like to know what that smelly green stuff is. It makes you think, doesn't it?"

"About what? The decomposing leftovers in our mothers' refrigerators?" In her haste to escape, Renie almost tripped over a child's plastic cricket bat.

Moving down the walk toward the Dunk Monument, Judith shook her head. "No. I'm talking plants. I asked the same question earlier, after we—" She stopped, staring at the coat-of-arms etched in stone. "What's wrong with this picture?"

Renie regarded Judith with a peeved expression. "What is this, Twenty Questions? It's a coat-of-arms, vertical band showing impalement, three court jester symbols dexter, three money bags sinister, and three lions rampant in the middle, which is no doubt called something else in heraldic terms, but I forget. So what?"

Judith was looking smug. "Okay, Ms. College of Arms, what does it *mean*?"

A couple of adventurous four-year-old boys were trying to figure out how to climb the monument. An absence of footholds and a lack of height daunted the pair, who took one look at the cousins and fled to the safety of their chattering mothers.

Renie had been about to offer Judith a snappish retort, but changed her mind. "Okay," she sighed, "I guess you're serious. Impalement refers to dividing the shield between two families. Quartering is when they go for four, obviously. In this case, we're looking at the court jesters on our left, which is probably Sir Lionel Dunk in his Master of the Revels role. On our right are the money bags, which usually represent wealth, often from banking. The lions in the center show courage and nobility and all those other traits that the rich and wellborn brag about."

Judith nodded eagerly. "That's what I thought."

"Then why ask?" Renie was growing vexed again.

Judith ignored her cousin's pique. "The money bags would be the Ravenscrofts, right? Aunt Pet's father, Sir Henry, made his money in The City. So the two families depicted on this shield are the Dunks and the Ravenscrofts." She paused fractionally, decided not to test Renie with another query, and continued: "Which means that this isn't the original monument. It was erected long after Sir Lionel's death, probably in this century. Or maybe just a few years ago. Didn't Charles or Claire mention that Aunt Pet paid to have the thing restored?"

Now Renie was looking thoughtful. "Yes, you're right. That may be when they added the Ravenscroft arms to the Dunks'. Maybe Sir Lionel's original shield showed him wearing pantyhose."

Gazing up at Sir Lionel's statue, Judith grinned. "Well, men did wear hose in those days. In fact, the old boy had good legs." Slowly, the grin faded. Judith was still staring up, but now her eyes drifted beyond the monument to the mellow stone walls of Ravenscroft House. Through a break in the plane trees, she could see the turret room where Aunt Pet had sat in her armchair and watched the village comings and goings. "She was lucky to have such a good view. Your mother gets rear-end collisions on Heraldsgate Avenue. Mine has the birdbath."

Wryly, Renie nodded. "But they do other things. Sometimes. It sounds to me as if Aunt Pet didn't do much except look out the window. And annoy her relatives."

The cousins strolled back down the path, circumventing a little girl pushing her dolly in a tiny pram. "I'm getting a picture of the family over the years," Judith said as they turned by the soldiers' monolith. "And some of the village, too."

"So?" Renie nodded at two gray-haired women who eyed the cousins with frank curiosity. Clearly, strangers were rare in Little Pauncefoot. "How does that help solve the mystery of who poisoned Aunt Pet?"

"It doesn't. Yet." Judith held her breath as they left the green and passed by the foul-smelling plants. "But there's a pattern emerging. Aunt Pet was a control freak. She used her wealth to run the lives of her relatives. Threatening them with money—or the lack of it—is pretty evil. Not that I condone laziness or greed. But it's wrong to make people feel like puppets, dancing to a financial tune. I see Petulia Ravenscroft pulling strings. Maybe she was always that way, but certainly as she got older—and physically impaired—she took advantage of their fear.'' At the arch under the gatehouse, Judith stopped abruptly. ''Yes, *fear*. Fear of not inheriting anything, fear of having to go to work, fear of being poor. And fear of *what else*? What did Aimee fear that made her run off with her young man? Did Janet Tichborne fear something that drove her out of Ravenscroft House? Or get herself killed, as Bridget believes? What kept Colonel Chelmsford away for forty years and then brought him back with a box of men's toiletries? Was that fear?'' Judith paced the expanse under the gatehouse, absorbed in her questions.

Renie proved sympathetic. ''Don't forget Nats and Walter Paget. It's one thing for Claire—who isn't my idea of a man-eating tigress—to tell Nats she can't marry Walter. It's something else for Nats to go along with it. This morning Nats acted like somebody who's run up the white flag. She was sulky, she'd lost her fire. And why was Walter excluded from the will? It not only bothers me, it makes me feel guilty.'' To prove her point, Renie scanned the amber walls of the gatehouse. ''This shouldn't be ours, it should be his. Heck, we've never even been inside.''

Judith followed Renie's gaze. ''Let's fix that right now,'' she said, marching up to the solid oak door with its small stained-glass window. ''Maybe Walter is receiving guests.''

Somewhat to her surprise, he was. At least he was in, opening the door to the cousins and looking surprised. Judith was taken aback. Her excuse for calling on the steward stumbled on her tongue:

''Mr. Paget! We were . . . ah . . . just now getting back from the inquest and thought we'd . . . um . . . ask about the horses.''

''What you thought,'' Walter said coldly, ''was that you'd inventory your inheritance.'' He stepped aside and made a stiff bow. "By all means, look about. You can occupy the place immediately."

Judith started to protest, then went dumb as she saw the neatly packed boxes in the middle of the living room. While the furniture remained, it appeared that all personal effects had been removed. In spite of the bare spots, the room exuded a masculine aura. Judith regarded Walter with shock.

"You're moving out? How come?"

Walter's aplomb was ruffled, but he didn't seem to care. "What difference does it make? The gatehouse is yours, you scarcely know me, and nobody else gives a bloody rap."

Renie's temper, which had been simmering for some time, now erupted: "Hey, we don't want this gatehouse! We can't keep it up and we'd have to sell it, which will bring the IRS down on our necks. Maybe the Inland Revenue, too. So screw off before I torch the place and collect the insurance and put it all on the roulette wheel in Reno. As far as I'm concerned, we'll sign a quitclaim deed or whatever and let you have it free and clear." As an afterthought, Renie glanced at Judith. "We will, won't we, coz?"

Judith caught herself swallowing hard. She and Renie had no moral right to the property. Aunt Pet had misconstrued the facts about the cousins' English ancestors and acted on a whim. And yet Judith hated to let the gatehouse go. After eighteen years of living from pillar to post with Dan McMonigle and finally returning to her family home, the lure of the gatehouse was tempting.

But the family home was now Hillside Manor; legally, it belonged to Judith. Gertrude, Aunt Deb, and the other surviving members of the older generation had signed it over so that she could take out the remodeling loan. Judith loved the house. She loved living there with Joe. Yet with guests usually occupying the second floor and sometimes the downstairs as well, she often felt as if she had no place of her own. Indeed, there were times when she seemed to be a guest, too, living in the third-floor family quarters on the approval of her senior relatives.

"We should talk to a lawyer," Judith temporized. "We'd want it done properly." She could stall. She should discuss it with Joe. She mustn't be rushed into a decision.

Renie was eyeing her cousin with mild dismay. "Well—okay. Maybe Arthur Tinsley can advise us." Renie's anger had fled. She turned back to Walter, who still looked glacial. "Don't move out on our account. You're not really quitting your job, are you?"

Walter gazed at Renie as if she had the IQ of a penguin. "Certainly I am! How can I stay here . . . *now?*"

Judith had gathered her wandering wits. "You mean your broken engagement?" she said boldly.

To the cousins' astonishment, Walter burst out laughing. It was not a happy sound. "Engagement! What a bloody farce! There was no engagement. Natasha lives in a fantasy world. It's a good place for her." He had now turned grim, crossing his arms and watching the cousins with impatience.

"I guess," Judith said in as pleasant a voice as she could muster, "we'll be leaving."

Walter said nothing. The cousins left.

"You want the damned gatehouse." Renie's voice conveyed disgust and disbelief.

Judith sighed. "I don't, really. But we shouldn't act impulsively. That's what Aunt Pet did, and that's how we got into this mess in the first place."

Renie didn't seem entirely convinced but she let the matter drop. "So why are we headed back to the village instead of the main house?"

"Huh?" Judith seemed surprised at the direction they were taking down Farriers Lane. "Oh—I suppose that subconsciously I was thinking about seeing Arthur Tinsley. Shall we?"

Renie shrugged. "I'd just as soon have this gatehouse thing straightened out now. It'll only get more cumbersome once we're home."

"I suppose." Judith's tone lacked enthusiasm. The cousins retraced their footsteps past the green. The sky had clouded over again. "Walter is immune to Nats's charms," Judith said after a long silence. "Why? No chemistry?"

"There was for Nats," Renie replied. "Somewhere along the line, Walter must have led her on. Or at least not discouraged her. I don't buy that part about Nats living in a fantasy world. She strikes me as hardheaded."

"Me, too." Judith and Renie rounded the corner by The Old Grey Mare. Across the road, the golden stones of St. Edith's had lost their luster under the darkening clouds. Judith stopped, her eyes scanning the church and its adjacent graveyard. "Maybe Nats was using Walter, just to get at her trust fund. He seemed available, and she's a good four years away from reaching thirty, which is the other stipulation for getting hold of the money."

"If that's the case," Renie said, waiting for Judith to uproot herself from the cobbles, "Nats didn't love Walter anyway. So why is she suffering from terminal pique? With her looks and inheritance, another sucker shouldn't be hard to find."

"True," Judith agreed. "Nats gave in too easily. Claire's not intimidating. What went on between those two when they had their little chat?"

Renie frowned. "Some other bone of contention, like money?"

Judith didn't respond. She was still staring at the church across the road. Suddenly, she whirled and started off past the inn. Renie hurried to catch up.

"Now what?" Renie asked on a grumbling note.

"Walter," Judith said, approaching the medical and legal offices. "What was he doing at Fleur Karamzin's grave?" Firmly, she pressed the buzzer for Dr. Ramsey.

"Hey," cried Renie, "you want the lawyer, not the doctor."

But Judith shook her head just as Eleanor Robbins opened the door. The receptionist's face turned bleak when she saw the cousins.

"Just a quick question," Judith said in an apologetic manner. "Where would we find Mr. Pettigrew?"

"Mr. Pettigrew?" Eleanor gave a little start. "Why, whatever for?"

Judith started to fib, then remembered Eleanor's perceptiveness. "We're still sleuthing. We need to interrogate him."

"Right," Renie chimed in, reacting badly to Eleanor's raised eyebrow. "You know, smack him around a bit, melt his dentures, set fire to his cat."

Judith glared at Renie, then gave the receptionist a sickly smile. "My cousin gets carried away. She's joking, of course. Do you have Mr. Pettigrew's address?"

A battle was raging in Eleanor's eyes. She obviously didn't want to do the cousins any favors, but she also wanted to get rid of them. The phone rang, turning the tide in favor of cooperation.

"He lives with his niece in Old Church Lane, Great Pauncefoot. But," she added over her shoulder, "you might still find him at the pub."

Judith closed the door. "We'll have our pint yet," she said, looking a bit smug. "I wish I liked beer."

"English beer is better than ours. Stout, that's the ticket. Otherwise, I only drink beer when I wallpaper. Unless I'm forced into it," Renie added.

"So I've noticed." Judith's tone was wry. "You haven't done your own wallpapering in twenty years."

"That's because our upstairs toilet keeps blowing up and flooding the rest of the house," Renie replied with a trace of indignation. "The insurance pays for the repair jobs. I let the paperhanger drink the beer. That's why the match is off in our bedroom."

Judith kept the comeback to herself. They had crossed the High Street and were in front of the pub. Over four hundred years, The Hare and the Hart had settled, giving it a crooked appearance. But inside, the common room was dark and cozy. A half-dozen patrons were lined up at the bar, drinking from thick, tall glasses. All were men over sixty, but the most ancient was also the most recognizable: Judith and Renie sidled up to Mr. Pettigrew.

"Hello there," Judith said loudly, assuming that her prey was deaf. "Could we buy you a drink?"

The other five men cried, "Here, here!" Two of them banged their almost-empty glasses on the bar. Judith blanched.

"Okay," she said more softly, turning to the barkeep, who was a balding man of middle age. He had narrow shoulders, a sizable paunch, and eyes the color of the dark beer he was serving. Judith gave him an off-center smile. "Let's have a round for everybody."

The ritual completed, Judith and Renie perched on each side of Mr. Pettigrew. "We're doing research," Judith shouted. "On the Ravenscrofts. We understand you were their steward for many years."

Mr. Pettigrew sipped the ale he'd been working on before the cousins' arrival. "Why the devil are you screaming?" he asked in a low baritone voice. "Are you deaf?"

Judith gave a little jump. "Oh—no! I . . . Excuse me." She attempted another smile.

"You were at Ramsey's," Mr. Pettigrew said, making it sound like an accusation. "The inquest, too. Who would you be then? Yanks? Canadians?"

Judith explained as succinctly as she could. Mr. Pettigrew nodded slowly. He was very thin, though not exactly frail. In his younger years, he had probably been the wiry type, with deceptive strength. His lined face was weathered and dry, like an autumn leaf. But the blue eyes that looked out from under the wispy strands of white hair were shrewd.

"Ask me then," Pettigrew murmured.

The old man's receptiveness rattled Judith. She didn't know where to start. "You retired when Walter Paget came along, isn't that so?"

Mr. Pettigrew snorted. "*Miss Ravenscroft* retired me. Young Paget must have a job, and I was sent packing. Oh, Mrs. Karamzin saw to it that I left with a tidy sum, but all the same, I'd rather have stayed on. What did I know after fifty years but being steward at Ravenscroft House?"

Judith calculated that Mr. Pettigrew would have been well into his seventies when Walter Paget pulled the job out from under him. "You'd earned a rest," she said in an ameliorating tone.

Mr. Pettigrew snorted again. "A rest! Digby Pettigrew isn't one to rest! I've worked ever since—handyman, groom, harvester. Keeps me fit. No, I'm not resting until I'm in my grave.''

Renie leaned forward on the bar to catch Mr. Pettigrew's attention. ''Why were the Ravenscrofts so anxious to hire Mr. Paget? It sounds as if you were able to handle the work.''

Digby Pettigrew swiveled slightly on the barstool. ''So I was, and do twice the job of a younger man. Lazy, they are. But oh, no, Miss Ravenscroft had to take on this lad with no more experience than falling off a haycart. Set on him, she was, right from the start. And everyone else must go along with her. That's the way it always was at the big house. She's gone now, and good riddance, I say.'' He swallowed the last of his ale in a gulp.

The subject of Walter Paget having seemed to reach a dead end, Judith switched to Aimee Ravenscroft, Fleur Karamzin's twin. Digby Pettigrew frowned into his fresh glass of ale.

''Miss Aimee,'' he mused. ''And Miss Fleur. Couldn't tell them apart when they were small. Full of life, they were, bouncing all over the place. But they changed when they got older. Miss Fleur was jolly, always ready to laugh. Miss Aimee, now—she was different. Moody-like, and given to tantrums. On her head or on her heels—you'd never know with that one. Fought something fierce with her mother and old Miss Ravenscroft. No surprise there when she ran off with her young man. Come to a bad end, that's what Miss Ravenscroft said, and for once, she might have been right. I heard Miss Aimee and her man died from drugs. Terrible thing, drugs. Why don't people learn?''

''Who was her husband?'' Renie asked. ''Assuming they were married, that is.''

''They married, all right.'' Mr. Pettigrew nodded grimly. ''Better if they hadn't. Miss Ravenscroft wouldn't have disowned her, maybe. Lived abroad, died abroad, buried abroad. Served them right. Why can't people stay where they belong? I've never left Somerset. Missed both wars. Too young for the first, too old for the second. But I was no shirker. I did my duty on the homefront. Whatever was asked of Digby Pettigrew, that's what was done.'' The old man raised his glass, perhaps saluting himself.

Renie hadn't given up on her original question. "Aimee's husband—did you know who he was?"

Mr. Pettigrew gazed at Renie with something akin to pity. "Of course not. He was a Yeovil lad. How should I know him?"

Marveling to herself at the insularity that still existed among the older generation of Englishmen, Judith moved on to Colonel Chelmsford. "You must know him—he lives next door to the Ravenscrofts."

"That I do." This time the nod was slightly less grim. "Old bore, if you ask me. To hear his war stories, you'd think he was the Duke of Wellington. Kept my distance, I did. Not that it was hard to do—he never came 'round."

Judith had been absently sipping her beer. Halfway down, she realized that Renie was right—the strong dark brew was definitely a cut above the American variety she bought for Joe at Falstaff's Market.

"But he did come by last Friday," Judith pointed out. "It seems there's some property dispute. I suppose that's what has caused the bad feeling between the colonel and the Ravenscrofts all these years."

Mr. Pettigrew chuckled, revealing ill-fitting dentures. "That! Chelmsford wants a—what do you call it?—easement or such so that his cows can get down to the river. He hasn't got but four. The bank is steep on his property, but it slopes by the Ravenscroft stone wall. I hear he wants ten feet of that wall removed to make room for the cows. Well, maybe the young people will accommodate him now that Miss Ravenscroft's gone."

For a few moments, both cousins were silent. To Judith, the fence dispute sounded minor. Of course, the wall was probably as old as the house. Steeped in tradition, Aunt Pet would have resisted taking down any of the stones. No doubt she had fought all sorts of change. But her supposed refusal of Colonel Chelmsford's request hardly sounded like a motive for murder. Or, for that matter, worthy of a bitter feud.

"Aunt Pet certainly didn't like the colonel," Judith remarked at last. "They must have fought over more than the stone wall."

Under his worn tweed jacket, Mr. Pettigrew shrugged. "They did at that. It was always like cat and dog between them." Finishing his free beer, he removed a pocket watch from inside his jacket. "Ah! Two minutes after two. The Great Pauncefoot bus comes by at two-oh-nine. I must be on my way."

Judith and Renie hurriedly downed their own drinks, accepted murmured thanks from the other patrons, and escorted Mr. Pettigrew to the door.

"You've been very helpful," Judith said as they stepped out into another soft spring rain.

Mr. Pettigrew looked skeptical. "Can't see how. There's no explaining a woman like Miss Ravenscroft. Thwarted, that's what she was. Women are poor losers when it comes to love." The old man toddled off down the High Street, using the cane for only sporadic support.

Judith and Renie were in hot pursuit. "Hey—Mr. Pettigrew!" Judith caught up with him in front of the greengrocer's. "What's this about love?"

The shrewd blue eyes took on a disparaging cast. "Love! Makes the world go 'round, they say. Could be so. I had a wife who . . . but that's a long story, both bitter and sweet." Anxiously, he glanced at the road some fifty yards away. "Pardon, ma'am." He nodded at Renie. "And ma'am. I'll be missing my bus if I don't hurry."

"We'll flag it for you," Judith volunteered, keeping close to the old man's side. "Did Miss Ravenscroft love and lose? Is that why she was . . . ah . . . 'thwarted'?"

Despite the cane, Mr. Pettigrew's gait was nimble. "I was a mere lad at the time, working the stables. Miss Ravenscroft was eighteen, handsome in her way, perfect carriage and excellent seat on a horse." They had passed the butcher shop and were turning the corner, heading for the library. "She fell in love, as young girls do. Her father reluctantly encouraged the match, since the boy's family was county but the bloodlines were mediocre. His parents pushed him, but the lad had a roving eye. Oh, he courted Miss Ravenscroft, but his heart wasn't in it." Panting just a bit, Mr. Pettigrew stopped at the edge of the road. He wore an air of expectancy and kept his eyes on the oncoming traffic from Yeovil. A middle-aged couple and two teenagers were also waiting for the bus. "The next thing you knew, it was all off. The lad had gotten another young lady in trouble, as we used to say. Bun in the oven." Mr. Pettigrew winked. "Miss Ravenscroft was never the same. Two minutes," he said, checking his watch again. "The bus will be here in two minutes."

Judith noticed that the other waiting bus riders were eyeing Mr. Pettigrew and the cousins curiously. "Yes, um . . . Who was this fellow? The beau, I mean."

Mr. Pettigrew frowned at Judith. "I thought you knew. Didn't you mention a feud between the families? Miss Ravenscroft was madly in love with the colonel's father, Clarence Chelmsford. Bit of a rogue, if you ask me. Ah well—that's life. Here's the bus. It's been a pleasure."

Mr. Pettigrew queued up with the others and got on the red and white vehicle. Judith and Renie were left, if not in the dust, at least in a daze.

SIXTEEN

"I NEVER HAVE time to work on the jigsaw," Judith complained, referring to the puzzles she kept on a card table in the living room at Hillside Manor. "The guests enjoy them, but I miss putting the pieces together. I suppose figuring out the lives and loves of Little Pauncefoot is the next best thing."

"Better," Renie declared as they trudged back to Ravenscroft House. "This is a real-life puzzle. The problem is, the pieces may not fit. Has it occurred to you that all these events may be isolated?"

But Judith shook her head. "They aren't, though. Clarence Chelmsford was the great love of Aunt Pet's life. Dora overheard her mistress and the colonel say something that sounded like 'cadence' or 'valence.' I'll bet it was 'Clarence.' Mr. Chelmsford died in February. Maybe the colonel had gotten around to bringing Aunt Pet some keepsakes from his father."

"She kept them, even if she threw Chummy out." Renie scuffed at a withered seed pod, then wrinkled her nose. "Phew—there's that smell again. It's worse than the paper mills at home."

Trying to ignore the awful odor, Judith walked faster. "Old sins cast long shadows, as they say. The lives of the Ravenscrofts and the Marchmonts and the Karamzins are entwined with the rest of the village. The staff, too—

Mr. Pettigrew, Mrs. Tichborne, Dora Hobbs, even Harwood.''

"Harwood isn't a real person," Renie said as they stealthily passed through the archway of the gatehouse. "He's wax." Furtively, she looked over her shoulder to see if Walter Paget was lurking somewhere, watching them. "Say, coz, we never got around to calling on Arthur Tinsley. I still think we should talk to him about how to handle this inheritance thing."

Judith kept her eyes on the winding drive. "Right, we'll do that. Real soon. Tomorrow morning, maybe. Now I want to call the hospital and see how Mother is doing."

"It's six in the morning at home," Renie pointed out, giving Judith a curious look.

"I know," Judith said as they approached the main entrance to the house. "That's a good time to call—the nurses change shift at seven, so I'll be able to get a full report on how Mother got along last night."

"Then go for it," Renie urged. "If it were my mother, I'd do it."

Judith gave a faint nod. Gazing up at the facade of the house, she saw the Nine Muses reposing in their niches. Which was Melpomene, the muse of tragedy? Judith voiced the question aloud, but more to herself than to Renie.

"The one who's holding the bottle of Prozac," Renie answered impatiently. "How would I know? I like history, not mythology. Give me real people every time."

Judith wasn't inclined to argue. Inside the house, all seemed unexpectedly quiet. If the police were still present, there was no sign of them. The door to the drawing room was closed, which might indicate that the family members were closeted there to plan the funeral.

"Let's go use the phone in the library," Judith suggested. "Then we're going to make some notes."

The phone call went through with efficiency. It took a few moments, however, to reach the nurse who was in charge of Gertrude. When she finally came on the line, Judith spoke in an uncharacteristically obsequious manner.

"Ramona, is it? What a lovely name! Yes, I'm Mrs. Grover's daughter. I hate to bother you, but I'm concerned

about Mother. Even a slight fall at her age can be dangerous. And sometimes she's a bit foxy about telling me
things. How is she doing?''

Ramona the Nurse didn't respond immediately. Judith
wondered if they'd been cut off. She glanced at Renie, who
was trying to keep an impassive face on the other side of
the big desk.

''Your mother is gone,'' Ramona said at last in sepulchral tones.

Judith reeled in the leather chair. ''*Gone?* You don't
mean . . . You can't mean . . . ?'' The ghastly question hung
in the room, causing Renie to freeze in place.

''Mrs. Grover checked out last night,'' Ramona explained in the same morbid voice. ''Her doctor saw no reason for her to stay on and she was anxious to go home.
Naturally, with the high costs of hospital care, we don't
encourage patients to remain when it's not medically necessary. Mrs. Grover assured us that her daughter would take
excellent care of her.'' There was another pause, though
much briefer. ''Would that be you or a sister?''

The relief, which was now mingled with confusion on
Judith's face, had allowed Renie to relax momentarily. But
Judith's next words weren't entirely reassuring.

''I'm the only child. I can't take care of Mother. I'm in
England.'' A desperate note had crept into Judith's voice.

''That will be difficult,'' Ramona allowed. ''Excuse me,
a patient is buzzing. Good day.''

Judith sat with the receiver balanced precariously in her
hand. ''Damn! Mother did a bunk! She told the doctor I
could play nurse. Now what?''

Renie considered. ''The Rankerses are probably taking
over. Maybe it was too complicated to explain.''

''Maybe.'' Still juggling the receiver, Judith sighed. ''I
hate to impose on Carl and Arlene. They're so good-
hearted, but this is asking too much.'' Impulsively, Judith
rang again for the overseas operator and put another call
through, this time to the toolshed on Heraldsgate Hill. ''I'm
calling Mother,'' she told Renie. ''It's six-thirty. She might
be awake, especially if she had an uncomfortable night.''

The first eight rings caused Judith no concern. The second eight had her chewing her lower lip. By the time the count had reached twenty-five, Judith hung up.

"Maybe she's sleeping," Renie suggested, now exchanging her frown for a feeble smile of encouragement.

"Maybe," Judith said without conviction. The cousins sat in silence for a full minute before Judith suddenly passed the receiver over to Renie. "Call your mother. She always wakes up early. She'll know what's going on. I hope."

Renie jumped back from the phone as if it might bite. "Good grief, Mom will talk for hours! I'll be in debt up to my ears! How about calling Carl and Arlene?"

"They're probably fixing breakfast for the B&B guests. I don't want to bother them." Judith pressed the phone on Renie. "Come on, coz, this is urgent!"

It was, and Renie knew it. Sighing, she grasped the receiver. Two minutes later, her mother's voice was humming in her ear.

"Dearest! Where are you? What's happened? Are you all right? Did you get sick? Have you been hurt? Did you lose Bill? I'm listening to the morning news, and the most terrible things are happening!"

"I'm fine, Mom," Renie finally managed to get in. "Judith is fine, too. So are Bill and Joe." She glanced at Judith, whose teeth were now clamped on her lower lip. "We're calling about Aunt Gertrude. Judith can't seem to . . . ah . . . find her."

Deborah Grover's voice took on a note of umbrage. "Well, how should I know where Gertrude is? Does my sister-in-law ever call to tell me anything? No, not her— she sits over there in that nice remodeled apartment of hers just a stone's throw from her daughter and never lifts a finger to dial *my* number. She could be dead for all I know." It sounded as if the thought was not altogether displeasing to Deborah Grover.

Judith was now wringing her hands. Renie was wringing the receiver, as if she could choke the information out of her mother. "Where *is* Aunt Gertrude exactly?"

Renie's mother sniffed audibly. "I'd be the last to know. Ordinarily, dear, that is. By chance—merely by chance, you realize—your Auntie Vance, who isn't nearly as big a *poop* as your Aunt Gertrude, filled me in. She and Uncle Vince have taken Gertrude up to their house on the island for a few days. Gertrude had to go somewhere, after they threw her out of the hospital.''

Hastily, Renie put a hand over the mouthpiece and re-layed Gertrude's whereabouts. ''How did that happen?'' Renie asked her mother, not wanting to cause Judith further alarm. Yet.

''Your aunt can be so ornery.'' Deborah Grover emitted a put-upon sigh. ''And don't I know it, after all these years of playing bridge with her. Just last week, she wouldn't speak to me for two days because I didn't bid my hand. Or so she said. I had thirteen points but *no* suit. Now how could I bid no-trump with cards like that? She insisted we would have had a small slam, just because *she* opened. Well, sometimes Gertrude takes *terrible* risks. Oh, she had fifteen points and a slew of spades, I'll admit, but how was I to know? I passed at three diamonds. I see no point in—''

''Mom!'' With her free hand, Renie clutched at her hair. ''Mom,'' she repeated in a softer voice, ''tell me about *now*. How Aunt Gertrude . . . um . . . left the hospital.''

''Under a cloud,'' Deborah replied with malice. ''She accused the nurse of cheating at cribbage. You know your aunt, she will *not* give in. She always has to be right. The nurse wouldn't apologize *and* she refused to play with Gertrude anymore. So your aunt said, 'Fine, then let me out of here.' You know how she is—if Gertrude can't play cards, she'd rather be *dead*. The doctor came to check on her, and she told him off, too. She always has to have *her say*, as she puts it. The poor man must have been at wits' end when she unplugged her roommate's heart monitor. Then she lit a cigarette. Such a filthy habit, and it's not allowed in hospitals, thank goodness. No wonder the doctor decided to send her home.''

Renie was nodding in a dazed fashion. ''Well, certainly. Except she didn't go home, she went up to the island with Auntie Vance and Uncle Vince, right?''

''That's right,'' Deborah agreed. ''They'd come down to

visit her in the hospital—of course they stopped to see me for a bit and brought some lovely clam chowder—I do wish they could have stayed longer, but they're just like you, always in such a hurry to be off.'' The note of reproach in her mother's voice caused Renie to wince. ''They got to the hospital around seven, just when the nurses were wheeling Gertrude's roommate off to intensive care. Or was it the nurse they were taking away? I don't recall. Anyway, after some *discussion*, your aunt and uncle promised to take Gertrude with them. It's a good thing, if you ask me. The only person who can get the better of your Aunt Gertrude is your Auntie Vance.''

On any given day, Auntie Vance could get the better of Ivan the Terrible, as both Judith and Renie well knew. With her rough tongue and good heart, Vanessa Grover Cogshell was a study in contradictions. She was also capable of holding Gertrude's head under water until she cried ''Uncle.'' Which, if she were crying for Uncle Vince, would do no good, because he'd probably be asleep. He usually was, except when driving. Even then, there was often some uncertainty about his level of consciousness.

''It sounds,'' Renie said, trying to keep her voice even, ''as if things are under control.''

''I should hope so,'' Deborah responded. ''The Rankerses are feeding the cat. And taking care of the B&B, of course. Such nice people—I do wish they'd drop in here more often. Arlene always has such a lot of news. I spoke with her on the phone the other day, and she told me that Sophie Weinerhoffen's gall bladder had—''

''Mom,'' Renie interrupted gently, ''I really should go so I can tell Judith about Aunt Gertrude. She's been pretty worried. You know how that is.''

''Oh!'' Deborah's gasp was palpable. ''I do! Worry—that's all I've done since you and Bill left town! You can't imagine how relieved I'll be when you're safe at home! Just last night I was talking on the phone to Mrs. Parker, and she said that—''

Frantically, Renie poked a random button on the receiver. An ear-splitting squawk ensued. ''Hey, Mom! I think we've got transmission problems! I'd better hang up! Love you!''

"What, dear? What was that you uttered? Now Serena, don't go out in the rain without your plastic bonnet—''

Renie poked another button. "This interference is *deafening*. Don't worry, everything's great, take care.''

"Don't worry about *me*,'' Deborah Grover said, at her most pitiful. "I'll be all right, alone here in my squalid little—''

Holding her head, Renie hung up. "Sometimes you have to be cruel to be kind,'' she murmured. "Or something like that. *Your* mother got tossed from Good Hope Hospital. You're lucky they don't cancel her membership plan.''

Judith groaned. "Oh, jeez! What did she do now?''

Renie told Judith everything. Her previous desire to spare her cousin the gruesome details had been obliterated by Deborah Grover's martyred whine.

"They'll outlive us yet,'' Renie said in conclusion. "Wait and see. When we're gone, they'll both bitch about what rotten daughters we were because we croaked from aneurisms and left them in the lurch.''

Numbly, Judith nodded. "At least Auntie Vance may be able to cope with Mother. Oh, dear.'' Raising her head from where it was lying on the desk, Judith tried to shake off the most recent dual maternal experiences. "Maybe I'll call Mother tomorrow.''

Renie made no comment. Judith stared off into space for some time, then finally gave herself a good shake. "Let me show you the will. If it's still here.'' She opened the desk drawer cautiously. "Ah!—it is. I'm almost surprised.''

Quickly, Renie read through the lines of spidery blue ink. "It's just as you—and Tinsley—said.'' She sighed, as woefully as her mother. "We've got to get out of this mess, coz.''

Judith lifted an eyebrow. "The inheritance? Or the murder?''

"Both,'' Renie said firmly. She started to push the single sheet back at Judith, then suddenly retrieved it. "You're right,'' Renie said, gazing at the handwritten will. "There *is* something odd about this paper. It's short.''

Judith stared. "Short?"

"Right. It's off a standard eight-and-a-half-by-eleven-and-three-quarter tablet used in the U.K. But this is only about ten and a half inches long." Renie noted Judith's uncertainty. "Hey, don't argue—visuals are my life. I'm a graphic designer, remember? Find a ruler, measure it. You'll see. Part of the page must have been cut off." Renie, who wasn't wearing her glasses and was farsighted, held the sheet at arm's length. "See? It's too smooth to have been torn, so it must have been cut."

Renie was right. Judith held the page up to her nose and saw the merest waver at the top, probably made by scissors. "Why would anybody cut this off? It starts out with 'The Last Will and Testament of Petulia Henrietta Victoria Ravenscroft'—which is perfectly logical. What else could it say?"

Renie considered. "Maybe she made a mistake, cut it off, and started over."

Judith disagreed. "Aunt Pet would have torn it up and used a fresh sheet. She might have been an advocate of the 'waste not, want not' school, but this paper is cheap. The date is at the bottom. So is the part about leaving us the gatehouse."

For some moments, the only sound in the library came from the ticking of the mahogany long-case clock. Renie pulled the sheet back in front of her, scrutinizing the date. "It's dated 24 April of this year, which would be right. But are the codicil and date written in the same ink as the main part of the will?"

It was Judith's turn to study the single sheet again. "Ink variations notwithstanding, it's definitely her handwriting throughout. The date's another matter. There aren't any numbers in the will itself to make a comparison."

"Maybe she switched pens," Renie suggested. "Or even bottles of ink. Let's say she wrote out the part about the family, just like it was in the earlier will. Maybe she did that Saturday morning or even Friday after Arthur Tinsley left. Then we came along, and were so filled with good English breeding despite our half-assed superficial American ways, that she wrote the gatehouse section later."

Judith's nod came slowly. "That's very possible." She hesitated, feeling she had missed something.

But Renie had moved on: "What else is in that desk? Have you looked?"

Judith had, in a cursory manner. "I found the will sitting right on top in one of the drawers. The rest seems to be household ledgers, old bills, and a bunch of stuff pertaining to the All Fools Revels. Apparently Aunt Pet kept her personal papers in her room. I suppose Charles and Claire keep theirs at their London flat."

Renie gave a short nod of agreement. Judith let her eyes roam the tall bookshelves, drawing a modicum of comfort from being surrounded by great works in a worthy setting.

"Aunt Pet," Judith said, seemingly from out of nowhere. "The old photo in her nightstand—I'll bet it was Clarence Chelmsford. He looked familiar because he resembled his son, Chummy."

"Brilliant." Renie's tone was wry. "So what?"

Judith made a self-deprecating gesture. "I was trying to add some detail to the big picture. The colonel brought that photo of his father, which must have been taken about the time of the ill-fated romance."

"Coz—we're getting nowhere. I thought you were going to make notes." Renie slung one pants-clad leg over the arm of the oak chair.

Judith blinked. "It's not a painting, it's a tapestry. Just like the ones that are hung on these walls." She waved a hand at the falconry scenes flanking the library door. "Each thread is separate, but when they're woven together, they create a—"

"—bunch of bull," Renie interrupted. "So what if we've got two different young women in two different generations taking a hike out of Little Pauncefoot? Who cares if Aunt Pet pined away for Clarence Chelmsford? I love history, but at the moment, I don't want to go back beyond last Friday. Who knew Aunt Pet had already made out that will and that it would stand up in court? The only person who comes to mind is Arthur Tinsley, and he doesn't have a motive."

Having had Renie take the wind out of her sails, Judith

was drooping behind the desk. "True. It's just that I'm fascinated by little scraps of people's lives, and I always feel as if . . . Ah!" Judith sat up and snapped her fingers. "That scrap of paper you found in Aunt Pet's desk—what did it say?"

Briefly, Renie looked confused. "I don't remember . . . oh! It was a date." She started to shrug, then gawked at Judith. "It was in April, like the twenty-ninth. No, it was the twenty-seventh."

Judith beamed at Renie. "What year?"

Renie concentrated again. "There was no year. It was just the month and day. The year part had gotten torn off in the drawer, maybe."

Judith sprang out of the chair. "Let's go see if we can find it. By the way, did you say 'torn' or 'cut'?"

Renie was hurrying after Judith, racing out of the library and up the main staircase to Aunt Pet's third floor suite. "I said 'torn.' But come to think of it, the scrap could have been cut."

"Exactly," Judith agreed as they reached the top of the stairs and knocked on the door to Aunt Pet's rooms. "Now let's see if we can—Hi, Dora," she said as the maid opened the door. "Do I smell smoke?"

Flustered, Dora backed into the sitting room. "No, certainly not. Well, a *teensy* bit, perhaps. It's no cause for concern." Her cheeks were very pink, and she stopped short of the door to her mistress's boudoir. "*Really*. I'll see to it." With surprising agility, she whirled around, entered the bedroom, and slammed the door in the cousins' faces.

Dora hadn't thrown the latch. Judith and Renie stormed into the room. Dora was pouring a glass of water into the wastebasket. She looked up, an embarrassed expression on her wrinkled face.

"I miss her so," she said, as if that explained everything. Maybe, Judith thought, it did. Dora started to cry. Judith put an arm around her shaking shoulders.

"You see," Dora went on, trying to stifle her tears, "I had no family of my own. Miss Ravenscroft was like a mother to me. And she lived ever so long. While she was alive, I was *safe*. Now she's gone, and there's nothing that stands between me and . . .'' The quavery voice faded as Dora buried her head in Judith's breast.

Judith patted her gently. ''I know. The very elderly are our barricade against mortality.'' Fleetingly, she thought of Gertrude, facing off with Auntie Vance. The two old women danced through her mind, dueling with cribbage boards and soup ladles. As long as they could carry on the good fight, Judith was safe. Of course it was an illusion, but there was comfort in it, all the same.

''Sludge,'' Renie said in a disgusted voice. ''There's nothing in this wastebasket now but sludge.''

Over the top of Dora's head, Judith eyed the still smoking burned-out mess. ''Was that emptied today, Dora?''

''What?'' The maid had stopped crying. With an unsteady step, she drew away. ''Oh! No, Millie would have done, but she gave notice.''

Judith nodded once, then fixed Dora with a kindly, if probing, eye. ''Dora, did you set a fire in there over the weekend?''

Dora was aghast. ''Oh, never! That is, not until now! I wouldn't burn anything of Miss Ravenscroft's! But she's gone, so it doesn't belong to her anymore, does it?''

Judith's expression grew puzzled. Her gaze followed Renie, who was on her hands and knees, and had pulled out a desk drawer.

''If there's any more of that paper scrap here, I can't dig it out,'' she announced. ''I've already wrecked two fingernails.''

''It doesn't matter,'' Judith said in a vague tone. ''I think I know what it said.''

Renie stood up. ''You do? Have you replaced logic with psychic powers?''

Judith gave Renie a crooked smile. ''Maybe. The rest of the paper gave the rest of the date—which was last year. What else? It couldn't be this year. The twenty-seventh is tomorrow. Aunt Pet couldn't have written that—she died on the twenty-fifth.''

Dora began to cry. Again.

* * *

Arthur Tinsley had gone home early, according to the small sign on his office door.

"I'm not walking to Mon Repos again," Renie declared, looking as if she were taking a solemn oath.

Judith started to argue, but stopped. "We won't have to," she said, waving frantically. "Alex! Yoo-hoo!"

The red Alfa was purring down the High Street. Alex swerved to the curb, almost hitting a planter of petunias. Judith asked for a ride. Alex asked her where to. Judith told him. Renie took one look at her previous perch under the dashboard and shook her head.

"Forget it. I'm not going." She leaned against a lamp-post and crossed her arms in a defiant manner.

Judith knew better than to plead. Besides, she didn't blame Renie. "Okay," she agreed, leaving the curb to whisper in Renie's ear. "But go to the library. Look up hyoscyamine. I'll meet you back at the house in half an hour."

With ill grace, Renie gave in. Judith slid into the Alfa and gave her driver a smile. "We're trying to do something about the will," she said as Alex turned onto the main road. "We'd like to get this gatehouse situation squared away."

Alex showed little interest in the cousins' problems. "I won't be thirty for over a year. What shall I do meanwhile? I'm not as keen as Nats on getting married."

It occurred to Judith that Alex was unusually subdued. He was also sober. Or so she thought, until he turned to look straight at her. The black eyes were definitely glassy. Involuntarily, Judith reached for the wheel.

"Careful, Alex," she said nervously. "Here's the bridge."

Alex responded like a robot, scarcely looking at the road, but somehow managing to avert disaster. "Nats will find someone now that Paget's out of the running. She'll do well enough." Alex was growing downright morose.

They passed into the vale with its farms and orchards. Judith was on edge, poised to make another grab for the wheel or to hit the brake. She wondered if he was in a suicidal mood. Making an effort, Judith tried to cheer Alex.

"You'll have the interest to live on until you're thirty,"

she said, gritting her teeth as Alex swerved over the imaginary center line.

Alex scoffed. "It's next to nothing! Damn Charles anyhow!" Pressing down on the accelerator, he drove so fast that Judith had to yell at him to slow down or they'd roar right by the Tinsley house.

"What's wrong?" she asked, relieved to be turning into the drive of Mon Repos. "Are the family finances in trouble?"

Braking to a stop, Alex cradled the wheel and sighed heavily. "It's a disaster. We got the bad news this afternoon. Charles has bungled everything. He's no businessman, if you ask me! I used to think Aunt Pet put him in charge and then set him an' Claire up. Now I wonner." Alex's words were growing slurred. "Was't t'other way 'round?"

Feeling conspicuous sitting in the red sports car, Judith opened the door and put one foot down on the driveway. "How do you mean, Alex? About setting up Charles and Claire?"

Alex was now draped facefirst over the steering wheel. "Matchmaking . . . thas what it was . . . Always Aunt Pet's way . . . T'hell w' love . . ." He appeared to pass out.

Judith hoped Alex would feel better after a nap. She got out of the Alfa, heading for the walk with its close-cropped privet hedge. When she reached the front door, it was already open. Lona Tinsley, now attired in a forest-green cashmere sweater and a Black Watch tartan pleated skirt, glared at her guest with unfriendly blue eyes.

"My husband is resting after his arduous weekend," she announced in her chilly voice. "If you'd checked with his office, you'd know he's not accepting any more appointments this afternoon."

Judith put on her most pathetic manner. "Oh, dear! I'd so hoped to see him about the will. Now I'll have to go to the police. But," she went on, just a trifle slyly, "I'm sure Mr. Tinsley is much too modest to want to be a hero."

Mrs. Tinsley's tight little face couldn't quite conceal her curiosity. "What sort of hero?"

Judith wore her most ingenuous expression. "Why, in

solving the murder, of course. Oh, I'm a firm believer in
the police—my husband is a policeman, after all. But I
know how they have to follow procedures. It's so time-
consuming. And meanwhile, the perp—the criminal, I
should say—may abscond. That's why I feel that your husband should share his special insights with *someone*. If he
hasn't already, I mean.''

Now Lona Tinsley looked not only curious but per-
plexed. It was obvious that she felt her husband wouldn't
have known an insight if it fell on his head from a fourth-
floor window.

''Really, I couldn't say . . .'' In what was no doubt a rare
fit of confusion, Lona opened the door all the way and
asked Judith to step inside. ''Do sit,'' she said, indicating
the tidy parlor. ''I'll fetch Arthur.''

Judith sat on a muted plaid sofa. The parlor was so clean
and uncluttered that it could have been a showcase at Donner & Blitzen Department Store. The only ornaments were
a cut-glass vase filled with spring flowers, a trio of Chinese
bowls, a gilt-bronze mantel clock with an ivory face that
had no numbers, and a wedding picture in an austere silver
frame. Even the fireplace was pristine, with a clean grate
and three artistically placed logs.

Judith took advantage of her hostess's absence to study
the wedding picture. It was, expectedly, of Lona and Arthur. She wore a fitted beige jacket over a matching fluted
skirt; he was attired in a dark three-piece suit. Lona's hair
hadn't changed a bit; Arthur's had receded quite noticeably.
Judith guessed that the photo had been taken some ten years
earlier.

''I'm sorry,'' Lona Tinsley said from somewhere behind
Judith. ''My husband isn't here. He must have gone for a
walk. He often does, when he's low in his mind.''

Embarrassed at having been caught staring at the photograph, Judith awkwardly sat back down on the sofa. ''He
is? Low, I mean. Is that because of Miss Ravenscroft?''

If Lona Tinsley had noticed Judith's snooping, she gave
no sign. ''I suppose,'' Lona answered a bit uncertainly.
Arranging her pleats carefully, she sat down opposite Judith. ''Miss Ravenscroft was a valued client of many years'

standing. But Arthur is also distressed over *other things*."

Having somehow found a chink in Lona's armor, Judith pressed her advantage. "You mean the murder?"

"Oh, that!" Lona dismissed murder as if it were the common cold. "No, I'm referring to his responsibilities. Arthur takes his work very seriously." The chilly visor dropped down again over Lona's face. "Excuse me, I'm speaking out of turn. If you'd care to give me your information, I'll pass it on to my husband."

Judith, however, was shaking her head sadly. "Responsibilities!" she echoed. "They're such a burden for conscientious people. The worst of it is when others step in and manage to make a mess of things. Like the missing will," she added pointedly.

Lona's unblemished skin darkened. "How could you guess?" She seemed genuinely astonished. "Why, that's it! Arthur *knows* he didn't lose that earlier will. Someone must have stolen it. But who?"

"But why?" Judith evinced sympathy. "That's the real question. The only people who would have benefited by the August will are in Swaziland."

Lona nodded vigorously. "That's precisely what Arthur says. It makes no sense. But it shows Arthur in a poor light. What will people think if word gets out that he can't keep track of his clients' important legal documents? Is it any wonder that he's sick at heart?"

Judith clucked her tongue. "Village gossip must be cruel. Is Arthur sure he had the original will in his office?"

Lona's color, which had started to return to normal, now deepened again. "Not the original. He'd brought that to Miss Ravenscroft on Friday. He left it with her. But he had a copy at the office. That's gone, too, though I can't think how anyone could have taken it. He didn't see any clients on Saturday, except Colonel Chelmsford."

Judith successfully concealed her surprise. "The property dispute, I suppose," she murmured.

Lona shrugged. "I really couldn't say."

"Who works with your husband?" Judith asked, wondering at the back of her brain why Colonel Chelmsford would consult Arthur Tinsley on a matter that was clearly a conflict of interest for the solicitor.

"He has a secretary, Mrs. Radford. She's been with him for years. In fact, she was trained by Arthur's father. But she didn't come in on Saturday. There was no need, especially since the colonel didn't have a scheduled appointment."

Judith was about to inquire more deeply into Mrs. Radford's background when Lona continued: "In fact, Mrs. Radford left at noon Friday. She spent the weekend taking care of her grandchildren in Yeovil."

The secretary wouldn't have known about Aunt Pet's desire to make a new will. It sounded as if Mrs. Radford was out of the running. Judith had almost hoped that her maiden name was Paget. Or was there another missing link? Judith frowned.

"Say, Mrs. Tinsley, do you know what Emily Ravenscroft's name was before she married George?"

Lona frowned back. "Who?"

"George Ravenscroft, the missionary. You know, the one in Swaziland."

"Oh." Lona shook her head. "No, I've never met them. I don't believe they spend much time in England. I've only lived in these parts since Arthur and I were married eleven years ago."

Judith understood that Lona Tinsley still would consider herself a relative newcomer to a village such as Little Pauncefoot. "You're from . . . ?" Judith prompted, for lack of anything more pertinent to say.

"London. Well, Tottenham, actually. But I lived in Kensington for some years with my first husband." Primly, she lowered her gaze until it rested on the plain gold wedding band. "He was a doctor. That's how I met Arthur."

Judith tackled the obvious question at an oblique angle: "I'm married for the second time, too. My first husband died young."

Lona's neatly coiffed head came up. "Oh—so did mine! Isn't it tragic?"

"Yes, it is," Judith replied automatically. *No, it isn't. Not when it gives you a second chance at life. Not when your first husband is trying to drink and eat and otherwise abuse himself into the grave and would just as soon take you along with him or send you to the funny farm.* But Judith let the expected reaction stand. "Was he ill?" she inquired in a neutral tone.

Lona nodded. "His heart. He'd had the condition all his life. Such irony—but then he wasn't a heart specialist." She gave Judith a tight, wry smile, as if Death had played a terrific joke on the doctor.

"I see," Judith said, and while she didn't, her thoughts were running off in other directions. "Arthur was a patient, I take it."

"Yes." Lona was no longer smiling and had stood up. "It's getting rather late. If you'd like to tell me whatever it was you came to see Arthur about . . ." She let the sentence fade away.

"Oh—sure." Judith also stood up. "It's about the handwritten will. Arthur's seen it, of course, but he may not have noticed that there's something odd about it. Being a solicitor, he'd probably be able to explain it. It's possible that the peculiarity might indicate who murdered Miss Ravenscroft."

Lona Tinsley was now looking very puzzled. "If Arthur's seen it, why didn't he mention this 'peculiarity'?"

Judith picked up her handbag and started for the door. "He may not have noticed it. I didn't either, the first time I saw it. Will you have him call me at Ravenscroft House?"

"Certainly." The mask was back in place. If anything, Lona was even more glacial, especially when she looked outside and saw the recumbent form of Alexei Karamzin. "Who is *that?*" she demanded.

Judith's grin was feeble. "My chauffeur. He's sort of tuckered out."

Lona made no comment, except to close the door. Judith hurried to the Alfa, where she gave Alex a sharp shake. He rolled over onto the passenger seat, snoring lustily.

With a sigh, Judith shoved him out of the way and got behind the wheel. Fortunately, she was used to the stick shift in Joe's beloved old MG. She was also relieved that she didn't have to be driven by a drunk. Reminding herself to stay on the left-hand side of the road, she managed the half-mile to the village without incident. Halfway up Farriers Lane, she spotted Renie, who was studying the plantings in the village green's border.

"Want a lift?" she called, coming to a full stop.

"Sure," Renie replied, moving toward the car. "Where's Alex?"

Judith pointed to the bucket seat. "Push him under the dashboard. It's his turn."

Renie did as she was told. With pleasure. The cousins returned to Ravenscroft House.

SEVENTEEN

SINCE IT WASN'T raining, Judith had no compunction about leaving Alex in the car. She removed the keys, however, and handed them to Harwood, who was at the door. The butler did not look pleased, but said nothing.

"Where is everybody?" Judith asked, taking off her jacket.

Harwood pursed his lips. It was obvious that he didn't think it proper to confide the whereabouts of family members to virtual strangers. On the other hand, Miss Ravenscroft had remembered them in her will.

"Mr. Charles is in the library. Mrs. Charles is in her room. Miss Natasha has gone out." Taking the cousins' jackets, Harwood also took two unsteady backward steps. "Will that be all?"

"That's great," Judith said cheerfully. "I mean, that's all. Thanks. Very much." She gave herself a shake, wishing she were more experienced in dealing with upper-class British servants of the old school. Her only background was Phyliss Rackley, which didn't count, since she was a fellow American and inclined to take orders only under duress while offering a great deal of criticism in return. As for discretion, Judith's cleaning woman probably thought it was a disease. One of these days, she'd come down with a life-threatening case of it, too. Phyliss was highly suggestible.

It was almost five o'clock, which caused Judith to

hurry out to the kitchen. Mrs. Tichborne was nowhere to be seen, though judging from the fresh vegetables laid out on the counter, she was in the vicinity.

"Let's call Doodles before he leaves the office," Judith said, going to the phone. "There's a London directory under the counter. Can you look up his number?"

"Under Doodles? Probably not." Renie made a face at Judith. "What's his real name? I don't remember—I didn't have the pleasure of meeting the guy."

"Woodley Swinford," Judith replied a bit impatiently. "He's the animal insurance agent."

"I know that part," Renie replied, flipping through the pages of the big London phone book. "I just couldn't remember his real name."

But Renie found a listing, in Maida Vale. "It might be his home," she said. "Maybe he works out of his house."

Judith punched in the numbers as Renie read them off. Doodles answered on the second ring. Judith asked her questions; Doodles gave his answers. Judith hung up, a mystified expression on her face.

"There's been no claim," she said, still standing by the phone. "Not from the Marchmonts, not from anybody at Ravenscroft House. I'm baffled."

"I'm hungry," Renie said, grabbing a raw carrot from the counter. "So what?"

"Let's go," Judith said, racing out of the kitchen.

"Where?" Renie asked, swiping another carrot but following on Judith's heels.

"The stables. I want to see if Balthazar is still there. Dead or alive."

Retrieving their jackets from the small closet off the entrance hall, the cousins hurried out into the mild early evening air. A cursory glance showed them that Alex was still sleeping in the Alfa. They passed him and continued through the gardens.

The Ravenscroft stables were a wondrous sight, at least from the standpoint of Judith and Renie, whose nodding acquaintance with American barns was limited to ramshackle cowsheds from which they had occasionally bought cut-'em-yourself Christmas trees. A mug of hot chocolate and a teenager in a Santa hat provided the atmosphere. Thus, they were unprepared for the splendor in which the Ravenscroft hunters lived.

"Wow!" Judith gasped, amazed at the orderliness and cleanliness of the high-roofed building that housed the bloodstock. "This is like an equine Four Seasons."

Chewing on a carrot, Renie also admired the animal luxury. She had a quibble, however: "It still smells like horse . . . stuff," she remarked. "Look, their stalls have nameplates, just like corporate executives. Why do I figure these dumb animals are smarter?"

Before Judith could answer, a rangy lad in his middle teens appeared seemingly out of nowhere. "Wot may I do ye fer?" he inquired, scratching his armpit.

"Where's Balthazar?" Judith asked with a slightly startled smile.

The youth shrugged. "Balthazar be gone. He were at the end."

Sure enough, Balthazar's nameplate remained in place. But the stall was empty. Judith glanced at the other horses, who eyed the cousins with well-bred curiosity. Orion. Circe. Diablo. Columbina. Fricka. Scorpio. The names resonated with romance. Judith smiled tautly as she thanked the stable boy and went back out into the pasture.

"Well?" Renie inquired, still wrinkling her nose. "Aren't you going to ask about my library adventure?"

Judith was chewing on her lower lip. "Oh—right. What did you find out about hyoscyamine?"

"Little Pauncefoot's research materials are very limited," Renie said as they headed back toward the formal gardens. "You'd be appalled. But I found a source book for poisons. Hyoscyamine comes from such plants as henbane, mandrake, nightshade, and thorn apple. The last one is also known as Jimsonweed, and it smells bad. It's not indigenous to the U.K., but was discovered by English colonists at Jamestown. Hence, the corruption to Jimsonweed. It's been imported to this country over the years, and because of its showy summer flowers, the English plant it despite the fact that *it smells worse than horse stuff.*" Renie shot Judith a look of triumph.

At the bottom of the stone steps that led to the rose arbor, Judith stopped in her tracks. "You mean—those foul plants along the village green are Jimsonweed?"

Renie gave Judith a quirky smile. "They fit the description in the book. That's why I was studying them when you drove up in the Alfa. The fruit appears in the fall and contains little black seeds," she went on, obviously trying to recite from memory. "The whole plant is poisonous but the leaves are the most toxic. If you noticed, there were still some pods lying on the ground."

Judith had noticed, vaguely. "So if you knew about Jimsonweed, you could gather the leaves, grind them up, and slip the stuff inside a chocolate."

Renie nodded. "But most people probably wouldn't know it was poison."

Slowly, Judith began to ascend the steps. "Maybe." She turned to look over her shoulder at Renie. "Do you remember what Dr. Ramsey said after Aunt Pet died?"

"That she was dead?" Renie narrowed her eyes at Judith's back. "It seemed like the right call at the time."

"No, you idiot," Judith snapped, increasing her pace as they reached level ground. "I mean about Aunt Pet's symptoms. Dr. Ramsey said he'd treated some kids with similar problems. Maybe he suspects the source, but he can't be sure because several of those other plants grow around here, especially the varieties of nightshade. What do you bet those kids were playing on the green and ate something off the Jimsonweed? Word would get out in a place like this. Everyone would know the stuff was poison. It would be necessary to warn parents."

Renie grew thoughtful. "Yes, just like warning our kids when they were little not to eat seeds or berries that they found in the yard. So much of what grows in an ordinary garden can be lethal. You hear about accidental poisonings every summer."

Judith was looking at her watch. "It's five-thirty. Dr. Ramsey will have gone home. Let's go see the colonel."

"What for?" Renie demanded. "He won't want to see us."

"I'll think of some reason why he should," Judith said,

then abruptly reversed in front of a rectangular lily pond. "We'll take the shortcut. Maybe we can avoid the locked gate as well as the dogs."

Judith's shortcut turned out to be more dangerous than she'd envisioned. Having returned to the pasture, the cousins followed the stone wall to the river. Colonel Chelmsford was right about access for his cows: The wall stopped just above the riverbank, which sloped easily on the Ravenscroft side. But the hill grew very sheer on The Grange's property. Judith and Renie had to create footholds to climb the short distance.

They came out at the rear of the house, which up close showed signs of deterioration. Catching her breath, Judith knocked on the back door.

Colonel Chelmsford was in his shirtsleeves, holding a pipe in one hand and a newspaper in the other. His recognition of the cousins dawned slowly.

"You again," he muttered as one of the dogs barked from somewhere in the house. "Well?"

"Where's Balthazar?" Judith asked, forcing urgency into her voice. "We're told he was brought here last night. Mr. Swinford is furious!"

The colonel's eyes bulged. "Swinford? Who the devil is Swinford?"

"The insurance agent," Judith responded, still seemingly disturbed. "He thinks there's some sort of scam. The police don't take insurance fraud lightly."

"Bloody hell!" shouted Colonel Chelmsford over the dog's persistent bark. He appeared torn between slamming the door in the cousins' faces and letting them in. Turning almost purple, he finally stood aside. "Come in, come in, no point in standing around half-in, half-out."

"Thanks," Judith said, losing some of her bogus steam as she and Renie entered the long, utilitarian hallway. "So where's the horse?"

Colonel Chelmsford tucked the newspaper under an arm, then pulled on his pipe. It had gone out. He cursed again, but under his breath.

"Balthazar's not here. I merely kept him overnight. Now what's this business about insurance fraud?"

Judith nodded sagely. "I figured you shipped him off in that truck this morning. You seemed very anxious to catch up with the livestock haulers."

"They came early," the colonel grumbled. "It'd never do for anyone to be on schedule. Usually, they're late. People today have no sense of time."

Next to Judith, Renie was running a hand through her short chestnut hair and looking mystified. "Excuse me, I think I missed something. Balthazar is alive and well?"

Judith nodded, then turned her attention back to the colonel. "He's at another farm, I assume?"

"Of course," Colonel Chelmsford replied. "Montagues' place near Compton Bishop. Fine people. Good horse sense. Now tell me what this is in aid of."

Having gotten the facts out of the colonel, Judith wasn't sure how to proceed. "It seems as if someone was trying to collect a big insurance policy on Balthazar—as much as fifty thousand pounds. He was supposed to be destroyed, but Natasha Karamzin wouldn't stand for it. She and Walter Paget went through the motions, but afterward, Nats rode Balthazar over here instead of calling Mr. Swinford, the insurance agent. Since I gather you don't have the facilities for keeping horses, at least not for long, she asked you to have Balthazar shipped to this other farm. How am I doing?"

"First-rate," Chelmsford said, amazement evident on his cherry-ripe face. "How did you guess?"

Judith gave a small shrug. "It's not exactly a guess. We didn't hear any trucks come to Ravenscroft House last night. Walter loves those hunters, so he wouldn't do anything as inhumane as shooting one of them. Yet Balthazar isn't at the stables. If he left, it had to be under his own power. *Ergo,* the horse couldn't be dead. Either Natasha or Walter had to ride him somewhere, and the obvious choice was The Grange. You've got a barn, and it's not likely that Charles or Claire would come snooping around here before you could move Balthazar to a permanent spot."

Renie was looking almost as dumbstruck as the colonel. "You mean that drama we saw last night was a sham? Coz, why didn't you say so?"

Judith turned a sheepish face to Renie. "Because I didn't know for sure until we went to the stables just now. Heck, I couldn't tell one horse from another anyway, unless they'd been put back in their stalls with the nameplates. Which they were, except that Balthazar's stall was empty and the stable boy verified that the horse was gone. Charles must be wondering why he hasn't heard from the insurance agent."

Colonel Chelmsford's color was returning to its normal ruddy shade. He was pacing the narrow hallway which was littered with old newspapers, empty pails, cardboard boxes, and sacks of dog food.

"Miss Natasha asked a favor," he said, more to himself than his unexpected guests. "Imagine my surprise! As if the Ravenscrofts ever asked a Chelmsford for anything these past seventy years! But I—we—owed it to them, and she has a pretty way about her when she wheedles. She told me Charles wanted to sell Balthazar, but she wouldn't have it—he was her favorite. If I could find a home for him nearby, she'd be able to ride him occasionally. Well, why not? I said. Pleased as punch to put one over on Charles and the rest of that ilk. So I kept the horse for the night and had him brought 'round to Montagues'. They were delighted, I can tell you. The animal is a superb specimen."

Midway through the colonel's explanation, Judith had derailed. "You owed the Ravenscrofts—for what? Your father's betrayal of Miss Petulia?"

If Colonel Chelmsford was surprised by the American stranger's intimate knowledge of village lore, he gave no sign. The colonel wasn't a curious type by nature.

"Not precisely that, no," he said slowly, working with tobacco pouch and match to restart his pipe. "It was what came after." Taking a deep puff, he fixed a surprisingly moist eye on Judith and Renie. "Dora Hobbs, to be exact. The Ravenscrofts took her in. Well, they had to, perhaps, since her mother was Lady Cordelia's maid. She died in childbirth. But the Ravenscrofts did right by the baby, in their way. True Christians and all that." The colonel puffed on his pipe, and scanned the ceiling. "Dora was my father's love-child. She's my half-sister. Never know it to look at her, but there it is. Life's a funny business, eh?''

Judith gulped and agreed that it certainly was.

It was after six when the cousins returned to Ravenscroft House via the main road. They had walked slowly, mulling over the information gleaned from Colonel Chelmsford.

Having established Balthazar's well-being, Judith couldn't figure out a way to tie in the attempted insurance fraud with Aunt Pet's murder. If Charles needed money because he had unwittingly helped bankrupt the estate, then it would have been in his best interest to keep Aunt Pet alive as long as possible. Or so Judith reasoned.

Nor did the startling revelation about Dora Hobbs aid in solving the mystery. Indeed, it seemed to Judith that Dora herself didn't know her father's identity. The colonel had gone on to explain that he had only found out about his relationship to Dora several weeks after Clarence Chelmsford's death in February. Clarence had left a letter, written many years earlier, admitting his liaison with the Ravenscroft lady's maid. He had also expressed remorse for treating Petulia Ravenscroft ''like a cad'' and asked his son to take her some mementos. Petulia, in turn, had treated the colonel with scorn. She was not of a forgiving nature. Or so it seemed—except that she had obviously kept the items that had belonged to her former suitor.

''I imagine Aunt Pet had a lot to say about Dora living at Ravenscroft House,'' Judith remarked as they headed past the gatehouse. ''Maybe she felt that if she could never be Clarence's wife and have a child by him, she'd keep his baby.''

''She kept her in her place,'' Renie noted. ''Dora wasn't treated like a daughter, but turned into servant.''

''That would fit Aunt Pet's way of looking at things,'' Judith said, half-hearing the song of a treecreeper as it climbed up the trunk of an oak, searching for insects. ''She'd provide a home for Dora, but she wouldn't raise her to the same social plane.''

Approaching the rear of the house, Judith and Renie were admitted by a frazzled Mrs. Tichborne. ''All these meals!''

she complained, hurrying back into the kitchen. "The family must hire more help. I can't be expected to cook constantly."

The cousins offered to pitch in, but the housekeeper had her pride: "Never let it be said that Hester Tichborne doesn't give satisfaction. Besides, I've got things under control. We'll eat at seven-thirty."

"Won't your duties ease up when the Marchmonts and the Karamzins return to London after the funeral?" Judith inquired.

Cutting chicken with a cleaver, Mrs. Tichborne gave Judith a patronizing look. "Who can say? The funeral is Thursday. Then Friday, the art appraisers are coming in. Saturday is the livestock auctioneer. Come Sunday, they'll probably have the vicar hold a jumble sale. Then they can set up their bed-and-basket or whatever they call it. Neon signs, no doubt, and a name like 'California Suite.' " Mrs. Tichborne was still grumbling as she turned the heat on under a large sautee pan.

Despite Renie's obvious anxiety to get out of the kitchen and into clothes suitable for eating, Judith lingered. "Things are moving pretty fast, I guess. They're selling some of the paintings?"

The housekeeper dripped oil into the pan. "Mr. Charles is trying to circumvent Miss Petulia's stipulations about keeping everything intact. We'll soon see if that's possible. If not, there won't be tuppence left for anyone."

Now Judith began to feel a sense of guilt about the gatehouse. "Where's Walter?" she asked suddenly.

Mrs. Tichborne shrugged. "Who knows? I thought he'd stay for the funeral. But then again, why should he?"

It was not a question that Judith could or was expected to answer. But on a whim, she had one of her own for the housekeeper: "Say, who dressed up as Mary, Queen of Scots, this year?"

Mrs. Tichborne's expression became pained. No doubt unpleasant memories were stirring somewhere under that tightly drawn coiffure. "Mr. Karamzin," she said at last. "His sister was Lord Darnley."

"And before that?" Judith pressed on.

"Mr. Tinsley," the housekeeper replied promptly. "He filled in for Mr. Charles, who always wanted to be a queen. Once he and Miss Claire married, Queen Mary was always his role. But last year, he and Mrs. Marchmont were in Greece. The only reason he did Lord Burleigh this year was because he'd put on too much weight to get into Mary's dress."

Judith took a deep breath. "And before that?"

Mrs. Tichborne looked away. "Mary was somebody different every year, I think. Mr. Tinsley, Dr. Ramsey, even Colonel Chelmsford, though he looked ridiculous. But he was thinner then."

"So the year that Janet . . . left," Judith said doggedly, "it was who?"

"Harwood," the housekeeper replied through tight lips. "Ordinarily, he wouldn't participate, but Walter Paget got himself thrown and was laid up for almost a week. Harwood took his place, and wouldn't you know, *he* tripped over Mary's petticoats and concussed himself. Walter came out of the hospital in Great Pauncefoot just as they were taking Harwood in. Harwood swore it was a judgment on him for behaving in such an unnatural and ungodly fashion."

Trying not to think too long on the butler dressed as the graceful, ephemeral Mary Stuart, Judith asked a final question:

"So the Queen's costume is stored here at Ravenscroft House?"

Mrs. Tichborne nodded. "Darnley's, too. And Burleigh's and Essex's and Raleigh's and the Four Marys' and—"

"Queen Elizabeth," Renie put in. "Who played her?"

Once again, Mrs. Tichborne gazed at the cousins. Now a small, pinched smile played around her thin lips. "Miss Ravenscroft, who else? Oh, these last years she never left her room, but she'd sit there in the turret window wearing Good Queen Bess's costume, wig, crown, and all. The villagers would wave and bow and scrape as if she were indeed the royal monarch. I do think the old lady enjoyed herself ever so much. Playing the Queen suited her."

"I imagine," Judith murmured, her thoughts flying in

several directions. Leaving the housekeeper to her duties, the cousins went upstairs to change. Fifteen minutes later, they were in the drawing room where Harwood was serving drinks to Claire and Charles.

After requesting scotch, Judith realized that her attitude toward Charles had changed in the past hour. No longer did she see him as merely an ambitious, semi-comic figure, but a blunderer who would stoop to chicanery to cover his tracks. But Judith was used to dealing with all sorts of people, including those of whom she didn't approve. Her polite manner was only slightly strained.

"I'm sorry we won't be here for the funeral," Judith said, sitting down between the Marchmonts. "My cousin and I really must leave Wednesday morning."

"Nonsense," Charles snapped. "The police won't allow it. You'll stay until they say otherwise. As will we all," he added in annoyance.

"What about Walter?" Judith asked, with a discreet glance at Claire.

Charles snorted. "What about him? He can give notice, move out, vilify the family name—it doesn't matter. He's still required to remain in Little Pauncefoot. If you ask me, he probably poisoned Aunt Pet. It'd be just like him to bring the old girl sweets."

Showing an uncustomary spark of anger, Claire bridled. "It would *not*. Walter doesn't grovel. He would never have tried to influence Aunt Pet through . . . *bribery*."

"Bah!" Charles shot back. "Of course he would! Paget knew which side his bread was buttered on. Didn't he try to marry Nats? Fortune-hunting, that's what your Mr. Paget was doing. It's a good thing you warned Nats off. A man shouldn't marry above him. In my opinion, it never works. Might as well marry a Chinawoman or a Mormon."

Claire flew out from her seat, startling Judith. "Charles! What a thing to say! *You* married *me*!" Her cheeks showed two spots of bright pink.

Charles regarded his wife with mild curiosity. "Yes? So I did. But that was . . . different." He had the grace to turn away.

Setting down her drink, Claire put a hand over her face

and fled the drawing room. Judith and Renie exchanged questioning glances; Judith followed Claire into the hall.

To her credit, Claire was getting the upper hand on her tears. "Charles can be so beastly! There was a time when he considered me a feather in his cap!"

Judith gave Claire a consoling pat. "There's no class so conscious of itself as the middle class. Even in America. Everybody claims to be part of it. Which isn't right, since then there'd be no other classes at all."

Claire's mouth wrenched itself into a pathetic smile. "It's not quite the same over here. People still have . . . aspirations. At least in my husband's peer group."

Judith started to make a remark, but Claire wasn't finished. "Aunt Pet took a fancy to Charles. He was young, eager, hardworking. After she turned over the family's financial management to him, she decided it would be wonderful if we married. I was barely twenty-three. I was terribly unsophisticated. Growing up in Swaziland doesn't offer much opportunity. To gain social graces, that is. By the time I came to England to go to school, I was at that awkward age. Only much more so than other adolescent girls. I never got over it. Not really. And Charles was ten years older. He worked in The City. He had Auntie's blessing. I mistook age for *savoir-faire*. At least he wasn't scampering about in a loincloth, shooting blowdarts at strangers. So I let Auntie talk me into marrying him. Sometimes it's seemed more like a merger than a marriage."

Judith nodded sympathetically. "I had a feeling that maybe it wasn't a passionate love affair. Alex hinted as much." She lowered her voice and gave Claire another reassuring pat. "It's understandable that you would seek . . . comfort . . . elsewhere. Walter Paget is very attractive."

"*Walter*?" Claire's face was faintly incredulous. "Yes, I suppose he is. In his way. Oh!" The color reappeared in Claire's cheeks. "You think I . . . that Walter . . . Oh!" She began to laugh, a sound bordering on hysteria.

Judith stepped back. "No?" she said in an embarrassed voice. "I'm sorry, I didn't mean to jump to—"

Claire's laughter was reduced to a giggle. This time, she patted Judith. "Infidelity is a terrible thing. I'd never dream of it, and Charles is a good man. In his way. But he *is* a trifle weak.''

Fleetingly, Judith wondered if Claire had guessed her husband's desperate plan to recoup the family's financial losses. Judith's own reaction to Charles might be harsh: How many bill collectors had she hoodwinked, evaded, and paid with rubber checks during her marriage to Dan McMonigle? It wasn't fair to judge a person under extreme pressure.

But Claire wasn't talking about money. "He doesn't know. Yet," she said, and Judith wondered what she had missed.

"He doesn't?" she repeated, feeling foolish.

Claire shook her head. "Maybe it doesn't matter now that Auntie is dead. I never felt that it did, not even at the time. But Auntie had such definite *ideas*."

"Certainly," Judith said, still at sea. "It's always best to be . . . ah . . . candid."

Claire's nod was enthusiastic. "Exactly. That's what I felt when I spoke to Nats last night. It was all so stupid. Nats wanting to marry Walter. How could she, when they were cousins? But of course she didn't know, because Auntie wouldn't tell her. Why the shame? It wasn't Walter's fault that he was Aunt Aimee's son.''

EIGHTEEN

JUDITH ASKED HARWOOD for a second scotch. It was, after all, at least twenty minutes until dinner. She was strangling on the latest family scandal, wishing she could get Renie alone. But Renie was deep in conversation with Charles, presumably about the proposed art sale.

Claire hadn't returned directly to the drawing room. Nats arrived, however, still looking sullen. She ignored Charles, and asked Judith if she knew of Alex's whereabouts.

Judith slapped a hand to her head. "He's out in the car," she blurted. "Or at least he was about an hour ago when we went over to The Grange. We came in the other way, so you didn't see him. Is it raining yet?"

Nats started for the door, then turned back to Judith. "You went to The Grange? Whatever for?" She had lowered her voice, and was watching Charles surreptitiously.

Judith saw no reason to lie. "Balthazar," she whispered. "We just wanted to make sure he was okay."

The color drained from Nats's face. Again, she glanced at Charles, but he was engrossed in talking to Renie.

"Have you . . . ?" Nats jerked her head in Charles's direction.

240

"Of course not," Judith answered. "It's none of our business. But he'll find out. Eventually."

Apparently reassured, Nats again headed for the door. Judith called after her, "If you don't see Alex, look under the dashboard."

To Judith's surprise, Nats wasn't startled. "I always do," she said, and left the drawing room.

Claire returned almost immediately, looking remarkably composed. "Dinner smells delicious. I was just checking everything with Tichborne. Charles, do you think we should keep her on when we start the bed-and-breakfast?"

Charles looked dubious. "It depends. Don't you enjoy cooking, m'dear? Occasionally?"

The front door chimes sounded, causing Harwood to leave his post. Claire let out a little squeal.

"Oh! I forgot! I invited Dr. Ramsey and his girlfriend to dinner! He's been ever so kind."

Renie, who had gone to the bar to mix her own screwdriver in Harwood's absence, shot Claire a curious glance. "Dr. Ramsey has a girlfriend?"

Claire giggled. "She's not a *girl*, of course. She's a widow, with grandchildren. But Dr. Ramsey lost his wife last year to leukemia, poor thing. And Mara Radford's such a nice woman. She works for Arthur. That's how she and Dr. Ramsey met. Years ago, that is. Arthur and the doctor have shared the building since . . . Oh, I've no idea. Almost forever." Faintly flustered, Claire also did her own bartending, mixing a second martini.

Dr. Ramsey was wearing what was probably his best suit, a charcoal model that had grown snug. By contrast, Mara Radford's black wool crepe was far more fashionable than Judith would have expected from a resident of Little Pauncefoot. The rest of Mara was more predictable. She was short, plump, and cheerful. Her silver hair was swept up and held in place with a rhinestone-studded clip. Judith guessed that she was in her mid-fifties, with no pretensions. The warmth Mara exuded made Judith happy to exclude her from the list of suspects. Still, the occasion was intriguing—Judith was able to put a face on another village name.

Evincing what seemed like genuine pleasure, Mara shook

hands with the cousins. "The American visitors! You're the talk of the village!" Her smile revealed very white, even teeth. Suddenly, she sobered. "Along with less pleasant things, of course. Poor Mr. Tinsley is all undone. He went home early today with a headache."

"My," Judith remarked as Charles handed Mrs. Radford a glass of white wine, "he and his wife must have a lot of complaints between them. I understand she often suffers from ill health."

Mrs. Radford sniffed. "She claims to. Mrs. Tinsley claims many things, I'm afraid. It doesn't do to listen to her. She's a great one for wanting attention."

Dr. Ramsey, cradling a hefty scotch, had joined Mara and the cousins. Claire and Charles were at the door, inquiring after Alex, who apparently was being dragged into the house by his sister.

"Now," the doctor said in a kindly tone, "don't disparage Lona Tinsley. She helps put food on my table, after all. Every doctor needs at least one patient with a lively imagination."

Mara Radford gave Dr. Ramsey a sweet little smile. "You're right, of course. And I should never criticize my employer's wife. It's a nasty habit I got into early on when I worked for Mr. Tinsley's father. Mrs. Tinsley—Mrs. *Edward* Tinsley, Arthur's mother—was a real harridan." Catching Dr. Ramsey's baleful glance, Mrs. Radford wagged a finger at him. "Now, Lawrence, don't deny it. Everyone in Little Pauncefoot knew what she was like, with her strict chapel ways. When she came down the High Street, people would hide—including the merchants. She was fierce."

Having checked on Alex, Charles now joined the group. "Old Mrs. Tinsley?" He chuckled, rather darkly. "I hardly knew her, but she and Aunt Pet had their innings. Quite the character was Mrs. Tinsley. I'm told she kept her husband and her son under her thumb, all right."

Mrs. Radford nodded, her silver hair shining in the wan light of early evening. "She tried to keep everybody under her thumb. Always giving me orders on the phone—errands and such, that had nothing to do with the job. Lona Tinsley would do the same, but I learned my lesson from Arthur's mother. Be polite, be tactful, but be *firm*.'' Mara nodded her head twice, her creamy chins jiggling.

Now that Claire had also entered the circle, Judith edged away, trying to catch Renie's eye. The cousins made contact. On the pretext of freshening their drinks, they moved toward the bar. Harwood eyed them with his usual mixture of deference and disdain.

Renie proffered her half-full glass to the butler. ''Touch this up, will you, sweetie?'' She gave Harwood a coy look. Harwood almost but not quite curled his lip.

Judith turned away from the butler and kept her voice down. Indeed, she barely moved her lips.

''Walter is Aimee Ravenscroft's son, by her no-good Beatnik husband. According to Claire, they became revolutionaries in Paris and shipped Walter home when he was eighteen.''

Renie's eyes widened. ''Revolutionaries in Paris? Weren't they a couple of hundred years too late? Why didn't somebody tell them Marie Antoinette's a lot shorter than she used to be?''

''Shut up,'' Judith muttered. ''You know what I mean, by seventies standards. Anyway, Aimee and Mr. Paget finally O.D.ed—but that was later. Aimee's twin, Fleur, took Walter in and let him work as a stablehand. Fleur pleaded with Aunt Pet, and finally got her to agree to make Walter the Ravenscroft steward. Now we know why he was putting flowers on Fleur's grave. His aunt had given him a home— and a job. But Great-Aunt Pet never quite forgave Walter for being Aimee's son. That must be why he was left out of the will. He certainly felt left out of the family. Walter was so embarrassed by his great-aunt's attitude that he didn't want anyone to know he was related. That suited Pet just fine. Claire said her aunt felt he'd been raised improperly, and thus wasn't worthy of being elevated to true family status. You know, like Dora being illegitimate. The old girl had really fixed ideas about social class.''

''The jewels,'' Renie hissed. ''Why didn't Aunt Pet rat on Aimee to her sister-in-law, Genevieve, about the theft?''

Judith gave a slight shrug. ''Who knows? Some rivalry

between them, maybe. Or Aunt Pet's need for control. Like Janet Tichborne, Auntie enjoyed her little secrets. They're a source of power for some people.''

Renie clutched her screwdriver. ''Phew!'' she gasped, almost inaudibly. ''This place is full of them!''

Judith shrugged. ''Not really. It's a village. Everybody everywhere has secrets. But in a small community like this, people are linked to an unusual degree.''

Renie didn't dispute the point. Instead, she sipped her drink and regarded the Marchmonts and their guests. ''So Nats and Walter are cousins,'' she said, still speaking very softly.

''Exactly. But Nats didn't know until Claire told her last night. Aunt Pet didn't want anyone to find out that she'd given in to Fleur by letting Walter work and live here. Aimee was anathema after she ran off with her Beatnik.''

''No wonder Walter seems self-conscious,'' Renie remarked. ''He's been caught between two worlds. Aunt Pet was right about that. His upbringing must have been very strange. Then he suddenly finds himself at Ravenscroft House, smothered with tradition and some very Victorian ideas.''

Judith was about to comment on Walter's understandable bitterness. But Nats had come back into the room and was heading for the bar.

''I held Alex's head under water for five minutes. *Running* water,'' she added hastily. ''He ought to be able to come down to dinner once he dries out.''

''Try rehab,'' Renie muttered. ''That'll dry him out.''

Nats, who was accepting a vodka martini from Harwood, didn't hear Renie. Judith couldn't refrain from asking the obvious question: ''Does your brother always drink so much?''

Nats grimaced. ''No. Oh, he drinks more than is good for him when he's in a party mood or in some kind of trouble. But I've never seen him drink so . . . consistently as he's done this weekend, which certainly has been no party. I suspect, then, he's up to his neck in debt—again.''

There was no opportunity for further discussion of Alex's drinking habits. Harwood had slipped out from behind the bar to ring the dinner gong. On this Monday night after Aunt Pet's murder, Judith thought it sounded more like a death knell.

As the group began their exit from the drawing room, Judith's morbid thoughts were interrupted by Mara Radford. She gave Judith a mischievous smile and spoke in a low voice:

"You mustn't mind me going on about the Mrs. Tinsleys. I've been with Arthur and his father before him so long that I feel like family."

Passing through the hall, Judith also smiled. "I understand. My cousin's mother worked part-time as a legal secretary for the same man for over forty years."

Mara nodded. "Exactly. And don't tell me that people never bring their troubles to work. You hear everything, which is why I'm rather fed up with Lona Tinsley's poor health."

Judith laughed as they entered the dining room. "It's a good thing her first husband was a doctor. She must have saved on office calls."

The smile disappeared from Mara's plump face. "She wasn't married to a doctor." The small, perfect mouth turned down in disapproval. "If you ask me, she wasn't married at all." Mara moved away, taking her place between Charles and Dr. Ramsey.

Judith goggled after Mara. But there was no immediate opportunity to probe further. Dinner conversation centered on children—the Marchmont twins, Mara's three granddaughters, and the baby that Dr. Ramsey's son and wife were expecting in a matter of weeks. Judith, who was seated between the doctor and a very depressed Alex, paid minimal attention. She sensed that the diners were carefully avoiding the topic of Aunt Pet's death. But of course children made for much more pleasant chitchat than murder.

Claire suggested bridge after dinner, but Charles vetoed the idea. Bridge, he seemed to imply, was too frivolous for a house in mourning. Dr. Ramsey stated that it had been a long and tiring day for everyone, so perhaps it was best to make an early evening of it. He and Mrs. Radford took their leave just before nine. Alex had already gone back upstairs. Charles asked Nats to join him in the library. His tone was ominous. Judith watched them head for the main staircase, and wondered if Charles intended to quiz Nats about Doodles Swinford's reaction.

"Dr. Ramsey was right," Claire announced, yawning widely. "The past two days seem like a year. I'm exhausted. I'll head for bed. If you don't mind."

The cousins insisted that they didn't mind in the least. Left alone in the parlor, Judith told Renie about Mara Radford's comment regarding Lona Tinsley.

"Weird," Renie said, standing in front of a Gobelin tapestry depicting The Hunt. "Maybe Mara is wrong. Maybe she wanted Arthur for herself. Maybe," she added quickly, reassessing her suggestion, "I'm nuts. Who'd really want Arthur, the quintessential dry stick?"

"Good point," Judith replied. She sipped her cognac, letting her gaze wander to the tapestry behind Renie. "I wonder if Nats is telling Charles the truth about Balthazar?"

Renie shrugged. "I don't see why it matters. They'll make a mint off the art collection alone. I think Charles panicked."

Thoughtfully, Judith gazed at Renie. "Yes, I think he did. Isn't that . . . interesting?"

"Huh?" Renie didn't sound as if she thought it was. "Say, you never told me why you knew about what was on that scrap of paper that got stuck in the desk drawer. You said it was last year's date. Why do you think so?"

"It's a logical conclusion," Judith said. "It can't be this year, because the twenty-seventh isn't until tomorrow. If Aunt Pet made out a will last April, then maybe it's from the draft she wrote. The question becomes where's the rest of it?"

"I don't see why you assume the date's off a will," Renie said. "Why not a letter? Maybe Aunt Pet was writing to George and Emily in Swaziland."

"Because," Judith countered, "we know she made a will a year ago. We also know that except for leaving us the gatehouse, it was basically the same as the one that was found in her desk. I imagine she always wrote out everything herself and then had Arthur Tinsley—or Mara Radford—transcribe it.'' Judith would have elaborated, but Charles poked his head in the parlor. He looked drawn and lacked his usual *bonhomie*.

''Oh,'' he said in a tired voice. ''I saw the light on under the door and wondered who . . .'' He gave a small shrug. ''Sorry. I believe I'll go on up to bed.''

But Judith had a question for Charles. ''Say, when was that memorial to the Dunks completed? The new one, that includes what I assume is the Ravenscroft arms.''

Charles looked blank, then tapped his temple. ''I remember now. It was restored in time for our wedding. Twelve years ago, come June.''

Renie had wandered away from the tapestry to stand by a seventeenth-century Venetian chair. ''What happened to it?'' she inquired, leaning on the gilt-edged back.

Charles shrugged. ''It was struck by lightning during a severe winter storm. Sir Lionel was knocked right off his perch. For some reason, the original stone base wasn't the same type that was used in most of the other buildings around here, including Ravenscroft House. A rebel Dunk, with radical ideas, I suppose. Aunt Pet wanted consistency, so they tore up the base and rebuilt it. They also stuck Sir Lionel's ear back on. Or was it his nose?'' Charles frowned, apparently trying to picture the damaged statue.

''It's very handsome,'' Judith said in a noncommittal tone.

Charles harrumphed. ''It should be. It cost the world. But for once, Aunt Pet didn't balk at expense. She never even flinched when she got the bill. I know, I was there at the time. Claire and I were man and wife by then.'' He grew wistful, perhaps recalling happier days.

Staring into her cognac, Judith let Renie speak for both of them. ''Go ahead, Charles, tuck yourself in. We're fine. By the way,'' she continued, with a meaningful look at Judith, ''we don't intend to keep the gatehouse. We think Walter should have it. *All things considered*.''

''What things?''

''Family things,'' Renie replied calmly. ''We came, we

saw, we listened. Beatniks, hippies, angry young men and women—we've lived through it all.''

Charles flushed. "You know?'' he gasped. "I only found out just now from Nats. How . . . ?''

Renie waved a hand. "My cousin has a unique way about her. She meets somebody, and two minutes later they're spilling their guts. Walter deserves the property. He's family. We're not.''

Judith gave Charles a sheepish smile. "Renie's right. We'll have everything straightened out before we leave.''

"That's awfully good of you,'' Charles said, almost stammering. "Walter will be grateful. Someday. He can be a stormy petrel, you know.''

"He can be one in the gatehouse,'' Renie said. "Good night, Charles.''

With a small wave, Charles left the parlor. As the door closed behind him, Judith sprinted across the room.

"Where are the cops?'' she demanded, as if Renie ought to know.

"Gee, coz, how about at the cop shop? Where else would they be?''

Judith shook her head impatiently. "No, they were holding forth in this very room. Now they've gone. Have they solved the case, or given up? Is the Yard coming in? Why isn't somebody on duty, watching this place? Constable Duff, I suppose, making the rounds on his bicycle. Damn! Why does England have to be so law-abiding? Why can't they be violent, like us?''

Renie drained her glass. "They're violent enough. They just do it with less noise. How many bodies do you want to rack up on this trip?''

Judith, however, was already out of the parlor, heading for the stairs. "I'm not worried about the body count. Come on, we're going to the library.''

"What for?'' Renie asked, attempting to take two steps at a time to catch up. "Are we calling your mother again?''

"No,'' Judith answered, sprinting across the landing. "We're calling the police.''

"Whew!'' Renie breathed. "That's better! For a second, I thought we were in trouble!''

* * *

Inspector Claude Wattle wasn't in. The desk sergeant—or at least that was who Judith presumed had answered the phone—was reluctant to pass on a message, especially from an American. Judith relayed her ties to Ravenscroft House. The sergeant succumbed. If the inspector thought it necessary, he'd call back. Judith hung up.

She gritted her teeth. "Dare I call Mother at the island? What if Wattle calls back?"

"He won't." Renie was standing by one of the tall bookshelves, fingering a vintage copy of *Martin Chuzzlewit.* "Besides, your mother never talks very long."

Resignedly, Judith put through the call to Auntie Vance and Uncle Vince's island home. They had moved there from the city upon Uncle Vince's retirement as a taxi driver. Uncle Vince had been a good taxi driver, as long as he stayed awake. Certainly his fares always felt relaxed in his company. At least until the cab began to drift aimlessly through the streets.

Auntie Vance answered in her typical ear-rattling manner: "Hello? Judith? What the hell are you doing, calling from England? You think I don't know how to take care of a semi-invalid? Hell's bells, I've been married to your uncle for almost forty years! He may not be sick but he sure as hell is nuts!"

Judith—and the rest of the family—were used to Auntie Vance's critical attitude toward her mate. Indeed, Auntie Vance tended to be critical of everything and everybody.

"I'm checking on Mother," Judith replied, and immediately realized it was the wrong thing to say. "I mean, I wanted her to know I was thinking about her."

"You're *thinking*? This *is* news!" cried Auntie Vance in mock surprise. "But it sure as hell isn't worth the money you're forking out to tell me over the phone. You could have sent a postcard. Or have you learned to spell yet?"

As ever, Judith tried to take the badgering as it was intended. Except that with Auntie Vance, she was never quite sure what was *really* intended. "If I could just talk to Mother for a minute . . ."

Though Vanessa Grover Cogshell's tongue was as tart

as—and saltier than—Gertrude's, she was much more reasonable. "Okay, I'm taking the phone to the old fart now.
Good God, Judith, how do you put up with her? She's
ornery as a goat and dumb as a bag of bricks! If you don't
get home soon, I'm going to row her out in Uncle Vince's
leaky boat and drown her!"

Gertrude's raspy voice could be heard away from the
phone. "Mind your manners, Vanessa. Have I told you
lately you're getting fat as a pig?"

"Shut the hell up, you miserable old . . ." Auntie Vance's words became muffled, for which Judith was thankful.

"Hi, Mother," Judith said, forcing cheer into her voice
and rolling her eyes at Renie, who was now sitting on the
edge of Charles's desk. "How do you feel?"

"With my fingers," Gertrude snapped back. "Now
what? Haven't you got anything better to do than sit around
and make expensive phone calls?"

"I've been worried," Judith said calmly. "In fact, I feel
guilty, being on vacation while you're in pain and Auntie
Vance and Uncle Vince have to—"

"You ought to feel guilty," Gertrude broke in. "What
else are children for? As far as I'm concerned, you should
feel so blasted guilty that it ruins your whole trip. Ha-ha."

Judith knew, of course, that Gertrude wasn't really
laughing. Unless she was so pleased to have one-upped her
sister-in-law Deborah in the Only Daughter's Guilt-Ridden
Stakes.

"Look, Mother," Judith said, still reining in her annoyance, "I actually can't keep this phone tied up. How are
you doing?"

"As I please," Gertrude shot back. "At least," she
added, lowering her voice and speaking closer to the
mouthpiece, "as much as your Auntie Vance will let me.
That woman is a *terror*. And she *has* put on weight. Her
backside is—"

Now reassured as to her mother's well-being, Judith decided to break off the call. "I have to go now, Mother.
There's a ruthless murderer on the loose. Ha-ha."

"Ha-ha? What's funny about *that*?" Gertrude retorted.
"It wouldn't be the first time, where you and your dim-

bulb cousin are concerned. All the same, don't put any nickels up your nose, kiddo. So long." To Judith's chagrin, Gertrude hung up first.

"She seems to be doing well," Judith said in a bemused voice.

"No kidding," Renie murmured. "Say, speaking of ruthless murderers, do you think Bill and Joe would have heard about Aunt Pet's poisoning?"

Anxiously, Judith sat back in the chair, eyeing the phone. "No. They're off in the Highlands, and probably haven't seen a newspaper. Certainly not a TV. Gosh, *we* haven't seen the news since we got here. I gather Aunt Pet took the papers, but Dora's probably set fire to them by now."

Renie considered her cousin's words. "Yes—you're right. This hasn't been a media circus, thank goodness. And if we're isolated here in Somerset, Bill and Joe are really cut off from the world. Which is good. For all of us." She leaned on one hand, regarding Judith in a confidential manner. "Now tell me why you're so anxious to get hold of Inspector Wattle. You know how I hate to be left in the dark."

"I didn't mean to," Judith said with a feeble smile. "It all just came to me while I was talking to Charles. One thing kept popping up from everybody in the last few days. It had to do with what—"

The phone rang then, a soft burring sound. Afraid that someone else in the household might answer, Judith snatched up the receiver. To her relief, Inspector Wattle was at the other end. He didn't sound pleased about being contacted by the American tourists. Judith sought to placate him.

"I know you'll think I'm being silly," she began, hearing a faint click on the line, "but a number of pieces of information have fallen . . . uh . . . into my hands. Verbally, for the most part, but along with studying the personalities of the suspects, I think it might be crucial to . . ." She paused, wondering nervously if someone was listening on an extension. "If you could dig up Sir Lionel Dunk's monument."

If Claude Wattle was incredulous, Renie was stupefied.

She gaped at Judith. Judith, in turn, blanched at Wattle's response. He didn't brook interference. He despised amateur meddling. He couldn't take seriously suggestions from any laypersons, *American visitors* in particular.

"I know it sounds goofy," Judith broke in, "but I've had some experience—"

"Experience!" huffed Wattle. "You watch the telly. See 'ere, Mrs. Flynn, we've brought in the Yard. They've got their experts, topnotch, dealing in evidence *and* personality. Psychological profiles, we call 'em over 'ere. We may seem backward to you Yanks, but we're on top of this."

"I'm sure you are," Judith said, "and if that's true, then is it all right if my cousin and I leave Ravenscroft House tomorrow or early Wednesday? We have to meet our—"

Wattle, however, was speaking right over Judith: "— first thing in the morning. We need daylight for a proper job of it. Cutting tools, a stone mason, the works. Wouldn't want the locals complaining that we'd defaced Dunk, would we?"

"What?" Frowning at Renie, Judith clutched the receiver. "You mean you're really going to open up the monument after all? How did you know?"

The inspector chortled. "Now, now, Mrs. Flynn, those other North American colonists aren't the only ones who always get their man. Or woman. I told you, we brought in the Yard. They know what they're about. Ta-ta for now."

Hanging up the phone, Judith made a face at Renie. "He's figured it out, too. Or Scotland Yard has. Oh, well. I said I had faith in the English police, didn't I?"

Renie nodded. "So why do you look like a plate of warmed-over worms? You should be relieved. We can go meet Bill and Joe. However," she added ominously, "you go nowhere until you tell me everything."

For the next fifteen minutes, Judith did just that. Renie evinced shock at first, then began to realize that her cousin's theory was sound. As ever, it was logical.

"How do you suppose the police figured it out?" Renie asked in semi-wonder.

"The same way I did," Judith answered promptly. "The

clues always pointed to one person and one person only. It was just a matter of hitting on the precise motive.''

The phone rang again, but this time Judith didn't pick up the receiver. "It can't be for us," she said, rising from behind the desk.

But it was. As the cousins left the library, Mrs. Tichborne was hurrying up the stairs. Mr. Tinsley had called Mrs. Flynn. He'd only just gotten the message from Mrs. Tinsley about Judith's visit.

Judith and Renie returned to the library. Arthur Tinsley apologized profusely for the delay, but said his wife had come down with neuralgia. What sort of "peculiarity" was Mrs. Flynn referring to in the handwritten will?

With a distressed glance at Renie, Judith summoned up her courage. "It's the gatehouse clause," she hedged. "We want to sign it over to Walter Paget. Can you make the arrangements?"

A sharp breath of surprise came through the receiver. "Are you quite sure this is what you meant?" the solicitor asked in his most precise voice.

"Mean—or meant?" Judith frowned at Renie.

Arthur didn't answer directly. Judith could picture him furrowing his brow and fidgeting with his pen, while deliberating on the matter at hand. At last he said that he could meet with the cousins Monday at one o'clock. "Is that satisfactory?"

It wasn't. Juidth explained that she and Renie wanted to leave on the first morning train.

"Well." Arthur cleared his throat. "I realize it's after ten, but would it be possible to meet tonight?"

"Ah . . ." Judith sounded faintly dismayed. "Aren't we rushing things?"

The solicitor's tone warmed slightly. "No, I assure you. It's a simple matter. If we do it now, it will expedite your departure." He paused, apparently considering his next words with his usual care. "If you like, I could come to Ravenscroft House within the next half-hour. Will Mr. Paget be present?"

Judith was forced into an evasion. "I'm not sure where Mr. Paget is. Does he have to be there?"

"No," Arthur replied. "I merely thought it might be . . . helpful. Shall I see you around ten-thirty?"

Judith agreed, but added an afterthought: "Meet us at the gatehouse. Just in case Walter is home, okay?"

Arthur was more than willing to accommodate the cousins. Judith and Renie got their jackets, then went downstairs.

"Let's check on Walter," Judith suggested. "Just in case."

Renie looked worried. "Are you sure that's a good idea? In fact, is any of this a good idea?"

Judith gave Renie a crooked smile. "You're the one who wanted to surrender the gatehouse. Are you having qualms, coz?"

"Not about *that*," Renie replied, obviously still disturbed. But seeing Judith's face set with purpose, she gave in. "Okay, let's get this over with."

For a split second, Judith hesitated. Renie was right to be cautious. It wasn't wise to act on impulse. Maybe they should put everything off until morning.

Then again, maybe morning would never come.

NINETEEN

A HALF-MOON RODE high above the river as the cousins started for the gatehouse. Clouds, weighted with the damp chill of the sea, were moving in from Devon and Dorset. More rain, Judith thought, but that was typical of capricious April.

There were no lights in the gatehouse. "Maybe Walter's there, but he's gone to bed," Renie suggested.

"Maybe." But Judith sensed that the house was empty. It conveyed an air of being spurned by its long-time resident, as well as its would-be owners. "Desolate," Judith murmured, more to herself than to Renie.

A gust of wind made Renie shiver. "Let's go. Even if he's there, we don't want to wake him up. There's no telling what he'll do."

Judith set her mouth in a grim line. "No, not even with good news. Walter may not see things that way, given his state of mind."

But Judith didn't head back to the house. Rather, she led Renie down Farriers Lane, past the village green. The trees cast long dark shadows, their trunks groaning, the leaves sighing in the wind. The cousins stopped suddenly as a flashlight played through the shrubbery.

Judith grabbed Renie's arm. "Who's that?" she asked, her heart beating faster.

Renie peered into the green. "I can't tell," she whispered. "Somebody's moving around the Dunk memorial."

"Jeez!" Judith now shuddered. "Let's go to Tinsley's office. He'll have to stop there first to draw up the deed."

Renie, however, balked. "We said we'd meet him at the gatehouse. Let's go back. This is creepy."

Taking several indecisive steps in a semi-circle, Judith kept watching the wavering flashlight. At last it became stationary. Judith edged closer to the green, but the moon disappeared behind a cloud. She could see nothing except the faint amber glow.

Renie nudged Judith. "There's a car parked at the end of the lane," she whispered. "I don't recognize it."

Judith turned. "Is it the police?"

"No," Renie replied. "I think I could make out one of those black and white so-called Panda cars."

The wind had picked up sharply, cutting through the cousins' light jackets. Renie brushed her hair out of her eyes; Judith pulled her collar up to her chin.

"You're right," Judith said finally. "We'll wait by the gatehouse."

Judith and Renie had just turned back when another car came down the lane. This time they recognized the gray vehicle as belonging to Arthur Tinsley. He stopped when he saw the cousins, rolling down the window and motioning to them.

Judith and Renie hurried to the car. "Walter doesn't seem to be around," Judith explained, still speaking in a whisper. "Shall we go back to Ravenscroft House?"

"No need," Arthur said. "I haven't been to the office yet. Come along and we'll fill out the papers there. It's grown quite chilly. I'll make tea."

Judith didn't see how they could politely refuse Arthur's offer. She had dealt the hand herself; she had to play it out. Two minutes later, they were in the waiting room where Mrs. Radford presumably held forth during business hours.

"The tea things are here," Arthur explained, turning on a desk lamp. "So are the forms. This won't take but a minute. I can deliver them to Mr. Paget tomorrow. Assuming, of course, that he'll be in."

Judith said nothing, but exchanged a quick glance with Renie. Arthur had his back to the cousins as he fiddled with a state-of-the-art tea maker.

"I prefer the old-fashioned method," Arthur said in a fretful voice, "but Mrs. Radford is all for efficiency. Still, the tea tastes quite good. Is Irish Breakfast satisfactory?"

It was, the cousins assured Arthur. He fiddled some more, apparently not as efficient as his secretary. At last, the tea seemed to be steeping. The solicitor turned to a file cabinet and produced the appropriate documents. Sitting at Mara's desk, he explained the procedure. Either cousin could fill in the blanks, but both would have to sign.

"Joint ownership, you see." He gave Judith and Renie a thin smile.

Renie did the honors and signed off. Judith hesitated, reminded herself that she couldn't miss what she never had, and added her signature, too.

"Well done," Arthur said, nodding approval. "Most generous. Ah! Our tea is ready. Sugar? Cream? Lemon?"

Renie requested sugar; Judith asked for cream. Arthur produced both, then put a hand to his head. "Oh, my! I almost forgot—do forgive me. Since you're not citizens of the Crown, there's one other document you must sign. It has to do with taxes and such. It's worded in a most complicated manner, but it's a mere formality. Here." He slid a piece of paper in front of the cousins. Judith tried to read it, then stopped.

"I need my glasses," she said, reaching for her purse. Her elbow struck Renie's arm, knocking the teacup to the floor. The tea spilled, and the china broke into a dozen shards.

"Oh, no!" Judith cried. "I'm sorry! Let me pick up this mess!" She bent down, then suddenly jerked her head up to fix Renie with angry eyes. "You're such a klutz, Serena! If you ever learned to eat and drink like something other than a pig at a trough, I wouldn't get involved in these embarrassing situations!"

"Hey! Since when did you ever . . ." Renie paused, blinked, and grabbed Judith by the collar of her jacket.

"I've had enough of your big mouth. Apologize, fatso, or we're taking this outside!"

"*Fatso!* How dare you!" Judith shrieked. "You make Bugs Bunny look like Elmer Fudd was an orthodonist! Okay, let's go! I'll meet you in the High Street."

Judith and Renie practically fell over each other getting out the door.

"Nice pick-up," Judith gasped.

"You only call me Serena when you're seriously mad," Renie said, between gulps of air. "And I'd never *really* call you fatso."

"Right," Judith said, now panting hard. "Faster, Bugs."

The cousins were running toward Farriers Lane when they heard footsteps pounding behind them. Judith turned just where the unidentified car was parked at the end of the village green. Arthur Tinsley was waving his arms, calling for them to stop. As he drew closer, Judith saw that he was also waving a gun.

"Don't do it, Arthur!" Judith called, trying to keep the panic out of her voice. "You're already in way over your head!"

"Don't move!" Arthur had assumed a marksman's stance, which ill-suited him. He reminded Judith of a toy soldier who had been knocked askew by his owner.

But that didn't mean that his aim would be false. Judith and Renie sidled closer together, standing nervously by the edge of the green. There was no sign of the flashlight now. The wind moaned in the trees and a few drops of heavy rain began to fall. Judith swallowed hard, then spoke in a voice that was supposed to be loud and clear, but was neither.

"You've already killed two women," she croaked, leaning on Renie. "Janet Tichborne, twelve years ago, when she rejected your advances. Tomorrow, the police will find her body in the Dunk Monument. Aunt Pet saw it happen from her turret window. She didn't realize it at the time, but a year ago, when you filled in for Charles as Queen Mary, she remembered the last time you played the part. You knocked out poor Harwood, and took his costume. He was sent to the hospital and you partnered Janet's Bothwell.

Her mother told us how Janet danced with her partner, but Harwood couldn't dance—he'd been lame since World War II. So someone had taken his place—you. The old lady saw you carry Janet—''

"Enough!" Arthur's voice cut like a rapier. He lowered the gun slightly, gesturing to his left. "The green," he said. "Move to the green."

Holding on to each other, the cousins backpedaled to the walkway which led off Farriers Lane. Arthur was now only ten feet away, gripping the gun with both hands. Judith considered screaming, but there was no one to hear. The shops on the High Street were closed, the almshouses were too far away, and the gatehouse had seemed empty. As for the inhabitants of Ravenscroft House, they were either asleep or too well insulated from any distant noise.

"How did you know?" Arthur Tinsley asked, his voice not only dry, but thick.

Judith summoned up the power to speak. "The new will. Oh, the will was meant to be the motive, to divert suspicion. But nobody knew about it except you. And Aunt Pet. She didn't make a new draft. It was too difficult with her arthritis. The only part she could write was the short paragraph about us getting the gatehouse. She was going to have you redo the old one, from the previous April. But you took the original draft, with the new amendment, and cut off the date she'd written on top. That made the paper shorter than it should have been. You added last Saturday's date at the bottom of the page using her pen and ink, and inadvertently kept the pen. We went through the desk and everything was there—except the fountain pen. I realized that when I saw Dr. Ramsey writing in his office. I remembered how you accidentally took Charles's pen and put it in your pocket. It was a habit, and it betrayed you." Judith stopped for breath. She also stopped backing up. She and Renie had almost reached the Dunk memorial.

"Aunt Pet confronted you with her realization about Janet's death," Judith said, now sounding hoarse and tired. "Maybe she mentioned it as early as last April. Maybe she taunted you. Maybe—"

"She tormented me!" Arthur shouted. "Hints, innuendo,

skirting the issue! It amused her, like pulling the strings of a puppet! Finally, during this year's All Fools Revels, she accused me outright! Imagine! After all these years!'' The hands that held the gun shook. Judith flinched and Renie let out a small, stifled cry.

"You set it all up," Judith said, barely above a whisper. "You had started bringing her chocolates, to placate her and hope that she'd stop talking about what happened to Janet. But she wouldn't. In fact, she finally accused you of Janet's murder. So when you found out that the family would be here while she made a new will, you used the Jimsonweed to poison her chocolates. She claimed to have a keen sense of smell, but that's dubious. It was Claire who first noticed the smoke last Friday afternoon. Aunt Pet wouldn't admit to losing any more of her powers."

Judith paused, trying to rally her voice. "You couldn't know when Aunt Pet would eat the fatal dose, but you had the original will from last April. After she was dead, you were in her room, hiding the handwritten version where it could be found and everyone would assume that it was new. The will she made in anger last August was never lost— you burned it in the wastebasket to make it look as if Dora had started another fire. But she swore she didn't. She may be a pyromaniac, but she's not a liar. You had to be sure the new will would be valid to provide a motive for the heirs. Only you could have done all those things. That's why I had to eliminate everybody else as a suspect. You thought your secret would never—"

"Stop!" Arthur was close to hysteria. Somehow he managed to steady the gun. It was pointed straight at Judith. "I'd hope to make this easier. Mrs. Tichborne told me about the police planning to dig into the Dunk Monument. The fool had listened in on your phone conversation with Inspector Wattle. She had no idea that when she repeated the information, your fate was sealed. If you'd signed that second paper and drunk the tea, everyone would have thought you were overcome with remorse for killing Miss Ravenscroft to get the gatehouse. But no, you had to spoil a tasteful exit! Now I'll have to shoot you, just like in those miserable American gangster films!''

Shaking with fear, Judith and Renie held on to each other. They heard a click. And then a shot. Each of them expected to feel terrible pain. But it was Arthur Tinsley who fell to the ground, writhing in agony.

The cousins collapsed against each other, rocking to and fro. They were oblivious to the rain that was now pelting down, and to the wind that howled among the trees. They were only barely conscious of the two dark figures who rushed past them.

"Coz!" Judith gasped.

"Coz!" Renie squeaked.

"Fuzz," said a familiar voice.

One of the two figures started walking back toward Judith and Renie. He shoved a gun in a shoulder holster under his dark canvas jacket. Then he grinned and hurried to Judith.

It was Joe Flynn.

The man who was still bending over the fallen solicitor was Bill Jones.

Both cousins threatened to faint. Instead, they started to laugh and cry at the same time. Renie rushed to her husband's side, choking on tears and laughter. She fell in his arms just as he stood up and almost toppled both of them.

"Hi, Bill," she said, sounding almost normal. "Catch anything?"

Bill glanced down at the unconscious Arthur Tinsley. "I think so. But so did you."

In a relatively quiet corner of the Waverly Bar just off the Royal Mile in Edinburgh, Joe Flynn and Bill Jones were threatening to kill their travel agent.

"I told you, we never got as far as King's Cross Station Friday morning," Joe said, still in wonder. "Paul called me just after you left for Little Pauncefoot and said he'd forgotten to ask how much we were paying for the privilege of fishing in Scotland. I thought he meant our lodgings."

"But he didn't," Bill put in, shaking his head. "Joe's brother was referring to the fees that are charged on most Scottish rivers because they run through private property. You wouldn't believe what they ask. Our whole trip didn't cost as much as the fee for just four days of fishing.''

Judith and Renie both looked suitably flabbergasted. In the past twelve hours since leaving Ravenscroft House, they hadn't yet had the opportunity to hear a coherent version of their husbands' aborted fishing adventure.

Joe sipped at his glass of ale. ''When the travel agent mentioned—in passing—that we would pay a fee once we got to Scotland, I thought he was talking about a license, like at home. But that was just the beginning of what turned out to be way beyond our means.''

Judith couldn't resist a small barb. ''I thought Paul had all sorts of influence through his job as a diplomat. Why couldn't he finagle something for you?''

Joe's green eyes rested on his wife's face. He looked nettled. ''He could—if he'd had time. But it would take at least a week, and while Bill and I were sorting everything out and figuring what to do next, Scotland Yard called.''

Judith and Renie knew this part of the story. One of the divisional commanders had been so impressed with Joe's ideas about an unsolved disappearance that he'd asked to meet with the American homicide detective. Since Bill had expressed interest in seeing Scotland Yard, Joe had taken him along. During the course of the meeting, Bill had made some suggestions about the psychological makeup of both the possible victim and the putative criminal. Again, the divisional commander had been impressed. He had asked the Americans if they'd like to go to the scene of the alleged crime. When they discovered it had occurred—if indeed it had occurred at all—in Little Pauncefoot, Joe and Bill had quickly backed off. They had no desire to show up where their wives were spending a cozy weekend with the Marchmonts.

Consequently, they had spent Saturday at Oxford and Sunday at Cambridge. Upon their return to London Monday morning, there was a message for Joe. Strange as it seemed, there had been another incident at Little Pauncefoot. This time there was no doubt about it being a homicide. The Yard was being asked in. While it was highly unlikely that the two cases were connected, would Detective Flynn and Professor Jones care to go down to Somerset?

Given the fact that their wives might be in mortal danger, Joe and Bill jumped at the chance. They had each tried to call Ravenscroft House from London, but had gotten a busy signal both times. It had been early evening by the time they had been updated by Inspector Wattle at his Yeovil headquarters. Checking into The Old Grey Mare, they had again tried to telephone Judith and Renie. And again, the line had been tied up. After a late—and virtually inedible— dinner at the inn, they had gone off with a flashlight to explore the Dunk Monument, which they knew the police planned to open up in the morning.

"It's a good thing you were armed," Judith said to Joe, recalling the events that had led up to the near-fatal encounter on the green.

Joe signaled the barkeep for another round. "I insisted on being issued a sidearm. I told the Yard people that for Yanks, a gun in our holsters triggered our brains. Without a piece, we were helpless. They weren't happy about it, but they gave in after I threatened to buy an antique blunder-buss."

Bill was nodding in approval. "That was good shooting. You only winged that lawyer. He'll be able to stand trial."

Renie edged closer to Bill. "And you had him all figured out, never even having met him! I'm so proud!"

Bill gave a small shrug. "If Janet Tichborne was mur-dered, but her body was never found, it was probably a man who killed her. The Yard had her background on file. I'll skip the technical jargon, but basically she used men to prove her worth, no doubt because her father had died so young and she needed masculine approbation. Her tactics were successful with her peer group, but when she came up against an older man—and it turned out that this Tinsley was almost forty—her tricks backfired. Tinsley had been dominated by his mother. He'd never had much luck with women, and he fell right into Janet's trap. When she tired of him, he rebelled. Violently."

Judith hastened to agree. "Did he ever! He strangled her and carried her off to the unfinished Dunk Monument, where he buried the body. The workmen never noticed, and completed the job a short time later. If they smelled anything strange, they probably thought it was that blasted Jimsonweed. And Aunt Pet watched it all, but wasn't sure what she'd seen. There was so much horseplay during the festival that she didn't find it odd that Mary, Queen of Scots, was carrying Lord Bothwell across the green. But then Janet disappeared. So did the costume.''

One thing had puzzled Renie all along: "Why didn't Aunt Pet figure it out sooner? She was sharp. It shouldn't have taken twelve years. Or eleven, if she twigged to it last April.''

"Her mind was sharp, yes," Judith agreed. "But remember how she fought getting glasses until the past couple of years? I suspect she hadn't been sure of what she'd seen. It would be hard to distinguish some of the men's costumes. And of course Bothwell's outfit was never seen again by anyone because Janet was wearing it when she died. The fact that Janet disappeared wasn't suspicious to Aunt Pet. Her own great-niece had run away in her teens. It was only much later, when Janet was never heard from, that people began to suspect foul play. It was well and good for Mrs. Tichborne to say her daughter would never go off without a word. But teenagers do that, and a mother's protests often are taken with a grain of salt. Then last April, Aunt Pet saw Arthur dressed once again as Queen Mary. She had her glasses by then, and it must have dawned on her what might have happened. She couldn't know, which was why she threw out hints. Arthur got rattled. He undoubtedly denied everything, but Aunt Pet was shrewd. She could tell from his manner that she was right.''

Bill was nodding again. "Miss Ravenscroft couldn't tell the police because she had no proof. Even if they dug up the monument and found the body, it wouldn't be possible to make a case against Tinsley. An old lady with failing eyesight wouldn't make a credible witness.''

Pulling two cigars out of his jacket pocket, Joe offered one to Bill and flicked on a lighter. "What I envy most about the English system is that a confession is admissible as proof of guilt. If we were home, this case would go right out the window.''

There was a pause as another round of ale and a platter of mixed hors d'oeuvres were delivered. Renie elbowed the others out of the way while she plundered the selections. The bar was busy on this misty early evening in April. The Flynns and the Joneses were seated at a table by an arched window that looked out onto the stalwart gray stone buildings of the old town.

Boldly, Judith dared to reach for an oyster on the half-shell. ''We were meant to believe that the estate was the motive. But the estate has diminished, and it certainly wasn't in Charles's interest to kill Aunt Pet. Besides, it was out of character. He panicked after her death, which proved he couldn't have been the murderer.''

Bill leaned into the table, lowering his rich voice, ''That's what makes all this so interesting—delving into the personalities. I think I got more out of the murder investigation than the IMNUTS conference.''

Joe clapped Bill on the shoulder. ''Stick with me, William. Back on the job, I can provide you with a new perp every day.''

''No thanks,'' Bill replied, looking somewhat grim. ''Once is enough.'' He turned to Judith. ''How long did Miss Ravenscroft intend to string Tinsley along, I wonder?''

Judith smiled faintly at Bill. ''I have a feeling that once Aunt Pet got the new will out of the way, she would have insisted that Arthur turn himself in. She may have actually thought he'd do it. Honor and all that. Instead, he killed her. His values weren't Victorian.''

Bill was sampling two kinds of cheese. ''Tinsley's marriage gave him away, too. Scotland Yard had checked into the background of everyone involved. They discovered that Lona Tinsley hadn't been married to a doctor, but had worked for one. He was a psychiatrist who Arthur consulted after having a partial breakdown following Janet's murder. That's how Arthur and Lona met. She'd had a stillborn baby out of wedlock in her youth. I suspect the experience had made sex unappealing to her. But she wanted the respectability of marriage. Arthur wanted sanctuary, which a wife could give him. The wedding took place less than six months after Janet was killed.''

Judith was nodding vehemently. "Mara Radford suspected that Lona had never been married before. Mara's a good judge of human nature.''

Renie nodded, a sweet pickle poised at her mouth. "Working in a law office will do that for you. My mother's experiences as a legal secretary have made her wise in the ways of people.''

Bill wore a dubious expression. "It's only empirical knowledge,'' he said, never willing to concede a point in his mother-in-law's favor. "But it's true that Lona Tinsley was obsessed with respectability. If it even became known that she'd had a baby, there had to be a husband. She'd lived a lie for years.''

"She'd lived dangerously,'' Judith noted, "without realizing it. Her husband was also living a lie. Of course they provided each other's cover, if unwittingly. It's very sad.'' Brightening, Judith stole another oyster, right out from under Renie's hand. "What a fateful year! So much happened twelve years ago, about the time that Janet disappeared. That's what kept cropping up with everybody we talked to. Not everything was tied into Janet's murder, but I sensed it couldn't all be coincidence.''

Renie, who had dribbled melted butter down the front of her silk blouse, was shaking her head. "Gosh! What a weekend in the country! I sure hope Walter gets over his sulk about the will now that we've given him the gatehouse. Moving into The Old Grey Mare was a bad idea, unless Millie's given notice. Again. Say,'' she went on, turning to Judith, "where was Claire going when she sneaked out of the big house Sunday afternoon?''

Judith laughed. "It wasn't to see Walter. She was off to Colonel Chelmsford's, to find out why he'd called on Aunt Pet. I just assumed she was going to the gatehouse, but she must have walked right past it.''

Joe and Bill both gazed askance at their wives. "That gatehouse,'' Joe began.

"It's on a river,'' Bill remarked.

Judith choked on a swallow of ale. "There's no fish," she spluttered.

Renie dropped a sesame wafer in her lap. "Tiddlers. All tiddlers. You know, undersized, small fry, wee baby fish, as they say here in Scotland."

Joe and Bill exchanged skeptical glances. "It would have made a terrific *pied-a-terre*," said Joe.

"I'm not so far from retirement," commented Bill.

"We're not far from dinner," Renie put in, wolfing down the last hors d'oeuvre. "Where are we going?"

Bill consulted a small piece of paper. "It's called The Witchery, quote, 'the most haunted restaurant in town.' " He refolded the paper and put it back in his jacket. "We're told it has some eerie special effects."

The cousins' faces both fell. "I don't like scary stuff," Renie asserted. She jabbed Bill in the ribs. "Hey, you know how I hate horror movies! What a dumb choice for a restaurant!"

"It sure is," Judith chimed in, glaring at Joe, who was motioning for their tab. "Why do we have to go someplace creepy? Do you want us to stay awake with nightmares?"

Joe lifted an eyebrow at Bill. "The worst of it," he said in a resigned voice, "is that they're serious."

Bill nodded. "I know. But are they crazy?"

Joe shrugged. "Don't ask me. You're the nut guy. I'm just a cop."

The cousins ignored their husbands. "Why did we let them choose in the first place?" Renie groused. "We're the trip planners. Didn't we just redo the entire final week of our vacation to accommodate *them*?"

"Ah . . ." Judith looked a trifle sly. "In a way . . . I just hope they like staying at the bed-and-breakfast in Orkney."

Joe turned apoplectic; Bill's square jaw jutted. "*Orkney*?" they chorused.

Judith grew smug. "Very rural, very isolated. Gorgeous scenery, peaceful pastures, rugged coastline. Only a third of the seventy islands are inhabited. There's fishing, too. It's free." Judith tried to keep a straight face.

"Free?" Joe was incredulous.

"What kind of fishing?" Bill asked, his expression skeptical.

Renie started to enumerate on her fingers: "Wild brown trout, salmon, halibut—you name it, they've got it."

Bill wasn't convinced. "How can it be free when everyplace in Scotland costs a bundle?"

"Thank the Norsemen," Renie said. "There's some ancient treaty that allows free access to all the Orkney waters. *We* did our homework."

Over the table, Joe and Bill exchanged high fives. Only after they were through shaking their heads in disbelief did they turn back to their wives.

"Hey," Joe said, suddenly serious, "what will you two do while we're fishing? Orkney sounds kind of out-of-the-way in terms of activities." Inhaling on his cigar, he blew smoke.

Glancing at Renie, Judith shrugged. "We'll think of something."

Judith could also blow smoke.